AIR & FIRE

RUPERT THOMSON

AIR & FIRE

Rupert Thomson was born in Eastbourne, England, in 1955, and graduated from Cambridge University. He lives in London.

AIR & FIRE

RUPERT THOMSON

VINTAGE CONTEMPORARIES

VINTAGE BOOKS

A DIVISION OF RANDOM HOUSE, INC.

NEW YORK

FIRST VINTAGE BOOKS EDITION, JUNE 1995

The Library of Congress has cataloged the Knopf edition as follows:
Thomson, Rupert.
Air & Fire/Rupert Thomson. 1st American ed.
p. cm.
ISBN 0-679-42506-3
1. Baja California (Mexico)—History—Fiction.
2. French—Mexico—Baja California—Fiction.
I. Title. II. Title: Air and fire.
PR6070.H685A74 1994
823'.914—dc20
93-8429
CIP
Vintage ISBN: 0-679-74730-3

Manufactured in the United States of America
10 9 8 7 6 5 4 3 2 1

All Kate's

' – Of the four elements that comprise the universe, God gave this country only two: air and fire.'

> – Francisco de Ulcoa, on his arrival in Lower California, 1539

' – Among people like the Californian Indians, and in a land like theirs, not many significant events occur which deserve to be recorded and made known to posterity.'

> – Johann Jakob Baegert

Acknowledgements

I am indebted to the following people for providing me with places to work during the past two years: Francis Pike, Martha Crewe (again), and the entire staff at Santa Monica's Hostel in Zanzibar – Natty, Martin, Mary, Teddy, Faith, Willy and, most of all, my good friend Mr Sam Mkwaya.

In order to write this book, I had to do a great deal of research. Particularly valuable to me were Monsieur Jean Roret, Dr A. J. Monhemius, Professor Fred Norbury, Tom Jaine, Adela Arrambide and Isela Rueda. I am also grateful to the Musée D'Orsay in Paris, and to the British Library, the Science Museum Library, The Royal Institute of British Architects and the Victoria & Albert Museum Library in London.

Lastly I would like to thank Imogen for being a wonderful agent and to wish her well in whatever happens next. I would also like to thank everyone at Bloomsbury, especially Liz, Ruth, Sarah, Mary, Lucy, Nigel, Alan and David, for continuing to support my work and for becoming, over the years, a kind of second family.

This book is dedicated to the memory of Kamps Veeran.

APRIL

1

The sea had turned red overnight.

Suzanne faced into the early morning breeze, her hands curling round the cool metal of the rail. She was standing on the narrow deck above the midship's house, the funnel towering behind her, a crop of ashes drifting downwards through the air. It was shortly after dawn on the 17th of April. She had been on board ship for more than three months. Her hands tightened on the rail, and she looked down. An infinity of red water, shifting and tilting under a pale sky.

There would be an explanation, of course. Some refraction of the light peculiar to the tropics. Or perhaps they were passing through the grounds of some great carnage: whales slaughtered for their fat, or seals for their skins. Though, strangely, it was men that she could see, an army of men laid out in rows, the blood draining from their wounds, spiralling upwards through the water, until at last each individual vein was empty. Then their skin would shine like snow and the ocean would glow above their heads, red as a basket of geraniums. She faced into the breeze once more, smoke from the steamer's funnel unwinding across the sky. There would be an explanation. Someone would know.

They were sailing due north now, into the Sea of Cortez, and the southern tip of California had appeared on the port bow, a long talon of volcanic rock pointing out across the water. It belonged to Mexico, though Mexico showed little interest in it; it was a land adrift, peopled by Indians and half-breeds – and now, she thought, by the French as well. She strained her eyes to take in every detail. The soil was the colour of an autumn leaf, somewhere between brown and gold. The ridges looked sharp to the touch. And scarcely a trace of vegetation to be seen. Brown land, red water. Paris had been left so far behind.

Altering her grip on the rail, she thought back to a summer morning the year before, late summer, one of the last days of August. The windows of the drawing-room stood open and she could hear doves murmuring in the garden. She even knew which dress she had been wearing – a white satin gown striped with bands of black velvet. The dress had been a gift from Théo, her husband. He had chosen it on account of its short sleeves which were fashionable that year and which also, so he said, showed off the beauty of her arms.

It must have been a Sunday since they were taking breakfast together at the octagonal table by the window. She could recall the exact moment, her hands closing round the handle of their silver coffee-pot. She could still feel the carved vines against the inside of her fingers as she leaned forwards to fill his cup, as she listened to herself pronounce the words that she had been planning:

'I'd like to come with you, Théo.'

The curtains shifted as a draught moved into the room. The air smelled of leaves as they begin to decay, that first hint of change.

Théo contemplated her across the table. It was a look that she remembered from their first meeting in the parlour of her parents' house in Dieppe. It seemed to pause on her face and then pass through; she might have been transparent, made of glass.

Though her announcement had caught him unawares, she could see that he was in no doubt as to what she was referring. She met his eyes, and her gaze did not waver. She wanted him to know that her request was in earnest.

'And what do you propose to do about the house?' he asked, his voice poised, almost light, his alarm exquisitely disguised.

'I have spoken to Madame Marcelline.' Madame Marcelline, their housekeeper, had been in their employ ever since they were married. 'She would be happy to take care of things while we're away.'

This did nothing to quell Théo's uneasiness; perhaps he even sensed a conspiracy. 'It will occupy the best part of a year,' he reminded her, 'when you consider the voyages out and back.'

'Which is a long time,' she said, 'to be separated from the man you love.'

Smiling faintly, he let his eyes wander across the cool satin elegance of her dress and then out into the comfort of the room in which they sat.

'It will be primitive,' he warned her.

'Dieppe,' she said, 'was primitive.'

Less than a month later she was ordering six gowns, three of foulard, three of mousseline-de-soie, fabrics that would be ideal, her dressmaker said, for a lady living in what she called 'the torrid zone'. Two months after that, she watched dust-sheets settle on the furniture, imitating the snow that had fallen in the night and now lay on the trees and rooftops that she could see through the window.

She heard a whistling behind her, soft and low, almost the same pitch as the ship's engines. The cabin-boy's face rose into view, his eyes scanning the narrow deck.

'It's all right,' she said. 'There's nobody else about.'

It had become a ritual, to meet him here at dawn, the ropes knocking and tapping against the mast, the cluster of white ventilators breathing their warm steam into the air. Sometimes they would talk; other times they would just lean against the rail and feel the soothing beat of the propellor and watch the water fold away from the side of the ship.

'You couldn't sleep, Madame?'

'I didn't want to sleep.' She looked down into his face, his features gathered tightly, almost braced, his dark curls corkscrewing in the breeze. 'Did you see the water?'

He nodded.

'What is it?' she asked him.

'I don't know. I saw something like it once before, but that was off Java.' Only twelve years old, but he had sailed the circumference of the world three times. He seemed burdened by experience, wearied, aged by it. She often wished that she could give him back some portion of his childhood. 'It could be weed, I suppose.' He shrugged. 'You see so many strange things.'

So many strange things.

Two nights ago she had been returning from a dinner in the Captain's quarters with Théo when a member of the crew scuttled from the shadows, plucking at Théo's sleeve with fingers that were callused, black with grease. 'Monsieur,' he whispered, 'we're entering a land where legends are born.' And then, as Théo prised the sordid fingers loose, 'You won't believe your eyes.'

Later, in the safety of their cabin, Théo dismissed the encounter. He had travelled by sea many times before, and he was familiar with the superstitious nature of sailors. They would sit on deck late into the night, he said, and hypnotise each other with tales of planets that dropped sizzling into the ocean and fish with the eyes and breasts of women.

'It's all nonsense, of course,' he said. 'And besides, did you not notice, the fellow smelt most unmistakably of liquor. Why, he was almost drowning in the stuff!'

Suzanne did not dispute this and yet she had to admit, to herself, not to Théo, that the sailor's words had thrilled her.

Théo stood by the porthole, frowning.

'Isn't it more likely,' he said, turning to her once again, 'that we're simply entering a place about which much remains unknown, a place where the imagination, especially, it would seem, the imagination of sailors, can take hold and run riot?' He stood over her, his face lit with exhilaration at the clarity and precision of his reasoning.

'It's more likely,' she said, 'yes.'

Though it occurred to her, as she smiled up at him, as he took her hand in his and touched it to his lips, that they were already in a place where the imagination, to use his phrase, had taken hold. That she was even there at all, sitting in the cabin of a ship that was bound for Mexico, was the purest act of the imagination. Hers, not his; he would never have been able to imagine it, had she not compelled him to.

The cabin-boy jumped. When she turned to look at him, he was standing with his head tipped at an angle, his toes gripping the deck.

'I thought I heard something,' he said.

Not for the first time during the voyage, Suzanne realised her debt to the boy. The *SS Korrigan* was a tramp steamer. It was in the business of carrying cargo, and its crew was unused to passengers – unused, especially, to women. Monsieur Groque, the Captain, would address her during meals or on the bridge, but he had to labour to produce even a few civilities, and it was no surprise to her that he reverted to the most foul language the moment her back was turned. As a woman she was, at best, a source of discomfort and inhibition. At worst, she was invisible – no, worse than invisible: a jinx, an evil omen, a pariah. Only the cabin-boy would speak to her with any measure of normality, though he had sworn her to secrecy, fearing what the crew might do to him if they found out. She had kept her promise, and nobody knew of their assignations, not even Théo; still, the boy's head swivelled at every creak.

At last he satisfied himself that nobody was calling him. He seemed to uncoil, his muscles loosening against his bones. He was like a dead thing coming back to life.

'When do we arrive?' she asked. 'Tomorrow, isn't it?'

He nodded. 'Midday.'

'So we can see each other one more time,' she said, 'and by then one of us will know. About the water, I mean.'

He moved to the rail beside her, and his head dipped on his neck. 'What will you do there,' he asked, 'in Santa Sofía?'

'My husband's building a church.'

'Is he a priest?'

She laughed. 'No, he's an engineer.'

The cabin-boy ran his hand along the rail, following a sudden twist in the metal. It had buckled during their passage round Cape Horn. That same night a wave had snatched one of the lifeboats from its cradle. They had not seen the lifeboat again.

'He builds things,' she added. 'Out of metal.'

'Metal? Why metal?'

'I don't know. Perhaps because it lasts.'

'Suzanne?'

The voice had come from below.

'It's him,' she whispered. 'My husband.'

But the cabin-boy was already slipping through the narrow gap between the ventilators.

She crossed to the stair-head and peered down. Théo stood at the foot of the steps in a dressing-gown and leather slippers, his black hair still disarranged by sleep.

'In heaven's name, Suzanne. What are you doing up there?'

It was at moments like this that she could feel the fifteen years that lay between them. She did not see the difference in age as an obstacle, however; she saw it only as a place where irony could happen, a gap that tenderness could close. She knew that she had disconcerted him – ladies of her station ought not to climb ladders – but she decided to make light of it.

'Have you noticed the water, Théo?'

He had not.

'Take a look,' she said.

But Théo did not move towards the rail. He remained at the foot of the stairs; he seemed suddenly to be plunged in thought. 'I think I'll write a letter,' he said.

'A letter? Who to?'

'Monsieur Eiffel.' He looked up at her again and she saw that he was smiling. 'I shall inform him that my wife has turned into a monkey.'

Laughing, she began her precarious descent.

She slept late on the morning of their arrival. By the time she woke, Théo had already dressed. He was wearing his black frock-coat and a pair of elegant pale-grey trousers, and he carried a malacca cane with a carved silver head. They would be landing in three hours, he reminded her.

They took breakfast on the bridge, accompanied by the Captain, the Quartermaster and the Chief Engineer. The usual food was served: dry biscuits, fried eggs sliding on a bed of grease, coffee with no milk. Though it was the last meal of a long and perilous voyage, there was no sense of occasion. If they had been putting into Hong Kong or Shanghai, perhaps it would have been different – but Santa Sofía? Perhaps, after all, there was nothing to celebrate. They ate in silence; the ship steamed northwards, its metal plates vibrating gently.

The Captain hunched over the table, as if his breakfast were a mirror and he were studying his reflection. Suzanne watched him fork a dripping yolk into his mouth, the web of muscle pulsing in the thin flesh of his temple. She had to speak, if only to distract herself from her disgust.

'I wondered if you'd be good enough, Captain,' she said, 'to explain what has happened to the sea.'

The Captain stopped chewing. His eyes lifted, pale, faintly mocking, empty of intelligence. 'I beg your pardon, Madame.'

'The sea's red,' she said. 'I wondered why.'

'Scared you, did it?'

Suzanne looked away. There was so much that she did not know, and the Captain seemed to take pleasure in seeing her ignorance confirmed – not only confirmed, in fact, but reinforced. During the past three months she had often asked him if she might be shown the stokehold or the engine-room. He would grunt, invent excuses, prevaricate. The ship was a mystery to her, and he had set himself up as guardian of that mystery. It was entirely typical of his behaviour that, though it was she who had enquired about the sea, it was to Théo that he directed his reply.

It transpired that the change in colour was caused by a myriad of tiny organisms floating just below the surface. As a natural phenomenon, it was customary for the time of year, though it led, he said, to 'a great many tall tales'. There was once a tribe of Indians, for instance, who believed that it was a sign from the gods, instructing them to make a human sacrifice.

'They thought the sea had turned to blood.' The Captain grinned. 'Savages,' he said, and, picking up his fork, he pierced the skin on his second egg.

Théo pursued the subject with the Captain, for he too was eager to acquire some knowledge of the region, but Suzanne found, in any case, that she could no longer listen. The inside of her head was slowly turning, as if she had been fastened to a wheel. Heat rose off her in a blast. She had to concentrate on the table, the stains and burns, the ridges in the grain of the wood.

She had been married to Théo for more than five years and they still did not have any children. She had miscarried twice. Théo did not know. The first time it happened, she had not even realised that she was pregnant. She had been walking down the stairs when she felt something break inside her, run down her legs. She stood in the hallway and lifted her skirts. The blood had filled her shoes.

She wrapped all her clothes in old copies of the newspaper and left the house. It was evening. The sky had filled with stunned light; the streets lay dark and still beneath. She set off towards Les Halles and did not stop until she found a brazier that contained a few glowing embers. It was a place where five roads met, but she saw no one. She dropped her bundle into the flames. Watched the paper catch, the clothes begin to blacken. Every now and then she stirred the fire with a stick from the gutter. She stayed until she was certain that nothing remained. It took a long time. Her shoes were glazed kid; they would not seem to burn. At last she returned to the house and took to her bed, saying that she was ill.

Some days later, when Théo asked her about the dress – it was one that he had bought for her, from her favourite shop on Rue de la Paix – she told him that she had lost it. 'Lost it?' he said. 'How could you lose a dress?' But she had run out of words. All she could do was shrug and turn away.

'Are you not feeling well, my dear?'

This question coincided with her thoughts so neatly that, for one moment, she could not be certain where she was. Then, looking up, she remembered and had to invent an excuse.

'It's just the heat, Théo.'

'This is nothing,' the Captain said. 'Wait till July.'

'Do you need some air?' Théo asked her.

She summoned a smile for him. 'I feel fine. How long until we arrive?'

Théo studied her for a moment longer then he reached up with his napkin and dabbed his mouth. 'An hour.' He turned to the Captain for corroboration.

'Aye,' the Captain murmured. 'Close enough.'

'Then we ought to be able to see the town by now,' she said and, leaving her chair, she launched herself towards the window that overlooked the bow.

But she could only see the land stretching away in both directions, a land stripped of all adornment, musty and jagged.

Then she noticed a cloud to the north-west, a thin white cloud that lay perfectly horizontal in the air. It was so straight, it might have been drawn with a ruler; Théo might have been responsible for it. Looking more closely, she realised that it was not a cloud at all. It was smoke, rising in thin columns from the land below. She could just make out two chimneys, some huddled buildings, the dark arm of a harbour wall.

'I can see it,' she cried.

The two men joined her at the window.

'Aye, that's it,' the Captain said, 'godforsaken hole that it is.'

But Théo was smiling.

'At last,' he murmured. 'The work can begin.'

2

My dear Monsieur Eiffel,

I wrote to you from Panama in January and again from Santiago some weeks later, but as I have little faith in either of the two postal services, I am writing to you once more on the assumption that this is the first that you have heard of me.

That I should mention Santiago at all will no doubt cause you some concern since our original plan, as I am sure you remember, was to put in at Panama, transport the church by rail to the west coast and then proceed northwards by steamer into Mexican waters. This plan was thwarted owing to the untimely dynamiting of a government train by a notorious group of revolutionaries. Any assessments as to when the line might once again be operational were vague, to say the least. After a conference with the Captain of the *SS Korrigan* I decided that it would be as well to continue south, reaching Mexico by way of Cape Horn. Though it would add two months to our journey it seemed the course of action that would offer least threat to our cargo which was, after all, our primary concern. Before too long I was to regret this decision, for we encountered the most ferocious storm, not only ferocious but persistent too, lasting, as it did, a full seventeen days. A section of the bulkhead split, and it seemed at one moment as if we all might perish. It was during that day that we sighted another vessel struggling, like we were, against the elements; it is difficult to express the degree of succour that it afforded us, to know that other men were sharing the same dangers, the same exhaustion.

Suffice to say that we survived the rigours of Cape Horn. On the 2nd of March we put into Santiago for extensive repairs, and it struck me then as an immense irony that, had the National Assembly supported the Panama Canal project, as you supported it, out of a sense of duty to the nation, we might have been spared many of the hardships of the preceding two months. Our sojourn in Santiago was, in many respects, delightful, but it was a relief to be under way once more. Our passage up the coast of South America was accomplished without incident, and the first day of April found us lying off Mexico. They say that one knows when one is entering the Gulf of California on account of the numerous sea serpents that appear in the waters alongside one's vessel, but, I must say, I have noticed no such phenomenon. Is it not more likely that we are simply entering a part of the world about which much remains unknown, a part of the world where the imagination – especially, it would seem, the imagination of sailors – can take hold and run riot? They were eager to assure me that it was a fact, that the serpents had been seen. I pointed downwards through the floor. 'In the hold of this ship,' I said, 'there are two thousand, three hundred and forty-eight component parts which, when assembled, will fit together with the greatest perfection. That, gentlemen,' I said, 'is a fact.' Sea serpents or no, we will arrive at our final destination this morning, some four months after leaving Le Havre.

You may remember that I was anxious regarding my wife's desire to join me on this undertaking. I need not have worried. She has acquitted herself admirably. After my many attempts to discourage her, mentioning, above all, the very real danger to her health, it will no doubt amuse you to hear that she has proved to be a far better sailor than her husband. While I lay below deck, prostrated by the most tenacious bouts of seasickness, she was usually to be found up on the bridge, sketching! She knows that I am writing to you and asks me to convey her most respectful regards. Please accept mine also, with your customary kindness, and know that I am, as always, your humble and obedient servant,

Théophile Valence.

3

Wilson Pharaoh dreamed that all his veins were filled with gold; he only had to cut his wrists and he would be rich.

Awake, there was a moment when he still believed the dream. That he could take his hunting-knife and open up a vein. That gold would pour in liquid abundance from the wound. He had seen maps of his own body, drawn up by a mining company of international repute. He had seen the proof with his own eyes.

He lay still, limbs swimming heavily at some distance from his body. Mosquitoes hung in the air. They were greedier here than anywhere that he had ever been. Kill one in the morning and you could watch your blood spring clear across the room.

His eyes moved along one edge of a green tin ceiling, down a yellow wall. This was not his hotel. He turned his head slowly on the pillow, discovered a girl sleeping beside him. One glimpse of that narrow face, that cataract of coarse black hair, and his memory returned.

He saw Pablo Fernández wiping the counter with a rag, his eyebrows reaching high on to his forehead and curving slightly, like the arms on spectacles. Pablo ran the Bar El Fandango, a cantina at the back of town. He also owned the hotel where Wilson was staying.

'There's a couple of men here say Americans can't drink.' Pablo slid the words casually past his thin dark lips, his eyes angled sideways and downwards.

Wilson glanced along the bar. The couple of men in question were Indians. Men hired by the company to mine copper. Men who carried future grievance in their bellies like an embryo. They were Seri Indians, famous for their treachery: you could never read their faces, but you could be sure that one of them would have a knife.

Wilson could not back down or walk away. He knew it, and Pablo knew it too. He could think of few distances more dangerous than the distance between the bar of El Fandango and the door. At least twenty men had perished in the space of those few yards. So there was really only one response:

'Line them up, Pablo.'

He had been drawn into a contest that lasted half the night. They drank cactus liquor from tin mugs, with strips of salted fish to take away the taste. Pablo distilled the liquor himself, in a shack behind the bar. The first shot lowered your voice an octave. The second almost blinded you.

There followed a bewildering sequence of events, one of the last of which would have been Wilson's delivery to the mildewed sheets of none other than La Huesuda, the skinniest whore in the Gulf of California – she was so skinny, you could gather her in your arms like a bundle of sticks. She was short too; her shoulder knocked against your hip-bone if you walked together down a street. It had been agreed in the cantina that whoever lost the contest would be expected to spend the night with her, all expenses paid. Wilson could not remember losing, though he supposed he must have. Not remembering and losing were two horses that pulled the same cart.

He leaned on one elbow, looking down. From her hairline to her nostrils was one long curve, except for a slight dip that signified the bridge of her nose. Her mouth had fallen open, as neat as that first notch you cut in the trunk of a tree before you set about the work of felling it; the breath sizzled past her teeth like lard heating in a skillet. He was looking down at her with some curiosity. She claimed to be descended from a tribe of Amazons who, according to legend, had once ruled the waters of the gulf. They were believed to have captured men in order that they might breed from them. Afterwards the men were put to death. Dressed in black pearls that had been threaded on lengths of wild flax, the Amazons would dance until the moon changed shape, and it was said that the thunder of their feet could be heard for miles around, and on the mainland too. Nobody could ignore that sound. Women carved holes in cactus plants, hollowed out the middles and hid their man inside. Even to this day, if they heard a storm coming, the Indians would often hide their men.

La Huesuda did not dance on beaches, nor had she been known to put men to death – business was slow enough already, God knows – but she did christen herself Pearl, which was in keeping with her lineage, and she painted the name on the wall of her house in letters so tall that they could be read from a ship anchored in the harbour. The people of the town were not impressed. They saw less with their imaginations than their eyes. They called her La Huesuda which, literally translated, meant 'the Bony One'.

Though her nostrils shrank whenever the name was used, she could often be found in Mama Vum Buá's establishment on the waterfront, eating plates of jerked beef and refried beans in an attempt to put on the inches that would bring with them not only trade, but credibility as well. For as José Ramón, the customs officer, said, if she was descended from a tribe of giant women, then how come she was only four feet eleven?

A ship's horn sounded, long and mournful.

La Huesuda murmured something, licked her lips, but did not wake. Wilson Pharaoh quietly left the bed.

Unlatching the shuttered door, he pushed it wide and stepped on to a small balcony that overlooked the port.

It was early morning. The water, tight and pale, glittered in the harsh light. Boys were diving off the south quay. Dogs pushed blunt muzzles into piles of trash.

Another low moan from the ship's horn. Wilson shielded his eyes against the glare. A steamer edged past the headland, trailing smoke across an otherwise clean sky. He wondered if they could read her name yet. He wondered if they could see him standing on her balcony like some advertisement.

'Hey! American!'

He faced back into the room. La Huesuda was leaning on her elbow, her black hair sliding sideways past one shoulder and down on to the stained pillow.

'Did you pay me yet?'

'The others,' he said. 'They paid you.'

'How much did they pay me?'

He was almost ashamed to answer, and his shame took the shape of courtesy. 'I believe it was twenty pesos, ma'am.'

'Ma'am?' She let out a rasp of laughter. A pelican lifted, startled, from a nearby roof. 'If you like,' she said, 'you can have me again.'

He stared at her. He was not sure that he had even had her once; in fact, he was rather hoping that he had not.

She mistook his alarm for hesitation. 'Half-price,' she said, 'since it's morning.'

He leaned against the balcony, his arms spread along the warm wood of the rail, and shook his head. 'Thank you kindly,' he said, 'but no.'

'I'm too skinny for you, is that it?'

There was a sudden crack, and then a splintering. The sky tilted, shrank; the doorway jumped into the air. Then Wilson was struck square in the back.

For a moment his vision blackened and he could not breathe. There was no feeling in his body. He hauled some air into his lungs, and let it out. Then hauled some more.

He looked round. He was lying in the street with pieces of timber splayed out around him, like rays around a sun.

'Holy Mother of Jesus,' came a voice from above. 'My balcony.'

Slowly he sat up. Everything was very quiet. The town seemed clear to him for the first time, both in its nature and its promise. He felt he could see through it, as if through glass, to what it held; he felt that it would yield.

A ball of dried mule-dung rebounded off his shoulder. Two of the Vum Buá girls stood at the corner of Avenida Aljez and showed him their tongues. He managed a smile. It scared them, and they fled. Somewhere up above, La Huesuda was still running through a list of saints and martyrs, anyone, in fact, who was even remotely connected with Christ. There were also some names that he did not recognise. These would be gods of her own, he supposed. Amazons, no doubt.

In climbing to his feet, he almost fell. It appeared, after all, that he had hurt himself.

'Hey, American,' La Huesuda shouted. 'What about my balcony?'

He squinted up at her, with her chicken's legs and her eyes of mingled green and brown, like the skins of over-ripe avocados.

'If you'd fucked me like a man,' she shouted, 'none of this would've happened.'

Shutters were beginning to open further down the street.

He tried to hold his patience together. 'I'd be grateful,' he said slowly, 'if you would throw me my clothes.'

There was a long moment while she stared down at him through narrowed eyes, then she withdrew. His clothes flew from the dark hole of her room like dirt scratched by a cat. He began to dress. His right ankle was already swelling, so he did not bother with his boots.

'Where are you going?' La Huesuda shouted as he limped away.

'Where do you think?' he replied.

The only doctor in town was a Frenchman by the name of Bardou, and he lived on the Mesa del Norte. All the French people lived up there. It was cooler. There was one main street, known as the Calle Francesa, and a small square with wrought-iron benches and a lemon tree. The Calle Francesa had been paved with stone, its blue-grey cobbles shipped all the way from Paris. Plane trees, also imported, had been planted down both sides of the street, though they were still too young to afford much shade. The houses had been designed with the pale skin and the thick blood of the Northern European in mind: verandas on all four sides, high ceilings in the downstairs rooms and a central corridor running from front to back, a kind of breezeway. They had as many windows and transoms as it was possible to have while still leaving four walls standing – though, as Wilson knew, the air did not move during the summer months, no matter how much encouragement it was given.

Wilson had seen Bardou in the lobby of the Hôtel de Paris on several occasions, but he had yet to make the doctor's acquaintance. The doctor was an educated man, by all accounts. He spoke English fluently and with an American accent, owing to the fact that he had studied for many years in Boston, Massachusetts, and it was said, in this connection, that he had assisted at the autopsy of none other than Abraham Lincoln himself. The doctor's drawled vowels were accompanied by gestures that were so frequent and elaborate that his hands must, sooner or later, Wilson felt, even despite themselves, produce a silk scarf or an egg or a dove in flight. Accordingly, it was with a somewhat sheepish air that he presented himself, boots in one hand, at the doctor's front door.

He was greeted by Madame Bardou, the doctor's wife, who showed him into a quiet room at the end of a corridor. She spoke to him in French and then, seeing that he had not understood, apologised in English.

'It's me who should apologise,' Wilson said, 'for troubling you at such an hour.'

She smiled quickly – not at him, but past him, somehow; he felt it dip over his shoulder, dart beyond him, the way birds do when they are trapped in houses. She lowered her head, and, murmuring an excuse, withdrew.

He let his eyes wander round the room. Blue silk lined the walls to elbow-height, giving way to panels of dark, lacquered wood. Here, in steel frames, hung an array of certificates, diplomas and commendations, almost too numerous to count. On the far wall there were three silver medals mounted in a glass case. Every medal and every piece of paper bore the name 'Bardou'. It began to look as if the tales of his many accomplishments had not been exaggerated.

Wilson limped over to the window. They were an unlikely people, the

French. In San Francisco, when he was a boy, he had spent his days on the waterfront with the white fog surrounding him and the world invisible, mysterious, beyond. Then the fog would thin and lift, and boats would emerge, ropes dripping, often as many as twenty in a single morning. He remembered French sailors jumping ship, whole crews sometimes. Let loose in a city that was new to them, they were as simple and eager as children; they seemed to expect gold to fall out of the sky like rain. Very few of them had any luck. They ended up opening restaurants or getting themselves killed. Small sad articles in the evening paper. And here they were again, in Mexico, with their hands waving on their wrists like meadow flowers in the wind and their silk umbrellas hoisted against the sun. A different breed of Frenchman, but no less conspicuous.

He heard a voice in the corridor and turned in time to see Bardou step into the room and close the door behind him. Bardou had shaved that morning, and his cheeks were pale and sleek. He wore a starched white shirt and a waistcoat tailored from some exquisite cloth – violets laid out upon a field of gold. His every movement was confident and precise. You could tell right away that he had spent many hours in the company of great men.

He joined Wilson by the window. Resting his hands on the sill, he filled his lungs with air and then turned back into the room.

'Do you smell that, Monsieur?'

Wilson lifted his nose towards the ceiling and sniffed. Surely the doctor could not be referring to the odour of mule-dung and dead fish that seemed suddenly to have invaded the room?

'The bread, Monsieur,' the doctor said. 'The bread.'

'Ah,' Wilson said. 'The bread.'

There was a baker in town by the name of Jesús Pompano. For some time now, various members of the French community had been trying to teach Jesús Pompano how to bake bread. They had specific requirements. They wanted a loaf that was eighteen inches long. It had to be crusty on the outside, and soft and fragrant within. They even had a name for it: it was called, they said, a 'baguette'.

Jesús Pompano was a Mexican, from the province of Arispé. He knew how to bake Mexican bread. He could turn out doughnuts too, and almond biscuits in the shape of angels, and sweet rolls dusted with cinnamon or sugar. But he had failed, so far, to produce anything that even remotely resembled a baguette. Wilson knew this from personal experience; he had been living off Jesús Pompano's mistakes for weeks.

'I hate to say this, Doctor,' Wilson said, 'but it smells a little burned to me.'

The doctor sighed. 'To me too.'

'I guess you'll just have to be patient. I'm sure that Señor Pompano is doing his best.'

'Patient?' The doctor's hands lifted into the air beside his ears and opened wide. Wilson held his breath but no egg hatched, no dove took wing. 'We've been waiting for weeks,' the doctor said. 'Months. All we're asking for is bread.'

Wilson had been present when Monsieur Morlaix, a mining-company executive, called in at the bakery to explain once again the notion of a baguette to Jesús Pompano. Morlaix had the face of an ageing cherub, his curly hair grey and thinning, his mouth set in a pout. He took a sheet of paper and drew on it. 'There,' he said. 'That is a baguette.' Jesús leaned down and studied the drawing. Then he stood back. 'It looks like a sausage to me,' he said. 'Maybe you should try the butcher.'

Looking up, the doctor saw that Wilson was smiling.

'But you didn't come here to listen to my obsessions.' The doctor moved away from the window and, holding a scented handkerchief beneath his nose, inhaled. 'It's your ankle, I take it.'

Wilson nodded. 'I fell.'

The doctor motioned him to a chair and then knelt down in front of him. Wilson was ashamed of his feet, which were black with dirt from the journey up the hill, but the doctor did not seem to notice.

'You're American, aren't you?'

'That's right. I was raised in San Francisco.'

The doctor was probing Wilson's ankle with pale fingers. 'I find it strange that you should leave a beautiful city like San Francisco for such,' and his eyes lifted momentarily to the window, 'for such barren shores as these.'

'It's only barren on the surface, Doctor.'

The doctor continued to probe the ankle, as if it might reveal to him the mystery of that last remark. 'There's copper here, of course,' he mused, 'and manganese – '

'It's not copper that I'm talking about,' Wilson blurted, 'but gold.'

The doctor stared up at him. 'I didn't know that there was any gold.'

'Well, it's not exactly common knowledge.'

'I see. Then you're in no particular hurry.'

Wilson did not follow.

'The injury, it's not very serious,' the doctor said. 'Some torn ligaments, a little bruising. However, you would be wise to rest it.'

'For how long?'

'One month at least. Maybe two.' He saw the look on Wilson's face. 'Unless, of course, you want to risk permanent damage. And the gold will wait, will it not?'

Wilson nodded gloomily. 'I guess.'

The main ward in the hospital contained about thirty beds, at least half of which were occupied. All the patients, so far as Wilson could judge, were Indians. Each bed had been swathed in a fine gauze netting; the sick men looked like flies caught in some sticky spider's web.

'Are they all company employees?' Wilson asked.

The doctor nodded. 'Most of them.'

'I hadn't realised there were so many injuries.'

'We're doing what we can,' the doctor said, 'to improve the safety of the mines.'

Wilson recognised the change in tone, similar to the way in which a man reaches for his rifle when he sees a stranger about to trespass on his property. He resolved to keep more of his thoughts to himself.

At the far end of the ward the doctor held the door open for him, and they passed into the surgery. A long table with a veined marble top stood in the centre of the room. There was a stone sink in the corner, and a row of shelves that glittered with the tools of a doctor's trade – scalpels, knives and saws. There was only one window, high in the wall.

The doctor told Wilson to lie on the table.

'There's no cause for alarm,' he said, white teeth showing in his smile. 'I do not intend to operate.'

Wilson gave himself up to the Frenchman's hands, the same hands to which the President of the United States had been entrusted, even though he was dead. His head jangled. He could not tell whether it was the cactus liquor beginning to take its toll or the result of that fall from the balcony. He supposed that it might well be both.

'It's a difficult business.' The doctor was bending over Wilson's foot, binding the ankle in tight bands of gauze. 'The soil in this region is a soft, wet clay. Very unstable. Even with heavy timbering it can collapse.' He began to apply plaster of Paris to the gauze. 'But you, as a prospector, would have a better understanding than most of the perils involved.'

'I do most of my work on the surface,' Wilson said. 'I have come to mistrust tunnels.'

'Even so, I'm sure that you have witnessed many accidents.'

Though Wilson had not, in fact, witnessed even a single accident, it seemed ungrateful, in the circumstances, to deny it. Accordingly, he recalled an incident where a man had fallen thirteen hundred feet to his death after being overpowered by a noxious gas. It had happened in Nevada.

'There,' the doctor said. 'You see?'

Wilson lay motionless, content with the silence and the soothing coolness of the marble against his forearms and the back of his head. It did not seem to him that he had lied. He could still remember reading the article in the *Illustrated News*. The accident had been described in such a vivid and realistic style that he did honestly feel as if he had been there.

While the plaster dried, the doctor left the room, returning some minutes later with a pair of wooden crutches.

'These will help you to move about,' he said, 'though I suspect you'll find small spaces difficult.'

'Small spaces?' Wilson peered at the doctor over his chest.

'Balconies, for example,' the doctor said. He handed the crutches to Wilson, his lips tightening into a furtive smile.

The hospital clock was striking midday when the two men left the building. They stood on the south veranda looking at the town below. The houses had roofs made from sheets of shining tin. The streets looked swept. But mesquite and ocotillo were beginning to disrupt the symmetry, and away to the east, where the mountains lifted steeply against the sky, Wilson could see a number of shanty dwellings pieced together out of driftwood, scrap metal, wild flag.

His eyes shifted east, towards the waterfront. The ship that he had noticed earlier was now docking in the harbour. It was a freighter, out of Le Havre. You saw ships like it in every port from Seattle to New Orleans, carrying timber, grain or fruit. Three masts, a funnel that could use some paint, engines of low power. An ocean tramp.

He watched the hawsers fly from the deck to the quay, where they were deftly looped through heavy iron rings. Coal barges were already nudging against the starboard bow. It did not look as if the ship would be in Santa Sofía for long.

'Do you know, Monsieur,' the doctor said, 'what is the cargo of that vessel?'

Wilson did not.

'It's a church.'

'A church?'

The doctor's smile broadened, but he chose not to elaborate. He too, it seemed, would have his mysteries.

'I'm afraid I must leave you,' he said, checking his watch. 'I have other patients to attend to.'

'You've been very kind,' Wilson said. 'What do I owe you?'

The doctor raised his hand in front of him, palms outwards, and turned his head away.

'When you find your gold,' he said, 'then perhaps one small, how do you say,' and he rolled his forefinger against the inside of his thumb and held it up.

Wilson could just see the sky through the gap. 'Nugget?'

'Yes.' The doctor beamed. 'Nugget.'

'You've got yourself a deal,' Wilson said.

He had reached town a month before, stone-broke and weak as a deadwood fence, his face buried in his mule's coarse mane, and all his tools hanging off her flanks and chinking like a kitchen in an earthquake. The sun stamped on the back of his neck, his shoulderblades, his hat. When he raised his head he saw two brown trains on the beach, waves rustling against their wheels, and thought he must be tumbling into madness. Then buildings appeared. Workshops, furnaces. A railway line. Smoke climbed from a tall brick chimney. Sawblades poured gold on to a soil floor. He pinched his eyes. A woman was standing on the road, her feet spread wide in the dust, as if she were about to draw a gun on him. That was all he needed.

'Who are you?' he asked.

Her name was Mama Vum Buá.

She stared at him. 'You want breakfast?'

What he wanted was water.

'No water,' she said. 'We got coffee.'

He took the coffee. You did not argue with Mama Vum Buá.

She was a Yaqui Indian, from the province of Sonora on the mainland, but sometime during the previous century the pure blood of her family had been corrupted by a renegade Jesuit priest. Her eyes were not brown, as you might have expected. They were a startling cobalt-blue. She was ashamed of the colour – it set her apart from her people, whom she loved

– and she found her contempt for anything foreign almost impossible to conceal, especially if it involved religion too. There was an old withered quince tree in the yard behind her restaurant. 'It was planted by some missionary,' she would hiss. 'No wonder it didn't bear no goddam fruit.'

Like many Indians in Santa Sofía, she wore copper rings on her fingers and her thumbs: twelve of them – one for every child she had conceived, living and dead. She had strung a handful of bronze Mulege pearls on a length of catgut and fastened it around her neck. She arranged her hair in the traditional Yaqui style, three braids coiled on her head, and she always appeared in the same dress, yellow with red flowers, though it had been washed in salt water so many times that the colours had faded to cream and pink. She chewed quids of some fiery local root that stained her gums and palate red, and when she smiled, which was not often, she always smiled out of the right side of her mouth. Wilson had taken to her instantly, her belligerent manner, the hiss and rumble of her speech. No morning was complete until he had breakfasted at Mama Vum Buá's place.

It was almost one by the time he limped into her yard. He laid his crutches on the ground and sat himself down at his usual table in the shade. Three Indians in cloaks stared blankly at his foot. A few minutes passed. At last the Señora emerged from the darkness of her kitchen. She stood in the sunlight, blinking, fists on her hips. When she saw Wilson, she hawked and spat. A rope of red liquid looped through the air towards him, landing in the dust close by.

'You're late this morning.'

'I had an accident – '

'You fell off a balcony. I know.'

'It just collapsed. I didn't – '

'In your underwear. You want eggs?'

Smiling, he lit the butt of a cigar and aimed the glowing tip at the harbour. 'They say there's a church on that ship.'

She tilted her head sideways, as if listening for hymns or prayers or something that might give the church away – but there was only the clank of the conveyor belt and the dull whining of flies in the midday heat. She let her breath out fast and spat into the dust so hard it bounced.

'You want tortillas?'

He nodded.

'Coffee?'

'Yes.'

Wilson heard voices chattering behind him. He looked round. Six of the Vum Buá girls were waiting by the date palm, two of them naked but for twenty-pound flour-sacks with holes for arms. One was swamped by a grown woman's dress; it wrapped around her twice and trailed in the dirt. Another held a dead fish by the tail.

Mama Vum Buá had eight daughters, none of whom had yet reached womanhood. They had dark eyes and funny, jagged teeth, and their black hair was tied back with dried kelp or fishing twine or bits of frayed rope. They had Indian names that were so long and unpronounceable that he had christened them First, Second, Third, etc., according to their height. Every time he sat down to his breakfast, they would sidle up and twist themselves around the nearest trees or chairs like ribbons, their eyes all wide and shiny. Sometimes he would entertain them with coin tricks he had picked up from a retired gunslinger in El Paso. Other times he would bring his guitar along. While he waited for his coffee to cool he would sing them songs in his tuneless voice, songs about broken hearts and America and fields of gold. Since they could not understand the words, it did not matter what he sang about, though he would never sing anything that contained obscenities. This morning he planned to tell them about a man who was so dumb that he tried to leave the second floor of a house without using the stairs. He could already hear their ancient, cracked laughter as he traced his descent in the air with his hand.

He was still wondering how to begin the story without mentioning vice of any kind when he noticed a small crowd gathering on the quay. He recognised Monsieur de Romblay, the Director of the mining company. He could also see a group of Indians, dressed in white shirts and clean breeches. They were clutching a variety of pipes and drums and whistles. It looked as if Monsieur de Romblay had come down to the waterfront, along with certain other select members of the French community, to meet the boat that had docked that morning. It was a welcoming party, and there would be music.

'Tell us about your foot, mister.'

Wilson turned to the girls. 'What?'

'Tell us what happened to your foot.'

His eyes drifted back towards the quayside. Two figures had just appeared on deck. A man and a woman, her arm linked through his. The band struck up a tune that Wilson did not recognise, and the two figures began to move down the gangway. The man wore a Panama hat and a black frock-coat. The woman wore a yellow dress that belled out into the air below her waist, and her parasol balanced at a jaunty angle on her shoulder. He wondered who they could be. Were they someone's relations? Could they be royalty? He leaned back in his chair. One thing, at least, was clear: they were French.

'Come on, mister. Tell us what happened.'

His foot ached inside the plaster cast. His shoulder ached too. He did not feel well. But he could not take his eyes off the scene that was unfolding on the quay. The man and woman had climbed into an open carriage, with Monsieur de Romblay in attendance. A whip arched and snapped. The carriage sprang forwards. Wilson suddenly saw that it would have to pass within a few feet of the table where he was sitting.

As the carriage approached, he straightened in his chair and, taking hold of his hat by the crown, lifted it into the air. The woman's head turned at that moment and she saw him. Her eyes were green, the shape of leaves. They seemed to be resting on her face; if the wind came, they might blow away and then she would be blind. She smiled, as if to reassure him, and vanished behind the wall of the Señora's restaurant. He did not see the carriage again until, pale-pink dust blossoming around its wheels, it took the bend that led up the hill to the Mesa del Norte.

The world bent at the edges and a fringe of sweat broke out on his forehead. Slowly he returned the hat to his head, slowly he lowered himself down into his chair. He sat without moving for some time, his hands clasped in his lap, his thoughts becalmed. The sight of that woman had run into him like something molten, had run into every part of him, and would set.

When he looked up again, the Vum Buá girls had gone. He could hardly blame them; he had not provided much in the way of entertainment. Only one of them remained, squatting in the dirt, oblivious to everything. She was carefully crushing ants with the tip of one finger. He lifted his cup and blew across the rim.

Mama Vum Buá put a basket of tortillas on the table, then she stood beside him, shielding her eyes, and peered out towards the boat.

'Any sign of that church yet?'

But Wilson had seen something far more unusual, far more sacred, than a church, and could not answer.

4

Towards dusk on the first day Suzanne left the Hôtel de Paris and walked south, along the Calle Francesa. She was wearing a white dress, a simple dress, fastened at the throat with an ivory cameo that had belonged to her mother. The sun had already fallen behind the wall of mountains to the west, and a fan of mauve and crimson rays had opened in the upper sky. She felt as if she were giving off light as she walked; she could have been a piece of the moon. Her new town, her new street. This new earth beneath her shoes.

Of course every place had its share of spells. Even the city she had left behind held many secrets underneath its skin. Only last year, while digging foundations for the Opéra, they had uncovered some ancient oyster beds, thousands upon thousands of shells, and several labourers had died of mysterious and disfiguring diseases. But there was nothing to compare with a new land, about which little was known, in which all the secrets lay waiting. The sailor's words came back to her. *You are entering a land where legends are born.* Her hopes rose; a smile reached her lips. Perhaps there was even a child in this town, a child who expected her.

She was passing houses where the other French people lived. The lit rooms seemed to crouch down, then leap up again as the kerosene lamps flickered. Screens had been fastened to the windows, and moths whirled against the fine wire-mesh. She walked within a few feet of a veranda that had been shielded by columns of jasmine and bougainvillaea. She could hear voices murmuring behind the leaves.

After the stealth of sailing up into the gulf, after all the tensions and conspiracies, she had not been prepared for the effect the town would have on her. By the time she stepped out on to the deck that morning, a crowd had gathered on the quay below, hundreds of faces gazing upwards – native women selling copper jewellery, soldiers in grey uniforms, boys with shaved heads and voices like ravens. Not since Santiago had she seen people in such numbers. There was even a band of musicians, Indians dressed in white shirts and moleskin breeches. Their faces were serious, though it was not, she thought, the seriousness of concentration. It was more as if their minds were somewhere else. And their version of 'La Marseillaise' reflected this: it was shrill, chaotic, disembodied.

At the foot of the gangway Suzanne and Théo were greeted by Monsieur de Romblay. With his globelike cheeks and his tight, swollen belly, Monsieur de Romblay looked as if he had been pumped full of air. He wore a blue frock-coat with a velvet collar, and smelled strongly of lemon cologne.

'The national anthem,' he declared, 'played on some of the traditional instruments of the region.'

'Really?' Théo said in a voice that made it perfectly clear to Suzanne that he had not, until that moment, recognised the music. 'Most remarkable.'

'I thought that, on this occasion,' Monsieur de Romblay said, 'the short version would suffice since, as you may have gathered,' and he aimed a wry smile at the ground, 'the Indians are not exactly renowned for their musicality.'

Suzanne had been studying the Director's face, the sly shifting of his eyes beneath their lids, the way his smile tucked into his plump cheeks. He seemed familiar, and she did not know why; certainly she had never met him before.

'Unfortunately my wife could not be here to greet you,' Monsieur de Romblay was telling her. 'She is at present arranging your accommodation.'

He turned to Théo. There was a small problem, he said. The house that they had been assigned was not yet ready. Instead, they were to occupy a suite of rooms in the Hôtel de Paris – at the company's expense, of course.

'You see,' he said, 'we thought you weren't coming.'

Théo could not conceal his surprise. 'But I wrote from Paris, Monsieur. I wrote to you.'

'You said February. It's now April.'

'We were delayed. The Panamanian railway was out of action. And then there were the storms – '

Monsieur de Romblay smiled into the air. 'That may be. But I fear that you have arrived at the wrong time.'

'I don't understand, Monsieur.'

'It's almost summer. Nobody builds in the summer.'

'We could always carry out the work during the hours when it's cooler,' Théo suggested.

A chuckle began deep inside Monsieur de Romblay. 'They don't exist, Monsieur.'

'Don't exist?'

'Cool hours. There's no such thing. Not in the summer.'

'I'm sure we can arrive at some solution, Monsieur de Romblay. That, after all, is what I'm here for.'

Théo cast a despairing look at Suzanne, but Monsieur de Romblay was already ushering them towards an open carriage.

'It's hardly surprising that we're late,' Suzanne ventured in a light tone as she took her seat opposite the Director, 'when you consider how far we've come.'

'Some people who sail round the Horn,' and Monsieur de Romblay paused, and his chuckle surfaced, '*ma foi*, they never arrive at all.' He enjoyed this joke of his so much that he had to produce a handkerchief and mop the tears from his cheeks.

Suzanne could not help liking him, despite the peremptory manner in which he had treated Théo. She thought that he was probably just establishing his own authority. He was the Director of Mining Operations which, in a town like Santa Sofía, was tantamount to being mayor. He was the Director and he wanted everyone to understand that, and once they did, it could be forgotten. It was a curiously provincial trait, and all of a sudden she knew what it was about him that struck her as familiar. It was not his face, but his voice. His accent.

'Forgive me for asking, Monsieur,' she said, 'but are you from Normandy?'

'I was born in Calais.'

'I thought so,' she exclaimed. 'You see, Monsieur, I grew up in Dieppe.'

'Then we're neighbours.'

'We are now,' she said.

Théo was looking at her with some perplexity, and she could guess why. She seldom spoke of her years in Dieppe – and when she did, it was never with any great fondness or nostalgia. But she had just realised that this coincidence, the link between her and the Director, could be worked to their advantage. Out here they might need allies, and Monsieur de Romblay, judging by the kindly look that he was now bestowing on her, was already close to being one.

Turning away from the Director, she noticed a man sitting in the shade of a tree. The man had a moustache. As she passed by, he raised his hat and smiled. It was an open smile, entirely without guile; it had no other motive than to show respect. She just had time to smile back before the man was hidden by a building. But his gesture lasted in her memory. This would be a friendly town.

She had reached the small square that marked the end of the Calle Francesa. She leaned on the stone parapet; it was still warm from the sun. The sky had darkened, but she could just make out the shape of the houses in the valley below, built in neat rows, like beans planted in a garden. Voices floated upwards. A dog barked once, then barked again – a strangely reluctant sound.

She stepped back from the parapet, uncertain what to do next. The breeze that drifted off the land smelt like a knife found lying at the bottom of a drawer, an unexpected blend of aniseed and rust. There was no freshness in it, nothing green, and yet it was dry and pure, it seemed to come from some high, clean place.

Looking left from where she stood, she could see the dirt-road bending away from her, over the brow of the hill, circling round behind the hospital, then dropping down into the part of town they called El Pueblo. It was still early, not even seven o'clock. She was not tired. A short flight of steps on the east side of the square took her to the road. Once there, she only hesitated for a moment before setting off down the hill.

There were rocks and potholes, and deep grooves worn by the wheels of carriages; she had to tread carefully, or she might fall. Two men rose through the darkness towards her, bent almost double by the loads that they were carrying. They stopped as she passed, not to rest but to stare. They spoke a language she could not identify. She heard it rasp across their tongues, grazing the air behind her as she walked on.

It was darker still in El Pueblo, as dark as the cupboards of her childhood. Sometimes a blade of light showed, bright, then fading, bright again – a candle seen through a crack in the side of a house. She could sense people moving past her down the street, or backwards into alleys, passageways, openings in walls, though it was only the movement that she sensed; she saw nothing as definite as a hand or a face. It could have been animals – dogs, perhaps, or pigs. One doorway spilled a cloudy yellow glow which reminded her of the apple cider her father used to buy for her at country fairs when she was young. She stood on the line where the light ended and the shadows began, and peered in. A single kerosene lamp hung from a rope that had been slung across the room. A family was gathered on the dirt-floor below, all eating with their fingers from the same tin bowl. Flies tangled in the air above their food. On the far wall Christ turned his eyes to the ceiling, as if he could not bear to look. She drew back from the door, moved on.

She took the first left-turning she could find. For a while she thought she was alone in the alley, then she noticed the girls in pale dresses who were leaning against the wall. They had flat faces and whistled softly through their teeth as she passed by. It was like the sound that the wind makes in trees. A sound as thin as needles. She walked faster, turned left again. She could not allow herself to think that she might have made a mistake in coming down the hill. Instead, she longed for a time when she knew the town, where to go for company – where not to go at all. But how would she ever know unless she confronted her ignorance?

Ahead of her, on the corner, she saw an old woman hunched over a fire, poking at the embers with a stick. She wished that she had chosen a different street: this travesty of her visit to Les Halles slowed her heart. But she did not feel that she could retrace her steps.

As she approached, the old woman looked beyond her, cackling. She glanced round. A crowd of children had gathered in her shadow. They must have been following her, but now they were standing still, fanned out behind her like a bridal train. There was a moment of quiet when only the spit and crackle of the fire could be heard, then they were moving closer, holding out their hands. They were asking for something. They used the same word, over and over again. She did not know it.

'I'm sorry,' she said, in her own language. 'I have nothing.'

'Sorry,' they cried, imitating her. 'Sorry.'

'Really, I have nothing,' she said. 'Look.' And she held her empty hands away from her sides.

But she might have been inviting them to admire her, for they clustered round her, touching her dress.

'Next time,' she said. 'Next time I'll bring you something.'

'Time,' they chanted. 'Time, time.'

She walked in the direction that would return her to the Mesa del Norte. The children followed her until the road began to climb and then they faltered, let her draw away from them. She did not look back again until she reached the hospital. They were still standing at the bottom of the hill, their faces tilted, pale in the darkness.

Entering the hotel lobby almost blinded her; she had to pause inside the door and let her eyes adjust. The wood floors stretched away, gilded under the electric lights. Minerals glittered in their oblong glass cases. Crimson drapes softened voices to a murmur, though, as she moved forwards, there came a sudden shout of laughter from the lounge. Through the curtained doorway she could see Théo sitting in a circle of their new acquaintants. She recognised the Director's blue frock-coat.

'Ah, Madame Valence.' His short arms convulsed and, with a flurry of elbows, he propelled himself out of his chair. 'May I present my wife?'

Madame de Romblay rose from the chair beside him. She was a handsome woman, in her middle-fifties.

Suzanne took her hand. 'I'm honoured, Madame.'

'What a charming creature.' Madame de Romblay offered her profile as she spoke, the words spilling over her shoulder. They must have been intended for her husband. 'I do hope that you're settling in, my dear.'

'Yes indeed, Madame. Thank you.'

Madame de Romblay had eyes the colour of tin and a nose that seemed profoundly attracted to her upper lip. When she smiled, her teeth slanted back into her mouth. Suzanne's first thought was that she had assumed the airs of her husband, though without the underlying humour.

'And this is Monsieur Castagnet,' Théo said, moving to her side. 'He has very kindly offered to assist me in the event of any construction difficulties.'

'We're not anticipating a great many of those, Madame.' Monsieur Castagnet bowed low.

Suzanne noted the large square face, the amused eyes, the forehead scored with lines. 'If the two of you are to be working together,' she said, 'then I can be perfectly confident of the outcome.'

Smiling, Monsieur Castagnet bowed again.

'And now, if you would excuse us,' Théo said, 'we really must retire. It has been a long day.'

He took Suzanne's arm and ushered her towards the stairs. Once they were alone, he turned to her.

'Where have you been?' His voice was hushed, fretful.

'I went for a walk.'

'A walk? Where?'

'Nowhere in particular,' she said.

'You didn't go into the town, I hope.'

'I walked along the street,' she said, 'then down the hill a little way.' She opened the door that led to their suite and moved beyond him, into the room.

'There were children,' she said, removing her gloves. 'They wanted something, but I didn't know what. Sweets, I suppose. Or money.'

'You shouldn't have gone down there, Suzanne. It's dangerous.'

'Dangerous?' She put surprise into her voice – though there had been a moment, she remembered, when she had felt uneasy. Those girls in pale dresses, air whistling between their teeth.

'Yes.' He turned away, frowning, and touched the bevelled edge of the mirror with one finger. 'Of course.'

'But we're living here, Théo. Surely we cannot live in fear.'

'We can live with propriety, however.'

Something gave way in her; she went and stood beside him, took his arm. 'I'm sorry,' she said. 'Perhaps it was foolish of me.'

As she spoke, the building shuddered. The shutters on the window rattled. She tightened her grip on his arm.

'That's the smelting works,' he said. 'When I told Monsieur de Romblay that I was looking forward to a good night's sleep, he just laughed. "You'll be lucky," he said.' Théo shook his head. 'That fellow takes great delight, it seems, in making fun of me.'

She smiled up at him. 'I love you, Théo.'

He sighed and patted her hand. 'I'm going to turn in. And you, my dear, you must be tired too.'

She nodded. 'I am.'

But she stood for a while longer by the window, looking out into the night. Many of the lights across the street had been extinguished. The Gulf of California lay far below, one shade darker than the sky. And it was then that she thought of the cabin-boy and felt a loneliness descend. She remembered how avidly they had listened to each other's stories, for they each believed the other's life to be more exotic than their own. But there had been no time to meet him again. No chance to compare their findings about the colour of the sea, no chance to lean against the rail and watch the water folding away from the side of the boat. No chance to say goodbye. That morning, as she climbed into the Director's carriage, she thought she saw a figure high up on the bridge, a figure with eyes like splinters and a head of curls. But when she waved, the figure had not waved back. She felt the disappointment sink into her, the way rain sinks into sand and darkens it. Her breath misted the glass. She wished that events would not so readily assume the shape of punishments.

Then she heard Théo call her name and, turning away from the window, she moved across the room towards him.

5

Hôtel de Paris,
Santa Sofía,
Lower California,
Mexico

20th April, 189 –

My dear Monsieur Eiffel,

A second letter, following swiftly on the heels of the first, seemed called for, if only to reassure you that we have arrived at our destination without further mishap.

Santa Sofía is a most unusual town, dividing as it does into three almost completely separate parts. The centre is laid out on a grid pattern, three avenues wide (each one bearing the name of an indigenous mineral) and ten streets deep, coming to an abrupt end one kilometre inland in a steep wall of sandstone and pumice. The mineworkers, predominantly of Indian extraction, are housed here in rows of identical dwellings that were built for them by the company and, though insufficient time has passed for the houses to have achieved much of a sense of individuality, the character of certain tenants can be deduced from the speed with which their properties are becoming dilapidated. To the south, high on an inhospitable ridge, a modest company of Mexican soldiers (or *rurales*, as they are known) has been garrisoned. Their commander, Captain Montoya, is the local representative of the Mexican Government. As such, he is held responsible for policing the entire area, and he can also be called upon to intercede between the French and the Indians, should any disagreement or unpleasantness arise; I can make no comment on the gentleman, since I have not yet had the pleasure of his acquaintance. The French, meanwhile, are to be found in the northern section of the town. We have made our home on a plateau that plays host to any passing breeze and is therefore considerably more comfortable than the valley below. The Mesa del Norte (known, colloquially, as Frenchtown) comprises one wide street that seems familiar and reassuring at the outset – with its paved surface and its rows of plane trees planted down both sides, it is faintly reminiscent of a Parisian boulevard – though this familiarity is, in itself, strange and not a little disconcerting. It is here that we are quartered, in the local hotel, having been assured that a house awaits us.

And so to the work in progress – though the word 'progress' is hardly appropriate in the circumstances. The assembly of this particular church ought to be a simple enough process (and would be, if we were in France), but a number of difficulties have already arisen. Owing to our late arrival, we shall be building during the hottest months of the year. It is for this reason, I surmise, that we have so far been unable to muster an adequate labour force, though Monsieur de Romblay assures me that men will be found, even if he has to sacrifice a few of his own workers from the mine. In any case, we cannot yet begin the assembly since the foundations, which were to be laid in advance of our arrival, have been installed without the proper care and attention, and will have to be scrapped and then rebuilt. Perhaps, after all, this is just the confusion that surrounds any project at the outset.

I trust this letter finds you in the best of health, Monsieur. You would do me a great service if you would convey to your daughter Claire my very best wishes on the occasion of her birthday; it seems strange to be asking this of you in April, and yet, by the time this letter reaches you, the sentiment will, I judge, be an appropriate one. I am, respectfully, your most humble and obedient servant,

    Théophile Valence.

6

The doctor had told Wilson to rest, which was no great hardship if you lived in a fine house with maids and ceiling fans and a veranda. All Wilson had was a single room on the first floor of the Hotel La Playa. A narrow bed stood in the corner, its springs so exhausted that his spine touched the floor when he lay down. A striped blanket hid the mattress. There were no sheets. There was no closet either. Someone had driven nails into the wall instead. Three copper nails, green with rust. Still, they served as a place to hang his jacket and his hat. Plaster had tumbled from the ceiling, exposing joists of blackened wood and, over by the door, he could see between two floorboards down into the room below. There was a stubborn smell of cooking-fat and sour sweat. At least he faced the street, though. That was something. At least he had a view.

There were two chairs backed up against the wall, both as weak on their legs as newborn calves. He pulled one towards the window. It wasn't a bad room, really. He had known worse. It just wasn't a fine house with maids and ceiling fans and a veranda, that was all. He poured an inch of whisky into a cracked glass. Then he lit the stub of a cigar and settled back.

That morning Jesús Pompano had burned the bread again. Wilson sensed it the moment he woke up – a taste of ashes in his throat, that charred edge to the air. As he reached for his crutches he glanced out of the window. A thin column of smoke lifted from the roof of the bakery.

Downstairs in the lobby he went looking for Pablo, thinking they could discuss this new development, but there was no sign of him, only a boy scraping vulture droppings off the floor with a piece of palm bark. Pablo would not have been much use anyway; it was still only eight in the morning. Pablo never spoke a word before midday, not to anyone. It was a matter of principle.

Wilson found Jesús slumped on a sack of grain in the bakery, his chin propped on his fist. Flour clung to his eyebrows and his pale, heavy mouth. He looked old before his time.

'Those French,' and Jesús blew some breath out, and it turned white as it passed through his lips, 'they'll be the death of me.'

'Another failure, I take it.'

'See for yourself.'

Wilson crossed the stone floor and rested his crutches against the counter. He peered into the mouth of the oven. Three blackened loaves lay smouldering on their baking tray. One of them had split open, as if somebody had taken an axe to it; a wisp of steam rose from the fissure like an apology. He turned away, leaned an elbow on the counter.

'Now they're telling me I have to build a sloping oven. *¡Chingada Madre!*' Jesús cleared his throat and spat through the doorway, then he stared at the floor again and slowly shook his head.

'A sloping oven?' Wilson was not sure if he had understood.

'It helps with the moisture. You have to have moisture, they tell me. Without moisture it can't be done. Well, let me tell you something. I can't stand moisture. I loathe it. Moisture makes me puke.'

'I saw the doctor yesterday,' Wilson said. 'He's getting impatient.'

'Is he the one with the fancy waistcoats?'

'That's him.'

'He's the worst. Always down here, poking around.'

'He just likes his French bread, that's all.'

'He should have stayed in France, then, shouldn't he.'

Wilson grinned.

'They'll be the death of me, those French.' Jesús shook his head again. A cloud of flour rose into the air and hung in a shaft of sunlight, looking suddenly as if it were made of gold. As Wilson watched, the middle of the cloud disintegrated; the cloud became a halo. The baker still sat gloomily below. It seemed to Wilson that he had been witness to a prophecy, which was his to do with as he wished.

'It will come right in the end, Jesús,' he said, and felt quite confident in his prediction.

Jesús looked at Wilson for the first time since Wilson had walked in. 'What did you do to your foot?'

He must have been the only person in town who had not heard. He had been too preoccupied to see beyond the four walls of his bakery. An earthquake could have happened. A flood. He would not have known.

Wilson drank from his cracked glass. Through the window he could see the tilting iron rooftops of the town, the steep escarpment of the Mesa de Francia and the clean blue sky beyond. In the foreground a space had been cleared, about the size of a small town-square or a ceremonial arena; Wilson could imagine that an Indian tribe might dance on that red dirt, and call it sacred. As he stared down, a man passed through his line of vision. The man was buttoned into a black frock-coat, and held a white umbrella above his head. In his other hand he clutched a handkerchief; every now and then he would reach up and dab his throat, his forehead, the back of his neck. On his feet he wore a pair of immaculate white spats. A Frenchman. No doubt about it.

The Frenchman advanced to the middle of the arena and stood still, facing east. Then he turned about and faced the mountains in the west. His shadow crouched behind him. He began to walk westwards, his legs stiff, his stride exaggerated. He was counting the number of paces, measuring the ground. When he could go no further, he stopped and nodded to himself.

Then, suddenly, he was running back the way he had come. It was a strange sight, a man running with an umbrella above his head, especially when that man was a Frenchman. You rarely saw a Frenchman running; there was no dignity in it. Without taking his eyes off the man, Wilson lifted his glass and drank. The man was holding up his hand as he ran and Wilson could now see why. Some Indians had filed into the square. They were carrying pieces of grey metal; some of the pieces were large, and required the combined efforts of six men. It seemed important to the Frenchman that the pieces be set down in certain precise locations, but the Indians were having trouble following his instructions – or maybe it was simply that they did not see the point. Arms were being waved, heads shaken. The pieces of grey metal moved from one place to another. Then, sometimes, they moved back again. Wilson was highly entertained by the charade; it might almost have been arranged on his behalf, something to keep him amused during the long hours of his convalescence. But his smile faded as the Frenchman, pale with exasperation, turned his face up to the sky. He was the man from the boat. The man who had walked down the gangway with that woman on his arm. The man who had sat beside her in the carriage. A jolting began somewhere under Wilson's ribs. He poured himself another shot of whisky, swallowed it.

Almost a week had passed since he had raised his hat to her and still he had not been able to banish her image from his mind – her yellow dress, her eyes like leaves, her hair tumbling blonde and bronze on to her shoulders. He dredged his past for some comparison, but he could only think of the girl he had known in Monterey when he was sixteen.

Her name was Saffron and she had been older than he was, almost twenty. She wore a shapeless green satin dress and no shoes. He had seen her in the street when it was raining, her bare feet turning puddles into crowns of water round her ankles as she ran, her red hair trailing in the air behind her. Later, she sat on his lap in the back of a saloon and her mouth tasted of brine, but her body was as firm as his belief in heaven under that slippery green dress.

He was not the only lover she had – there were others; he knew of at least two – but he was grateful to be counted among them, to be sharing her favours. In his innocence he felt privileged. And she had never lied to him. From the beginning he was made to understand that jealousy was something he was not entitled to. There was an odd purity about the girl, for all her promiscuities; twenty-five years later, he still felt a kind of skewed respect for her.

They would sit on the quay, among the coiled ropes and fishing nets, and watch the fog roll in, and it would fold around their shoulders, reach between their faces, and all the harbour sounds closed in – the creak of hawsers, sailors' curses, cats in heat – and he would push his hands beneath her clothes and taste the weather on her lips, and there was fear in it, her pa would strap her if he knew, which only made the trembling more. But the danger did not issue from her family. One night a tall man showed; old he seemed then, though he had probably been less than thirty. He strode out of the fog and pulled a gun from his overcoat and fired. It sounded as if he had hit a tin tray with his fist. They fled, but there were no more shots. They crouched in a warehouse stacked high with salted mackerel and listened for his tread. None came.

'Passion done spoiled his aim.' She was panting, and her eyes glittered through her hair. 'He's not like you. He wants to be the only one.'

Again he felt the privilege of being close to her and, later that night, with the moon dull on the water, he told her that he loved her.

'Oh Will,' she said, 'not you as well.'

'I don't mean nothing by it.' He stared at the moon on the water. He stared so hard, he thought he might shatter it.

'Will,' and her voice was as soft and biased as a mother's hand, 'you don't have the first idea.'

Then, one morning, his father shook him awake with the news that he had hitched them a ride on a covered wagon heading east, and it was leaving directly. He folded his bedroll, his mind still flat with sleep. It felt like one of those Chinese paper lanterns he had seen on Montgomery Street. You bought them flat and then you had to shake them out. Sometimes it was hours before his mind opened and there was light in it.

He followed his father down the narrow stairs and out on to the street. The sun had not yet risen, but the sky was warming up on the horizon, a blush of light that made his father's eyes look fierce and clean. A man in a crumpled hat drove past them in a cart. A second man was balanced on the tailgate. He had rolled his sleeves up and he was dipping his hand in a barrel and his pale arm swung this way and that, like he was sowing seeds. But it was water that he was throwing on the street, salt water to hold the dust down. It must have been summer.

He huddled in the back of the wagon, pressed half-way off the bench by a man whose broadcloth coat was sticky with liquor and the grease of hogs. A cock crowed on a nearby roof; he could see its shape cut out against a strip of sky. His father handed him a tin mug with an inch of cold coffee in the bottom. He drank it down.

The wagon rocked and rattled east. As the town became memory, he began to think of the girl with the red hair and the green satin dress. If only he had asked for a lock of that hair of hers, a snippet of that dress. He had nothing but a name, held inside him, like a smooth stone in the darkness of a pocket. If only that tall man's bullet had nicked his cheek. He did not even carry a scar he could remember her by. And it was too late now. And though he passed through Monterey several years later, on his way north, to Oregon, he never did see her again.

A clock struck two somewhere. He drained his glass.

It had been his custom, during the afternoons, to walk up the hill to the Hôtel de Paris, which was the fancy place where all the French people stayed. He had noticed an old upright in the lobby. The wood had warped in the heat, and the keys had stiffened, but it was still a decent piano – a Chickering, from Little, Brown & Co. of Boston. He would sit on the maroon plush stool and run through pieces that he used to play in San Francisco – ballads, marches, Negro melodies, fragments of opera from Europe, even hymns. It took him back to the years when he worked in the saloons around Portsmouth Square, the Empire and the Alhambra, La Souciedad, the Rendez-vous, ten bucks a night and another ten in tips if he was lucky, say if Bill Briggs dropped by, or Jack Gamble with his diamond stick-pin flashing like a whore's eye on his shirt, ten bucks at least, those were the days. And then it took him further back; his mind would empty out and he would reach way down, deep into the past, and play dance tunes that his father used to whistle when they lived by trapping beaver in New Mexico, and Rodrigo Feliz, the houseboy at the hotel, would watch him from behind the bar, with his eyes the colour of wet leaves and his girl's mouth. But the music Wilson kept returning to was *Carmen*, by a Frenchman called Bizet. He had first heard *Carmen* on a trip back to San Francisco in the eighties. It had some fine tunes in it. His fingers got restless just thinking about it.

Before his foot broke, he could make his way up to Frenchtown any time he pleased. Even now he played most afternoons, but it required a measure of tenacity and planning. One thought, one image, sustained him: the woman in the yellow dress. His eyes lifted to the plateau where the carriage containing her had gone. He knew nothing about her; all he knew was that he had seen her face. And she was married – he knew that too. Mama Vum Buá had told him about the ring she wore. 'Solid gold it was, and thick as rope,' the Señora had said, her blue eyes growing still more blue. 'She must get awful tired carrying that thing around all day.' He knew nothing about her, and yet there was a new shape to his days, a sense of expectation. Not that he expected anything. Another glimpse of her, maybe. That was all the closeness he could hope for. That was all he asked.

He corked the bottle and, reaching for his crutches, hoisted himself to his feet. If he was going up to the hotel he had to move now. Two reasons. One: he would be less likely to run into La Huesuda and have to endure another lecture on his clumsiness and his sexual inadequacy (she always slept in the afternoon). Two: the waterboys made deliveries to Frenchtown after lunch and if he timed it right he would be able to hitch a ride on the back of their cart.

He was half-way down the stairs when his good foot caught in the banisters. In an attempt to save the damaged one, he almost toppled headlong and broke everything else. He was beginning to lose his faith in manmade structures. Maybe he should forget about playing the piano for the time being. Maybe he should forget the whole damn thing. Half-way down the stairs, he stood quite motionless, the sweat cooling on his face.

There had been a terrible winter once, in the Sierras with his father, when they had dug hole after hole, when they had moved earth, washed it, moved earth, washed it, week after week of bloodied hands and all for a couple of dollars a day, just barely enough to keep them from dying. Yet there was always someone near by, someone in the next placer or someone they just plain heard about, who had lifted sagebrush at the edge of a creek and found so many pieces of gold among the roots that he had taken the next ship to New York to live like an American King Solomon. It did not matter how bad things got. There was always something to keep you from trailing home to a life with no shine in it. Though maybe he should track Pablo down before the week was out, and speak to him about a room on the ground floor, just until his foot was mended.

7

From bats' wings at dusk, whispering through the deadened air, to the stubborn clanking of water churns at dawn, Santa Sofía was a place of incongruous sounds, but no sound was more incongruous, perhaps, than the sound of Bizet's *Carmen* being played on an out-of-tune piano in the middle of the afternoon. Suzanne found the piano downstairs, pushed against the wall in a distant corner of the lobby. She lifted the lid. The white keys were as discoloured as a horse's teeth. Two black keys had gone missing altogether. The piano did not look as if it had been used for years. And who would play *Carmen*, anyway? People thought it vulgar, hysterical. She stood beside the maroon piano stool, one elbow cupped in her hand, her fingers curled against her chin. Perhaps her dreams had served the music up to her. Perhaps she had imagined it.

The Hôtel de Paris was as luxurious as she and Théo could have hoped for, given the desolate surroundings, and the suite of rooms in which they had taken up temporary residence was the best in the hotel. There were armchairs upholstered in striped damask and floors of polished oak, and all the walls had been lined with silk – the drawing-room in peacock-blue, the bedroom in scarlet. The brass bed was said to have belonged to one of Maximilian's generals. Théo thought the décor more appropriate to a bordello than a hotel, and certainly, waking in that scarlet chamber on the first morning, Suzanne could not imagine where she was. Then she noticed the sky, a flawless blue, immaculate and hard, and she remembered. 'Mexico,' she whispered to herself. 'I'm in Mexico.'

She saw very little of Théo during the week of their arrival, but that was only to be expected. She did not mind – in fact, if anything it suited her. She was able to take the days at her own pace.

In the mornings she sat on the hotel veranda. From her table she could look down a barren hillside of rocks and cactus to the narrow coastal strip where most of the town's industry was to be found. Beyond that jumble of brown buildings lay the Sea of Cortez, palest blue, too lazy to achieve a tide, yet capable, so Théo had told her, of the most sudden and violent storm that was known locally as El Cordonazo or 'the Lash'. While she gazed at the view which, even at an early hour, would seem to undulate in the heat, Rodrigo, the houseboy, would bring her coffee in a glass cup, a basket of fresh rolls and a French newspaper that was never less than six months out of date. Rodrigo moved with a kind of slovenly grace which was only appealing because he was young, and which would in time, she felt, become grotesque. He always had a smile for her, though, and he would leave small gifts on her table – sometimes the flower from a prickly pear, sometimes a piece of fruit. It was Rodrigo who showed her the library behind the office, shelves of novels, journals and almanacs that had been discarded by previous guests, some in English, the rest in French, and it was Rodrigo who then offered to carry her selections up the stairs for her. She spent whole afternoons in her drawing-room, reclining on the ottoman by the window. She sketched, she read her books; she slept. There were no more expeditions of the kind that she had undertaken on her first evening. She did not seek the land out; she was content to let it come to her.

Her first visitor was the Director's wife. A sharp, two-syllable knock on the door heralded a flurry of emerald silk skirts as Madame de Romblay launched herself into the room. Her tin eyes glittered; her tea-gown foamed with Irish lace.

'Forgive me for disturbing you like this. I was just passing.' Her mouth opened in a mirthless smile. 'In a town the size of Santa Sofía, one cannot help but be just passing.' She placed one hand against her collar-bone and stooped to examine the gilt frame on a miniature. 'How are you, my dear?'

'I'm very well, thank you.' Suzanne always had the feeling that Madame de Romblay's questions, though innocent and conventional on the surface, were probing after some much deeper and more unhappy truth. 'Can I offer you something?'

But the woman was already half-way to the fireplace, her eyes scanning the silk-lined walls, her pale-green sunshade twitching on her shoulder. 'It's not a bad hotel, though it's not what you're used to, I'm sure.'

'I'm not used to staying in hotels at all,' Suzanne replied. 'Actually, I'm quite enjoying it.'

Madame de Romblay surveyed her from the far end of the room. 'We are so few here. I'm afraid that you'll be bored.'

'I came here to be with my husband, Madame. I did not expect a constant round of entertainment.'

'Well, we do our best.' With a fatalistic sigh, Madame de Romblay opened a fan that was inlaid with mother-of-pearl and began to beat the air beneath her chin. 'There will be a dinner, of course,' she said, 'to welcome you both.'

'I shall look forward to it.'

'Oh yes, and my husband asked me to assure you that you'll not be inconvenienced for much longer. Your house will be ready by the end of the week,' and Madame de Romblay's eyes lingered on the books and journals that littered surfaces throughout the room, 'then you'll have something to occupy you at last.'

Later, Suzanne stood at the window and watched as Madame de Romblay emerged from the ground floor of the hotel. The drawing-room still seemed disrupted by her presence. The air churned.

It was the doctor who appeared next, using his professional status as an excuse for a visit which was, Suzanne suspected, entirely social.

'And how are you feeling, Madame?' He spun gracefully into the room on slippered feet, the tips of his moustache as sharp as the points of pencils, his hair slick with pomade.

She admitted to being somewhat tired.

'A long voyage,' the doctor said. 'A new climate.' He opened his hands and brought his shoulders up towards his ears. 'It's only to be expected.'

'And what do you prescribe, Doctor?'

'Rest, Madame.'

'I've been resting a good deal,' she told him.

'Excellent.' The doctor nodded to himself. His sleek hair caught the light and flashed. 'One must conserve one's energy. I insist that my wife rests for at least an hour every afternoon. She finds it most beneficial.'

Suzanne had met Florestine Bardou the day before, on the Calle Francesa. The two women stood on the street, their faces shaded by the fringed rims of their parasols. Florestine had been wearing a plain grey dress which constrasted most strangely with the luxuriant convolutions of her name, and she had the habit of lowering her eyes when she was speaking as if she were in the presence of someone far more important than herself. Suzane was beginning to understand how this might have come about.

'Well,' the doctor was saying, 'I just hope that life won't be too dull for you. I hope that you will not become too,' and his eyes lifted to the ceiling as he searched for the word, 'too jaded.'

She smiled. 'The town doesn't seem to have had that effect on you, Doctor.'

'No?' The doctor glowed. He was not a man to be dismayed by compliments.

That afternoon, as she followed his advice and rested for an hour, she heard the piano again, only this time it was not *Carmen*, but something that she did not know. It sounded like a ballad or a show-tune, she decided, as she closed her eyes. She dreamed of people dancing in a barn, with bales of hay stacked high against the walls, rush-torches casting shadows on a sawdust floor.

In the evening she looked for Rodrigo. She found him on the veranda, idly flicking dead flies off the tables with an ancient copy of *Le Temps*. When he saw her, his eyes brightened.

'You have been reading?' he asked.

She smiled at his mangled, lisping French. 'A little.' She let her eyes drift out over the Sea of Cortez. The water had absorbed the fading light, its surface the colour of woodsmoke, or hyacinth. It was after five o'clock. People would soon be arriving for their aperitifs.

She turned back to Rodrigo. 'I thought I heard someone playing the piano this afternoon.'

'Yes, Madame.'

'Do you know who it is who plays?'

'He is American.'

'There's an American here?'

'Yes. He plays the piano. Always in the afternoon.' Rodrigo smiled, and his sharp teeth showed. 'He is a good man,' Rodrigo said, 'but he is,' and he revolved one finger in the air beside his ear.

'Mad?' she said.

'Yes.' He grinned. 'Mad.'

The following afternoon, towards three o'clock, Suzanne was woken from a light sleep by the opening bars of Schubert's 'Marche Militaire'. She rose from the couch and crossed the room to her dressing-table. She had determined to seek out the American and make his acquaintance. It would be a welcome diversion; it would also be a chance to practise her English. She had only met one American before. In the summer of 1889 Buffalo Bill Cody had brought his Wild West Company to Paris as part of the

World Fair. During his stay Mr Cody had visited the Eiffel Tower and, after he had signed his name in the guest book, she and Théo, among others, had taken him to lunch. He had been a man of some considerable charm, despite his long hair and his peculiar clothes.

She made one final adjustment to her dress, then left the room. When she reached the bottom of the stairs, however, she hesitated; she did not advance into the lobby. The American was seated at the piano, less than twenty feet away. He was playing with such vigour that he remained entirely unaware of her. She drew back into the shadows.

Light flooded through the windows behind him. His face was hard to see. He sat with a straight back, his hat wedged down to his eyebrows, his fingers jumping on the keys. She thought she recognised him, and did not know from where. Then she remembered. He was the man who had lifted his hat to her on that first day. It was, in fact, the same hat. It was the hat that she had recognised, not the man.

She took another step backwards, the heel of her right shoe touching the bottom stair, her thumb set sideways against her mouth. The American reminded her of somebody from her childhood in Paris – the gardener, perhaps, the lamp-lighter or the postman. It was not the lowliness; quite the reverse. It was the unacknowledged stature. Not the prescribed role, but its secret counterpart. These had always been people she could trust, people who would not give her away. She remembered one with particular fondness, a man with a voice like logs hauled over rocks. She knew him as Monsieur Épaules. He was the water-carrier. Every morning he would tramp up the back stairs with two pails suspended across his shoulders on a wooden bar. The pails would be brimming with water, yet he would never spill a drop. The palms of his hands were so rough, it seemed as if he had been made from bits of trees. He wore a velveteen suit of darkest green, and he carried an earthy smell about with him; being close to him was not unlike being in a forest. She did not think that she had ever seen him out of breath, even though, in those days, they had lived in an apartment on the seventh floor. Perhaps he rested on every landing. Somehow she doubted it. She never found out whether Monsieur Épaules was his real name, or whether he had invented it for her – his own wry summary of his place in life, a statement of his limitations.

He would always stop and tell her tales about where their water had come from that morning – which spring, which reservoir, which well – and he wore a flask of thick glass on a cord around his neck that contained, he said, a water that could not be surpassed, a water so rare that it was almost holy. And he would cross himself in the dark air of the stairwell, and she would too. The very last time that he delivered water to their house, just prior to their departure for Dieppe, he poured her a small glass of this most precious liquid. He held the glass out to her. She took it in both hands. He smelled more than ever like a forest on that last day. His dented silver pails stood on the floor like held breath.

She brought the glass up to her lips. The edge where you drank from was thick and smooth. She took a sip. The water tasted bitter, almost like metal. That was because it was filled with minerals, he told her. It had come from under the ground, from a place a kilometre down. It was virgin water, he said, clear and bright and pure.

She held the glass out for him to take.

He shook his head. 'Drink it all up. It will keep you strong until the day when you return.'

It was to be almost twelve years before her family moved back to Paris. She must have been eighteen by then. She was already in love with Théo, and he lived in Paris, yet her first impulse on returning was to seek out Monsieur Épaules. But the city had changed during her absence. The twenty thousand water-carriers of Paris had been trampled by the march of progress. They no longer existed. They had been replaced by pipes.

Her father thought it was a good thing, of course, as did Théo. They were always talking about the advantages of 'constant supply' in those self-important voices that men so often use. She did not care a fig for 'constant supply'; she liked whatever the opposite of it was. This new, modern city was most certainly a disappointment. She felt as if she had been cheated, betrayed; she felt, too, that she had broken her word. For the first few weeks she never went anywhere without peering at everyone she passed, without scanning the streets and pavements for a glimpse of a man in velveteen that was the colour of a forest. Even later she would think of him, and wonder where he was. She hoped that he was still alive somewhere, and that his virgin water had kept him strong.

Back in her room, sitting at her writing desk, she stared through the window at the landscape that she had insisted on seeing. When she first set eyes on the American, spied on him from the shadows at the bottom of the stairs, she had the feeling of returning to a piece of the past that had happened without her. He had allowed her access to a pleasure that she had always been denied. In that moment, sitting at her writing desk, she felt as if her presence in the town was proper, natural – even earned. She felt as if she were about to be compensated for her many disappointments. This place would afford her some redress.

8

The cart shuffled to a halt outside the Hôtel de Paris. Wilson slid down off the tailgate, pulling his crutches after him. He thanked the boys for the ride.

'Any time, four-legs.'

They fought briefly over the reins, then the cart moved on, its high silver churns tottering and clanking. 'Water,' the boys cried, in their hoarse voices. 'Fresh water.'

Wilson shook his head as he watched them go. There was no respect for Americans in this town, no respect at all.

Still shaking his head, he swung round on his crutches, and there she was, standing at the foot of the hotel steps, with her green eyes the shape of leaves and that tumbling, dark-blonde hair. In a town the size of Santa Sofía coincidences were no cause for astonishment; in fact, they were practically a way of life. Yet he had been relying on coincidence for so many days now with no result that this coincidence, long overdue, took him completely by surprise. The sight of her at such close quarters when he had only imagined her at a distance closed the spaces between the beatings of his heart. He went to lift his hat, but it fell from his hand. One of his crutches toppled.

Gracefully she leaned down, retrieved the hat.

'Here,' she said.

'You speak English?' He had not expected this.

'I teach it.' She corrected herself. 'I used to teach it. When I was young.' She laughed.

'You speak it very well.'

She looked away into the sky. 'You know, it's strange. I did not think that I would need English,' and she brought her eyes back down to his, and they were filled with the sky's light, 'not here, in Mexico.'

There was not the slightest trace either of shyness or flirtation in her manner. Her parasol revolved slowly on her shoulder, like the wheel of a cart that has turned over in a road. He was the shy one. No words would come to him.

'You are the piano player,' she said.

He admitted it. 'Though I'm a little rusty, I'm afraid.'

'Rusty? What is rusty?'

'It means I'm out of practice.'

'But I heard you from my room. You're good. You are, how does one say it,' and the shadow at the corner of her mouth lengthened as a smile reached her face, 'you have enthusiasm.'

It was for you, he almost said, but could not. He thanked her instead.

'Will you play today?' she asked him.

'If you would like me to.'

Her smile widened. 'Shall we go in?'

'Give me an orange juice and a beer, would you, Rodrigo?'

Rodrigo eyed Wilson across the cool zinc counter. Rodrigo was polishing a glass. Wilson would have laid odds on the fact that Rodrigo had been polishing that same glass for half an hour.

'You're going to play the piano, Señor Wilson?'

'Maybe.'

'You must like the piano very much.' Rodrigo's eyes reached beyond Wilson's shoulder to the Frenchwoman who was now taking a seat at the table by the window.

'I do.'

'You must like it very much,' Rodrigo said, 'to come all the way up here with that bad foot.'

'It's good for it. The doctor told me. It's exercise.'

'Exercise. I see.' Rodrigo was still polishing the glass, only much more slowly now.

'An orange juice and a beer,' Wilson said, 'when you're ready, that is.'

'No beer today, Señor.'

'I'll have two orange juices then.'

'What about yesterday?'

'What about yesterday, Rodrigo?'

'You didn't pay me for yesterday. Or the day before.' Rodrigo made a few languid calculations on his fingers. 'You owe me forty-five pesos.'

Wilson sighed.

'I know, I know,' Rodrigo said. 'One day you'll find your gold and then you'll pay me everything.'

When Rodrigo brought the drinks, some ten minutes later, Wilson turned to the Frenchwoman and apologised. 'You know, the oranges come from Mulege,' he said. 'It's about forty miles south of town. The time it takes Rodrigo to make a glass of juice, I reckon he probably goes down there and picks them himself.'

'It doesn't matter. I'm not in a hurry.' She smiled. 'We saw Mulege from the boat. There were many palm trees. And a rock shaped like a hat.' She sipped at her drink. 'And you, Monsieur,' she said, 'where are you from?'

As if he, too, were a species of fruit.

'San Francisco,' he said.

'San Francisco?' The name had the effect of widening her eyes and softening her voice.

'That's where I learned to play the piano.'

He found himself talking about his childhood, San Francisco in the early days. You could only mine for gold from April until October, and the city was almost empty then. In the winter everyone returned. There were not enough jobs to go around. Pay was low. His father had worked down at the docks unloading cargo. Only five dollars a ton, but he was lucky to have a job at all. It seemed to rain all the time. There was great poverty, great frustration. People got killed over nothing, and the punishment for murder was death.

The city was so new, unformed. Many of the streets did not even have names. He would make them up himself. In those days the cost of storing merchandise was more than the merchandise itself was worth. Goods were often dumped outdoors, simply abandoned. There was a sidewalk close to where Wilson lived that was built out of sacks of flour from Shanghai. He called it Chinese Flour Street. There were others too: Saucepan Alley, Tobacco Way –

'The street where I grew up,' he said, 'it was always called Piano Street.'

'There were pianos?'

'A dozen of them, maybe more. And some still worked. That was how I learned to play, right there, in the middle of the street. With people passing by. Sometimes they would throw me money.'

'Did you play concerts for them?'

Wilson nodded. 'I even did a funeral once.'

A friend of his, John Goode by name, had died of pneumonia. Wilson had played the 'Funeral March' by Chopin for John Goode's family as they carried the boy's coffin up the street. It had rained that day and he could still remember the feeling of his fingers slipping on the black keys.

He stopped and looked at her. She was gazing down into her glass. 'I'm sorry,' he said. 'Maybe I talked too fast.'

'No, no,' she said. 'I understand almost everything.'

At last she looked up and wonder filled her face so full, it almost seemed as if it could have been poured. He saw that he had brought her some kind of happiness, though he did not know how, nor could he begin to guess.

'Pardon me for asking, ma'am, but what's your name?'

Her hand moved to hide her mouth. 'Oh, I'm sorry, Monsieur. How impolite of me.' But she was smiling – or at least her eyes were, leaves narrowing and sharpening at the edges.

'It's nothing,' he said. 'We just forgot.'

'I am Suzanne Valence.'

He rose to his feet and, after first wiping his hand so as not to soil her glove, offered it to her.

'Wilson Pharaoh,' he said.

'I'm delighted to meet you, Mr Pharaoh,' she said. 'Now please, I beg you, tell me more about Piano Street.'

Wilson placed his glass on top of the piano and lifted the lid. The keyboard seemed to grin at him. For the last week he had been making his way up to the Calle Francesa every afternoon – it had taken real determination; once he had even walked – and he had played the piano for an hour each time, but he had been denied even a glimpse of the woman in the yellow dress. Only the day before he had decided to give up on it: the piano, the woman – everything. Now it turned out that she had been staying in the hotel, one floor above, that she had been listening to him all along. And here he was, about to play for her in person! The tips of his fingers rested on the keys. He would begin with something spritely, a dance tune that his father used to whistle.

It was a while later and he was just embarking on a piece of Schubert when the doctor ran lightly up the hotel steps. As he entered the lobby he saw Suzanne, and bowed from the waist. 'Madame.' Then his eye fell on Wilson, over at the piano. 'Ah, Monsieur Pharaoh.' He launched himself across the room. 'But I am sure that I told you to rest. Or is my English so bad?'

The doctor was wearing a different waistcoat today, but it was no disappointment: a brocade design in colours that could only be described as burgundy and lightning.

'Your English is not bad at all, Doctor. Your English is very good.'

'Then what am I to understand? That you cannot live without music? That, without this,' the doctor clutched at the air, 'this opportunity for self-expression, your life would be a misery?'

'A little piano practice,' and Wilson spread his hands. 'Surely that cannot hurt.'

The doctor leaned down, a glint of mischief in his eye, and lowered his voice. 'And the company of a beautiful woman,' and he tapped Wilson on the shoulder with the backs of his fingers. 'Am I wrong, Monsieur Pharaoh?'

He waited until he saw that Wilson could not find an answer, then he stood back, rolling one wing of his moustache between finger and thumb. A smile darted nimbly from one part of his face to another.

'Try to rest, Monsieur Pharaoh. Just a little. For me.' And, dusting one palm against the other, the doctor spun on his heel and glided from the room. His waistcoat flickered in the gloom of the long corridor that led to the back of the hotel.

'What did he say?' Rodrigo asked, in Spanish.

Wilson spoke over the staccato notes of *Carmen*. 'Well, Rodrigo, it was just like I said the other day. He told me to keep playing. For the exercise.'

'Mr Pharaoh,' came Suzanne's voice from the far end of the room, 'you are the most terrible liar.'

'Yes, ma'am. That's true.' And the distance between them gave him the courage to voice the first thought that came to mind. 'But I would never lie to you.'

A few minutes later, he walked back across the room towards her, walked into her soft applause.

'I remember when that was first performed in France.' She smiled. 'Everybody hated it.'

'It's one of my favourite pieces,' he said.

'Mine too.' Her smile widened. 'And now you have brought it here,' she said, 'to Santa Sofía.' She turned her glass on its base and then lifted her eyes to his. 'Tell me, Monsieur. Do you like it here?'

It was not something he had thought much about. He shifted in his chair. 'It's a town full of strangers. There's nobody that belongs, not really.'

'You're talking about us,' she said, 'the French.'

'Not just the French. The Mexicans, the Portuguese.' He leaned backwards in his chair. 'See, twenty years ago there was nothing here. No town, no harbour. Maybe there was a mission, maybe that. But nothing else. Everyone who came here, came from somewhere else. Even the Indians.'

'Do you think that you will stay?'

He looked down at his foot and grinned ruefully. 'It looks like it.' And before she could ask any questions that might embarrass him, he said, 'And you, how long will you stay?'

She shrugged. 'It depends. Two months. Perhaps three. I do not know how long it takes to build a church.'

He pictured the deserted square, just a piece of red ground, quite empty, then he saw a Frenchman running, a white umbrella in the air above his head.

'So you're here to build the church?' he said.

'My husband is.' She paused. 'Have you heard of the Eiffel Tower, Monsieur?'

He had not.

'It's the tallest structure in the world. It was built by a very famous man in France. His name is Gustave Eiffel. My husband works with him. My husband is an engineer.'

He watched the pride rise into her face and colour it. He saw how much she loved her husband and how, for reasons of convention, she was doing her utmost to conceal it.

'He worked on the designs with Monsieur Eiffel and now he will assemble it. Here, in Mexico.' She laughed. 'There are two thousand, three hundred and forty-eight pieces.'

She turned to the window, and he looked at her without her knowing, the coil of hair beside her ear, that lilac groove beneath her eye, the same colour that you find on the lip of certain shells, the same smoothness too. While they had been talking, the day had darkened, and she was watching her own people as they stepped out of their houses to sample the evening air. The men wore top hats and pale linen suits. The women, balanced upright in their great hooped dresses, reminded him of spoons in cream. A new moon tilted above the sea. Couples strolled beneath the plane trees, the sky's last light violet, uncanny. The women seemed to have no feet; they floated along the street, and their fans slid open and shut, like cards in a gambler's hand. He heard her sigh.

'It's beautiful,' she said.

'It can be.' He leaned forwards. 'On nights when the moon's full, it shines so bright you can sit outside and read a book.'

She nodded, smiling. She was in the kind of mood where all previous belief suspends. Then it was over.

'I should go.' She rose with some reluctance from the table. 'I hope that we shall meet again.'

Wilson had risen from the table too, but he could not think of the words that people used when they took their leave of each other.

At the door she paused and looked back at him across the room. 'I did not thank you for the music.'

'It was my pleasure, ma'am,' he said.

That night, as he slept, he saw a woman shed her dress, her shoes, and then, as he embraced her on sheets that smelled of lavender and summer grass, she fell into more than two thousand pieces, and only her husband, waiting in the corridor outside, knew how to put her back together.

The following morning Wilson was once again the victim of coincidence, though this time it was in no respect a fulfilment of his wishes.

He had woken before dawn, and found he could not sleep. For a few moments his bed still smelled of summer grass; he could dream, at least. Then, as the darkness faded, hammers began to ring outside his window, each blow widening the gap between his dream and the world, between sheets that smelled of summer grass and no sheets at all. It was the church – the early shift. There would be no sleep now. He sat up, reached for his clothes.

On his way down to the waterfront he met Namu, one of the local fishermen, returning from a night out on the water. Namu was walking up the street with hunched shoulders and wet hair. He looked cold. Redness veiled the whites of his eyes.

'The French are having a dinner,' he said. 'They wanted yellowtail or barracuda. I got both.' He smiled, the gap showing between his teeth. 'I haven't slept for two days.'

The arrival of the French had been a stroke of luck for Namu. There was an almost constant demand for big fish, the kind that Indians would

never think of eating. Namu sold most of his catch up on the Calle
Francesa. He made a good living.

'So when are we going out on the boat again, Señor?'

Wilson showed Namu his foot.

The fisherman's eyes travelled from Wilson's foot up to his face and
then back down again. 'We could always use you as an anchor.'

Wilson's smile lasted until he came round the corner of Mama Vum
Buá's cantina and saw La Huesuda, whom he had been successfully
avoiding for days, standing under the quince tree eating refried beans
out of a pan. His smile soured. He should have realised that she might
be here at dawn – a night's work, then one last snack before turning in.
He should have known.

But it was too late now. She had heard something alter, a sudden
increment of tension in the silence, the scrape of his crutches on the
ground as he stopped dead. She twisted round; her black hair swung
against the backs of her knees.

'How are the beans?' Wilson said. 'Good?'

She was wearing a lemon-yellow dress that could have been made
from spun-sugar, but there was nothing sweet about the look on her
face. The saucepan jumped out of her hand. He watched it land in the
dust, roll over once.

'You been past my place recently?'

'Yes, ma'am,' he said. 'I have.' Several times in fact, while she was
sleeping.

'You seen it?'

He guessed that she must be referring to the ladder. It stood propped
against her bedroom window, the rungs made out of pickaxe handles,
old rope from the harbour, bits of fruit crates. 'I've seen it. It looks
pretty solid.'

She moved to within a few feet of him. Up close the whites of her
eyes were orange. One finger swerved upwards and stabbed the air below
his chin.

'I'm standing on the street the other night,' she said, 'and I meet a
guy. He's had a few drinks, now he wants a good time. So he comes
back to my place. Then it turns out he's got to fucking climb a ladder
before he can screw me.' The heat of her anger pushed Wilson back a
step. 'If you laugh,' she said, 'I'll fucking kill you.'

He did not even smile.

'The guy takes one look at the ladder and says no way. He won't even do it up against the wall. One look at that ladder and he's gone off the whole idea. You,' and she poked him in the chest with two fingers, 'have ruined my business.'

'I've ruined mine too.'

He looked past her shoulder. The sun balanced on the horizon, seemingly uncertain of its course. Its gold light coated everything – innocent, deceptive. It told lies about the sea, the trees in the back yard, the saucepan on the ground; it told tall tales about their value. He reached up with one hand and rubbed his eyes. There was a smell coming from somewhere, a smell that was like eggs cooking in a pool of rancid fat.

'I'll make it up to you,' he said. 'As soon as my foot's better, I'll make it up to you. That's a promise.'

She did not speak. She just aimed this look of bitterness at him from out of her narrow eyes, from out of the sweet spun-sugar of her dress.

He turned away from her and limped towards his table.

'It's no good thinking you can run away,' she shouted after him.

'I'm not running,' he said. 'Look at me.'

She had only been gone a few minutes when a voice called from behind the pale-blue shutters of the cantina.

'Somebody out there?'

'It's Señor Wilson. I've come for my breakfast.'

The shutters burst open, bounced back off the wall. Some pieces of plaster landed on the ground below the window. Mama Vum Buá peered out, her eyelids bloated with sleep.

'You're late this morning,' Wilson said.

'If you're going to be funny you can go up the road.'

He grinned. Up the road was an eating-shack called La Concha. You only had to step through the beaded curtain to feel the first twinges of dysentery.

The Señora appeared in the doorway, wearing her usual dress, the one that used to be yellow and red. She summoned a sound from deep in her throat, a sound commonly associated with geese, and sent her spit soaring clear across the yard. He heard it land in the peaceful water of the harbour. Turning her face towards the sun, she began to scratch her arms. Her blunt toes kneaded the dust.

'That church,' he said, 'remember?'

'I remember.'

'You know why we couldn't see it?'

Mama Vum Buá drew her shoulders up towards her ears. Her mouth curved downwards. She kept her eyes imperiously shut.

'It's in pieces,' he said, 'that's why.'

'What happened? Somebody break it?'

He laughed. 'Nobody broke it. It's supposed to be in pieces. It has to be assembled.'

'Ah.'

'A very famous man designed it, apparently.'

Her eyes were open now, and slanting at him, across her cheeks. 'Who?'

'His name's Eiffel.'

The same downward curve of the mouth. 'Never heard of him.'

'He built the Eiffel Tower.'

'The Eiffel Tower? What's that?'

'It's the tallest building in the world.'

Her eyes moved lazily out towards the horizon. 'I can't see it,' she said. 'Can't be that tall.'

Wilson could not keep from smiling.

'What's so funny?'

'Nothing.' He leaned back in his chair. 'I'd like some of those eggs of yours, Señora, if you please.'

But she was staring at him, suspicion drawing her eyebrows down towards the bridge of her nose. 'Something's funny. You wouldn't be laughing if something wasn't funny.'

'And coffee,' Wilson said, still smiling. 'Plenty of that good coffee.'

9

'It is an honour and a privilege, not to mention a relief,' Monsieur de Romblay began, 'a relief,' he continued, lifting his voice above the laughter, 'to be able finally to welcome into our midst Monsieur and Madame Valence who are here as representatives of one of the most prestigious construction companies in France, if not the world, the Compagnie des Établissements Eiffel – '

Suzanne felt her attention begin to wander. Her eyes drifted away from the Director and out across the table – the glinting clutter of silver and glass, the red flowers arching out of their wide bowl, the tallow candles releasing the occasional twist of black smoke into the atmosphere. Gathered round her in the dining-room was the cream of Santa Sofía society: Eugène and Léonie de Romblay, the hosts; Émile Bardou and his wife, Florestine; Marie Saint-Lô, his assistant at the hospital; François Pineau, the accountant; Pierre Morlaix, the safety engineer; Jean-Baptiste Castagnet, who was in charge of timbering and lumber; and, lastly, Captain Félix Montoya, commander of the military garrison. The men were dressed in black coats and white cravats, the sole exception being the Mexican, who had appeared in a scarlet tunic with silver epaulettes and a broad felt hat which was now recumbent on a chair, its plumes shifting in the down-draught from the electric ceiling fan. The women wore evening gowns of silk and taffeta. Marie Saint-Lô had decided on emerald-green, which complemented her pale skin and her brown hair – though, by leaving her neck and shoulders bare, the dress accentuated her stocky, somewhat earthbound figure. Madame de Romblay had chosen a particularly unambiguous cerise. The doctor's wife had settled for dove-grey. All three had adorned their hair and their décolletages with sprigs of jasmine and cactus blossom, and scent-vials glittered in their gloved hands. Suzanne was wearing mousseline-de-soie in lettuce-green, trimmed with pompon roses, and pale-shrimp suede gloves to the elbow, and, looking round the table, she did not feel that she was overdressed.

They were nearing the end of a dinner that had been a revelation. An hors-d'oeuvre of spiced bouillabaisse was followed by fillets of yellowtail and barracuda, caught in the waters off the island of San Marcos. For the entrée Madame de Romblay offered a choice of quail or pigeon, both trapped locally by Yaqui Indians. With the fish she served a chilled Chablis, with the fowl, a Bordeaux. (It transpired that, unknown to Théo, both wines had travelled in the hold of the *SS Korrigan*, along with the town's new church.) Dessert consisted of segments of Mulege orange preserved in pomegranate brandy and, for the more enterprising, a bowl of pitahaya, the fruit of the organ-pipe cactus, whose spiny, ash-green skin could be peeled away to expose a deep red meat which tasted, Suzanne thought, like strawberries that were almost, but not quite, ripe. With dessert Madame de Romblay suggested a garnet wine from San Ignacio. It had been produced by Jesuits, she claimed, and was one of the few aspects of Jesuit teaching in which the Indians had shown any interest. It closely resembled port, both in its colour and its flavour, and was, in fact, most palatable. Théo had already drunk three glasses.

Suddenly the table rocked with laughter and Suzanne looked up. Théo was turning to her with a smile of resignation on his face. It appeared that Monsieur de Romblay was approaching his finale.

'– late as a Valence. And if someone's very late, say about two months,' gusts of laughter were now sweeping the room and powder rose in clouds from the shoulders of the women, 'then you might say, "That was a real Valence." For many of the local people, as we all know, the Valence is a way of life. Perhaps,' and now the Director himself could not keep from joining in the hilarity, 'perhaps it's a blessing, no, more than that, a stroke of genius, that they will now be working with the original exponent of the Valence, none other than Monsieur Valence himself.'

Théo leaned forwards in his chair and executed a number of modest bows in all directions. He was still smiling, though his smile had grown somewhat bemused.

Monsieur de Romblay reached down and seized a glass of Jesuit wine. 'But seriously,' he said, 'we do welcome you both to Santa Sofía, and we hope that your stay will be a happy and rewarding one.' He raised his glass high. 'To Monsieur and Madame Valence.'

At last the time came for the company to divide, the men retiring to the library for cognac and cigars, the women to the drawing-room, where coffee and Turkish Delight would be served. As Monsieur de Romblay passed behind Suzanne on his way out of the room, she turned in her chair.

'A most amusing speech, Monsieur.'

Monsieur de Romblay bent close to her ear. 'I did not go too far, my dear?'

'My husband may be correct,' Suzanne replied, 'but he can take a joke. You should hear me sometimes.'

Perhaps, after all, she had drunk one too many glasses of the garnet wine herself. But the Director had thrown his head back and seemed to be threatening, in his merriment, to swallow the chandelier.

'You are certainly a welcome addition to our little throng,' he said, when he had regained his composure. 'Most welcome.'

In the drawing-room the women conversed among themselves, complaining first of the laziness of Mexican and Indian maids, then of the din made by the boys who delivered the water; there was also a brief and hushed discussion of some local root that was reputed to have aphrodisiacal powers. All this talk either concerned events that preceded Suzanne's arrival or presumed a degree of intimacy that she did not as yet possess, but she was content simply to listen, turning every now and then to gaze out of the window. The Director's house occupied the high ground at the south end of the Calle Francesa. She could look beyond the rooftops of the houses opposite to where the sea pushed against the gravel shore. She could see white smoke rising from the smelting works like the trunk of some ghostly tree. Away to the right and far below she could just make out the dim yellow lights of the harbour.

She had suspected that, sometime during the course of the evening, she would be examined by Madame de Romblay, so when she heard the chair beside her fill with rustling taffeta she knew, without looking, who it was. She could feel those cold tin eyes travelling across her clothes, her skin. She prepared a smile for the moment when she turned from the window, back into the room.

'Madame de Romblay, that was a truly exceptional meal.'

'You must call me Léonie, my dear.' Madame de Romblay lit a dark-brown cigarette and let the smoke spill from the corner of her mouth. 'We're such a small community here. We cannot stand on too much ceremony.'

Suzanne inclined her head, a gesture that was not unlike submitting to a guillotine. And then Madame de Romblay's voice, soft as the blindfold that would be used: 'How long have you been married?'

'Almost six years.'

Madame de Romblay's upper body moved sharply backwards. 'I would not have thought that you were old enough.'

The two remaining women had exhausted their conversation on the other side of the room and were listening with undisguised curiosity. But Suzanne could not think of a reply. Instead, she focused her attentions on Madame de Romblay's dress. A woman with Madame de Romblay's colouring should not be wearing cerise. It gave her neck and shoulders an unhealthy, mottled look. A darker colour would have been more flattering. Indigo, perhaps. Or heliotrope.

In the face of Suzanne's silence, Madame de Romblay felt the need to elaborate.

'You must have been very young,' she said.

'I was twenty.'

'So you are now, what, twenty-six?'

Suzanne admitted it.

'You don't look twenty-six, my dear.' Madame de Romblay appealed to the other women, and they duly shook their heads.

'Thank you,' Suzanne said.

Madame de Romblay tipped an inch of ash into the metal ashtray at her elbow, one eyebrow arching. 'He's a distinguished man, your husband.'

'He has done well,' Suzanne ventured, 'yes.'

'And how did you meet him?' Madame de Romblay leaned over and shut her cigarette inside the ashtray. While her back was still turned, she added, 'After all, the age difference, you must admit, is quite considerable.'

Suzanne smiled. 'My father taught at the École Centrale in Paris, and Théo was one of his best students. They became friends. Théo was often a visitor at our house.' Her smile spread as a lie occurred to her. 'In fact, I'm sure that I remember Théo babysitting me,' she said, 'when I was about seven.'

'How charming,' Madame de Romblay said.

But she knew that Suzanne had pre-empted her, and she knew that Suzanne knew, and the pot of coffee that had just arrived in the room provided her with an opportunity to excuse herself.

After leaving the de Romblays' house, Suzanne and Théo crossed the small square that she had discovered on her first evening. They stood at the parapet, looking down into the valley. A warm breeze rose off the sea and pushed against her dress.

'What do you think of our new friends?' he asked.

She understood his intent, however veiled. 'I do not regret coming here,' she said, 'not for one moment.'

He laughed. 'If our conversation were bridges, I fear they would soon collapse.'

'Oh?' She took his arm. 'And why is that?'

'We advance too quickly, before we have built the necessary struts and trusses to support us.'

'Sometimes,' she said, feeling daring now, feeling a sudden sense of release, 'I think you overdo the struts and trusses.'

He laughed again, though less readily. It was a reference to the tower that he had laboured on with such zeal and devotion, and it was a reference that was less than respectful. But she had wanted to dispatch his gravity with her light wand; she had meant him to understand that she loved him, not for what he had accomplished, but for what he was – not the engineer, but the man.

He turned away from the parapet, hands clasped behind his back. She followed him. They walked beneath the trees in silence. She watched the light and shade alternating on his face.

'Well,' he said at last, 'they seemed satisfied with the plans, though there was one rather awkward moment.'

She saw that he had not held her piece of gentle mockery against her. Perhaps he had understood her after all.

'What happened?' she asked.

He set the scene for her. When he entered the library that evening he saw that his architectural drawings had been laid out on the table, their corners held down by an assortment of natural paperweights – copper, mostly, as one might have expected, though there were also some specimens of various local minerals: gypsum, chalcedony, malachite and jasper; there was even, he remembered, a fossilised shark's tooth from the Pliocene era. This digression, so typical of him, might, at other times, have frustrated her, but on this warm night, with her arm linked through his, she found it impossible not to indulge him.

For many of the men gathered round the table, Théo said, this was a first glimpse of the church that would be built for them, since it had been purchased on their behalf by the head office of the company in Paris. They were murmuring and pointing, conferring among themselves, the air rich with the mingled fumes of brandy and cigars. Then François Pineau cleared his throat.

'He is the thin one,' Suzanne said, 'with the twisted upper lip.'

Théo nodded. 'He's the accountant.'

She smiled. It was as if, in describing the nature of the man's work, Théo had supplied the reason for his ugliness.

Monsieur Pineau cleared his throat and stepped back from the table. 'It's a curious notion, don't you think,' he declared, 'building a metal church in a town like this?'

The question was directed at no one particular person, but rather tossed into the air in order that somebody might reach out and catch it. That somebody was Théo, as, no doubt, it had to be.

'Curious?' he said. 'Why do you find it curious, Monsieur?'

'I don't know whether you are familiar with our climate, Monsieur Valence, but during the summer months the temperature often rises to thirty-five degrees, sometimes higher. In a church that is constructed wholly out of metal – ' He lifted one hand into the air. He had made his point; he did not need to go on.

There was a sudden hush in the library, as if this factor had not been properly taken into consideration, as if some dreadful blunder had been committed. All eyes turned slowly, inevitably, to Théo. This was the awkward moment to which he had alluded. He was not shaken, however, or cowed. He had been present when Monsieur Eiffel defended his tower in front of a hostile committee of the city council, and defended it on both structural and aesthetic grounds. This was not even a matter of aesthetics; this was simply a practical objection.

'I'm sure that your superiors in Paris would not have bought the church in the first place,' he replied, 'if they thought it inadequate for their needs.' Then, in case it seemed that he had merely put the accountant in his place, he turned to specifics. 'There will be insulation between the walls,' he explained, 'in the roof, too, if we can find a suitable material. Pumice has, I believe, been suggested.' He turned to Monsieur Castagnet, who nodded. 'There will also be a great many windows, as you can see. Draughts will be conducted throughout the building.'

'My dear Monsieur Valence,' and Pineau's lip curled in a sardonic smile, 'during the summer months, there are no draughts.'

'And in time, of course,' Théo continued, 'there will be fans. I hasten to remind you that we are living in a modern age. We need no longer be at the mercy of an unfavourable climate.'

'In time,' Pineau muttered. He would not be placated.

'Perhaps, gentlemen,' Monsieur de Romblay ventured, 'we are meant to suffer for our religion.'

Even Théo had laughed at that.

'The Director is not without a certain wit,' Suzanne observed.

Théo murmured his agreement. 'In any case,' he added, 'they will not have to suffer just yet. In fact, it will be a good two months before they have to start suffering.'

'Two months it may be,' Suzanne said, 'but I'll wager that Madame de Romblay has already reserved her pew.'

'I must say, I do not care for that woman.' Théo was frowning. 'There is something vulgar about her. Though the dinner was exceptional, of course.'

Suzanne smiled to herself as she recalled how Madame de Romblay had flirted with Théo, and how Théo had signally failed to respond. Théo did not understand flattery; he never took it personally or believed it, not for a moment. To him it was one facet of the art of conversation; it was purely an exercise in the social graces, pleasant enough, but essentially meaningless. When Madame de Romblay suggested that some of Eiffel's genius might have rubbed off on him, he immediately, and without self-consciousness or hesitation, launched into a discussion of the word and then departed for the wider pastures of semantics, leaving the poor woman far behind with a glazed expression on her face.

Suzanne's smile widened. There was something vulgar about her, he had said, as if it was something that he could not quite pin down – a hidden quality, some elusive trait. She remembered how Madame de Romblay had turned from Théo to Montoya, leaning into him, her tin eyes glittering through narrowed lids. She had been wearing a dress that made no secret of her breasts, and all the men, at some time in the evening, had let their eyes rest for a moment on those brazen slopes. Where for some they might have been emblems of seduction, for Théo they were merely vulgar. For the young Captain they appeared to present a positive threat. He seemed flustered, if not smothered, by her interest. As for the rest of the company it was rather as if she were lavishing attention upon a favourite hound. They displayed no signs of unease or embarrassment; the atmosphere was one of complicity. In fact, the manner in which her behaviour was tolerated suggested that this was an established routine, that the French thought of Montoya, and perhaps all Mexicans, as a lesser breed, a butt for ridicule, a source of entertainment. But if Madame de Romblay was vulgar, she was also dangerous – for what was that vulgarity but a craving for centre-stage; it was her right, her privilege, and the other women, Marie and Florestine, had left the field open for her. Suzanne saw that she would have to tread with the utmost care. She could make enemies here.

This meditation had brought them both to the front of the hotel, and Théo stood aside so she could climb the steps to the veranda. She paused under the sloping roof to draw the beauty of the night into her lungs. The air was dense and soft; she felt she could almost cup it in her hand. She looked away to the south. The moon had risen into the clear sky above the mountains. Her thoughts turned to the American. When she first addressed him, just below where she was standing now, it had been with a confidence, a kind of familiarity, which, had it been viewed from the outside, say by Madame de Romblay, would probably have seemed quite inappropriate – even, perhaps, shameless. But she had once again sensed a kinship between this new acquaintance and the water-carrier from her childhood; they shared the same kindliness, the same quiet strength. It had seemed entirely natural to seek him out and talk to him.

She took Théo's arm. 'When the moon is full, Théo, you can sit outside at night and read a book.'

The idea entertained him. 'Who told you that?'

'The American.'

'Is he that fellow with the broken foot?'

'His name is Wilson Pharaoh. He comes from San Francisco.'

'Typical American,' Théo said, 'to go filling your head with fanciful notions.' His tone of voice was understanding, though, and fond; he was only amused at the naivety of a foundling nation.

She pressed closer to him. 'I wish you were younger,' she said, 'so that I might have more time with you.'

He smiled down at her. 'I'm not dead yet.'

She lay on her back under the mosquito-netting that arched from the bed up to a metal halo near the ceiling. Its long sides billowed in the down-draught from the fan. She could hear Théo washing in the room next door – water splashing on to stone. It was their last night in the hotel. Tomorrow they would be moving into a house with a view of the sea. The garnet wine surged through her body; her blood weighed more than usual in her veins. One of her hands drifted upwards from her hip. Her skin rose to the touch of her nightgown.

'Make love to me.' She had to whisper, or he would hear.

'Please,' she whispered.

She wished that he desired her more often, with more urgency, with violence, if need be. She could imagine that he might hold her down by her hair, that he might take her by surprise, against her will.

But his love for her, every aspect of his love, seemed so measured. Methodical, precise. It had been the same during the voyage from Le Havre. In their cabin there had been two single bunks, and he considered it undignified, he said, to make love in a narrow bunk – though he had, on more than one occasion, the voyage being so long, felt driven to submit to this indignity.

The bed lunged and creaked as he climbed in. She listened to his breathing deepen. Then, without thinking, almost despite herself, she reached out and touched his shoulder. He shifted suddenly away from her.

'What is it?'

There was anger in his voice. She could not answer.

'I was almost asleep,' he said. 'You startled me.' He became gentler, more persuasive. 'You know that I have to be up early in the morning.'

'Of course, Théo. I'm sorry.' She turned away from him, lay on her side.

She felt him lift his head off the pillow and peer at her. She sensed his puzzlement, but knew it would not last. She closed her eyes and listened to her heart roll against her ribs. It was not long before the bed tilted and he sank back down into the sheets. Soon afterwards he was asleep.

She thought back to the summer when she met him. Though she was still only seventeen she had already been admired by many men, none of whom she cared for, not even remotely. Then, one afternoon, her father announced that Monsieur Théophile Valence, a former student of his, would be coming to their house for dinner.

When she saw him she could not look into his face. It was as if she knew that she would find what she had always wanted there, and was afraid suddenly. Her heart had vanished for a moment, completely vanished, like an animal falling into a trap, then it returned again, beating harder than before.

She remembered that she had stopped on the threshold to the drawing-room and watched the two men talking. It had been a hot day; evening sunlight gilded the arms of chairs, the raised piano lid, the crystal teardrops of the chandelier. Standing in the doorway, unobserved, it was his hands that she noticed first. They were not distinguished or refined at all. They did not taper, as men's hands were supposed to. They were not as smooth as ivory. She could see the veins knotting just above his knuckles as he gestured; she noted the big, square palm. They were, well, they were labourer's hands. And almost instantly the feeling took hold of her, as deep as if she was asleep and dreaming: the feeling that she wanted more than anything to surrender to his hands, to feel his hands descend and settle on her skin. Standing there she could, in fact, imagine this possession, and because she could imagine it, she knew that it would happen. It was the sweetest and most scandalous delight, to know this with such certainty before he even saw her.

At that moment her father noticed her, and he smiled and rose from his chair, saying, 'Ah, and here, at last, is my daughter – ' And she had to pretend to be moving forwards, forwards into the room.

But what she had imagined did not happen. Nothing happened. She could not understand it.

At the Chantilly Derby that year, wearing a new dress (moon satin, daring for the afternoon), she had accepted compliments from no fewer than eleven members of the nobility, including a distant cousin of Napoleon III and a count from the Piedmont in Northern Italy, eleven pairs of lips had brushed the back of her mauve kid glove, but she could remember sitting in front of her triptych of mirrors after yet another desolate encounter with Théo and fingering her dark-blonde ringlets and thinking: What is it? What is wrong with me? For the truth was, he did not seem to see her. He just did not seem to see her at all. Autumn came, and she lay in bed like a stone, not even blinking.

In desperation she consulted her closest friend, Lucille, who was two years her senior and had more experience of the world.

'Lucille?' she said. 'Am I ugly?'

Lucille stared at her, and then she began to laugh. She had a pretty laugh – like a bell, men often said – but that day it had grated.

'It's not a joke, Lucille.'

'It has got to be.'

'Just tell me the truth. I want to hear the truth.'

'You're beautiful, Suzanne. Everybody thinks so. I always wanted to look like you.'

Suzanne told Lucille about Théo.

'Perhaps there is something wrong with him,' Lucille suggested. 'Perhaps,' and she lowered her voice, 'he doesn't like women.'

Suzanne shook her head. 'He was engaged once. My father told me.'

Lucille sighed.

When she left that afternoon she took Suzanne's hand in both of hers. 'Men can be slow sometimes,' she said. 'Men can be blind.' She kissed

Suzanne on the cheek. 'He will come round, don't you worry. He will come round in the end.'

And he did, of course. In the end.

She felt cold suddenly. She moved closer to Théo in the bed – gently, imperceptibly, so he would not wake – until she could feel his warmth against her belly and her thighs. It was no reflection on her that he did not make love to her more often. He was under pressure, that was all. He had so much to do.

She wedged a pillow between her knees and brought the sheet up to the soft hollow between her chin and her lower lip. I am married to the man I love, she thought, and let the thought repeat itself, over and over, until the sweet wine cut her moorings, and she slept.

10

17 Calle Francesa,
Santa Sofía,
Lower California,
Mexico

30th April, 189 –

My dear Monsieur Eiffel,

It is two weeks since we arrived in Santa Sofía, and I am pleased to report that things are at last beginning to run smoothly. During the past two days I have been supervising the final stages of unloading. All the longitudinal elements are now laid out on site in the usual manner, along with the majority of the end posts and tie bars, and I find myself marvelling once again at the intrinsic simplicity of the system $1 B_2 4, 5 B_4 8$, etc. upon which all our endeavours are based. We have employed dry foundations, sinking to a depth of just half a metre; given the quality of the subsoil in El Pueblo and the nature of the shearing forces in this particular structure, there seemed no necessity to ensure against unequal settling. With the aid of Monsieur Castagnet, the timbering expert, we have fashioned a crude but satisfactory mast and a number of simple hoisting gins. Tomorrow we should be able to lift the first of the central arches into position.

I am aware that much of the above may sound pedantic, but it is a measure of our predicament. In a country as primitive as the one in which we find ourselves, nothing can be taken for granted; we must be grateful for small mercies. Though I have assembled a workforce of twenty-two men, they are, for the most part, Indians and have difficulty interpreting even the simplest of my directives. It is the clear and systematic methods on which our company prides itself, curiously enough, that seem to present an obstacle, since the ways of the native people are pervaded throughout by every conceivable illogicality and confusion. The most common word in their vocabulary is *'vara'* which, literally translated, means 'nothing'. They come and stand before me, and when I ask them why they have come, they say '*Vara*.' If I then ask them what they want, they reply again, '*Vara*.' It is quite maddening. Yesterday I received three successive '*Vara*'s from one man before I was able to elicit from him that he wanted to know when to report for work on the following day! At this point we were plunged abruptly into a new quandary, one that stemmed from differing approaches to the concept of time. Most of the Indians can only count to six, some only to three. (No Indian can say how many fingers he has; his reply will always be, 'Many.') Since we could not communicate the idea of five o'clock in the morning we had, in the end, to settle for 'early' or, in the revised version, 'much early'. You are probably far more acquainted than I am with these frustrations, Monsieur, and I realise that I will have to learn that most irksome of virtues, namely patience. If current progress is anything to go by, the project is unlikely to be completed before June.

As you can see from the letter heading, we have moved into our new home. Though sparsely furnished, it is perfectly adequate, and Madame Valence is finding a hundred small ways of rendering the interior more pleasing, as only a woman can. She has bought two rugs from a Mexican trader to brighten the bare wood floors, and fills the rooms with various species of cactus which are, she claims, a substitute for flowers. In the absence of any paintings, she will no doubt hang her own! She is so occupied at present that I scarcely see her from dawn to dusk. Our neighbours have shown us every kindness, especially the Director of the company himself, Monsieur de Romblay, who is a most personable gentleman and a raconteur of some note. I will endeavour to keep you informed of our progress, such as it is, and hope this letter finds you, as always, in the very best of health.

I remain, with the deepest respect, Monsieur, your most humble servant,
    Théophile Valence.

MAY

1

Suzanne had only met Captain Montoya once, at the welcoming banquet in the last week of April, and they had exchanged no more than the few required sentences, yet she had suspected, even then, that he would fall for her. It had not been hard to predict this infatuation; she had seen the signs in the mournful slackening of his face as he gazed at her across the table, and in the reverence with which he bent over her gloved hand and brushed it with his lips when she departed. Since that evening she had not thought of him at all except to smile when she remembered how Madame Bardou, the epitome of modesty and decorum, had caught a glimpse of his plumed hat on the chair and let out a shriek because she thought a cockerel had found its way into the room.

Then, one afternoon, she was woken from her siesta by a knocking on the door. Her maid, Imelda, always returned to her parents' shop in El Pueblo after lunch, so she was alone in the house. She drew a silk *peignoir* over her chemise and fastened her hair in a casual knot at the back of her head. It was the most silent hour of the day, and not a time when anyone would think of visiting. She assumed that it was Théo; he must have forgotten his keys. She stepped out into the corridor that ran through the centre of the house.

'Who is it?'

'It is I, Félix Montoya.'

Her surprise registered as an instinctive glance at the mirror, one hand moving up to adjust a stray twist of hair. She would have recognised his voice, even if he had not given her his name. He spoke French with an unmistakable accent, though he had assured her, on the night of the banquet, that he had learned the language at the most expensive school in Mexico City.

She unlocked the front door and then unfastened the screen door that lay beyond it. Captain Montoya was standing on the veranda in full dress uniform: a scarlet tunic with a stiff collar and silver epaulettes, tight-fitting dove-grey trousers, and high black boots garnished with a pair of spurs. Rows of silver buttons ran down the outside of his trouser-legs. He wore a cutlass, too, housed in an ornate, hand-hammered silver scabbard.

'Good afternoon, Captain,' she said.

He brought his heels together and bowed low.

'I'm sorry to disturb you at such an hour, Madame,' he said, 'but I have an invitation.'

Bowing again, he handed her an envelope. He would not look at her. She took the envelope. It had not been addressed, nor was there any name on it.

'It's for me?' she asked.

'It is.'

'Am I to open it now?'

He shrugged. 'As you wish.'

There was a tension and a carelessness about him. It was as if he were constantly in possession of some powerful emotion that he had to suppress, but whose existence was impossible to deny. She stared at him for a few moments then, when he still had not moved from the veranda, she asked him if he would like some refreshment before he continued on his way.

In retrospect she decided that perhaps she ought not to have encouraged him, though by then she was to realise that he would have seen encouragement even if it had not in fact been there. At the time she saw no harm in offering a little hospitality.

She led him into the parlour and showed him to a chair by the window. He sat down. The shutters had been drawn against the sun, and the room was cool.

'I will just fetch you something,' she said.

When she returned from the kitchen with a glass of lemonade, he was sitting with a straight back, his eyes angled away from her. The room had relieved him of some portion of his glamour; he seemed inert, weighed down, encumbered by all the metal he was wearing. She handed him the glass and watched him while he drank. There were smudges beneath his eyes – signs of sleeplessness. His moustache was made up of two entirely separate triangles. There was a line beside his mouth which would deepen if he smiled. When he had finished almost half the contents of the glass, he put it down on the table by the window and stared at it, as if it were capable of moving by itself.

'Is it good?' she asked him.

'Yes, Madame.'

She took a seat across the room from him and picked up the envelope.

'Now,' she said. 'The invitation.'

Reaching for her paper-knife, she slit the seal. Inside she found a card that requested the presence of Monsieur and Madame Valence at the private residence of Captain Félix Tortoledo de Avilés Montoya on the 11th of May at five o'clock in the afternoon, for tea. It had been written in crimson ink, with a number of loops and flourishes, the graphological equivalent, she supposed, of spurs and epaulettes. She experienced a sudden and almost uncontrollable urge to burst out laughing, a desire which was only heightened by the Captain's mournful and unwavering gaze. She did not have to look at him to know. In fact, she dared not look. She concentrated on the invitation – its scalloped edges, its crimson loops and flourishes.

'The eleventh,' she said.

'Yes.'

'That's a Tuesday.'

'Yes, it is.'

'My husband will be at work. He won't be able to come.'

'Then come alone.'

Though this was ostensibly his answer to the objection that she had raised, it also had the distinct ring of an order. There was no doubt in his mind but that she would come, and come alone, if she had to. It might even, she thought, have been his original intention, and it now occurred to her that, despite the conspicuous formality of the invitation, Montoya was a man who took no account of the accepted social proprieties.

That evening, after supper, when Théo had retired to his study on the first floor, Suzanne read for an hour on the divan, the invitation tucked between the pages of her book. Towards ten o'clock she climbed the stairs to bed. The study door stood open, but she thought that she should knock. When there was no reply, she entered. Théo was hunched over some plans, his back to her.

'Will you be much longer?' she asked.

He spoke without looking round. 'I didn't hear you knock.'

'Well,' she said, 'I did knock.'

'I'm sure you did. I just didn't hear it.'

She crossed the room and leaned against the window. She could hear the monotonous rumble of the smelting plant through the wire-mesh screen. The night smelled of jasmine and rust.

'Don't you find it hard to concentrate,' she said, 'with all this noise?'

'One can become used to anything.'

Smiling faintly, she moved away from the window and stood behind him, one hand on the back of his chair.

'We've been invited to tea,' she said.

'Really? Who by?'

'Montoya.'

'The man's a clown.' Théo unfolded a detailed drawing of the church and spread it on the table in front of him. The crash and rustle of the paper dismissed her.

'Clowns can be entertaining,' she said.

Still Théo would not look up.

'And besides,' she added, 'I think he has a certain charm.'

'You know that I'm busy.'

She was staring at her hand. White against the dark wood of the chair. And, beyond her hand, his back. The curve of it. Solid, black – immovable.

'Do whatever you think best, my dear.'

She doubted he had heard much of what she had said. Like the rumble of the smelting works and the heat, her presence lacked the power to disturb him. He was too preoccupied with the documents that lay before him.

It was only when she pulled her hand away from the chair and turned to leave the room that his eyes lifted. She thought she could feel him studying her as she walked out.

2

It was twenty past eleven by his father's gold watch when Wilson pushed through the corrugated-iron door of the Bar El Fandango. Pablo Fernández was sitting in the cool gloom, a heap of peanuts at his elbow. Staring straight ahead, Pablo would snap a shell open, toss the nut into his mouth, then let the empty husk spill out of the side of his hand. His eyes did not blink or flicker as Wilson passed in front of him; they did not move at all. Though Wilson had grown used to Pablo, he still found this manner of his unnerving; it was like dropping a stone into a pond and it just vanishing without a ripple. He sat down at the only other table and waited for the two hands on his watch to meet.

The Bar El Fandango was a wooden lean-to, with sky showing through the walls. The floor was clay, baked solid by the heat, its surface polished by spilt drinks and miners' phlegm. Pickled eggs crowded in a tin bowl on the counter. Close by stood a jar that bristled with viznaga spines – the poor man's toothpick. A turtle-shell and a pair of castanets hung from a nail above the bar. Bottles with no labels filled the shelves beneath. Cactus liquor. Pablo had told Wilson how the stuff was made. It was simple enough. You found the right kind of cactus, then you just cut the top off and added sugar. Seven days later a pure, clear alcohol dripped from a pinhole in the base. Seven days. That was how long it took. 'Just like the world,' Wilson had observed at the time. Pablo had not reacted – not for a moment, anyway. Then his head began to turn. It turned until it locked on Wilson's face. Then he stuck his hand out and Wilson had to shake it. 'Just like the world,' Pablo repeated, and his thin dark lips achieved a smile. After that, Wilson always knew when he had said something Pablo liked because Pablo would stick his hand out and Wilson would have to shake it. The smile would happen later. Sometimes not until the next day.

At twenty-five to twelve Wilson broke the silence.

'Don't it give you wind,' he said, 'eating all them nuts?'

Pablo could not answer, of course. Not at twenty-five to twelve. Wilson watched Pablo's thin, arched eyebrows lift and curl as his blunt fingers hunted among the peanut shells. The seconds ticked away inside Wilson's jacket pocket.

'You know, I just had a thought, Pablo.'

Pablo looked up.

'You know you don't talk in the morning? Well, maybe it would be a good idea if you didn't talk in the afternoon as well.'

Another empty shell slid from the side of Pablo's hand and hit the floor.

'And the evening,' Wilson added, after a moment's reflection.

Pablo just looked at him.

Wilson stood up. He reached across the bar and took a bottle off the shelf. He brought the bottle over to his table. He sat down again and folded his arms.

'What I'm trying to say is, maybe we'd all be better off if you didn't talk at all.'

Pablo said nothing.

'There's a couple of missions I heard about,' Wilson said. 'They're on the mainland. You can go there and nobody ever speaks to you. There's a word for it, I can't remember what. Calls for a bit of discipline, but I reckon you'd be up to it.'

Wilson leaned forwards. 'Then nobody would get hurt any more, see? Then nobody would bust their foot.'

Still Pablo said nothing. He studied a husk. His eyebrows had lifted high on to his forehead, as if he were appraising it.

'No need to rush into anything,' Wilson said. 'Just think it over.' He poured himself a drink and swallowed it.

Then he looked at Pablo again. 'It'd give me wind,' he said, 'that's for sure.'

It was two minutes to twelve.

When midday came, Wilson decided not to speak. Instead, he closed his eyes and dozed. The next time he looked at his watch, it was eighteen minutes past.

'About the room,' he said.

Pablo cleared his throat. First words of the day. 'What's wrong with it?'

'Nothing's wrong with the room. It's the stairs.'

'What's wrong with the stairs? They're good stairs.'

'My foot. That's what's wrong with the stairs.'

'You shouldn't have bust it, should you. Shouldn't go sleeping in strange places. With strange women.' Pablo shook his head.

'I was thinking,' Wilson said. 'Maybe I should take a room on the ground floor.'

'Can't help you, I'm afraid.'

'But there's an empty room below me,' Wilson said. 'I can see it through the floor. There's no one in it.'

'It's taken. They're all taken.'

Wilson gaped at Pablo. If this was true, it would be the only time in the hotel's history.

'It was Montoya's idea,' Pablo said. 'There's some new workers coming in. For the church. There's no houses for them, so they're putting them in my hotel. Fifteen of them,' he said, 'in three rooms.' His dark lips twisted.

'How long for?'

Pablo shrugged. 'As long as it takes.' He swept the rest of the shells on to the floor. 'I'm not happy about it either. They're paying me some cut rate that they decided on. The Government,' he said, and sighed. He brushed a few last fragments off the table, then ran the same hand through his hair. 'Have you seen anything of Jesús?'

'I saw him this morning,' Wilson said. 'Ramón's been giving him trouble.'

'Ramón's a parasite.'

Wilson had spent most of the morning with the baker, sitting on a sack of flour just inside the door. Jesús had suspended a wooden bar from the ceiling on ropes, and he was standing in his kneading-trough with both hands on the bar, trampling a mass of dough with his feet.

'This is new,' Wilson remarked.

'It's what they do in Austria,' Jesús said. 'An Austrian came through on a ship. He told me about it.'

'What about your oven? Is it finished yet?'

'Take a look.'

Wilson crossed the room, unlatched the iron door and peered inside. 'Well,' he said, 'it's got a slope, that's for sure.'

'A slope?' Jesús chuckled. 'That's called a sole, that is. I'm going to do it this time. I'm really going to show them.'

His refurbished oven and his adoption of European techniques had given him the kind of lift he needed. He could see his way forwards again. A baguette began to seem possible. He pumped up and down with his wide feet. The sweat dripped off his chin, moistening the dough beneath.

'Salt,' he said, and his pale, heavy mouth broke into a grin. 'Good bread needs salt.'

'I hope you washed your feet,' Wilson said.

'I trod in some shit before I started work.' Jesús took one hand off the bar and spread his fingers in the air. 'Well,' he said, 'it's only the French, isn't it.'

Wilson was glad to see that the baker's sense of humour had returned. This certainly was a new Jesús.

The only shadow on the day was cast by Señor José Ramón, the customs officer. Ramón toured El Pueblo a couple of times a week, in search of bribes. His trouser pockets were the deepest in town, but still his mother had to fit them with extensions every year. He appeared on the threshold of the bakery, his hands clasped behind his back. Blue-tinted glasses hid his eyes.

'You got anything for me?'

His hands surfaced and caressed each other. He moistened his lips. Like many corrupt and powerful men, José Ramón had an almost inexhaustible appetite for cake.

Jesús climbed out of his trough and reached behind the counter. He handed Ramón a brown paper bag. Ramón opened it, and peered inside. He just kept peering down until Jesús reached behind him once again and gathered a handful of sugar buns. Ramón held the bag out. Jesús dropped them in.

Ramón nodded and turned towards the door.

'Ah,' he said, 'American. You want to change some dollar? The rate is good.' He bared his teeth in a predatory smile.

'I haven't got any dollar.'

Ramón laughed. 'A poor American. Now that's something.'

He was still chuckling when he left the bakery and set off down the street. His pockets were so fat with bribes and sweeteners, he had to swing his weight from one leg to the other; it was the only way he could achieve momentum.

Pablo nodded at the description.

'Ramón more or less runs the town,' he said. 'This part of it, at least. He's set an import duty of two hundred per cent. That's on all imported goods. Flour, fruit – you name it. Just plucked the figure out of the air.

If you don't pay it, the goods are held in the warehouse. Guarded by a couple of Montoya's men. They're in on it too. If Ramón likes you, though, and you slip him a little something every once in a while, then he only charges you fifty per cent.'

'A little something?' Wilson could still see that brown paper bag, bulging with cakes and pastries.

'Well,' Pablo said, 'that's what he calls it.'

Wilson looked at his watch. It was time to hitch a ride up to Frenchtown. He hoisted himself to his feet and wedged his crutches under his arms.

'Vows of silence,' Pablo said.

Wilson turned in the doorway. 'What?'

'That word you were trying to think of,' Pablo said. 'It's vows of silence.'

On his way down Avenida Cobre, Wilson heard voices – a low muttering, a hum of anticipation. Half the population of El Pueblo had gathered in the square outside the Hotel La Playa. Wilson caught sight of Luis Fernández, Pablo's younger brother, and asked him what was happening. The first piece of the church was about to be lifted into place, Luis said. Some kind of arch. Wilson could see more than a dozen Indians crowding round a winch, under the anxious supervision of the man he now knew to be Suzanne's husband. He pressed closer, leaned one shoulder against the wall of the hotel.

The arch lay flat on the ground, its feet loosely bolted into concrete foundations. Cables had been fastened to the other end, some linked to the winch, some lying unattached. A long line of Indians waited at the apex. Wilson watched as they bent down, inserting their hands beneath the structure. Then, on a signal from Monsieur Valence, they straightened up. The arch rose a foot into the air. The Frenchman shouted another command. The winch let out a creak; the cables tightened. The arch began to lift. The Indians supported it, their chins tucked into their chests, their arms stretching above their heads. Then it was out of reach, and all they could do was stand beneath it staring upwards as the cables took the strain.

As the arch lifted, framing the houses beyond it and the clear blue sky above, Wilson began to get an idea of its size and shape. It was at least forty feet high, and built entirely from interlocking pieces of grey metal. He remembered Suzanne telling him about the number of component parts involved. Two thousand and something, she had said. Now he could understand it. The arch had been constructed in six sections, and each section was made up of – he counted – twenty-four pieces. The two sections that met to form the apex and the two at the base were straight. Only the two sections that created the actual shape of the arch were curved. He saw how cleverly the structure had been designed, so as to use the least number of curved pieces; they would be more difficult to make, and more expensive.

Halfway up into the sky, the arch suddenly slipped back. Several of the Indians scattered, fearing they might be crushed. But Valence shouted a command and the arch slipped no further. It put Wilson in mind of trying to land a big fish: it seemed to require the same skills, that balance of strength and gentleness, that sureness of touch. He watched closely as the men bent to the handle of the winch and the arch rose up again. This time there were no false moves.

Once the arch stood upright, the cables that trailed from its apex were gathered up and fastened to rings in the ground. Men darted to the base and bolted the metal feet into position. Someone let off a firecracker. People began to shout and clap. Valence stood back with his arms folded, and his face tilted upwards in what appeared to be a private moment of celebration – pride mingled with relief.

Through the crowd, Wilson caught a glimpse of Mama Vum Buá. She stood out from those around her; she shared none of their amusement, their jubilation. Her chin was lowered, and she peered at the archway through her eyebrows. She seemed dissatisfied, suspicious, and Wilson thought he knew why. This structure from across the sea, half metal and half air, was not her idea of a church. She did not recognise it yet. She was still waiting for her enemy to show its face.

Smiling, Wilson moved off down Avenida Manganeso. It was about time the town had a church of its own. When he first arrived in San Francisco with his parents, there had been no church. His mother had never forgiven his father for that. Though he could only have been three years old, he could remember the night she turned on his father, rain beating against the canvas roof, the candle shivering. He could not remember what she had said, only the sound of her voice. He heard the sound again years later, felling redwoods in Oregon. The moment when a tree admits that it can no longer stand. The agony and indignation as something strong begins to break.

She had married Wilson's father, Arthur Pharaoh, believing him to be a dealer in horses when, in fact, he was nothing more than a drifter, an opportunist, even, at times, a thief. The breadth of his shoulders and the energy that crackled in his heels had drawn her to him, but they only told part of the truth. He was an edgy, brittle man; he turned this way and that, like a branch caught in rapids. She had wanted to settle on the eastern seaboard, but he yearned for the West, those undiscovered places where life had yet to take shape, and she had, in the end, and against her better judgement, consented. During their journey across the country she became pregnant, an event which Arthur seized on with gratitude, claiming that it was the Lord's blessing from above and proof that the adventure that they had embarked upon together would bear fruit. It would do nothing of the kind, of course. No sooner had they reached San Francisco than he was leaving again, for the mountains this time, in search of gold. His wife and child were left to fend for themselves in a town where the winter rains had begun, where people lived in tents made out of flour-sacks, where the streets became so thick with mud that horses had been known to drown. With her hair scraped close to her scalp and her teeth already loose in her head, Constance Pharaoh submitted to yet another cruel awakening. She felt herself surrounded by heathens, murderers and Chinamen, and she took to carrying a bottle of carbolic acid with her whenever she ventured out; she said it protected her against disease and sin. In the absence of any church she built a kind of chapel inside the walls of her own skin, a place that would be hers alone to govern, a place where she would be free from all deceit. She could not keep her husband, but she could keep God. He, at least, would not abandon her.

Wilson shook his head as Avenida Manganeso delivered him on to the waterfront. He sat down on an iron bollard in the milky sunlight. If she could see him now she would despair. The drunkenness, the debts, the wanderlust. Image of your father, she would say. A bleak smile on his face, he stared out across the harbour. One small boat lifting and falling, one grey sail. It was Namu. He raised a hand, but the fisherman did not notice him. A pelican dipped over the water, ragged edges to its wings. Three beats and a rest, three beats and a rest.

'You seem melancholy today.'

He did not need to look round; he knew the voice. As he began to climb to his feet, a gloved hand touched his shoulder. 'Don't get up.'

'Melancholy?' he said. 'Your English is certainly coming on.'

She laughed. 'It's the same word in French.'

He turned his face towards hers. A plain cream dress, a straw hat. A basket on her arm. There were people who could reach down and lift you effortlessly out of where you were. It was almost a godlike quality. Suzanne was one of those people and, in the spirit of those people, did not know it.

'I bought some fish,' she said. 'Would you like to have lunch with me?'

He hesitated, not wanting to impose on her.

'I thought we could eat in the kitchen,' she said. 'My husband would not approve, but he will not be there.'

'Where is he?'

'He's having lunch with Monsieur Castagnet.'

Wilson nodded. 'I saw him earlier. Your husband, I mean. The first piece of the church has just gone up.'

'Thank goodness. He was beginning to think that nothing would ever happen.' A despondency settled on her for a moment. Then she shook the look out of her face and smiled down at him. 'Please come.'

'I would like it very much, ma'am,' he said. 'Though by the time I get up that hill, it will be closer to dinner.'

'Dinner then.'

She had pinned her hair up under her hat and, as she bent down to lift one of his crutches, he could see the valley between the delicate muscles at the back of her neck. It seemed that he was always discovering new natural places of beauty on her. But her beauty did not ache this morning. It was part of the lightness that she had brought with her, part of the elation that had risen through him the moment that he heard her voice. He wedged the crutches beneath his arms and turned to face the road that led to the hill.

'Race you,' he said.

The kitchen was a simple timber shack, linked to the back of the house by a short flight of stairs. It had a wood-burning stove for cooking on, and a row of copper pans hung along the wall, arranged according to size. There were two windows. One framed the lower slopes of the Cabo Vírgenes Mountains to the north-west. The other offered a view across El Pueblo; Wilson could see the ridge known as Mexico and the white wall that encircled Montoya's ranch. A century plant grew close to this second window. On his way down the steps, he had noticed how its lethal spikes had collected in the grooves of the tin roof. The Indians used these spikes as needles and even, on occasion, as weapons. He had not eaten since early that morning, and then only the inside of two blackened loaves that Jesús had given him. As he watched Suzanne slip the fresh fish into her shallow pan of oil, his hunger rose from the pit of his stomach, powerful and sour. She did not disappoint him. For lunch she served fillets of bonita fried in sweet garlic, a salad of capsicum and cucumber, and a dozen ripe figs, the colour of evening shadows. She opened some white wine too. Condensation poured down the outside of the bottle, pooling at the base. When he asked her how it came to be so chilled, she showed him the earthen pit below the house, lined with lava blocks and filled with ice. Her two canaries sang in their gilt cage. Wilson thought they sounded a little like wagon-wheels in need of grease, though he did not tell her that, of course. Instead they talked about journeys – his through Mexico by mule, hers on a steamer round Cape Horn. As he sat at the tilting wooden table, watching her prepare each new delight for him, he felt that he was receiving a gift that hardly seemed deserved. He would not have dared to imagine an intimacy such as this, and there were times during the meal when it humbled him. But then, risking a glance at her, he would witness the pleasure that she was taking in this small rebellion of hers, and he realised that he was in some way necessary to her. When he finally laid down his knife and fork he told her that it had been the best cooking he had tasted in a long time.

'Better than Mama Vum Buá?' She was smiling at him across the rim of her glass. He could feel the beauty rising off her face like heat.

'There's no comparison,' he said, lowering his eyes, 'though I do enjoy the company of her children.'

'How many children does she have?'

'Eight, I think. You can never be sure with her. She had four more that died.'

Suzanne's face dipped, and she was silent.

'Have you got any children, Wilson?' she asked eventually.

'Not that I know of.'

She smiled again, her face still dipped, one finger pushing grains of salt across the table. 'Have you ever been married?'

'Still waiting for the right girl, I guess.' He heard his voice across a distance, steady and light. His words were not his; they belonged to someone else.

She looked up, her cheeks flushed with the wine that she had drunk. Her eyes flashed and glinted, like earth when it is strewn with mica.

'But you have been in love,' she said, 'surely?'

He did not want to answer her. He did not see how he could talk of other women in her presence. He had the feeling that it might debase him in her eyes. That it might cheapen him, and spoil everything.

He shifted on his chair.

If he was to mean anything to her, he should now be telling her that he had never loved anyone – shouldn't he? It would prepare the way for his love for her. No past. No history. No seeds sown in him by any face but hers.

His love for her, which stretched in both directions, past and future. A love which overflowed the banks of the present to flood his entire life. What people called eternal.

So, yes. Deny the past, what little there was of it. Then maybe she would understand his love for what it was – unique, unparalleled, beyond compare.

He glanced at her – a quick, guilty look. She was still watching him, still smiling.

And suddenly he knew that he had got it wrong. The stories he did not want to tell her, she would eke them out of him. He saw that now. She would eke them out of him because he wanted more than anything to please her – even if it meant that he was sacrificing some pleasure, some ambition, of his own.

And something else. There had been his promise, hadn't there. Lightly given, lightly accepted – yet firm, remembered, serious.

'Surely,' she repeated, waiting.

He leaned forwards, let out a sigh.

Once, he told her, a long time ago in Monterey, he had loved a girl who had red hair.

3

As Suzanne passed through the screen door and into the house, the darkness suddenly closed in, wrapped around her head, and she had to rest one hand upon the banister. She had drunk too much wine. She was not accustomed to drinking, and certainly not during the day, but the spontaneity and ease with which she had improvised the lunch had induced in her a kind of recklessness. She did not move again until there was light in the hallway, until she felt that she could see.

Upstairs in the bedroom she reached into the bottom of her trunk and found her paint-box bound in a scarf of crêpe-de-Chine. She had been intending simply to show Wilson the paints, but now she had another idea. She took a vase from the table and filled it from the water jar.

When she returned to the veranda, the sun seemed to have fallen in the sky. The shadow of the house sprawled below, warped by the uneven slope of the terrain; the edge of the shadow rippled, reminding her of flags in wind. At the foot of the hill lay the sea. It stretched away to the horizon in alternating shades of lavender and jade. The American was sitting where she had left him, in an upholstered cane chair, his hands folded across his waistcoat, his hat pulled level with his eyebrows.

'Wilson?'

He tipped his hat back and sat up straighter. 'I was dreaming there for a moment,' he said. 'Must be the wine.' He leaned forwards. 'What's that you've got?'

She handed him the paint-box. 'It was given to me when I was a child,' she told him. 'Before that, it belonged to my mother.'

He admired it slowly, turning it in his rough hands, making it seem, for the first time, a thing of delicacy.

'Are you going to paint something?' he asked her.

'Yes, I am.' She smiled. 'I'm going to paint your foot.'

His look of alarm pushed her smile over into laughter. 'Look at it,' she said. 'It's so dull. It needs some decoration.'

'I don't know,' he said.

'Of course,' she said. 'Now what shall it be? A flower? An animal? Some gold at the end of a rainbow?'

'I don't want everyone to know my secret.'

'I guess not.'

He looked at her, one corner of his mouth curling humorously upwards.

'It's American,' she said. 'I learned it from you.'

At length they decided on a flower. But which kind? He let her choose. Then it would be a rose, she said. A red rose. And, propping his foot on a stool, she dipped her brush in the vase of water and set to work.

'Saffron,' she mused. 'It's a strange name for a girl with red hair.'

Wilson thought for a while. 'I believe her father was in the business of spices.'

She laughed; the stem of the rose jumped sideways. Sometimes his answers were so crooked and unlikely that she thought she must have misunderstood, but one look at his face would tell her she had not. It was only that he himself had no sense that what he was saying was anything other than commonplace and everyday. They were things that had happened to him, and that was how he passed them on – as fragments of a life, as facts. As she began to outline the petals of the rose she let her mind wander back through the story of the red-haired girl. Her father must have had some premonition of her effect on men, for she seemed to have lasted in Wilson's memory in the same way that a certain fragrance lingers in the place where spices have been stored – though she could not now remember what saffron smelled like, or even if it smelled at all.

'Did you ever see her again?'

'No,' he said. 'I never did.'

'Did you look for her?'

'I passed through Monterey a few years later. Somebody told me she'd got married. Maybe it was that man who came out of the fog.' He laughed quickly.

'Has there been anyone else?' She felt she could ask him almost anything, so long as she used the voice he used, and did not look up from her work. The truth could only be drawn from the thorns and petals of the rose.

His eyes explored the air above her head. 'No.'

She had embarrassed him, but she talked on through his embarrassment as if she had not noticed. They were doing favours for each other without acknowledgement, which was ground on which friendship could be built.

'But it must be lonely,' she said, 'when you are always travelling from one place to another.'

'You don't travel by yourself. Mostly you team up. Especially if you're heading into dangerous territory.' Wilson sat back in his chair, easier now.

He told her about a trapper, name of Mickey Noone. They were riding across the prairies of West Texas together. Noone was after hunting beaver on the Colorado River, the Gila too, but the beaver were strictly incidental. He just seemed to have a natural bent for killing things. His rifle always lay in his arms, one restless finger in the region of the trigger. One day Wilson had asked him what he liked killing best. Noone shrugged. 'It don't matter what,' he said, 'though, on general principles, I'd prefer an Indian.'

'I think I'd rather travel alone,' Suzanne exclaimed, 'than travel with such a man.'

'I don't believe he ever killed an Indian in his life.' Wilson smiled down at her. 'He was a terrible shot. Once I saw him miss a jack rabbit from six feet away.'

The rose, complete with petals, stem and leaves, had almost dried when they heard the grating of carriage-wheels in the street. From the shadows of the veranda they watched Montoya leave his carriage and climb the steps to the de Romblays' house. At this distance they could not see his face, only the scarlet of his tunic and the epaulettes that clung, like huge glinting spiders, to his shoulders.

'My God.' Suzanne had only breathed the words.

'What is it?' Wilson asked her.

She shook her head. 'I've just remembered something.'

Last night she had dreamed that she was standing in a house. It was late. No lamps or torches had been lit. There was not even a candle to see by. Only the moonlight falling through a high window, pooling on anything that had a shine to it.

She was standing at the foot of a stone staircase. She could look up and watch the stairs come sweeping down into the hall, almost like a river or a tide, each stair gifted with a silver edge. She could see details; the smooth wooden rail of the banister and how it curved towards her, curled into a snail-shell. She reached one hand out, let her fingers trace the curve and final circle of the wood.

She heard a shuffling close by. She had been expecting something to happen on the staircase – someone to descend, perhaps; but the sound had come from behind her. She looked round.

Two women were dancing with each other on the flagstone floor. They were Indian women, with oval faces and splayed toes. One wore a scarlet tunic. The other wore pale breeches with silver buttons. Otherwise they were naked. It was a slow dance; they scarcely lifted their feet from the ground. Round and round they shuffled, on their big square feet. Round and round. There was no music.

She had woken that morning believing the house to be Montoya's.

'Sounds like the uniform was his,' Wilson said.

'You know something, Wilson? He has invited me to tea.'

'Montoya?'

She nodded. 'Yes.'

'Then you'll be able to find out, won't you?'

'Find out what?'

'Whether it was his house that you dreamed about.'

They watched as Montoya emerged from the house up the street and climbed back into his waiting carriage.

'There are men like him in Paris,' she said, 'but I did not expect to find them here, in Santa Sofía.'

Wilson squinted after the carriage. 'He's not a typical inhabitant, certainly.'

She began to laugh, and found she could not stop. It was the thought he had given to his judgement, and the gravity with which he had delivered it. He, too, began to laugh.

'Though I don't know how I can talk,' he added, a few moments later, 'with a red rose painted on my foot.'

After Wilson had left, her smile faded and she sat on the veranda for a long time without moving. She was more shaken than she had realised. It was not the dream that had disturbed her, as she had let him believe. It was not the dream itself, but the nature of the dream.

There had been this, when she was young.

She had dreamed about her china doll. She had watched the doll come tumbling down a slope. Head over heels over head over heels. That tall blue summer sky above. And a faint breeze across the grass. And quiet. Just the china doll all folded up at the foot of the smooth green hill.

It did not happen quite like that, of course.

When she left her house the next morning she was not frightened in the slightest. There was no reason to be: no tall blue sky, no smooth green hill. It was the first time, and she had not yet learned to recognise the pathways, how they bend round without you noticing, how they bring you out in some new, remembered place.

She met her friend Claire at the edge of the woods, as agreed.

'What's the time?' Claire whispered.

Suzanne shrugged. 'I don't know. Early.'

It was a secret, this crime that they were about to commit, and yet they must have looked so obvious, two girls threading their way through the trees in clean white dresses. They might almost have been daring the world to catch them in the act, but the world had been asleep that morning; the world saw nothing.

The tip of Claire's nose was red and every time they hid behind a tree, thinking they had heard something, Claire sniffed.

'Be quiet,' Suzanne whispered.

'I am quiet.'

'You're not. You keep sniffing.'

'I can't help it,' Claire whispered back. 'I've got a cold.'

'Just don't sniff, that's all. Do something else.'

'Like what?'

'I don't know. Wipe it on leaves.'

The canal lay to the east of the town, beyond the woods. It would be a warm day later but, at that hour, the grass was sticky with mist; it licked at their brown boots, stained the toes and heels black. Suzanne listened to the birds sending their long calls looping through the trees. She could smell the bitter sap in the stalks of plants.

It was still early when they reached the canal. The apple lighters were tied up, two abreast, along the towpath. Here was the threat: the huge dark hulls coarse with rust and sloping steeply into water that was coated with a thick green scum. They were not yet full of fruit. That would take a few more days. Then they would be setting off for Paris. Paris was where the canal ended. Paris was where the apples went.

The two girls crouched in the bracken at the edge of the towpath. They had to be careful. Sometimes there were men.

Insects hovered on the slime below. No one came.

When Suzanne decided it was safe, they ran across the gravel and clambered on to the nearest lighter. Breathing fast, they crouched again.

The silence held. They climbed down a vertical metal ladder, and then they were standing in the hold. It was darker down there, though still open to the sky. The sweet smell of peel rose into Suzanne's nose. She began to fill her bag.

'Look at me.'

Suzanne looked up.

Claire was balanced on the hill of apples, her toes pointed, her arms held out sideways. She must have climbed back up the ladder and out along the walkway. It was strange. Claire was usually the more cautious of the two, but now she seemed to have fallen into a kind of trance. Perhaps she thought she was the girl who walked the tightrope when the circus came to town.

'We're supposed to be stealing,' Suzanne whispered, 'not doing tricks.'

Claire did not take any notice.

Before Suzanne could speak again, a noise began. A murmuring and then a drumming. Then a rumbling. She saw Claire's face tilt. As if the power of the trance were being tipped out of her. The apples jumped from under her feet, and one of her legs swung up into the air. She came tumbling backwards down the slope, and when she reached the floor she did not move.

'Claire?' Suzanne was still whispering. If she shouted, men might hear.

Claire was folded up against the side wall of the lighter. The apples had almost buried her completely. There was even an apple resting in the socket of her left eye. Her head looked funny on her neck, like a flower when the stalk has snapped. The tip of her nose was still red, and a clear liquid slid towards her upper lip.

It was then, in the silence that followed the avalanche, in that sudden silence, that Suzanne remembered the dream – the tumbling doll, the smooth green hill – and she dropped her bag and ran for the ladder. She cut her finger as she snatched at the first rung, but she did not look back, not once, not even when she was safe behind her bedroom door.

She filled her wet boots with newspaper and hid them in the cupboard; she would clean them with polish as soon as they were dry so nobody would know. She sucked her finger until the blood slowed down, then she undressed and put her nightgown on. She climbed between the sheets. They were cool against her feet, as if whole days had passed.

She lay in bed with her eyes wide open and waited for somebody to come and wake her up.

That afternoon a policeman visited the house. He sat in a chair, and she had to stand in front of him. She could still remember the dark cloth of his uniform, the bright metal buttons. He asked her whether she had seen Claire that day.

She thought carefully and then said, 'No.'

'Claire has disappeared,' the policeman said. 'Do you know where she might have gone?'

Again she answered, 'No.'

'Claire's your best friend, isn't she?'

'Yes.'

'But you have no idea where she might have gone?'

She shook her head. 'No.'

The policeman put his hands on his knees and prepared to stand up. She felt sorry for him suddenly. She would tell him something.

'She had one favourite place.'

Everything fell quiet then. She could hear a wasp trapped between the curtains and the window. Outside it was the end of summer.

'You know the boats on the canal, the ones they put the apples in? Sometimes she liked to go there.'

Suzanne rose shivering from her chair and moved to the rail of the veranda. The mountains were in shadow now. It would soon be dark. She could hear their maid, Imelda, moving inside the house. She had not even noticed the girl arrive.

The dream about the women dancing was the same kind of dream. Some coded version of the truth, a message in disguise. But she was out of practice. It had been years since this had happened. Six, at least.

It seemed to her, as she watched the dusk come down and the French begin to leave their houses, that the town was offering her some link back into her childhood. It could have been as simple as the presence of the sea: steamships and lighters moored along the quay, the smell of kelp and gutted fish and brine, that salt-water grittiness in the air. It could have been. But the feeling rose in her – and it was a feeling she could not dispel – that there was another side to this that she had still to understand, that it was not just some surface familiarity, some coincidence, but a deeper link, inside her mind, below the skin.

4

Towards midnight Wilson left the Hotel La Playa. He took the long route to Pablo's bar, passing through the church on his way. It was strange how the bare arches had the appearance of remains – some creature that had perished in the desert's grip and then been stripped by vultures; it was strange how the beginning could imitate the end. What he could not imagine, as he limped among the pillars and the stacks of metal, was what came between: the final shape of the building, its place in the life of the town.

It was dark on Avenida Manganeso. The only light came from the pool-hall, which was used for cock-fights and illegal lotteries. He stopped in the entrance. Three smoking oil-lamps lit the room. A man was sleeping on a table, with an empty bottle for a pillow. There was a smell of warm urine. Wilson moved on, his arms aching from the crutches. Stars massed in such numbers above his head that it looked as if somebody had spilled chalk-dust across the sky. As he passed along the north side of the municipal square he heard a baby crying, and then silence. At last he pushed through the door of the Bar El Fandango.

The first person he saw, leaning against the zinc counter, was La Huesuda. He could tell from the angle of her head on her neck that she already had a few drinks under her skin. He began to ease backwards through the crowd, but she noticed him. Downing a shot of clear liquor, she swilled it round her mouth, spat it on the floor, then elbowed her way across the room towards him.

'So,' she said, 'American.'

He touched the brim of his hat.

'Where have you been hiding?'

'Nowhere special,' he said.

'You've been lying low, haven't you. Avoiding me.'

He glanced down at his foot. 'I've been resting. The doctor told me to rest.'

Her eyes followed his.

'That's a pretty flower,' she said. Her voice had sharpened at the edges.

'It's not bad.'

'Who painted that on there?'

'A friend.'

'More than a friend, I'd say. That's a woman, did that.' Her thin face scraped the air. 'Am I right, American?'

He nodded.

'Mother of Christ.' Her eyes were knocking around in their sockets like two drunks in a cell. She was muttering some language that he did not understand. All teeth and saliva.

'Pearl,' he said, taking hold of her wrist, 'what's wrong with you?'

She twisted away from him. 'Get lost.'

'Pearl,' he said.

'Go fuck a goat,' she said, and slammed out of the bar.

One of the miners turned to him, 'Jesus,' he said. 'What did you do to her?'

Wilson did not answer. He was remembering the afternoon he had spent with Suzanne and how, after saying no to all the flowers he could think of, and all the animals, after saying no to lumps of gold – they would look, she said, like potatoes – she had decided on a rose. He had not been able to dissuade her. In truth, he had not tried too hard. Deep down he had thought that it might represent the love he felt for her and could not name, though he suspected that she was thinking of his heart and how he had lost it to a girl with bright-red hair. And now the Bony One, with the prickly insight that whores seemed to possess, had seen right through the veils and disguises to that secret truth.

'Nobody wants to fuck her anyway,' Pablo was saying. 'She's too skinny for fucking.'

'I had her once,' the miner said. 'It was like what you leave on your plate after you ate a chicken.'

Wilson sighed. 'I don't feel good about it. When my foot's mended, I'm going to build her a whole new set of stairs.'

Pablo's lip curled.

'I'm going to paint them some colour that's real nice for a whore,' Wilson said. 'Like pink, maybe. Maybe put in a few electric lights as well.'

'Sure you are,' Pablo said.

'I am,' said Wilson.

But somehow it was Suzanne that he could see, standing at the top of the steps in a white silk dress. And, as he watched, he saw the French gold wedding-ring slide off her finger. It slid right off her finger and dropped, spinning, through the air. It landed on a stair and bounced, missed the next two stairs, then bounced again, jumped over his boot and lay down in the dust like it was dead.

He drank quietly for a while, and the blood ran with smooth purpose in his veins, and he dreamed of setting his foot, his mended foot, on that first step, and of her smile as he looked up for reassurance. Clutched in his fist would be a lump of gold. Enough for ten thousand wedding-rings.

Raised voices brought him out of his reverie, and one voice louder than the rest. It was an Indian, his neck and forearms streaked with clay. A miner. He stood shouting in a circle of men. His hands shook as if he were carrying a fever, and his eyes were fastened on the ceiling, though there was nothing there but sheets of tin and smoke from cheap cigars. His words forced themselves out of his mouth; it almost seemed as if he was retching – a flood of words, a pause, another flood. His hair was spiked with sweat.

Wilson asked Pablo what was being said.

'He has seen a painted man.' Both Pablo's eyebrows lifted.

'A painted man?'

'The man was seven feet tall and he was naked,' Pablo said. 'He was standing at the entrance to one of the mines. He was painted half in red and half in black.'

'Who was he?'

'He is a warning.'

Wilson watched the Indians close in around the shouting man. They were pulling at his shirt and talking into his face, but he paid them no attention. He seemed to be receiving a voice from beyond the roof, and repeating what he heard.

'The painted man is an ancestor, and they must listen to him.' Pablo was still translating. 'He is angry with his people. They are betraying their heritage. They must return whence they came. This town should never have come into being. It is a place of blood and ashes. It is an abomination.' Pablo reached for a piece of rag and began nonchalantly to wipe the bar.

The miner uttered a single high-pitched shriek and dropped to the floor. His body thrashed like a hooked fish in the bottom of a boat. His eyes rolled back into his skull; his throat began to rattle.

Pablo looked up. 'He's an epileptic.'

'He's swallowed his tongue,' Wilson said. 'He's choking.'

He pushed through the crowd and, bending down, reached into the man's throat and pulled his tongue loose. Then he turned the man on to his stomach. The fit was over. Yellow vomit trickled from between the man's lips.

'Don't move him,' Wilson told the miners. 'Leave him be.'

He found some water in a bucket behind the bar and washed the bile off his hands.

'You saved him,' Pablo said.

Wilson shrugged. 'Maybe.'

The Indians had ordered more drinks. They were talking among themselves in rapid broken Spanish. Their prophet lay forgotten on the floor.

'This town isn't so bad,' one said.

'At least we're getting paid,' said another.

'If you can call five pesos a day getting paid.' This man had a short, twisted body and he wore a deerskin beret.

'It's five pesos more than you get scratching around in the dirt,' the first man said.

'Right,' said the second. 'And they build us houses.'

The man in the beret spat on the floor. The spit lay next to the epileptic's hand, like a coin tossed to a beggar.

'We're cheap labour is what we are,' he said. 'They're using us for work they wouldn't do themselves.'

Some of the miners were beginning to see with his eyes. And maybe they had a point, Wilson thought. He could still remember how many patients there had been in the hospital, and that sudden shift in the doctor's tone of voice.

'They don't care about us,' said the man in the beret, one arm thrown up in front of his face and curved like a bow. A space had cleared in front of him so he could express himself. 'They're only interested in feathering their own nests,' he said. 'They build themselves fine houses up there on the Mesa del Norte. They're even building themselves a church now – '

'Maybe Señor Wilson should pay the church a visit,' Pablo said. 'That would be the end of the church for sure.'

The miners laughed long and hard, repeating the joke among themselves, and then, when they had almost finished laughing, they translated the joke for those of the Indians who had not understood, and the laughter was handed on.

'That was very funny, Pablo,' Wilson said.

'I thought so,' said Pablo.

5

Tuesday came. You could tell that spring was almost over. The sky had stepped back, forfeiting all colour. The smelting works had shut down for repairs; only a faint chainsaw bit into the clean grain of the air. The silence of the desert could be heard, and the march of the heat across the land.

Though her enthusiasm for tea with the Captain had faded, Suzanne thought that she ought to honour the invitation. At four o'clock a victoria arrived for her. The driver wore an immaculate dove-grey uniform, complete with a red neck-tie and a belt of bullets slung diagonally across his chest. He helped her up into the carriage, then closed the door behind her. She heard him click his tongue. The carriage moved away. She had never been driven to tea by an armed man before. It was novel, if nothing else.

They passed French houses, silent in the afternoon. The rich scent of leather heated by the sun surrounded her. Soon they were descending the hill.

Montoya's ranch stood high above the town, in the mesquite scrubland to the south. As they came up the last of the road's tight curves, she saw the town cemetery. The ground was so hard on this barren ridge that gravediggers could make no impression on it. All they could do was scratch a shallow ditch and pile stones on to the corpse. It struck her as ironic that men who had died because they worked under the ground should be buried on the surface.

The carriage had come round in a long, dusty loop, doubling back towards the coast, and now she could see the house. It had whitewashed walls and a roof of dark-red tiles, and outbuildings at the rear for servants and horses. It stood alone on the ridge, unsheltered by trees, solid yet exposed; she would not have cared to live there. As they drew up outside, Montoya stepped out into the sunlight, hands clasped behind his back.

'I trust you had a pleasant journey, Madame.'

A smile flickered across his face and was gone. She saw how her presence unsettled him, and it softened her. She resolved at once to be kind to him.

'Yes, thank you, Captain,' she said, as she placed a gloved hand on his arm. 'It was very pleasant.'

Montoya led her across a sparse lawn to a terrace on the far side of the house. A banqueting table had been set up in the shade. Two Mexicans stood by with palm branches, in case a vulture tried to land. They both wore straw hats. One of the men had a bright-yellow face and yellow hands, and a cough that shook his entire body.

'He used to work on San Marcos,' Montoya said. 'The sulphur mines.'

He had prepared a feast for her. Quails' eggs, rock oysters, pomegranates. Iced cakes from the bakery. Fruit cordials. Even a bottle of sherry, produced by his great-uncle in Oaxaca.

'I did not know what you would like,' he said. 'I thought that if I bought many different things then perhaps you would find something to your taste.'

'That is most considerate of you, Captain.' Though it was more than considerate; she felt almost crushed by the weight of the food.

He sat beside her and leaned forwards, his chin mounted in the palm of one hand, and stared out over the sea. His eyes shifted one way then the other, as if the empty expanse of blue were filled with countless fascinating objects.

'You're not eating, Captain,' she said.

'I'm not hungry.'

'But all this food – '

He smiled miserably. 'It's for you,' he said. 'In your honour.'

There was a sense in which her own comfort depended on retaining a certain strict formality, a kind of tension between them, and yet the balance had to be precise or conversation would die out altogether. If only she could make him laugh, she thought; laughter would ease the passage of time. But she had yet to discover his sense of humour – if indeed he had one.

The silence stretched until the thick air seemed to hum. Once she thought she heard voices behind her. When she turned in her chair, the yellow man was grinning at her. His palm branch swayed and whispered above the untouched banquet.

After tea Montoya insisted on showing her the house. She passed through an ornate front door ahead of him and into a hallway with a high ceiling and a stone floor. And there, catching the light in a way she recognised, was the coiled snail-shell of wood. And there, as she lifted her eyes, was the staircase, curving round and up. Until that moment she had forgotten about her dream, and the realisation that it was true brought her to a sudden standstill.

'Is something wrong?' he asked her.

'I had a dream about this house.'

He bowed. 'I'm flattered.'

He must have thought she was trying to compliment him. He had not understood. But then, how could he? And she was not about to embark upon an explanation. Her dreams contained an element of danger, and she could hardly instil a sense of caution in somebody whom she did not know.

They moved on through the house. Montoya talked about stone floors and narrow windows – cool in the summer, warm in winter. He laid the flat of his hand against the wall, as if it were a horse's flank. She murmured her approval, but could not concentrate. She kept expecting to recognise something else – the next room, perhaps, or some object that would otherwise have gone unnoticed. She braced herself, as if for a shock.

But the shock did not come. No room had a secret to reveal, no new fragment of the dream, nothing.

Slowly, she relaxed.

'These are my ancestors,' Montoya declared. 'My family.'

They had reached the gallery, a dim room at the back of the house. One by one Montoya introduced the portraits, some distant, close to being forgotten, some still living, all with names as long as incantations or diseases. There was a reversal of the feeling that she usually experienced in a gallery. She felt that this was being done, less for her benefit, somehow, than for theirs, as if she were being offered up for their approval, as if, in fact, they were alive and standing in the room with her. She discovered that she was shivering.

'Are you cold?'

'A little.' She laughed. 'As if one could complain, in a place like this, of being cold.'

She stood closer to the paintings, close enough to see the brushstrokes, close enough to reduce Montoya's ancestors to mere techniques, details: a man with hair that glistened with pomade; a woman holding in her hands a gold mirror and an intricate lace handkerchief. Sometimes there were clocks and roses in the background, sometimes a cannon and a battlefield. She felt the weight of evidence accumulate. Montoya had clearly been born into a noble and distinguished family. Then why had he been sent to Santa Sofía, the very limit of the kingdom, memory's edge? Had he been exiled from the glittering circle that the pictures appeared to represent? She suspected this might be the case, but put it as subtly as she knew how.

'You are so far from your family, Captain.'

She watched his face go cold and still. It was enough to convince her of the soundness of her intuition. There was no need to pursue the subject, and yet she could not simply let it drop. She softened her voice.

'It doesn't seem to suit you. You belong elsewhere.'

There. She had withdrawn, leaving him a comfortable place in which he might explain himself. She had been kind.

But he was staring out of a narrow window, out across the landscape, brown and faded in the heat.

'It is in the nature of a test,' he ventured finally.

'A test?'

'Of character. That's what my father told me.'

He was waiting for her to speak, but she chose not to.

'A glamorous posting on the mainland,' and he drew down the corners of his mouth and shook his head, 'there would have been no challenge. This town may be remote but it is still, after all, a command. But you,' and he brought his dark eyes up to hers, 'why did you come?'

'I wanted to be with my husband.'

'And now?'

She gave him a steady look. 'You're insolent, Captain. I expect that's why they sent you here. It was your insolence.'

'Perhaps you're right,' he said.

Though her rebuke had been seriously intended, he had chosen to treat it as a joke. His voice remained light and mischievous, admitting no remorse, no guilt. She felt cheated. He had taken the confidence that she had given him, and used it against her.

She moved past him, towards the door. Somehow she felt that she had been robbed of the initiative, and that her departure from the room could be seen as a retreat. She heard him follow her, his spurs chinking every time a heel struck the floor. The sound was like a few coins in a pocket, a handful of loose change. It seemed to mock her. Was that all she was worth?

'It is almost seven o'clock. You should go, or people might begin to worry.' He was still behind her, speaking into her back. His words were ambiguous. They contained equal measures of menace and concern.

The carriage was waiting outside. Night had already fallen. To the north the furnaces had thrown an amber light into the sky, as if that part of town had been left out in the rain and then rusted. It was the only light there was.

'It's so dark,' she said. 'How will he find the way?'

'He knows the road.'

As she stepped up into the carriage, Montoya took her by the arm, asking her to wait, and before she could ascertain the reason he had turned and hastened back into the house. He emerged a moment later with a lit candle inside a dome of glass. She took the lantern, asking him what it was for. His smile was crooked in the tilting flame, unstable. It was so he could watch her, he said, as she travelled back across the town.

6

Wilson was woken by Indians shouting in the room below. They had arrived three days before, from the mainland. They were a tribe that he did not recognise, short querulous men with barrel chests and hair that hung in greased strands to their shoulders. Wilson had seen them through the gap in the floor. Sitting cross-legged, they scrawled sets of circles on the bare boards with a piece of charred wood. Then they tipped pebbles out of leather pouches. They would be up for hours, drinking and gambling, cackling, spitting. Their little stones would rattle through his dreams.

He lay down and tried to sleep, but his foot was troubling him and he was up again as the sun poured its light across the waters of the gulf. He watched the miners shuffling out on to the street. They could not have slept for more than an hour or two; it was no wonder they could scarcely lift their feet. And now they would be working underground, in temperatures of forty degrees, pitting their strength against the stubborn local clay. But that was how the Indians lived. They thought no further than the day or night that surrounded them. They always looked forward to the ripening of the pitahaya, but when the time came they never harvested or stored the fruit. They ate as much as they could on the first day. Towards sunset they could be seen sprawling on the ground, speechless, bloated, green in the face. He had once heard of an Indian who had received six pounds of sugar as payment of a debt. The Indian sat down in the dirt and ate his way through the sugar, every ounce of it, and died. Wilson did not doubt but that the story was true. They did not think ahead. There were those who said they did not think at all.

He rolled a cigarette and took it out on to the balcony. He sat on his weak chair, smoking peacefully. The ridge to the north-west had caught the sun. The rock glowed orange. The land that lay below still stood in shadow, the colour your fingers go when you gather wild berries. He could see a long line of men moving on the path that climbed up from the town. They would be heading for the Arroyo del Purgatorio, where a new bed of copper had been discovered. He still could not get used to the sight of so many Indians collected in one place. On his expeditions inland, his many fruitless searchings for the riches he believed were buried there, he had become acquainted with their customs. They were a nomadic folk, with no attachments to the land and few belongings. They travelled in small groups to where the food and water was, seldom sleeping on the same ground twice. They were simple, hopeful – credulous. In their daily lives they would walk for twenty hours without fatigue, but give them a vision of doom, a man painted half in red and half in black, and the light emptied from their eyes and their muscles cramped. It took something supernatural to happen before they believed their grievances were real. Their progress up the wall of rock seemed laboured now. He could not help wondering how it would end.

His gaze dropped down into the town. In the square outside his window men were already at work on the church. He had grown used to the ringing of hammers; if he closed his eyes he saw a score of blacksmiths making shoes for horses. Almost a month had elapsed since the tramp steamer had docked; four metal arches now stood on the ground, four hoops lined up in a row and linked by horizontal rods, like a wagon with the canvas off. He could see Monsieur Valence, seated on a packing-case in his black frock-coat, mopping the sweat from his forehead. The pale face seemed turned for a moment in Wilson's direction, and Wilson raised a hand in greeting. The Frenchman did the same. But that was the limit of their acquaintance. No word had yet passed between them.

He took up his guitar and ran his thumb across the strings. One jangled chord lifted into the air. In his enforced idleness, he had decided to write a song. It was about gold, of course, but it was also, in a curious way, about Suzanne as well. The words would have a kind of double meaning, if he could just get them right. He only had one line so far, which had come from the dream he had woken with on the morning she arrived: 'Gold fever, running in my veins . . . ' That was it. He had already decided to dedicate the song to her and, when it was finished, he would play it for her, one quiet afternoon, in the shade of a veranda.

His eyes blurred, took on distance.

A morning in the hills west of Salinas. A morning that had stayed with him. The sun slanting on yellow grass. Pale-green moss hung from the trees like the matted strands of fleece that sheep leave on fences. A cool morning, early fall.

They had stolen two horses the day before, in Greenfield. A good horse was better than money, his father always said. It might last fifteen years, which was more than money ever did. Money had this way of spilling through your fingers, even if you closed a fist round it. Money always found the one hole in your pocket. Money ran out on you every chance it got; it was even worse than women. These were lessons he had learned from his father, though as a teacher his father often contradicted himself. He taught out of bitterness instead of knowledge, that was the trouble. Take women, for example. It was not women who had run out on his father – if anything, it was the other way round – but it was not the son's place to point out inconsistencies; it was the son's place to listen. He owed obedience, still being only twelve years old, not yet a man. And that obedience, that listening, could pass for love. Were parts of love. When his father told him they would have to steal a horse or two to get through the winter, he went along with it. But the horses that they stole that day, a chestnut and a roan, from the back of the Staging Post Hotel, belonged to a marshal who happened to be visiting the town. They were fortunate to escape arrest, hitching a ride on a melon cart, switching two hours later to a doctor's wagon that was travelling in the opposite direction, then walking half the night. That was the nature of his father's luck: two-sided, like a coin.

But he woke the next morning with a feeling of lightness that he could not explain. He threw off the blanket and, leaping to his feet, tried to stamp the life into his stiff limbs. He saw that his father was still sleeping, so he set about gathering some kindling for a fire, just enough to boil water for coffee. It was a risk, but only a slender one; during the night they had climbed high into the hills and they were now shielded by oak trees. He drove two sticks into the earth, balancing a third above the flames. He slung the kettle on this third stick and sat back on his heels.

When the steam began to swirl across the face of the water, he went to wake his father. His father was lying there with his eyes open. He was staring up into the trees. His eyes wide open, like tins to catch the rain for drinking.

'The coffee's ready, Pa.'

His father did not answer. He just lay on the ground, still as fallen wood, and did not say a word. Did not even blink.

'What's wrong, Pa?'

He had never seen anybody who was dead before, and maybe this was what it looked like. Your eyes were polished till they were clean and so much silence was poured into you, it reached all the way to your fingers.

'Pa?'

His heart was threatening to jump between his ribs.

And then his father's lips moved. 'All I ever dreamed of was to find us some gold.'

His relief converted into faith, the faith his father had instilled in him. 'There's plenty more gold in the ground, Pa. It ain't all used up yet. There's plenty there.'

'That's all I ever dreamed of and all that happens is we end up running from the law.'

He leaned closer, his faith working his tongue for him, lending him the words. Maybe they were running towards the gold, he told his father. Maybe all their running, it was in the right direction. It was just that they didn't know it.

His father was still lying there, the shape of people when they put them into coffins. A faint smile altered his mouth, but it did not reach his eyes. His eyes were wide and frightened; they had that shine to them, the shine of something final. It was as if he were waiting for six feet of sky to come down and cover him like earth. As if he were so old that there was nothing left for him but that. And yet he seemed young too, no more than a child, and needed to be wrapped in something big like love.

Wilson reached into his pouch of tobacco and rolled another cigarette. He could not recall much else about that morning. He struck a flame on the wall behind him and touched it to the paper. He took the first bloom of smoke into his mouth and back over his throat. It was harsh Indian tobacco, grown in the hard ground. Harsh as memory.

There was one thing, now he thought about it. Something he had said to his father. Something that had been on his mind for weeks.

'Maybe we should go home, Pa.'

His father's head turned slowly on his bedroll. 'What good would that do?'

He could think of some good, actually, but he could not voice it, not with his father bending such a look on him. And just then the water, boiling suddenly, jumped out of the kettle, and he had to snatch it off the fire before it spilled some more.

They walked south, then east, with the trail losing heat behind them. Once they saw a group of horsemen cut out against the light above a ridge, but otherwise the world was theirs. No longer fearing capture and the branding that would surely follow it, they dropped down to the valley floor. On the third evening they felt secure enough to risk another fire. He roasted squirrel over a blaze of wild oak and, for want of any potatoes, baked some pale roots in the ashes. The squirrel tasted like rabbit, a pungent meat, but succulent. They cleaned their palates with some strawberries that he had gathered earlier on the wooded slopes. The next day they walked on, always east. His father did not talk at all, but he would often stop and lift his face, as if the air had spoken to him, as if it had said something that gave him cause to hope. To the north a range of yellow hills unfolded. The weather held, dry and crisp. He asked his father where they were headed, but his father would not say. The mystery walked beside them, always there, unsolved.

They walked for a month. Rising before dawn, sleeping at dusk. Moving all the time, and always in silence. He sang to himself so he did not forget he had a voice – 'Old Zip Coon' and 'The Banks of the Mohawk'. They soon left the yellow hills behind. The earth altered beneath their feet. Though September must have been over, the air grew dry and hot. They crossed parched valleys, dried-up riverbeds; they climbed through fields of sharp red rock. They were finding no fresh water now. His father taught him how to create water where none existed. You cut the top off a barrel cactus and then dug a hole inside, about the size of a quart bottle. Then you gathered brush and built a fire around the base. In a few moments sap would collect in the hollow place that you had made. Only two cupfuls, and bitter, but drinkable – and it could save your life. Again he asked his father where they were headed; again his father acted deaf. He could almost see the mystery, walking just ahead of them. It seemed to be leading the way. It was as real as his father, and no less inscrutable.

And then, one afternoon, they came over a stretch of barren ground, a few red rocks, some wiry grass, and there, opening in front of him, was a chasm that was wider and deeper than his eyes could understand, a great gap in the world. He stepped back, dizzy.

'The Grand Canyon.'

His father stood with his hands in his pockets and his toes close to the precipice.

'People say the devil got mad and tried to cut the world in two.' His father turned to him. 'Would you rather be home now?'

He could only gasp. 'No.' All the doubts were chased out of his head by the red-and-violet splendour of the place. All the words too. All the thoughts.

Later they climbed down to where the river, pale-green and lazy, coiled along the canyon floor. He stood on the bank, his shoulder touching his father's rolled-up shirt-sleeve. His father stared at the water with such defiance, it might have been the source of all his misfortune. But his voice, when he spoke, was gentle.

'Now this is something to remember,' he said. 'This place, us being here – that's something to remember. But not the rest of it.' His face opened; he hazarded a smile. 'At least I showed you something.'

His father had kept the secret for weeks – a child's desire to surprise him, a deep need to get something right at last.

Standing at his father's shoulder that afternoon, he was filled with equal measures of happiness and sorrow. When he saw the Grand Canyon again, years later, he could not find the place where they had stood, and yet the same feeling rose in him, a pull in two directions, a spirit divided against itself.

'Hey! American!'

He came back slowly from the past and peered down between the splintered staves that formed the railing to his balcony. Standing on the street below was the Bony One. He shifted on his chair, preparing to withdraw deep into his room.

'I'm sorry if I laid into you the other night,' she called up. 'I was feeling lousy. I had to take it out on someone.'

'That's OK,' he said.

'I just want to apologise. I was pretty hard on you.'

'Forget it.' Smiling, Wilson leaned against the wall.

'Really? You forgive me?'

'I do.'

'Hey, American!'

He leaned forwards again, looked down.

'Don't you think you're tempting fate,' she said, 'sitting on that balcony like that?'

7

It was the 21st of May, the doctor's fiftieth birthday, and Captain Legrand, master of the *SS Providencia*, had organised a dance in his honour. The *SS Providencia* had docked the day before with a cargo of timber, live piglets and, most important of all, champagne. Twenty-five cases of Clicquot had arrived from Paris, ordered for the occasion by Madame de Romblay (the doctor's wife being incapable, presumably, of such an extravagant gesture). The birthday dance was to be held on the rear deck. There was one problem, though. Since the freighter had been unloaded, it had risen in the water, and it could only now be reached by means of a vertical ladder on the starboard bow. This would be too hazardous for the ladies – for certain of the gentlemen as well. In the event, Captain Legrand had proposed an ingenious, if unorthodox, alternative. They would attach an armchair to a system of ropes and pulleys, and hoist the guests aboard. He had used the technique before, he said, in Chile, almost entirely without incident.

'I could donate a chair,' Jean-Baptiste Castagnet said.

But Monsieur de Romblay was frowning, one forefinger set diagonally across his mouth. 'Almost, Captain?' he said. 'What do you mean, almost?'

Captain Legrand was a vast, droll man. To see the Captain and the Director together, in conversation, was to be reminded of two majestic planets orbiting slowly, one around the other.

'It was the Mayor of Valparaiso's wife,' he said. 'She drank too much gin. On the way back down, the chair began to spin. She vomited on the heads of her citizens from a height of thirty feet.' He paused. 'They lost the election the following year.'

That evening, on the stroke of seven, the French gathered on the north quay. They were dressed in all their finery, as such an event demanded, though nobody could outshine the doctor. He had received a birthday surprise from his wife: a new waistcoat. Cream silk brocade, it was, overlaid with a tracery of ferns in palest green and gold. Three months in the making.

The doctor clapped his hands for silence. 'My colleagues,' he cried, 'my friends. Let us begin!'

They had agreed beforehand that they should choose straws to determine the order of their ascent. One by one they stepped forwards, dipped their hands into the doctor's opera hat. It was Florestine, his wife, who drew the shortest. Her eyes scaled the steep sides of the freighter, mollusc-encrusted, pocked with rust. Then dropped down, round and watering, to the yellow damask armchair that had been donated, as promised, by Monsieur Castagnet. Florestine, it now transpired, had vertigo.

There was some delay, but after a few drops of valerian and a soothing lecture from her husband on the psychological advantages of going first, the yellow armchair lifted into the night sky with Florestine securely strapped in place. She had a rosary plaited through the fingers of her right hand. Her husband's velvet cummerbund shielded her eyes. The French watched from below. Nobody spoke. The chair spun slowly on its rope, but Florestine did not so much as murmur. Soon only the soles of her shoes were visible.

When at last she appeared at the guard-rail, supported on her husband's arm, eyes glittering in a face that had drained of blood, the French rewarded her with an outburst of spontaneous applause. The yellow chair descended, empty now. High on the deck above, the doctor borrowed the Captain's megaphone and aimed it at the quay.

'Next!'

There was a moment's silence, some nervous laughter, then Suzanne stepped forwards. Théo helped to strap her in.

'I would have thought you'd prefer the ladder,' he murmured in her ear.

She smiled up at him, but did not answer.

He was paying her small attentions tonight, which could have been the result of the dress she was wearing, since it was a favourite of his, an evening gown of peach silk-satin, with bare arms, a looped neck held by ribbons at the shoulders and skirts that were patterned with chrysanthemum petals.

As she rose off the ground and the faces below her shrank, the chair began to turn clockwise. First she was facing the sea, then she was looking inland, towards the mountains. Then she faced the sea again.

She tried not to think about the Mayor of Valparaiso's wife. Instead, she summoned the image of her friend, Lucille, who at that moment was probably attending some dreary opera in Paris. How Lucille would have relished this.

She was swinging sideways now, over the guard-rail, and she could look down. The entire rear deck of the SS *Providencia* had been transformed into a ballroom. Chinese lanterns hung round the edges of the dance-floor, shedding exotic coloured light – cider, damson, lime. French flags had been draped across the forecastle and the bridge. On a rostrum at the stern, an orchestra was playing a polonaise by Ambroise Thomas. The armchair gently touched the deck and she was helped out of the harness by Florestine Bardou, who was almost ragged with exhilaration.

'It's a miracle, isn't it?' Florestine said.

Champagne had reached the town at exactly the right time; a ballroom had been created out of nothing; Florestine had survived her ordeal in the armchair – they were all miracles. It was hard to know which of the miracles she was referring to.

And suddenly the doctor was dancing towards them on the balls of his feet, his elbows tucked against his ribs, his hands spread sideways in the air as if he were walking a tightrope. His waistcoat seemed to arrive first. He gestured at the streamers and pennants that looped above the dance-floor. 'I should be fifty more often.'

'I should like to be fifty again.' The voice had come from above, and they all looked up. Monsieur de Romblay saluted them from an armchair in the sky.

'As for me,' Suzanne said, 'I should not like to be fifty at all,' which won her a burst of raucous laughter from the airborne Director.

Soon everyone was on board – and entirely without incident, as the Captain was swift to point out in his brief welcoming speech. The glasses were charged with iced champagne and Monsieur de Romblay stepped forwards to toast the doctor. The fact that they had something special with which to celebrate became in itself a cause for celebration. The drinking was reckless, even among the ladies, and by the time the first dances were over and the early supper was served, most of the party was drunk.

At the table on the top deck, with the night so still that the candle flames stood motionless and tall, Théo began to talk about bolts. The week before, a box of bolts had vanished from the construction site. They were particularly robust bolts, a full ten centimetres in diameter; they were used to attach the purlins, which formed the basis of the secondary structure, to the central structure of the arches.

'I do like a man who can tell a story,' Madame de Romblay said. It was not a venomous remark; she seemed genuinely amused by Théo's long-winded and technical introduction. She leaned towards him. 'Don't forget, Monsieur Valence. You promised me the mazurka.'

With a brief nod in her direction, Théo continued. The missing box of bolts had held him up for three days. He approached one of the more communicative Indians and tried to establish who had been left in charge of it. The Indian said, '*Vara*.'

'Literally, "*Vara*" means "nothing",' Théo explained. 'But they also use the word idiomatically, to mean "I don't know".'

He asked the Indian when he had last seen the box. Again the Indian said, '*Vara*.' He wondered whether the Indian had any idea what might have happened to the box. The reply was the same: '*Vara*.' He demanded the Indian's name. '*Vara*.'

Laughter rippled round the table.

Pineau interrupted. 'How long is this going to take, for heaven's sake?'

'*Vara*,' shouted Monsieur de Romblay.

By now everyone was laughing, even Théo, though, as Suzanne knew, he had by no means reached the point of the story.

He proceeded to describe how he had set up a search party, consisting of himself, a Mexican soldier, an Indian interpreter and 'Vara' too, since he suspected that four denials in a row amounted to some kind of confession, or at least suggested that the Indian had something to hide and might be party to the theft.

Monsieur de Romblay lifted his glass. 'I salute you, Monsieur Valence. You have penetrated one of the first mysteries of Indian logic. "Nothing" means everything.'

Théo tried not to look too pleased with himself. Just for a moment he resembled a head on a coin: frozen, stern, imperial.

'And did you find the bolts?' asked Marie Saint-Lô.

'Yes, I did,' Théo said. 'I found them on a piece of wasteground behind the town. They were in the possession of four of my Indian labourers. Do you know what they were doing with them?'

Nobody could guess. In fact, they did not want to guess. They wanted to be told.

Théo smiled. 'They were playing boule.'

The thought of four Indians playing boule with Théo's bolts was too much for the French. Laughter exploded against the still night air.

'Now for the best part,' Théo said. 'I asked them what they were doing. "There is no work," they said, "so we play." ' He leaned forwards, gripping the edge of the table. 'The theft of the bolts by the Indians had caused a stoppage at work. The effect of this stoppage was a sudden acquisition of free time. Having acquired this free time, the Indians reacted in a predictable way: they looked round for something to do. And what did they find?' Théo opened his hands. 'The bolts. They used the original cause of their predicament as its solution. Cause, effect, cause, effect, cause. A perfect circle.' He had become dishevelled in his excitement, his white tie loosening, one shirt-cuff dappled with Hollandaise sauce.

'It sounds like a Belgian joke,' Pineau said.

Monsieur de Romblay disagreed. 'It's a classic tale of the region. Absolutely archetypal.' He lifted a glass to Théo. 'You should be a logician, Monsieur Valence, not an engineer.'

'Perhaps the two are not so far apart,' said Théo, with becoming modesty.

Madame de Romblay appeared to be finding it difficult to grasp the twists and turns of the logic that her husband so admired. She was staring into the night with the vacant expression of someone who has been waiting for a carriage for a long time, only to see it drive past without stopping. Nothing could have been further from her mind at that moment than a mazurka, though that was what the orchestra was playing on the deck below.

'To the lost bolts,' cried Florestine Bardou, 'now happily found again!'

At least someone was benefiting from the seemingly infinite supply of champagne.

The night began to whirl. A huge moth flew over the supper table, blundered three times around a candelabra and crackled into nothing in the flames. Montoya, who had arrived late, presented the doctor with a brocade sombrero. Marie Saint-Lô flung her shoes into the harbour and danced barefoot with Captain Legrand. It was still only eleven o'clock.

Suzanne sat by the rail in the stern, a glass of champagne cooling the palm of her hand.

'Would you care to dance?'

She looked up. It was Montoya, Félix Tortoledo de Avilés, with his mournful eyes. His plumed hat nestled beneath his arm, like a chicken just bought from the market. Théo was right: the man was a clown. But the champagne had softened her. She would grant him this one dance and be done with it.

Folding her fan, she rose to her feet and placed one gloved hand on his arm. The music swooped down and spun her through the air. Dancing seemed as natural as breathing.

'I watched you all the way across the town,' he said.

She remembered the lantern he had given her and smiled.

'I watched your light ascend the hill.' He was staring past her shoulder, his eyes distant.

Still smiling, she turned her face sideways. There were two women dancing at her elbow. One wore a scarlet tunic with silver epaulettes. The other was naked from the waist up, her breasts gleaming from the exertions of the waltz. She only saw the women for a moment. Then Montoya whirled her away across the floor. When she could look again, they were gone.

She broke away from the Captain, moved quickly to the rail. The lights of the boat were reflected on the water. She could see black dots and dashes, punctuations in the shifting gold – the heads and arms of children swimming in the harbour. Further along the deck, François Pineau, the accountant, was tossing coins over the side.

'There's no point throwing money to them,' Pierre Morlaix was saying. 'They can't see it.'

Pineau's top lip curled. 'Exactly.'

'You're incorrigible.' Morlaix began to laugh.

Suzanne found her glass and held it against her cheek. The coolness burned her skin.

Montoya came and stood beside her. 'Is something the matter? Are you faint?'

'Leave me alone,' she said.

The two women had been so close to her; she could have reached out and touched either one – a glistening bronze shoulder, a ghostly epaulette. Her mind opened in front of her like an abyss. She could hear the safety engineer laughing.

A hot wind, rising off the water, gusted across the deck. All the candles guttered and then blew out.

'Time to leave,' somebody cried. Which must have been a joke, since it was not even midnight and the Captain had promised dancing until dawn.

But when she turned round, she saw Montoya step over to the doctor and shake his hand. His eyes met hers for a moment across the deck, then he was climbing backwards down the ladder. She watched his plumed hat vanish below the rail.

At the late supper Suzanne sat quietly while Pineau and Morlaix traded stories that served to illustrate the foolishness of the Mexicans, the foolishness, particularly, of the local representative of the Mexican Government.

'He's very young, is he not,' Marie Saint-Lô remarked, 'to be representing the Government?'

'Ah well,' the doctor said. 'His father went to school with Porfirio Díaz.' And, when she did not seem enlightened by the information, he added, in lower tones: 'The President.' He faced the gathering again. 'Apparently he was named after Félix Díaz. The President's brother.'

Morlaix swirled the cognac in his glass. 'Wasn't he the one who got shot?'

The doctor nodded. 'I believe so.'

'I still can't get used to that preposterous uniform.' A lock of Pineau's hair hung in his eyes. His twisted upper lip was sprinkled with drops of perspiration. 'What does he think he is? A general?'

'He's dashing, though.' Florestine Bardou sounded wistful, almost unconvinced.

'And am I not dashing?' cried the doctor. 'Even at fifty?'

Nobody could deny that, of course, not on his birthday, and certainly not in that new waistcoat.

Madame Bardou blushed.

But the subject could not be changed quite so easily. It was a favourite among the French, especially after dinner when the blood was high.

'He may be dashing,' Madame de Romblay said, 'but he's also mad, completely mad.'

'Did you know?' Castagnet said. 'He has a submarine.'

Madame de Romblay's eyelids drooped with pleasure. She had not expected support from such a reputable quarter.

'I've never seen it,' Morlaix said.

'He keeps it in Señor Ramón's boathouse,' Castagnet said.

Pineau chuckled sardonically. 'For a small fee, I imagine, knowing Ramón.'

Monsieur de Romblay wanted to know how Montoya had come by it.

'He bought it from the Pacific Pearl Company,' Castagnet said. 'I'm not sure if he ever uses it. It must be twenty years old by now. It would probably dive straight to the bottom.'

'One way of getting rid of the fellow,' Morlaix said.

Laughter swept the table.

'You know that boy who works in the hotel,' Madame de Romblay said, 'the one who plucks his eyebrows like a girl? Well, apparently,' and she lowered her voice and leaned over the table, 'he spends whole afternoons up at Montoya's place.'

'No!' Florestine Bardou put a hand to her throat. Though she would not initiate a story, she would, it seemed, become a willing accomplice in the telling.

'Oh yes, Madame.' Pineau leered. 'I've been watching him.'

'Two Mexicans live there too.' Madame de Romblay's tin eyes glittered, and her powdered shoulders were streaked with excitement's generous secretions. 'People say that the four of them,' and she dropped her voice still lower, 'indulge in vicious practices.'

'Whole afternoons?' Florestine Bardou had fixed on this single, lurid detail. Her hand still clutched her throat.

Suzanne was smiling. 'Actually, I doubt that.'

All eyes turned on her, but it was the eyes of Madame de Romblay that felt the closest.

'It's true, there are two Mexicans living with Montoya,' she went on, 'but they're both well over sixty. And one of them is poisoned from years of working in a sulphur mine. So I think vicious practices are probably out of the question.'

'And how, precisely, do you know all this, my dear?' Madame de Romblay knew how to use a simple question as an accusation. It was all in the twist she gave to the word 'precisely'.

'I've been to his house. He invited me there,' Suzanne said, 'for tea.'

The air softened with astonishment. Several of the company ostentatiously refrained from looking at each other. Across the deck, between two coloured streamers, Suzanne could see the moon, dented in two places, as if it had drunk too much and fallen several times.

One swift glance at Madame de Romblay and she knew that she had made a mistake. She had walked into the woman's limelight, pricked the rumour like some ludicrous balloon. You did not do that to Madame de Romblay. She saw that she was about to be punished for it.

'It was the strangest tea,' she said brightly, attempting to escape through humour. 'We ate oysters that had been harvested in the Bahía San Lucas. We drank sherry from his great-uncle's vineyard. There was no actual tea at all.'

She had hoped for laughter, but the silence lasted. The only response issued, as it had to, from the thin, painted lips of the Director's wife.

'You *drank* with him?'

'I didn't know you had been to tea with Montoya,' Théo said.

It was after two in the morning and they were taking the Director's carriage home.

'Well,' she said, 'I did tell you that I was going.'

Looking at him, she could sense him trying to remember. She did not have to try. She could recall that night's conversation word for word. His monotonous remoteness, his sudden scorn.

'You probably didn't hear me. You were probably too busy,' she said, 'with your work.'

He dropped away from her, into a long silence.

She listened to the carriage-wheels, the chink and jingle of the reins. The night was loud with all the champagne that she had drunk. She could feel his disapproval surfacing and knew that it would take the form of a rebuke. But waiting for it, that was hard. Knowing that it would come. When all she wanted to do was rest her head against his shoulder.

'You should not have said what you did.'

It was a relief to hear him speak, even though he was condemning her. She did not reply.

Such nonsense had been talked at the supper table, but there was one moment, towards the end of the evening, that she would always cherish. The candles had burned low. The white tablecloth was littered with melting sorbets, lobster claws, the skins of fruit. Pierre Morlaix was holding forth. She could see his lips, moistened, flecked with spit. She could see his scalp beneath a flickering of silver curls. It was the usual monologue. The locals could not be trusted. They were lazy, unhygienic, sly. Animals, really. No wonder the church was taking so long. And so on. Théo had not witnessed what happened next; he must have been downstairs, dancing the promised mazurka with Madame de Romblay. For, suddenly, there was a young boy standing in their midst. Only his shoulders and his shaved head showed above the table's edge; his eyes too – dark and sombre, bewitched by the place in which he found himself. He had been swimming; his wet skin shone. In his hands, held just below his chin, a pair of women's shoes. Water dripped from the silver straps. The sequinned heels blinked. But it was to Morlaix that Suzanne looked. It was Morlaix she remembered. His sudden silence, as if the blood had knotted in his brain. His mouth gaping, fishlike, the next boorish words already shaped. There was nobody at the table who was so drunk that they did not recognise the irony.

As the carriage drew up outside their house, a grim smile appeared on her face. Perhaps she had behaved badly, but she had not been alone. In fact, all things considered, she believed that she had behaved quite well. There was no reason why she should apologise. She did not feel the slightest remorse.

Towards morning she woke up. A long way off she heard the mournful cry of a coyote, but she knew that it was not the coyote that had reached down into her sleep. Her nightgown had gathered underneath her arms, binding her tight. She sat up in bed and threw the damp sheet back.

Théo lay sleeping under a single mound of white. It looked as if snow had fallen in the bedroom, and then drifted. A soothing image in a climate such as this, she thought, though certainly perverse. Then she heard a clink. She could not place the sound, and yet she knew it well. Another clink. It was measured, regular; it could almost have been the beating of her own frustrated heart.

As silent as that imagined snow, her feet landed on the floor. She slipped from the bed, moved to the window. The narrow gap between the shutter-blades afforded several different views. Through one, she saw part of the hard mud path that led past the kitchen hut. Through another, a portion of the kitchen roof. Through a third, the sea.

That clink again, somewhere below.

She pressed her face to the shutters, saw moonlight running down a sword. A gasp escaped her. She stepped back.

She sat on the edge of the bed. Her heart had gathered speed; it now outstripped the chinking of the spurs. She felt nothing for the Captain, nothing at all, and yet his secret vigil excited her. These were the sleepless nights that she had predicted for him. This was the hunger.

But it was dangerous knowledge. There would be nobody to tell.

She eased back, laid her head against the pillow. Instead of spurs, she willed herself to see a man's hand bouncing coins. Then just the coins. Then she spent them.

Her heart slowed down.

Her husband, whom she had always loved, still loved, would always love, slept blindly on.

8

17 Calle Francesa,
Santa Sofía,
Lower California,
Mexico

23rd May, 189 –

My dear Monsieur Eiffel,

Though it is fully three weeks since last I wrote, I am delighted to report that everything is proceeding according to plan. All the principal arches have been erected and assembled, their sections being placed end to end in the usual manner, immediately drifted, and then bolted. The purlins will soon follow. I have divided my labour force into two equal groups, one working an early shift, one working late. In this way the Indians are afforded some respite from the considerable heat, though it troubles them less than it does me. The arrangement is also far more suited to their temperament; the idea of pay may appeal, but the idea of work, especially eight hours of it, does not. I often think fondly of those intrepid men, each one vying with the other in his zeal, who worked up to sixteen hours a day in high winds, rain and snow, to build the tower that now bears your name, and fall to wondering how long the job would have taken had you attempted it in Mexico. During the idle hours between shifts I eat lunch with Monsieur Castagnet, a most genial man, and a capable one too (he it was who solved the dilemma of the lifting-mast by commandeering half a dozen railway sleepers to anchor the base). We have discussed the church in detail, and I have found myself referring him to your renowned monograph, *Mémoire sur les épreuves des arcs métalliques de la galerie des machines du Palais de l'exposition universelle de 1867*, and those early experiments that led you so ingeniously to determine the value of the modulus of elasticity applicable to composite members. Monsieur Castagnet has always demonstrated great loyalty to timber, but even he has no choice but to agree that the galvanised wrought-iron that we are using here is a truly remarkable material. When we return to the site in the afternoon, there are invariably half a dozen children climbing among the girders, as if the structure had been provided solely for their own amusement. I always feel that this forms the perfect counterpoint to our weighty lunchtime meditations.

Such problems as we have encountered here have rarely been of a technical nature; in Santa Sofía it is the human problems that abound. We had the greatest trouble, for instance, trying to explain the notion of a working-week to the local Indians. On the Monday of the second week of construction, six of them failed to report for work. We found them two days later, almost five kilometres from the town, grilling a rattlesnake over a fire! They seem to have only two measurements of time: a day, which lasts from dawn to dusk, and an 'ambia', which is the period of time that elapses between one harvest of their beloved pitahaya fruit and the next (three 'ambia's amount to approximately one year). If they work hard, I now tell them, the church will be finished by the next ambia. This, of course, they understand.

Property is another source of confusion. With the exception of a bladder or a cow's horn for holding water, a bow fashioned from the wild willow and a sharpened stick or bone for digging up roots, the Indians have no possessions. They simply do not understand the concept. This was illustrated last week, when a box of bolts went missing from the site. Construction was held up for three days while I endeavoured to ascertain their whereabouts; it seems that the role of an engineer in Mexico can stretch to encompass that of a police detective. Suffice to say that the bolts were recovered and are now in place on the central arches, where they belong. I have taken precautions against further thefts by enlisting the services of three Mexican soldiers from the garrison above the town. (I should just mention, in passing, that I have met the garrison commander, a gentleman by the name of Félix Montoya. In my opinion he lacks the experience to be able properly to discharge his responsibilities; he should be replaced as soon as possible – though this might be a somewhat delicate matter, since it lies beyond our jurisdiction.)

The living conditions – climate, diet, etc. – have also taken their toll. I was struck down only last week by a most unpleasant gastric infection, the result, I suspect, of eating a meal that had been prepared in a local restaurant, though the woman responsible was vociferous, to put it mildly, in her rebuttal of these charges. Whatever the true origin of my complaint, I was laid up in bed for almost two days with frequent attacks of vomiting and diarrhoea. My poor wife had to minister to me, and I am sure that I was not the easiest of patients. I have recovered now, however, and, though still weak, am back at work on the site.

Madame Valence is well (unlike myself, she has succumbed to no illness of any kind since our arrival) and is proving a most popular member of this small community, as you might imagine; Monsieur de Romblay seems to have taken quite a fancy to her. She sends her fondest regards, as do I, and I trust this letter finds you in good health – better, at least, than mine. I have the honour to be your most humble and obedient servant,

    Théophile Valence.

9

As soon as his boat had passed the harbour wall, Namu hoisted a sail and tried to coax some life out of the air. The patched canvas faltered, swelled, faltered again. Wilson could not help but think of the Pacific, less than a hundred miles to the west. The wind blew constantly on that side of the peninsula, hurling breakers shorewards, tormenting shrubs and bushes until they bent down, cowered, turned their backs. That same wind spent itself in the foothills of the Sierra de la Giganta mountains, and not even the faintest of breezes made it through. August and September could be fresh months on the Pacific coast, but in the valley where Santa Sofía had been built the air hung like a curtain of steaming velvet and the streets turned to powder.

Namu called to him and pointed at the sail. They had picked up a light north-westerly, and maybe that was the best they could hope for with June around the corner. Wilson spoke to Suzanne, who was seated in the bow.

'With any luck, we'll make it to San Bruno. Namu knows a place about a mile off shore. It's where the big fish go.'

She did not respond. She sat with her face angled away from him, her parasol turning absent-mindedly upon her shoulder.

He scoured his mind for something that he might have done to offend her, but he could find nothing.

'Suzanne?'

'I was wrong to come to Mexico,' she said, still facing away from him.

'No.' The word had escaped before he had time to think what it might imply. 'No,' he said, more gently, 'you weren't wrong. Your place is by your husband's side, surely.'

'He hardly even knows I'm there. And when he does, I only disappoint him.'

'Disappoint him? How?'

She sighed. 'He tried to warn me what it would be like. I didn't listen. I didn't want to understand.' She turned to him with a sad smile. 'I'm sorry, Wilson. I didn't mean to spoil the day with my bad humour. You're so kind to have arranged all this.'

All this. She made it sound as if he had arranged the sea and sky for her, those islands in the distance, that leaping fish. Of course he would have, if he could.

'You're not spoiling it,' he said. Though he was happier now that she had owned her mood; he could begin to find ways of dispossessing her of it.

He shifted down the bench towards her, then leaned forwards, forearms draped across his knees, hands dangling.

'Someone else who thinks of nothing but his work,' he said, 'is Jesús Pompano.'

The boat gathered speed; water chopped against the hull. He began to tell her the latest instalment in the story of the elusive baguette.

Only the day before, as he returned from breakfast at Mama Vum Buá's place, he had found Jesús waiting on the first-floor landing in his hotel. Jesús was tucked so deep into the gloom that he was hardly visible. If it had not been for the pale patches on his clothes, Wilson would not have noticed him at all. He showed the baker into his room and sat him down.

'What is it, Jesús?'

'I've got to hide.'

'Hide? Who from?'

'Take a look outside.'

Wilson went to the window. Something shiny was moving up the street. Something that flashed and glittered. He saw a hat, two legs. A man then. But not just any man. A man who looked as if he had been wrapped in sunlight.

The doctor.

He faced back into the room. 'I thought you had it all worked out, what with the new oven and your Austrian techniques and everything.'

The baker put his head in his hands. 'My mother died.'

Thinking some tragedy had befallen the Pompano family, Wilson brought the second chair in from the balcony and sat down beside his friend.

'I didn't know you had a mother,' he said. 'I mean, you have never spoken of her.'

The baker's shoulders twitched once, twitched again. They began to shake. Wilson could not tell whether the baker was laughing or crying. Then Jesús threw his head back, and there could be no doubt. His laughter swelled, and filled the room. He slapped his thighs; flour billowed into the air. Both men began to cough.

'Wilson,' Jesús said, 'you're a fool.'

Wilson stared at Jesús blankly. Hiding in doorways, laughing at the death of his mother, insulting his friends. Had the baker lost his mind?

'Don't you know anything about bread?' Jesús said.

Wilson had to admit that his knowledge was limited.

Jesús proceeded to define a mother for him. A mother was a spontaneous lactic fermentation informed by wild yeasts, otherwise known as a leaven. It was achieved by mixing flour and water in a bowl and leaving the mixture to mature. A mother had to be added to each day – another handful of flour, a little more water. A mother had to be nurtured and developed. When you came to make a loaf of bread you used some fresh leaven in combination with some of the original. A mother lay at the heart of all good bread. A mother was fundamental, irreplaceable. Without a mother, you could do nothing.

'It was some lecture,' Wilson said, turning to Suzanne.

Her melancholy had lifted, leaving her face clear and untroubled in the sunlight. All her keenness had returned.

'How did the mother die?'

He smiled. 'That was my next question.'

'I don't know,' Jesús said.

'Well, how does a mother usually die?'

'One of two ways. It has to be kept at a constant temperature, say between seventy-five and eighty-five degrees. If it gets too cold, it dies. But can you imagine it getting too cold in a town like this?' Jesús let out a mirthless chuckle. 'It also dies if you don't add to it each day. It gets too sour. But I could've sworn I added to it. I do it religiously.'

'So what will you do?'

'Start again, from the beginning. I've got no other choice.'

The long silence that followed this pronouncement made the knock on the door seem all the louder. Three knocks, each one separate, abrupt, demanding. A voice called from the landing.

'Monsieur Pharaoh?'

The baker looked towards the door. The flesh seemed to have slipped an inch on his face. 'The doctor?'

Wilson nodded. He scanned the room. There was no place to hide save underneath the bed. The gap between the floorboards and the springs was negligible, and the baker was not a small man. But there was nowhere else.

'Monsieur Pharaoh?' Another triple knock. 'It is I. Dr Bardou.'

Taking Jesús by the sleeve, Wilson pointed under the bed. Jesús nodded dismally. He dropped to his knees and began to insert himself into the gap. He was whispering the most terrible blasphemies against the doctor.

Wilson opened the door, and the doctor slid past him with the smoothness of a ball of lard in a heated skillet. He was wearing a waistcoat of raspberry, peppermint and gold, and his hair, slick with pomade, mirrored the brilliance of his patent-leather shoes. He looked almost supernatural against the decaying plaster of the walls.

'I was looking for Monsieur Pompano, but he is not at home. So I came to see you, Monsieur Pharaoh. My patient. How is the foot? You are resting it?' Not a breath was taken between sentences, and his eyes darted about the room. He seemed thrilled to have penetrated this new territory.

'Won't you sit down, Doctor?' Wilson said, hoping that he would not notice the light dusting of flour on the seat.

The doctor's hand polished at the air. 'No, no, Monsieur Pharaoh. Thank you. I cannot stay.' Then his head dipped sharply to one side. 'But I can smell bread. No, it's flour. Am I right, Monsieur Pharaoh?' He had danced forwards and was balanced on the ball of one foot, his dark eyes searching Wilson's face, one hand held out flat, palm uppermost, like a tray for drinks.

'The baker was here this morning,' Wilson said, 'to give me the sad news.'

'Sad news? What sad news?'

'His mother has died.'

'Oh, but I am sorry. Yes, look.' And he folded in half, his eyes not six inches from the boards. 'There is some flour on the floor.' He dabbed the white dust with one finger and examined it. If he had looked sideways at that moment he would have seen a man under the bed. 'But his mother died, you say? That is terrible.'

Terrible indeed, thought Wilson, as he watched the doctor straighten up. Especially for you, Monsieur.

'Poor Jesús,' Suzanne said, though she was laughing. 'He was under the bed the whole time?'

Wilson nodded. 'When the doctor had gone, it took him ten minutes to extract himself. "I've been breathing cockroaches and dust for half an hour," he said. "By Christ, if I'm not tempted to put a few new ingredients in the doctor's beloved bread."'

'He wouldn't,' Suzanne said.

Wilson laughed. 'He might.'

Namu called from the stern and pointed towards the coast. The land had flattened out; they could see a few thatch huts, some palm trees, a strip of volcanic sand.

'San Bruno,' Wilson told Suzanne. 'People say that a tribe of Amazon women lived there once, but there's no real proof, only stories that were handed down.' He stared towards the shore, its charcoal sand, the curved prows of canoes. 'It's just a fishing village now.'

10

Suzanne listened carefully as Wilson described the place that they were heading for. It lay just to the south of a sandbank that was almost a mile long. Each morning shoals of small fish swam through a channel at the southern tip, which made it a popular feeding-ground for bigger fish. If they anchored above the channel, Wilson explained, they would stand a good chance of catching bonita or cabrilla or yellowtail.

She interrupted him. 'But it's all sea. How do we know when we've arrived?'

Wilson asked Namu, and then translated the fisherman's reply for her. There were three different marks on the land, Namu said. When all three lined up in a formation that he recognised, then he knew he was there. He lifted his shoulders, grinned.

She watched Namu as he watched the land, and thought she saw the moment when the landmarks fell into place because his wide eyes sharpened at the corners. Soon afterwards he stood up and began to furl the sail. Next he had to fix their position on the surface with his anchor, a solid lump of rusting metal. It looked more like part of an engine than an anchor, and she said as much to Wilson.

'It is part of an engine,' he said.

There were rocks on the ocean bed below, he told her. If they used a traditional anchor, the kind with a straight piece and a smiling piece, it would more than likely just get stuck.

He had to help Namu heave the anchor on to the bow and roll it overboard. The two men could barely manage it between them. But over it went, and the rope uncoiled slickly, fizzled over the side as if it were being devoured by the sea. Uncoiled, uncoiled; it seemed the sea's appetite was boundless.

'It must be deep,' she said.

Wilson nodded. 'Fifteen fathoms.'

Namu took a wooden reel and unwound the twine. On the end of the twine was a lead weight, the shape of a teardrop, and a hook. He reached into a bucket at his feet and took out a mackerel.

She watched as Namu threaded the hook in through the fish's mouth, out through its gills, in through its body, out through its tail. It reminded her of sewing. He straightened the fish on the hook, then threw it overboard and put the reel and the line in her hand.

'Let the line pay out,' Wilson told her. 'It'll run through your fingers. When it stops running, that means you've reached the bottom. Then you reel it back in a few feet, so it's hanging above the floor. That's where the big fish are.'

She followed his instructions. The line slid across her palm and vanished into the water, just kept vanishing. A magic trick: there did not seem to be any reason why it should be moving. She tried to imagine what the line was passing through, what it would be seeing if it had eyes, and could not. Such a vastness lay beneath them; it was like an image of infinity.

At last the line stopped paying out, as Wilson had said it would, and she reeled it back and held it, as he was holding his, between her thumb and forefinger, almost as if she were testing its weight. She sat for several minutes with the line between her fingers. Nothing happened.

When Wilson reeled his line in, the bait had gone.

She decided to check her own line. The hook came up empty. Yet she had felt nothing.

'It's practice,' Wilson told her. 'It takes years.'

He fixed her hook for her, and she began again. Time slowed down, and then it did not seem to pass at all. Light glanced off the water. The boat seemed cushioned, in suspension; nothing changed or moved. Soon even her sense of place dissolved. It was not here that children walked in her shadow and moonlight ran down swords. Not here; somewhere else. She tried to summon Paris into her mind, and found that she could hardly remember it. Or rather, she could remember it, but it just did not seem real. The grey streets that she saw did not convince her. What had she loved? The city after rain. Dancing until she was almost asleep on her feet. The nightingales on the Rue de la Sorbonne. But their singing now seemed artificial, shrill, to her, a tune played on a music box. Rain was something she no longer understood. And dancing? She preferred not to think of that at all. The sound of a knife on wood broke into her thoughts, and she glanced round.

Namu was hacking two mackerel into pieces on the bench beside him, chopping the fish as fine as if they were parsley. When he had reduced them to a bloody pulp he moved down the boat, examining the pale stones that were wedged between its ribs. She had thought these stones might be decorations, or represent some kind of superstition, but she now saw that they had a specific, practical purpose. Namu selected a stone with a good flat surface and laid the crushed fish across it, then he took his hook, already threaded with a whole mackerel, and wound it round and round the stone. He threw the whole grisly parcel into the water and paid his line out fast. He looked up, saw that she had been watching. He grinned, and uttered a few quick words.

'What did he say?' she asked Wilson.

'Wounded fish. They smell the wounded fish.'

And sure enough, before too long, Namu was up on his feet, the line taut in his fist, the muscles standing out on his stringy arms.

'He's got something,' Wilson told her.

Namu would haul on the line and then pause, his head tipped sideways, as if he were listening to the fish below. Then he would haul on the line again. One final tug, a shudder of silver in the air, and the fish landed on the boards at Namu's feet. The length of an arm, and heavy too, if the blows it gave the bottom of the boat were anything to go by. She could feel the power of its convulsions in the soles of her feet. As Namu chopped another pair of mackerel, he began to talk to the dying fish. Wilson translated for her. 'He's telling it to quieten down. He's saying that everything's going to be all right.'

Namu spoke to the fish as you might speak to a child with a fever, his voice calm and comforting, soothing as a cool hand on your brow. It struck her that he cared for the creature he had killed. There was respect in the look he gave it, a kind of compassion too, perhaps even a little affectionate teasing at the continuing strength of its protestations, even though the battle was lost. She touched it after it had ceased to move; it felt as hard as muscle. There were many colours in its skin, pink and blue and yellow, the colours of dawn, but only when the light caught the scales at a certain angle. She thought of the doctor's waistcoats and mentioned the similarity to Wilson, who looked up from yet another empty hook and smiled.

At the end of an hour Namu had two more fish, almost identical to the first. It was close to midday by then, and time to set sail for the land.

'I don't think I'm very good at fishing,' she said, as she handed her reel back to Wilson.

'I didn't catch anything either,' he reminded her.

Namu spoke to Wilson. He pointed at the sky, then at the fish, and shrugged.

'He says we arrived too late,' Wilson told her. 'He says the small fish mostly pass this way just after sunrise. If we'd been here earlier, we would have caught forty or fifty.'

'Three, though,' she said. 'It's enough for lunch, surely?'

Wilson laughed. 'More than enough.'

11

Wilson chose a beach that was just south of San Bruno. It had a platform of flat rocks to moor against, and sea-grape clustered thickly at the water's edge, providing anchorage for the boat and some degree of shade.

'But this is beautiful,' Suzanne exclaimed.

He let his eyes travel beyond her, along the curve of blinding sand. The burnt-orange hinterland bristled with cardon and ocotillo. Out to sea, there were small islands, as rough and pink as grazed skin, and the sky above was that uncanny blue, so bright and hard that if you stared into its depths, it threatened to turn black.

While Namu gathered brushwood for the fire, Wilson put up the parasol that he had borrowed from the company store. Suzanne had brought a straw hamper and a Mexican rug with her. She spread the rug out on the rocks and began to unpack: plates, glasses, bottles of water and fruit cordial, knives and forks, two loaves of fresh bread, some green tomatoes and a few ripe figs.

She glanced up, caught him watching her. 'It's only a few simple things,' she said. 'It's nothing special.' Her eyes had captured so much light that it was hard to look at her.

He piled stones around the base of the parasol, then sat down close to her. They were silent, taking in the view. Dark-purple shells the size of dishes lay scattered along the shoreline, rolling and scuttling as the waves pushed up the beach, pulled back, pushed up again. Three pelicans flew north, their bellies no more than a finger's width above the surface of the water. Soon a crackling began. Namu was turning the fish on a wooden spit, and all its fats and juices were spilling down into the fire.

In twenty minutes it was cooked. The meat, pinkish-grey and succulent, fell into easy slices on their plates. It tasted so good, they could not pause to speak. They ate with their fingers, to be closer to the food; the knives and forks lay near by, still glittering and clean, parts of their lives that had been abandoned, disdained. Afterwards they crouched by the sea and washed their hands, returning to the shade of the parasol to lean against rocks or rest their heads on cushions.

With the brim of his hat pulled low over his eyes and his vision narrowed to a strip of blue water, Wilson began to talk about his feelings for gold. He wanted to try and explain how it was. He had been born in a wagon at the edge of a road in Iowa. Come to think of it, he was not so sure about the road. It could have been a track or a riverbed or just plain grassland, featureless and wide. Still, it was probably fair to say that he had been born in transit, on the way to somewhere. Born with movement in his blood. Later, his father would tell him of the many strange sights that they had witnessed on their journey west. A wardrobe standing by a river, its mirrored door ajar; snakes coiled among the rows of ballgowns that still hung inside. A four-poster bed beneath a tree (they spent the night in it). And, once, abandoned on the prairie, quite alone, a grand piano. Its stout legs bound with weeds. Wind whipping through the strings. A sound so mournful, they heard it for weeks after. Like everyone else they were forced to offload most of what they owned, fetching up in San Francisco with a few pans and a blanket. He had never had much, never wanted much. He could not imagine being rich. No, it was the idea of gold. The feel, the colour – the *idea* of it. It was out there someplace and you never quite knew where; it was the looking for it. It ran beneath your days like time itself. It measured just about everything you did. It was the joy you felt for no reason. The thought of gold pushed everything else to the sides of your head, like a room cleared for dancing.

He looked across at Suzanne, saw that she had understood.

'But tell me, Wilson. How did it begin?'

'Let me show you something.'

He sat up, took off his jacket and, borrowing Namu's knife, began to unpick the stitching on the lining. After opening the seam along one edge, he reached his hand inside. And slowly drew a piece of parchment out into the air.

'It's a map?'

He nodded. 'It's my father's map.' He spread the parchment on the ground and put stones on the corners to keep it flat. 'We travelled together many times looking for gold. We never did have much success. Then, one fall, the fall of '82 I think it was, we headed down to Reno. Reno, Nevada.'

His father sensed that his luck had changed. He said a man just knew sometimes. He claimed there was gold waiting for them at a gaming-table, a whole heap of it. He claimed it had the name Pharaoh written all over it. His father was not given to mystical episodes or premonitions of any kind – in fact, he had always poured mockery on fortune-tellers, calling them a pack of charlatans. His announcement was so unlikely, such a departure from the rule, that Wilson thought there must be something in it.

In those days the town of Reno had a reputation for lawlessness. Assaults were commonplace, even in broad daylight. Greed had men reaching for their guns; greed pulled the trigger. The time to arrive was just after dawn. Cold-streak gamblers would already be asleep. The rest would be locked deep into their games, with eyes for nothing else. There was less chance of trouble at dawn; they might even live long enough to sit down at a table and win themselves some money.

They walked in with the first fingers of light, one morning late in September. The desert floor creaked as the chill lifted. Wilson could see the low brown buildings of the town, and the mountains behind, violet and grey and mauve. The way it had been set with such deliberation in the middle of nowhere, it had the look of a place that could settle your destiny, if you were prepared to hand that power over. He took the keen air into his lungs and whistled under his breath. His thoughts were falling into line with his father's thoughts. The ground stood firm beneath his feet. Out here there would only be fine days.

On the edge of town, they passed a shack. A man was saddling up outside. His father hailed the man. Said they'd been walking through the night and could the man spare a drop of water for their thirst.

The man studied them across the horse's neck. 'Ain't got no water, but I could sell you a couple beers.'

His father said that beers would do just fine. The man named a high price, and his father paid. They sat in the shade behind a wall and drank from the cool brown bottles. When Wilson remarked on the man's avarice, his father shook his head.

'This here's a town of transactions. People came out here with money and threw it around, and the town sprang up like money was the seeds for it. The price of beer's steep because people can afford it. If the beer was cheap, then we'd be in the wrong place for what I got in mind. It's no more than I was hoping for. It's a good sign.'

During the next five days his father let it be known that he was a road agent, a gambler and a horse-thief. All the bad things he had ever done, he owned – and he invented some more, just to be on the safe side. The only shame in a town like Reno, or so he claimed, was a life lived according to the law. He boasted of robberies he had never committed, men he had never killed. His crimes swirled around him like some voluminous, embroidered cloak. They had arrived in town on Monday. By Saturday they were being shown into a private room at the back of the Lame Mule Saloon.

He had never seen his father play cards before. Imagining disaster, he could not watch. Instead he let the room absorb him. It was some place. Tall gold pillars, scarlet drapes. Walls that were said to be bullet-proofed with sheets of corrugated iron. Paintings of women, naked beneath transparent scarves. One had hair like Saffron's, and he stared until the face came too; even after fifteen years, he had not forgotten it. Then, towards midnight, the doors burst open and a burning girl walked in. Her face serene, but all her clothes on fire. Three men put her out with French champagne. Afterwards, she stood beneath the chandelier, her arms raised, the fingers on each hand spread out to form a crown. She seemed unharmed. A man in a white derby turned to him. The man had to shout to make himself heard above the whistling and the applause. 'Most nights she shows up,' he said. 'We call her Flaming Lil.' When Wilson looked round again, the girl had gone. The air filled with string music, and the watery slap and lick of cards. From time to time someone would kill someone else with a revolver and smoke would drift upwards from the barrel, mingling with the fumes of a gambler's cigar. One man, wounded or dead, would be removed, and the music would start up again and the game would continue. It got so he could tell the difference between the smoke from a gun and the smoke from a cigar: the gunsmoke had more blue in it. His father was smoking too, he noticed, when he could bear to look, the smudged black letters of the horse-thief's brand showing casually on his thumb as he brought his cigar up to his mouth.

Then came the decisive moment, at five o'clock that morning, when he snapped awake to see his father raise the stakes so high that all the players had dropped out but one, and that one player paused and then reached down, not for a gun, as might have been expected, but for a roll of parchment that had been sealed with wax and tied with black ribbon. 'I'm using this to match your stake,' the man said.

His father frowned. 'What in hell is it?'

'It's a map.' The man smiled. 'It could be worth more than all the money on the table. All the money in this room, for that matter. It's up to you.' The man leaned back, put two fingers to his jaw and waited, the same curious smile on his face, a bystander's smile, as if he were outside the game, as if it amused him to know what the outcome might be.

Smoke rose from seven motionless cigars.

The man did not look like a gambler. He wore no long-tailed coat, no white shirt with ruffles. There was no pearl-handled Colt revolver lying on the floor beside his chair. All the same he had an air about him.

It was as if the man knew his father, Wilson thought, shifting on his gilt chair in the corner. As if he were some kind of doctor and had diagnosed the fever that had brought them to the town. He was offering a piece of parchment instead of money, and he knew that Arthur Pharaoh would accept it. Maybe it was the inevitability of it all that amused him.

But his father was smiling too, a smile of recognition. He fanned his cards out on the table. Three queens. The stranger had nothing but a pair of tens. His father had won the hand.

Though there was more than eight hundred dollars in the pot, it was the map that his father reached for first. He turned to Wilson with the scroll clutched in his fist.

'This,' he said, 'is why we came.'

His father had astonished himself that night. He had become something that he had never dared to dream he might become, something that he had been known, in his fear, to scorn: a man who could cut the cloth of his existence and turn it into a suit of clothes that he might wear.

It was morning by the time they climbed the stairs to their room. Outside, the street stank of hogs and vomit but the map, it seemed, could sweeten any air. They spread it out on the table, weighed down with mining tools. It followed the outline of Lower California, from the Mexican border to the tip of the peninsula. Three women stood in the sea, below the Colorado river. They had brown skin and pointed breasts, and they wore skirts that were made of black stones hung on bits of string. Halfway down the east coast, just to the right of a grove of palm trees, the land was covered with a flurry of markings that looked like the transcript of someone's excitement. His father read anything that was legible out loud. The names of islands, towns and bays dropped into the still air of the room and sent out ripples.

'The Sea of Cortez,' his father breathed.

His eyes gleamed. There might already have been gold stacked in the room. His eyes were just reflecting it.

'And this is the same map?' Suzanne bent over the parchment, her face lit with the secrecy of it. Her hair had come unpinned. One curl hung against her cheek like the spring inside a watch.

'The very same,' he said.

'So you know where the gold is?'

He shook his head. 'I've no idea.'

'But the map – '

'There are sea serpents and women in black skirts. There are volcanoes. But I don't see any gold, do you?'

She leaned down, frowning.

'It's like wearing a cross,' he said. 'It doesn't mean that God exists. It just means that you believe He does.'

12

It was as they sailed past San Bruno, close enough to notice the bell suspended in the tower of the church, that the feeling came flooding into her. A sense that she had been left to fall into ruin, to decay. A sense that everything was over. She could see that girl, standing in a pool of ashes and champagne, the smoke still rising from her clothes. There were rooms in her and all the doors were open. Dead leaves blew across the floor. She could feel their gentle scraping against the inside of her skin.

She watched the village slip by, with a kind of desperation, as if by noticing it in all its detail she could save herself and break free. Those children poking among the fallen palm branches and the shells of crabs, those children turning to stare and then waving their thin arms. The boats drawn up on a strip of olive silt, their hulls as fine and curved as melon rinds. The church, pain-white against a cloudless sky. But she could not gather it; it would not wait for her. The view was a dismissive river. It just moved on past.

She did not know why. Perhaps it was the beauty and contentment of the day. The battle between Namu and the fish, a meal eaten by the sea. So much new knowledge. And she had found her beauty and contentment in the company of an Indian fisherman and a gold prospector from San Francisco. Imagine Madame de Romblay's face if she ever learned of that. Imagine Théo's.

A moment opened in her memory, its petals lifting to reveal a poisoned heart. How she looked up and out across the banqueting table on the *SS Providencia* and saw Théo distancing himself from her, disowning her. And how, later, as they rode home in the carriage, he held a silence that was heavy with rebuke and then, at last, and without looking at her, said, 'You should not have talked that way.' *Should not.* Later still, close to the house, he had added something kinder, a few words that sounded like advice. It astonished her how easily he could achieve distance from almost anything. They could have been two virtual strangers who would shortly separate and make their way to different houses for the night. They had no longer seemed to be linked by any bond or understanding. If they seemed close, it was only because they were sharing the same carriage. It was no more than geographical coincidence. Like statues in a park. Like planets.

The empty house; deserted rooms.

They shared a bed, and yet they hardly seemed to touch. His work. Responsibilities. The heat. It was love that was leaving, or had left. Not hers for him, she thought, but his for her. She was trying to gather it in, and it was slipping through her hands, like ice. The tighter she held on, the faster it melted. And when it was gone there would be nothing. No, less than nothing. Emptiness that once contained something always felt much emptier than emptiness that had never been otherwise.

She glanced up. The children, the boats, invisible. The spire almost gone. Tears were coming to her now. The sky, the land, the water, blurred. She wiped her eyes, and then looked round. She had not been observed.

'Wilson?'

He looked up, his hat pushed to the back of his head.

'I wish we didn't have to go back,' she said. 'I don't want the day to end.'

He was smiling, but he did not speak. Sometimes she would see him keep something to himself, not through want of a desire to offer it, but because it might be spoiled by words.

'Promise me something,' she said.

She saw that this would not be difficult for him.

'Promise me that we can do something like this again. Not this exactly. Just something like this.'

He gave his promise easily. Not lightly, but easily. And she knew that she could rely on him.

But what should it be? She recalled a tedious conversation with Florestine Bardou. The doctor's wife had mentioned the Misión San Ignacio which was, she claimed, one of the finest churches in Lower California. It had been established by the Jesuits in 1728 and completed, by the Dominicans, she thought, in about 1786.

'I hope ours doesn't take that long.' Then Suzanne saw that she had been flippant and also, perhaps, tactless. 'Have you seen it?' she asked quickly. 'The Misión San Ignacio?'

'Oh no,' Florestine said. 'I haven't seen it. But you must.' Her chin dropped; her forehead, wide and concave, seemed to expand. 'You're so much more adventurous than I am.'

Suzanne chose to deny this – politeness demanded it of her – and yet, in truth, she could not disagree. It struck her that Florestine Bardou lived through others, encouragement being the most active part that she could play, and even in her encouragement she showed humility.

She turned to Wilson once again. 'Have you ever heard of San Ignacio?'

'I went there once.'

'You have been there?' She could have cried out with delight at the coincidence, but then she saw Santa Sofía on the port bow, crouching in the shadow of the mountains. The chatter of machinery carried across the water. The harbour wall reached out, bent halfway along, like an elbow. It would soon be gathering them in.

'What's it like?' She spoke with urgency now.

'The town?'

'Yes,' she said, 'the town.' Men could be slow sometimes. They had to weigh everything, like shopkeepers.

'Well,' he said, 'it's famous for its trees.'

'There are trees?' She had not expected that.

'There are thousands of trees. Date palms, mostly. All in the same valley.'

She sat still, trying to imagine it.

'And its water,' he said.

'What's so special about the water?' she asked.

He thought for a moment, and then he lifted his eyes to hers. 'That it is there at all.'

Before she could ask him to explain, he pointed towards the land. 'Look. Your husband's waiting for you.'

'Yes.' But she did not look.

They had passed through the harbour entrance, and both Wilson and Namu were occupied with practicalities. Wilson stood close to the mast and began to haul the sail down. Namu's eyes were fastened on the quay, the tiller shifting in his grasp as he brought the boat alongside. It was accomplished with great tenderness – a mother laying down her child. Half a dozen boys squatted on the parapet above, their toes hooked over the edge. With their shaved heads and their pinched eyes, they looked capable of malice, but they caught the ropes that Wilson threw to them and looped them around the iron bollards. It struck her that one of them could have been the boy who appeared with Marie Saint-Lô's silver shoes, though she was not sure she would have recognised him now. She climbed the flight of stone steps that led up to the quay. It was not until she was standing on solid ground that she looked up. Théo was waiting at a respectable distance, his hands clasped behind his back. She could not see his face, only the winking of his gold watch-chain against the dark ground of his coat. The routine demands of mooring the boat, that sequence of small, sure actions, had given her time to recover her poise, had moored her too. When she waved, he lifted one hand and lowered it again, the gesture reassuringly mechanical, familiar. Her husband, waiting for her. She moved towards him, took his arm.

'Théo, this is the American I've been telling you about.'

Wilson swung his way along the quay on his crutches. She turned quickly and included him.

'Mr Pharaoh,' she said, 'this is my husband, Monsieur Valence.'

The men shook hands.

'It's a great pleasure,' Wilson said.

'And for me.' Théo raised a clenched fist to his mouth, as if it were a cup and he might drink from it. He coughed once. 'And I must thank you, Monsieur Pharaoh, for going to such trouble to entertain my wife, especially in your condition. Perhaps I could offer you a small aperitif?'

Suzanne smiled, not just at Théo's heavily accented English, but because she realised that he must have been assembling this little speech while standing on the quay, attaching one word to another, piecing the sentences together – and the construction was sound, of course, and the pieces fitted perfectly.

Wilson dipped his head. 'Thank you kindly,' he said, 'but I have to settle up with Namu.' He indicated the fisherman, who was standing some way off.

'Settle up? Ah yes. Of course.' The gap between Théo's eyebrows narrowed and he nodded, as if some weighty legal matter had been mentioned. Possibly he had not understood; out of politeness he would let his lack of understanding pass. 'Another time, perhaps.'

'Perhaps you would dine with us one night,' Suzanne said.

'Thank you,' Wilson said. 'I'd like that.'

'Good. Then I'll arrange it.'

She was distracted by a scraping sound that seemed to be coming from behind Wilson's back. She peered past his shoulder. The Mexican boys had gathered a few yards away. One of them had wedged his foot into a metal bucket and was limping round the quay. Two others were bowing, shaking hands, bowing again.

Wilson swung round and flung an arm out sideways, as if he would have liked to sweep them all into the water. They scattered – though the boy with the bucket on his foot clung to his fiction, scattering more slowly, more awkwardly, than the rest.

'Little devils,' Wilson said.

Lifting his hat to Suzanne, he pivoted on his crutches and moved away. The boys followed at a safe distance, some limping, some hopping, one with his bucket still attached. She smiled as she watched him go. It was partly the sight of the procession and partly this: she would have been willing to lay money on the fact that Wilson had never heard of an 'aperitif'.

'You've caught the sun,' Théo said.

'Have I?'

He touched his forehead, then his cheek. 'Here and here.'

'It must have reflected off the water,' she said.

'But you enjoyed yourself?'

'Oh yes. Very much.'

Though she was tiring now after her long day she hoisted her spirits for a moment. They were light, yet artificial; she was imitating her pleasure in the day for him. Underneath, she could hardly wait for sleep.

'You mentioned that we might invite the American to dinner,' Théo said, as they began to climb the hill.

She looked at him. 'What of it?'

'Wouldn't it be awkward?' he said. 'I mean, after all, he doesn't know anybody.'

'He knows the doctor.'

'Yes, that's true.' Théo walked in silence for a while. 'It's just that some of our colleagues don't seem to have a very high opinion of Americans.'

'Or of any other nationality, for that matter.' Suzanne smiled. 'But I'm sure Madame de Romblay would not be averse to a little extra male company,' she said, 'wherever it happens to come from.'

'Well,' Théo said, 'if you think it might be agreeable.'

When they reached the house, he mentioned that he would be dining with Jean-Baptiste Castagnet in the company offices that night. For once she was glad to be excluded. She did not have the energy for dinner. It was as much as she could do to wish Théo a pleasant evening.

She noticed his eyebrows lower. Her apparent equanimity had wrong-footed him; probably he had been expecting to have to defend himself. He would now be convinced more than ever of her capriciousness – or perhaps he would interpret it as his reward for having given way to her. It seemed that once men saw some kind of pattern in a woman then they clung to it. This acquiescence of hers did not conform to the pattern that had been assigned to her. Her fatigue became suspicious, even perverse.

She ate a cold supper on the divan by the window. Afterwards she read a novel. Every now and then she let the book close on her thumb and, resting her head against a cushion, dreamed of San Ignacio.

Towards eight o'clock a letter arrived. She studied the envelope that Imelda handed to her. It had been secured with a dab of scarlet wax that bore the seal of the Mexican Government. Thinking that this must be another of Montoya's invitations which she would be obliged on this occasion, to turn down, she asked Imelda if anyone was waiting for a reply.

'There was a coachman,' Imelda said, 'but he drove off.'

'Thank you, Imelda.'

As soon as she slit the envelope open and removed the single sheet of vellum, folded neatly in half, she knew what it would be. She did not need to see the fevered tangle of loops and flourishes or read the significance in his choice of ink (the hot vermilion of lips and hearts); she already knew. Montoya had brought his secret vigil to an end. He had declared himself.

At once she was curious to know what exaggerated form his language took, how the waves of his emotions crashed upon the page, but she could understand hardly a word of Spanish. In order to know what the letter said, she would need someone to make a translation for her, and that would be a delicate matter, most delicate. On a sudden, almost girlish, impulse she slid the sheet of paper back into its envelope and hid the letter inside one of the many cushions that littered the divan and then lay back, unable to keep herself from smiling at the thought that she had received a love letter that had been fastened with the official seal of a government.

13

Though almost a week had passed since the outing on the water, Wilson was only now addressing himself to the task of sewing his map back into its hiding-place. Dusk had fallen on the town, and he could hear men returning from the afternoon shift. He sat in his window with a needle and thread, an oil-lamp close by. He was not much of a seamstress. He had already pricked his left thumb and two of his fingers. Each time it happened he held the wound away from him and saw how the tiny bulb of blood swelled and glistened in the soiled yellow light. Yet he pressed on. His spade, his rifle and his pickaxe stood on the far side of the room. They had the look of old acquaintances, propped against the wall like that, all in a row; they seemed to be watching with a kind of quiet amusement.

Such was his concentration as he bent over the jacket that he lost the feeling in his good leg. He stood up and, leaning his weight on his walking-stick, circled the room. The plaster would be coming off next week. He could hardly wait. So much would suddenly become possible. He paused by the window. Stars glittered above the ridge, whole constellations; the tail of the scorpion curled down like a hook for a hat. He missed the sky above him as he slept. He missed that vast, overhanging silence. He even missed the irritations: sandflies, cactus thorns, the absence of shade. He sat down again. On with the jacket. Half the hem was done, a zigzag of stitches, a drunk's walk down the lining. As he took up the needle he thought of the journey he would undertake with Suzanne. The day before, he had spent part of the evening in her company, and she had talked of little else.

They had been sitting on the veranda of the Hôtel de Paris, the only people there. A night of almost inconceivable stillness. They could have been imprisoned in a vault; gold would probably feel like this, he remembered thinking, as it lay in windowless rooms beneath a bank. He had smoked half a cigar to keep the mosquitoes away and when he let the smoke drift out between his teeth it hung in the air, almost without moving, like a flower that blooms at night. He let her excitement wash over him, never taking his eyes off her face except to attend to his cigar or glance along the veranda to where Rodrigo was standing, or not standing so much as leaning, slouching against the doorpost in his pale silk shirt, as if he had no bones to hold him up. Only when she paused for breath did he betray some uncertainty about the venture. It was two days' ride across treacherous terrain, and he was not sure that a woman, any woman, would be up to it.

She absorbed the subtle compliment that he had paid her, but mocked what she called his 'lack of faith'. He had disappointed her, she said.

'After all,' she went on, 'we could always take longer. We could spend two nights under the stars. Or three.'

'With the rattlers,' he said, 'and the polecats.'

'Rattlers?' She studied him sternly. He could see that she suspected him of inventing dangers now, and she would rather challenge his authority than own up to any fear.

'Rattlesnakes, vipers, scorpions, tarantulas.' He smiled into the night. 'There's even a poisonous tree. If you sleep under it, you can go blind. And there's no water anywhere. None.'

'So I will have to make the journey alone,' she said. 'Is that what you're trying to tell me?' Her lips had hardened in defiance, a sharp edge to their usual soft lines. And yet a smile lay below the surface, waiting to emerge.

She was determined to go at any cost, and he soon tired of trying to discourage her. It had, in any case, been a show of undeniable perversity on his part, since there was nothing he would rather do than ride with her to San Ignacio. He could imagine arriving above the town with an hour of light remaining in the sky. It was always a shock to look down on the oasis after crossing the lava fields and plains of basalt that lay to the east. It was so lush suddenly, so tropical. All those green trees clustered in the valley, all that green water. It did not belong. It could not be real. It could seem almost cruel.

He could still remember the last time that he visited the mission. There had been a party for the *padre*, Father Lutz, who was going up country the following morning. His Indian converts had danced the fandango until daybreak, their sweat spattering the floor of the barn like rain. Even the Father had danced, his cassock swirling around his bare ankles, a flagon of wine balanced just above his eyes. Father Lutz was the kind of missionary the Indians could understand. They were still dancing at nine o'clock in the morning when the Father rode out of town with a cool cloth wrapped around his head. He had drunk too much of the local wine. He could not even lift an arm to wave.

Wilson looked up from the jacket lining and out through the window. One star fell in a breathless curve. Perhaps he would dance the fandango with her. If she did not know it, he would teach it to her. First the wheeze of an accordion. Then a guitar picking up speed, the click and chatter of the castanets. Her skirts spinning across the dirt floor, one curl coming loose and dangling like a spring beside her ear. Air the colour of crushed pomegranate. Rush torches blazing. Laughter. In many of the songs there would be obscene references to cacti and volcanoes, but they would be in Spanish and she would not understand. If she asked him for the words, he would sweeten them in his translation.

And later in the night they would stroll among the palm groves, beside the still green waters of La Candelaria. He would sing the song that he had written, the song about gold. She would listen, and she would understand only half of it. That was the beauty of the song. Later still, they would bathe, perhaps. Cool their feet, which had been scorched by hours of dancing. Wash the sweat and smoke from their bodies. And he would turn his eyes away as she took off her clothes because his love was of a size that could embrace all denial. *I don't want the day to end.* The words that she had uttered on the boat. It was his wish that she had voiced that afternoon. His one impossible wish. Impossible because unthinkable. Doubly impossible because it countered everything that he admired in her. Her faith, her purity, her love. If she were to betray those qualities and turn to him, then she would forfeit his respect. His love could only be denied or else consume itself. In her own sadness, though, she had not noticed his. He had been grateful for that. His sadness was something she must not be allowed to see. He would show her only joy.

A sharp pain arrowed through his thumb. He watched another ball of blood form on his skin. But he had almost closed the lining of his jacket. Only one more inch to go.

'Don't show it to anyone. Not to anyone.'

He saw his father leaning over him, a twist of black smoke rising through the glass shaft of the oil-lamp. The cords strung taut in his father's neck, the skin draped over them like canvas. The map spread beneath his gaze. It had been laid out so many times, in so many different rooms, that it had become obedient; weights were no longer needed to hold the corners down.

'Keep it sewed up in the jacket, sewed up good and tight. And keep your mouth sewed up likewise.'

His own mouth twisted away from his face when he spoke, like a steer fighting to escape the branding-iron. His eyes were always looking beyond the walls to some far horizon, some future time: the place where the map began, the moment when they entered it. But the place came no closer, and the time never arrived. All his father's luck had drained away and only fear remained. He was convinced that they were in danger. If they made one move towards the gold they would be ambushed and robbed – probably murdered too.

For almost eighteen months they traced a wary arc across the southern states – Texas, New Mexico, Arizona – keeping a safe distance from the line that marked the beginning of the map. They never stopped in any town for long. They switched hotels after dark, riding in rivers to become invisible, or splitting up and taking different trails so those in pursuit would not know which one of them to follow. They travelled under false identities. Sometimes they dropped down to the Mexican border, and spent a night in Tombstone or El Paso, but they always left the next morning, a feeling of ricochet as they headed north or east, into a land where nothing could happen. They stayed in red-light districts, near railroad tracks, on waterfronts. Places with names like Hell's Half Acre. Places with no name at all. Anywhere so long as it was cheap, anonymous. One night they watched an orchestra of ladies who were clothed only in their undergarments. For their own protection, the ladies played inside a cage that had been electrified. Three men had died trying to climb between the bars. In Fort Griffin they met a man who had no ears and no fingers, his punishment for stealing a fellow-miner's gold. Life descended into nightmare. Countless evenings where they were barricaded in some room, listening for footsteps on the stairs. His father kept his right hand thrust into the bosom of his coat, as if he had a gun in there. People took to calling him Napoleon. 'Big mistake, heading into Russia like that,' they would say. Or, 'How's the syphilis?' 'I'm not Napoleon,' his father would mutter. 'I'm nobody.' All he wanted was to feel safe. All he was seeking was refuge, invisibility.

'Not a word to anybody. Not one word.'

1882–1884. The lunatic years.

Wilson thought it must have happened during the poker game in Reno. When his father let that man reach below the table, knowing it could be a gun that he was reaching for. When, smiling, he let that man reach down. You have to be part crazy to orchestrate that kind of moment.

It was what dreams did to you if they did not come true. They made you mad with the constant glimpsing of them. The dreams were there, but only just. The heels of the dreams were always vanishing round corners, and when you reached the corner they were gone. Only you saw them; that was what made them so valuable, so terrible. Only you saw them. And when there were things that only you could see, then you were crazy for sure. A footprint on the sand, one snapped twig in a forest. The trail that you were following did not exist for anybody else. On you went.

'Keep that mouth of yours sewed up. Good and tight now. Good and tight.'

Some nights he woke with a cry, thinking that his father was bending over him with a needle and thread. He could feel a tugging at the corner of his mouth as the first stitch tightened. He could smell his father's bitter breath. *Hold still now. Just hold still.* Other nights he dreamed that the horror had already been accomplished. He would lie awake as morning came and would not be able to open his lips. He feared mutilation at the hands of his own father. Towards the end he had even feared death. They would be sitting in a hotel room in Bastrop or Santa Fe and he would see his father's head lurch round and fasten a mad but calculating look on him. He was the only person in the world who knew about the map. Could he be trusted with the knowledge? He slept in snatches during the daylight hours and lay awake all through the night. A son fearing his father, his father fearing everyone. It could not go on.

Seventeen months after that game of cards, his father was dead. In a boarding-house in Silver City. The name of the town cast an ironic shadow over the event. His father had never in his life sought any metal but gold. In that one sense you could say that he had been faithful. His chest had been crushed by a stagecoach as he crossed the main thoroughfare at midnight. Listening for the dreaded footsteps, he had not heard the wheels.

It was a decent boarding-house, with curtains in the windows and no gambling allowed. His father's hand lay on the clean sheet, fingers curled. Cracks ran lengthways in the nails. His father's wool shirt hung on the back of a chair, the breast decorated with medals of blood.

Exploiting his father's weakness, he did something he would never otherwise have dared to do. He took his father's hand. And held it.

'You got the map?' His father could only gurgle. He was drowning in his own fluids.

Wilson nodded.

'It's safe?'

He pressed his father's hand. 'It's sewed into my jacket,' he said, 'just like you showed me.'

'Never found it, did we?'

He could only smile down.

'On the grave,' his father said, 'I want some words.' His eyes cleared for a moment, a gap between clouds. Then he coughed, and his chin tipped backwards, and his voice filled with blood. Wilson thought that he might never hear the words.

At last his father found an ounce of breath.

'Still looking,' he said.

Two hours later he was dead.

The last stitch, double-strength, was now in place; the map was back where it belonged. And he was standing on the land that it described, ground that had taken his father's luck, two-sided though it may have been, and spent it all. He could have inked himself in, with a hat, a moustache and a broken foot, three inches to the south-west of the women with the pointed breasts. He was here, he was on the map, and yet he seemed no closer to anything. His father would never have imagined such disillusion to be possible. Bending over the needle, he severed the thread with his teeth, then tied the two tails in a solid knot.

He stood up, poured some water into a bowl. Then he began to wash. He was expected on the Mesa del Norte for dinner.

'I hear that you're looking for gold.' Monsieur de Romblay's face lowered over the table like a huge ripe fruit that might drop at any moment from its branch. 'Is that correct?'

'Yes, sir,' Wilson said. 'It is.'

Monsieur de Romblay nodded. 'I didn't think that you could have been drawn here simply by the beauty of the place,' he said with a smile, his face resembling a fruit more than ever as it glowed and dimpled in the candlelight.

There were a few sardonic chuckles. Then a man with a thin face and prominent knuckles leaned forwards.

'It would be better to go back to where you came from, would it not?' The man's name was Pineau. He was not a man for whom Wilson had developed any great fondness.

'Why do you say that?'

'Your country is famous for gold. California, Montana, even Idaho.' Pineau paused. 'But Santa Sofía – '

Wilson waited for the laughter to fade. Some people cannot resist trying to soil and ridicule your dreams. Maybe it is because they have none of their own.

'It is my contention,' he said finally, 'that, sometime in the future, it will be discovered that this entire peninsula is nothing less than an extension of the famous gold-fields of Northern California.'

You could have heard a dime land in the rug.

He sat back in his chair. It was the first dinner party that he had ever attended. The men wore shirts that gleamed like ivory. The women had jewelled necks and ears; flowers blossomed in their hair. He did not belong in such exalted company. He had washed with carbolic soap. He had trimmed his moustache. He had dressed in his best blue-flannel shirt, a black four-in-hand tie of his father's and pair of dark trousers which he had borrowed from Jesús Pompano. But still he looked like the men they put in fields to scare the birds.

'Do you have any proof of this,' and Pineau paused again, 'contention of yours?'

Wilson smiled to himself. 'Certainly, at the present time, I should be hard pressed to furnish you with proof to the contrary.'

The doctor chuckled. 'Bravo, Monsieur. Well said.'

Wilson glanced at Suzanne and saw his secret safe behind her eyes, invisible to everyone but him.

But Pineau would not let him alone. 'You would not be here,' he said, 'if you did not know something.'

Suzanne let out an exasperated sigh. 'Monsieur Pharaoh is a romantic,' she said, 'and romantics don't need proof. All they need is faith.'

'Faith.' Pineau curled his lip.

'My dear Suzanne,' said Madame de Romblay, whose head and shoulders rose out of a froth of purple satin, 'you make our American friend sound like a candidate for sainthood.'

Smiles travelled the length of the table. Wilson felt that he should smile too, if modestly.

But Suzanne did not smile. Her cheeks flushed and her green eyes seemed to bleach.

'Who was it, may I ask,' she said, 'who landed in California with gardening implements believing, in their naivety, that gold was so abundant that it could be raked out of the rivers?' Nobody spoke. 'I'll tell you who it was,' she said. 'It was the French.' She looked round the table, settling at last on the Director's wife, whose eyes were glittering at this betrayal of her nation, whose lips had snapped tight shut. 'We may think that we're superior, that we know more than others,' she said, 'but we don't. We don't know the half of it.'

Monsieur Valence leaned forwards, placing his hands flat on the tablecloth. He had folded his napkin into one tight square.

'Well,' he said, 'if we have all finished, perhaps we should adjourn to the veranda.'

'But we haven't finished,' Suzanne said, 'have we, Théo?'

Valence looked steadily at Wilson. 'Monsieur Pharaoh?'

Wilson had no choice but to struggle to his feet. As he turned away from the table he saw Suzanne lift her napkin into the air and suspend it quite deliberately above the candelabra. In seconds the napkin had caught fire. She dropped the burning cloth in the centre of the table and rose calmly from her chair.

'By all means,' she said. 'Let's adjourn.'

She did not appear for the coffee and brandy that were served on the veranda. Monsieur de Romblay took hold of the conversation and, working in unison with the doctor, steered it into a debate about the recent unrest among the miners, not exactly an entertaining subject, but less troubled than some. It was a discussion in which Wilson played little part since most of those present had by now reverted to their native language. Still, he could feel some of the tension in the air disperse. Now and then the doctor leaned over and translated for him. At one point he thought of mentioning the epileptic's vision, which could well have helped to undermine morale, but he held his tongue, fearing that he might make a fool of himself again. Indeed, his only contribution drew a snort of indignation from the accountant. He had simply observed that conditions in the mine were far from perfect. Monsieur de Romblay also bridled at the remark.

'We are not running a charity, Monsieur.'

Wilson kept silent after that.

It was not long before the doctor turned the conversation to his favourite subject: bread. Given the conspicuous lack of progress during the last few weeks, he suggested that they should consider recruiting a baker from France. Madame de Romblay said that, in her opinion, no baker worth his salt would agree to come. The Sister, Marie Saint-Lô, thought they should give the Mexican another chance.

'Apparently there has been a death in the family.' Marie Saint-Lô turned to the doctor.

'That's correct. I forgot.' The doctor sighed. 'Well, I suppose you cannot expect too much of somebody who is going through a period of mourning.'

'Who died?' Monsieur de Romblay asked.

'His mother, wasn't it?' The doctor did not seem sure.

Madame de Romblay shook her head. 'No,' she said. 'It was his aunt. I'm certain of it.'

'Monsieur Pharaoh?' the doctor said. 'Perhaps you could enlighten us?'

But Wilson only shrugged. He felt bloated and queasy. He could have opened his mouth and emptied the contents of his stomach on the ground, a temptation that was very nearly rendered a necessity a few minutes later when Pineau settled in the chair beside him.

'Monsieur Pharaoh,' and he put a hand on Wilson's shoulder, and Wilson could smell compost on the accountant's breath, 'they tell me that you can recommend a local whore.'

It was after midnight when Wilson put his glass of brandy down. Reaching for his crutches, he announced that he would have to be going. 'I could use some rest,' he said.

The doctor beamed up at him. 'I'm delighted to hear it. The message is getting through at last.'

Monsieur de Rombay joked, rather drunkenly, that Wilson should not consider looking for any gold until morning and, under the cover of good-natured laughter, Wilson wished the company a pleasant night, thanked Monsieur Valence for the most excellent dinner and then began to make his way round to the front of the house.

Halfway along the veranda, Monsieur Valence overtook him.

'There is a carriage,' he said. 'I will fetch it for you.'

Before Wilson could protest, the man had vanished.

Sheet lightning lit the heavens to the west, beyond the mountains. In other towns it might have heralded rain; in Santa Sofía, this did not seem likely. He stood at the top of the steps. His head ached from listening to hours of talk.

Then, as he looked up, the lightning came closer, laying bare the sky above the house, and there, in the shadows of the veranda, stood Suzanne.

'Wilson? Is that you?'

'Yes.'

'You're leaving?'

Stumbling over his words, he began to thank her for the dinner, but he encountered a look of such utter distraction on her face that he could no longer speak.

'Imagine,' she said, 'if the house had burned down.'

She was laughing. A sequence of notes, innocent and clear.

He stood still, uncertain what to say.

Lightning again: her face jumped out at him, a section of her dress, a jasmine flower behind her. It seemed to have the power to reveal her one moment and remove her the next, as if her existence were pure illusion.

'You're ashamed of me.'

He shook his head.

'I'm sorry, Wilson,' she said, 'I'm truly sorry. It was not the dinner I intended it to be.'

'It was a fine dinner,' he maintained stubbornly. 'I enjoyed it very much.'

She took a step towards him. The shadow of a hanging plant moved down her forehead and across her cheek, reminding him of fingers on the keys of a piano.

'He never touches me,' she said. 'He doesn't love me.'

She held his arm. He felt something land on the back of his hand and knew a moment later that it must have been a tear.

'Suzanne,' he said.

She wiped her cheek. 'Will you come again?'

'Of course.'

He heard the wheels on the street below.

'Look,' she said. 'Your carriage.'

When Wilson turned in his seat, looked back towards the house, she was still standing on the veranda, a branch of lightning stranded on the ground, a white flag in the darkness.

Somebody surrendering.

The carriage ambled down the hill. He could not fit his thoughts together. He could only see that napkin burning on the table, and her face above the flames, quite calm, absorbed.

14

During the night Suzanne woke up and heard voices. She was lying with her head close to the window, only a mosquito-net between her and the stars. The voices drifted up from the veranda; the words had lost their shape, turned into murmurings. Théo and another man. She sipped at the tea Imelda had prepared for her – to calm her, Imelda said. It tasted of grass and dust. She wondered how late it was, wondered if she should go downstairs. Sleep took her again before she could come to a decision.

In the morning she woke with the same dream in her head, the dream about Montoya's house. She could not be sure whether she had dreamed it again, or whether it was just a memory, fostered by sleep. She lifted the jug off the floor and poured some water into her china bowl. She washed slowly, the dream becoming clearer in her head, though she could only remember that one fragment: two women dancing in the hallway – that was all. There had been no reference to their appearance on the night of the doctor's birthday. She did not know if she should feel reassured.

She thought back to the time when she realised that she had the power of dreams, dreams that were like prophecies, dreams that came true. It had sent fear screaming through every layer of her skin. After the death of her friend she no longer trusted sleep. She saw beds as enemies. She even gave up eating cheese, afraid of what she might dream. But sleep lay in wait for her, knowing she would come, and she could not keep the dreams away.

Time passed; she became accustomed to the gift. She found that she often dreamed of people whom she did not know. It was like receiving a letter that had been intended for someone else; the dream postman had delivered to the wrong address. But what a relief that was. She could not be blamed for what happened. There would be no policemen calling at the house. Other times the dreams were commonplace or trivial. Always accurate, though. Once, for instance, she saw her father meeting a man on the road from Paris to Dieppe. The man was an old friend of her father's.

He wore a blue swallowtail jacket with gold buttons, and his horse was lame; she even knew which hoof. When her father came home, his face was lit with astonishment. 'Do you know who I met today?' Yes, I know, she thought. *And* I know what he was wearing. And his horse was lame too, wasn't it? But she did not actually say anything; she did not dare. It was only the servant classes who believed in signs and portents. She turned to their African maid, Olique, with her wide eyes and her credulous heart. Every Thursday Olique would pay a clandestine visit to the bookstall on the Rue Chartreuse, returning with pamphlets and treatises, almanacs and horoscopes, which they would then spread out on the dark oak table in the servants' kitchen. They would explain the present, explore the future. Excavate the past. Telling Olique about her power made it more bearable. She even felt a sense of privilege because Olique told her that, in the country she came from, only very few were chosen, and they were almost always women. She came to treat the premonitions as a thrilling edge to her existence rather than a core of fear and unease.

And then they stopped.

She had been married for less than a week. She could still remember entering the library on the first floor of their house on the Rue de Rivoli, the tall window standing open, a sheet of white sunlight on the carpet. Nobody had used the room in days; the air had settled, motionless and dense. She held her arms away from her sides as if she were naked and about to be dressed. That moment had, in fact, been like a kind of nakedness. She had been stripped of her power. Her gift had gone.

Standing in the library that morning with the doves calling from the garden and the books in their hushed rows on the walls, she did not know what she thought. From being open, her hands closed up; she felt her fists begin to shake. She ought to have been warned. Too much was being taken from her. She seemed to have to pay so heavily for anything she gained.

And now that Théo would not touch her any more, she thought, as she dried her face and draped the towel over a chair, now that the ghost of her purity had been summoned and was walking through the house, could her gift be returning? It made a kind of sense. It was so logical that even Théo would have been compelled to agree with her. She left the room and moved down the corridor, her hands shifting among the folds of her dress. The thought of her gift returning was like a shiver in the heat. She did not want to use that part of her – not any more.

The future was too volatile, too uncertain. There were things just out of sight that she would rather have no knowledge of, like other people.

It was late by the time she walked downstairs, and Théo was long gone. She thought that it must have been a relief for him to leave while she was still asleep, to be able to avoid what would certainly have been an awkward encounter. To think that she had almost set fire to the house. This morning the whole episode seemed ludicrous, beyond belief. She smiled faintly, had to shake her head.

In the parlour she found her breakfast, which Imelda had left out for her some time before. There was coffee, still warm in its blackened pot; a few sweet rolls; a bowl of peeled oranges and pitahaya, covered by a sieve; some fresh dates. She stood above the table, looking down. The world crackled at the limits of her vision, as if it had been fed with bolts of electricity. That fruit, for instance. Glistening in its prison of fine wire-mesh. That china vase, the hooped back of a chair, her paintings on the wall. Just ordinary objects, but each one invested with a shimmer, fizzing at the edges, rimmed in white. She could not explain it. She was just aware of it as she poured herself some coffee.

She ate her breakfast at the table, her robe draped over her shoulders, the pale silk hanging loose against her chemise. It was too hot to bother with the sash, too hot to dress. Beyond the surface of the table, through the window, she could see a section of the coastland. It looked like biscuit; if she reached out and touched it, it would crumble. Above it lay the sea, smooth and dull, the colour of slate. She lifted a slice of pitahaya towards her mouth, one black seed embedded in a strip of redness. She had held her second child on her hand, with Théo calling through the bathroom door. She had stared down at her second child, thinking nothing, only curious, perhaps. That black seed eye, that formless redness. The echo was too faithful. She put the fruit back on the plate and waved a fly away. To bear a child in this town. Her lips twisted in a wry smile. The conception would have to be immaculate. She sat back in the chair, her smile gone. She would not be drawing today, or reading, or embroidering. She would not be doing any of the things that women were supposed to do. She would not be doing anything at all.

The minutes passed with no division. Time had flattened into a single, smooth dimension, like the sea. Nothing separated one minute from another, or one hour from the next. As she stirred a spoonful of molasses into her coffee, her eyes moved to the divan. She reached out, took a cushion between her hands and, unfastening the pearl buttons one by one, felt deep inside and drew the hidden letter out.

She sat on the window-seat, her legs folded beneath her, the envelope caught between her thumb and her remaining fingers. The ocean filled the window, still and hot and flat.

At last she sat up straighter, reached into the envelope. Unfolded the single sheet of paper it contained. Her eyes travelled through the unfamiliar words, tangling in the loops of some letters, slipping down the tails of others. Not understanding it only fuelled her excitement. Not understanding it, yet knowing what it was.

'*Amor*,' she read.

She saw a man borne down a flight of stairs on an uneven tray of hands. Her belly tightened; a tingling began inside her. The letter slipped from her fingers, swooped to the floor. She lay back. She thought of the point at which the ocean touched the land. The sun beat down outside, reducing everything to silence.

She moved one hand through the opening in her chemise.

Amor, she thought.

She could feel a welling now, like water in a cup when it is filled too full. That moment just before it overflows. When it seems to tremble, higher than the cup's own lip.

One afternoon she had watched the Indians lifting sections of the church, sweat shining on their bodies, as if they had been coated with silver. The iron panels had been lying in the sun all day. She saw one of the Indians draw his hand back sharply, shake it in the air. They were burning their hands on pieces of Christ. Their bodies partly silver, partly wood. She could almost hear the sizzle of their flesh.

She moved her hand against her skin. Her head pushed back, she felt her breath ease past her lips. She was filling a glass of water as slowly as she could. The glass was almost full, but she was still adding water, drop by drop. The water seemed to bulge above the rim. Then she had to hold it there, hold it until she could hold it no longer, until the moment when it spilled, ran slickly down the outside of the glass.

She could tell from the position of the sun that it was afternoon. The shadow of the house lay distorted on the ground. The century plant spread its long three-fingered hand across the hot brown rocks. What she could see through the window at this hour had an artificial quality: a papier mâché landscape, propped up from behind.

She thought of the place that Wilson Pharaoh had described for her. A forest in the desert, an oasis; a place that had three dimensions, even though it only existed in her imagination. She had broached the subject with him a few evenings before, sitting on the veranda of the hotel.

'You never told me about the water,' she said.

'Water? What water?'

'The special water,' she said. 'At San Ignacio.'

Wilson smiled, his amusement almost fatherly. 'You haven't forgotten then?'

'Forgotten? Of course not.'

'It's fresh water,' he said, 'kind of green in colour. It's known for its purity. They say it comes from springs high in the mountains.'

She had shivered at the words. It was as if part of her memory had been distilled and stored in his. She thought of the man in Paris and his small glass vial, almost holy in the way in which he wore it like a cross around his neck.

'You have to remember that the town is surrounded by desert on every side,' Wilson went on, 'and the desert, the Vizcaíno, is merciless. It has killed many people. The water at San Ignacio is the only water for fifty miles around.'

'Does it have a name?'

'There's one pool among the palm trees where the water is said to be the sweetest. The Spaniards called it La Candelaria, but that's not the original name. The Indians were there long before. They called it Kadakaamana, which means "valley of the sedges". It refers to the sedge grass that grows at the edge of the water, long grass, very green, a good deal like rushes. Without that water, the grass wouldn't be there at all.'

'Kadakaamana.' She was already dreaming of the place.

'For the Indians it was sacred,' he said. 'The source of life itself.'

From her seat by the window she could hear the distant notes of a piano coming from the hotel across the street. Only today there was a difference. She began to smile. It was not Bizet's *Carmen* that Wilson was playing. It was 'La Marseillaise'.

She roused herself and, leaving the haven of the divan, ran up the stairs to dress. She had an idea now and it had swept away her lethargy of the day; energy had come from nowhere in a rush. She was halfway across the street, her parasol spinning on her shoulder, before she remembered the letter that had fallen from her hand and would still be lying on the carpet. She had to hurry back into the house. There the letter was, where she had abandoned it, unfolded, shameless, an open mouth confessing everything. She snatched it up, pushed it back into the envelope, returned it to its hiding-place inside the cushion. She could not believe that she had been so rash. Chastened, she left the house again, and it was with much greater composure that she set out across the street for the second time.

She had spurned all the muted colours in her wardrobe. Instead she had dressed in a gown of shell-pink foulard, and pale-green gloves with jade buttons. She had soaked a lace handkerchief in her favourite Guerlain. On her shoulder twirled a sunshade crowned with ostrich feathers, its handle finished in Japanese *cloisonné*. She crossed the threshold, stopping just inside the door. The lobby seemed deserted, apart from the man at the piano. Then she caught a glimpse of a shadowy figure, almost liquid, stooping in a sheet of light, the white glare where the corridor ended, where it opened out into the courtyard. But it was just Rodrigo, sweeping. She looked back into the room, which now seemed dark. Wilson noticed her, half-rose from his piano-stool.

'No, no,' she said. 'Don't stop.'

She stood at his shoulder and watched him play. Then she took a seat some distance away, by the window. She knew that he had been waiting for her. That the music was incomplete without her. She sat by the window, listening.

It was a while before she spoke.

'How did you learn it, Wilson?'

'I found the music in an outhouse back of the hotel. I thought I'd surprise you.'

'You had better be careful,' she said, 'or the French will be hiring you to play on special occasions.'

'Do you think so?' he said, almost hopefully. Then he looked down at his soiled red bandana, his collarless shirt. 'Not unless I smarten up a bit.'

'I apologise for last night,' she said.

'There's no need.'

She looked away from him. 'I doubt the others will be quite so understanding.'

In the silence that followed she could hear the panting of a train as it struggled up the hillside to the mine. The red velvet drapes on the window smelled of damp.

'Something else,' he said. 'Look.' And he spun on the stool and shot out his right leg.

At first she did not see it. Two feet, two boots. There was nothing strange in that. Then she realised, and had to laugh.

'But that's wonderful,' she said. 'How does it feel?'

'Like it belongs to someone else. I still need a stick to get around, but the doctor says it's just a matter of time before that goes too.' He grinned at her from beneath the brim of his hat. 'The expedition you had in mind,' he said, 'it won't be long now.' He swivelled on his stool and launched into the first bars of 'La Marseillaise' once more.

She waited until he reached the part he did not know, until he stumbled, then she stood up and walked towards him. 'Wilson?'

'Yes?'

'You speak Spanish, don't you?'

He took his hands off the keys. 'You could say that.'

'Can you read it?'

'Pretty much.'

'Do you think you could translate something for me? From Spanish into English?'

'Depends what it is.'

'It's a letter.'

'That shouldn't be a problem. What kind of letter is it?'

She stood behind him, studying the music that lay open on the stand. She could hear Rodrigo's broom on the tiles at the far end of the corridor. A kind of pendulum, measuring a time that passed more slowly.

'What do you like to eat?' she asked.

'To eat?' Wilson glanced up at her.

'Yes. What's your favourite food?'

He looked down, thought for a moment. 'Steak, I guess. Though it's months since I had it.' He glanced up at her again. 'Why?'

She turned away. She supposed that she could always ask Rodrigo. He ought to be able to get her some. His brother worked in the hotel kitchens.

She did not look back until she reached the door. Wilson was still sitting at the piano, and she could see from the angle of his head that he was confused.

She smiled across the room at him. 'Come to lunch the day after tomorrow,' she said. 'I'll cook some steak for you.'

15

Early the next morning Wilson was leaving the Hotel La Playa when he heard somebody call his name. He turned to see Monsieur Valence striding towards him, dressed in his usual black frock-coat, with his usual white umbrella hoisted in the air above his head. Less usual was the pair of cracked and dusty riding boots that he was wearing.

'Good morning, Monsieur,' the Frenchman said.

Wilson returned the greeting, and then stood back and allowed himself a smile. 'I see you've developed some more practical footwear.'

Valence surveyed his feet with faint embarrassment. It was as if he had been caught in fancy-dress.

'Soon you'll be wearing spurs,' Wilson said.

'Spurs?' The reference was lost on Valence. Then he understood, and shook his head. 'Ah yes. The Mexican.' A smile crossed his face, but only remotely, like a man on a horse seen from a distance, traversing a stretch of open prairie. He looked up, some as yet unrevealed weight behind his steady gaze. 'I thought, perhaps, that you might join me for a drink,' he said, 'if there is a bar in the vicinity.'

The only bar in the vicinity, Wilson told him, was the Bar El Fandango where, if you did not drink with the greatest caution, you were liable to lose consciousness and wake up in the bed of a woman you had never seen before.

'Perhaps a coffee then,' said Monsieur Valence.

Wilson led him down the street towards the waterfront, which was where he had been intending to go in the first place. They walked side by side with the ease of men who knew each other's measure and did not feel the need to stamp their own authority upon the silence. It was only when they drew close to the pale-brown wall of Mama Vum Buá's establishment that Valence stopped short, his face twisted out of shape by something that resembled dismay – or stronger than dismay, maybe, more like alarm.

'I cannot go here,' he announced.

When Wilson asked him the reason, he explained that he had been poisoned during his last visit to Señora Vum Buá's place and that he no longer trusted anything that she produced.

'A coffee.' Wilson spread one hand in the air. 'Surely a coffee cannot hurt.'

Some private war was being waged inside the Frenchman; his face had stiffened with the conflict. At last he took a deep breath and sighed. 'I suppose not,' he said.

Wilson sat down at the table beneath the tree. Valence settled gingerly beside him, as if he feared the chair itself might infect him with some terrible disease. The Señora was standing in the doorway with her arms folded. Her face had darkened, and she had bound her hair in three tight braids which jutted from her head like weapons. Wilson wished her good morning and ordered two cups of coffee.

Arms still folded, the Señora seemed to grow in size and stature before his eyes. Then she spoke:

'No.'

He stared at her. The Yaqui Indians were often named after their physical characteristics. Vum Buá meant 'high rock', but it could also be used to refer to a mountain. It was certainly appropriate this morning.

'I'm not serving that man.' She would not even look at Monsieur Valence. Instead, she rolled her head to one side and spat on the ground.

'Why not?' Wilson asked.

'He insulted my food.'

So that was it. Wilson thought it best to improvise.

'It was a mistake. He's come here today to make amends,' Wilson said, 'by drinking a cup of your good coffee.'

He sensed a lessening of tension in her stance.

'Señora,' he pleaded. 'Two cups of coffee.'

At last she withdrew into the dark interior. He could see her twelve rings moving supernaturally about.

'She is very proud,' Monsieur Valence observed.

Wilson was not sure how much of the exchange Valence had understood, if indeed he had understood anything at all. He decided not to enlighten him. Ignorance might be a happier state.

'They're a proud people,' he said. 'They work, but they don't like to serve. Service is not in their nature.'

Monsieur Valence did not appear to be listening. He held his left hand in his right, and was pressing his thumb into the palm. A fly landed on his shoulder and became invisible.

At last he spoke. 'You have not known my wife for very long, but I believe you are a friend to her.'

'Yes,' Wilson said, 'that's correct.'

'Has she said something to you? Has she expressed,' and the Frenchman looked up quickly, then looked down again, 'any dissatisfaction?'

It was Wilson's turn to hesitate. 'No,' he said, 'not that I can think of.' And it was, in some sense, true. He was too surprised at the bluntness of the questioning to apply his mind properly to the answer.

Valence continued to massage the palm of his left hand with his thumb.

Mama Vum Buá brought their coffee in two buckled tin mugs. It was the grey colour of certain rivers in the winter; grounds swirled in a sluggish spiral on the surface. It provoked in Wilson a curious and unexpected nostalgia for the north – or perhaps it was just the sudden desire to be far away, to be somewhere else.

'Two coffees,' the Señora said. 'You want eggs?'

Wilson felt the Frenchman shudder. 'No eggs,' he said. 'Not yet.'

'Something wrong with my eggs?' Her blue eyes glinted in her heavy copper face.

'First we've got to talk some business,' Wilson said, 'then I'll have some eggs.'

'Business?' She ambled away, cackling. 'Business.'

Monsieur Valence put one finger through the handle of his mug, but did not lift it to his lips. 'I fear,' he said, 'that she is losing her mind.'

For a moment Wilson thought he was referring to the Señora and was about to smile, then he understood. He felt his heart drop in his chest like a dead weight; it was like watching a sack of flour being heaved off the back of a cart. He could not speak.

Monsieur Valence had been watching him, and now seemed reassured to see that he was taking the matter seriously. Valence pushed his tin mug to the centre of the table.

'How is your ankle?'

'It's still weak.'

'Good.'

Wilson stared at the Frenchman, but the Frenchman did not even notice. He was one of those people who are incapable of seeing the world from outside of themselves, and are therefore denied a share in much of its humour.

'Since you must stay here in town,' Valence continued, 'I would be grateful if you could watch my wife.'

'Watch her?'

'Yes.'

'You make it sound like work for a policeman,' Wilson said, 'or a jailer.'

'Forgive me. It's my English. Sometimes it escapes me.' Monsieur Valence let out a sigh. And looked, just for a moment, like an ordinary person, with ordinary measures of weakness and fatigue.

He leaned forwards, hands on the table, shirt-cuffs resting against the edge. 'All that I am talking about is friendship,' he said. 'Do you understand me?'

'I understand.'

'I would be very grateful.' Without lifting his wrists off the table, the Frenchman spread his hands.

Wilson watched the Frenchman as he rose to his feet. 'As it happens,' he said, 'I'm having lunch with her tomorrow.'

'Excellent.' Monsieur Valence placed a banknote beside the mug of coffee, which he had not touched, and, retrieving his umbrella, stepped out into the sunlight.

As soon as the Frenchman had turned the corner, Wilson took the Frenchman's mug and drank the coffee down in three swift gulps. Then he sat back, stretched his legs. The street beyond the pool of shade looked white as chalk. He contemplated the banknote on the table. It was enough for twenty cups of coffee.

'Something wrong with it?'

He jumped. Mama Vum Buá was standing at his elbow with her arms folded and a toothpick wedged between her two front teeth.

'Your coffee,' she said. 'Is there something wrong with it?'

'The coffee's fine,' he said.

She reached down, picked up the banknote. 'What's this?'

'It's payment. The Frenchman left it.'

'It's too much.'

'I know.'

She fingered the money with a mixture of amusement and disgust. 'The fool,' she said. 'He don't know the value of what he's got.'

16

17 Calle Francesa,
Santa Sofía,
Lower California,
Mexico
30th May, 189 –

My dear Monsieur Eiffel,

At last I can be the bearer of unadulterated good news. During the past two weeks we have made excellent progress. In place now are the purlins which have had the desired effect of correcting the relative positions of the arches and, simultaneously, of bracing them by creating an indeformable whole. We are now proceeding with the panels. I estimate that the job will be completed by the end of next month.

There have been no more thefts of any kind, thanks to the assiduous attentions of the soldiers whom I employed to guard the construction site, nor have there been any further instances of absenteeism. Indeed, one could almost say that the Indians are becoming Frenchmen. They work hard, and are beginning to demonstrate a certain pride in their achievement. I think they could not, for a long time, imagine what it was that they were building, but now that the structure is taking shape before their eyes they have suddenly become enthusiastic. Only yesterday my foreman expressed a sense of wonder at my ability to turn such an 'unpromising heap of metal', as he called it, into something as worthy and elaborate as a church! He seemed to be suggesting that, in less ingenious hands than mine, the pieces of metal might not have amounted to anything at all. It was a most amusing moment; I only wish that you had been there, Monsieur, to witness it.

I apologise for the relative brevity of this letter, but it is late and I must rise again before dawn; continuing good progress is dependent on my presence on site at every hour of the day. Madame Valence is well, and conveys her warmest regards. I am with respectful esteem, Monsieur, your most humble and obedient servant,

Théophile Valence.

JUNE

1

'I love you,' Wilson said, and faltered.

Suzanne leaned forwards. 'Go on.'

He stared at the piece of paper in his hand. She had not been able to wait until the end of the meal. Through the kitchen window he had seen the hem of her dress, the heels of her shoes, rise up and vanish. She descended moments later, breathless, with a cushion in her hands. What she wanted translating, she told him, was hidden inside the cushion. What she wanted translating, he now knew, was a love letter.

His eyes dropped to the bottom of the page, and the signature, though florid, was still legible: Félix Montoya.

'Go on,' she said.

His mind as tangled as the signature, he returned to the top of the page. 'I think of you every moment of the day,' he said. 'You fill my thoughts the way the air fills my lungs. You are as natural to me as breathing. You belong around me, with me, in me.' He hesitated again.

'What's wrong?'

'It's difficult,' he said.

'But you're doing so well.'

She was watching him across the table, as if he were a magician – and maybe that was what he had become to her that day, turning a simple piece of paper into a declaration of undying love. Her teeth gripped her bottom lip, her green eyes glowed. He tried not to notice her body beneath the yellow dress that she was wearing, or to imagine how that silk might be removed, in the darkness of a bedroom, in the afternoon, and her nakedness revealed to him, her skin like gold lifted dripping from a river. She had risen into womanhood for him, and he could not look; she possessed it so entirely, with a natural authority that he had never seen before, in anyone. He had to lower his eyes; he had already looked too long. Instead, he stared at the words emerging from the Spanish, words he had never dared to say, words he had forbidden himself even to think of.

'I cannot exist without you. It is a nightmare for me to be so close to you, and yet so far away.' He had surpassed himself, he thought, in the quality of his translation. But his heart had been plucked from his chest, and there was a gaping, ragged hole where it had been.

He forced himself to continue. 'I think that the few hours we have spent together are the best time in my life. These few hours I have spent with you are jewels. No, more precious than jewels. More precious than anything. I love you – ' He put the letter down, began to laugh.

'Why are you laughing?' she asked him.

He could not say.

She reached out, touched his arm. 'Tell me.'

He shook his head. 'I must be going.'

'But you haven't finished your lunch.'

He looked down at the steak that she had prepared for him. Sirloin, she had said. His favourite. A dead thing on a plate.

'I'm not hungry any more.'

'What about the rest of the letter?'

'That's more or less it.'

'More or less?' She was not going to let him get away with that. 'Read me the rest, Wilson. Please.'

That hand on his arm again.

He looked at her quickly to see whether her eyes saw anything in his. But they were too full of the letter's light. He sighed. Picked up the sheet of paper, read the rest.

The last few sentences tortured him. They were so direct, naked almost. He put no feeling into the words; he read in a dull flat voice, hoping to bore her, but every time he paused, glanced up, there were her eyes, three feet away and glowing.

'You can never know how much I love you. I wish – God, how I wish – that there was something we could do.'

He looked at her once more. She was gazing out of the window, the window that faced south, over the valley. This was such agony for him, and she had not even noticed – and the worst of it was, he forgave her.

'It's something to do with a woman,' Jesús declared, with the air of someone drawing on a wealth of experience.

'Of course it's a woman,' Pablo said. 'The question is, which one?'

There followed an arduous silence: Jesús thinking.

No doubt he would be pushing his chin into the palm of his hand. No doubt there would be creases in the pale dough of his forehead.

Wilson did not look round.

'It's funny,' came the baker's voice again. 'I never heard him say anything about a woman.'

'That's because you're always talking,' Pablo said. 'You're always going on about your lousy bread. No one ever gets a word in edgeways.'

Wilson heard Pablo sweep a batch of peanut-shells and bottle-tops from off the counter. They clattered to the hard clay of the floor, and he thought nostalgically of the last time it had rained in his life. It must have been two years ago. But no time seemed longer than the time that lay ahead. He reached for his glass and drank. The liquor ran over his throat like oil, lit a fire when it hit his belly.

'Well, it's not the Bony One,' Jesús said at last, with just the slightest uncertainty in his voice.

Pablo snorted. 'Don't be a fool, Jesús. It couldn't possibly be her.'

'You got any better ideas?'

The way Pablo responded to this challenge, which was not at all, it could have been morning. But the entrance to the bar had filled with black, and bats swooped close to the ceiling, their shadows distorted and grotesque in the light of the kerosene lamp.

Wilson felt the two men's eyes sliding down the bar to where he stood, searching him for some clue as to the identity of the mysterious woman. He pretended not to have noticed; he did not even appear to be aware of the existence of a mystery. This was easily achieved. He had been drinking for two hours. He was heading for unconsciousness along a straight road, and no amount of talk was going to slow him down or deflect him from his destination. There was no place in this for friends. Friends were about as much use as mosquitoes.

Sometimes a phrase from the letter rose into his head, and he grimaced and scraped his boot against the gutter that ran along the bottom of the bar; he might just have stepped in a cluster of fresh mule-dung. He could only console himself with this one thought: Montoya's letter had gone on and on, his love endlessly repeating, an echo obsessed with itself. But then he remembered Suzanne's face, struck with a kind of awe, and glowing, as if the sun had been setting behind his shoulder. *To be so close to you and yet so far away. The hours I spent with you were jewels.* The letter was not bad. It was good – too good; he could not have written one like it. All his consolation dissolved. He thought of the plaster cast that he had kept as a memento, the ghost of a red rose showing through the dust. Like the light that hangs outside a brothel on a winter's night. Wincing at this new bitterness of his, this treachery, he swallowed the contents of the glass that stood in front of him. He was almost sick.

It had been hot in the kitchen hut. The air seemed scented with her, some subtle distillation of her skin. She had taken the letter from him and turned the paper in her hands.

'It's a bomb,' she said in a soft voice.

He stared at the dress that she was wearing. The skirt had been embroidered with lilies of the valley. A flower that stood for the return of happiness, she had told him once. The canaries sang in their gilt cage as if nothing ever changed.

'Yes,' she said, her voice still softer. 'A bomb.'

She slid the letter back into the envelope and pushed the envelope into the centre of the cushion. She fastened the buttons that held the cover in place. Then she held the cushion in both hands, and turned it slowly, one ear bent close, listening.

When she was satisfied that the letter could not be detected, she lifted her eyes to his. He sensed that she wanted some kind of reassurance, but he was not sure that he could give it to her. There was her feeling, which he did not understand, and there was his, which he could not admit. He felt like a man being torn apart by horses. He made one final effort. It seemed to require all his remaining strength.

'That bomb,' he said, 'you must be careful with it.'

'I will be careful.' Her eyes had opened wide.

'It must not go off.'

She shook her head.

'Take it upstairs. Put it back where it belongs.'

'Yes,' she said, 'you're right.'

She left the hut.

It was as if they had not spoken at all. An exchange had taken place in some secret space and would never again be mentioned. So quick, so simple – and yet it had exhausted him.

When she returned, he was waiting by the door.

'And now,' he said, 'I really have to go.'

This time she did not argue.

He slid his glass across the counter. When Pablo came towards him, he took the bottle out of Pablo's hand.

'Look.' Pablo spoke to Jesús. 'He wants the whole bottle.'

Jesús whistled. 'Must be some woman.'

Wilson ignored them both.

He drank the bottle dry and ordered another. The bar was filling with miners from the second shift. Voices, elbows, smells. Was there no peace anywhere? He took his empty bottle by the neck and smashed it against the wall. One of the miners put a hand up to his face. Blood gushed between his fingers. A wedge of flying glass had taken half his eyebrow off. Wilson told the man it was his own damn fault. Should've moved, shouldn't he. Should've ducked. He tried to hit the man, but the punch looped through the air, a good yard wide. He climbed on to the bar and started dancing. It was a routine that he had seen a troupe of Africans perform in a saloon in Leadville, Colorado, once. You had to stamp your feet and shake your fists and shout. His shouting took the form of curses. He cursed the Mexicans, the French, the Indians, the French again and, once again, the French. He undid his pants and pissed on Jesús Pompano's boots. Then he attempted something else the Africans had not featured in their act, a flying somersault across the bar. He did not remember anything after that.

2

Suzanne lay in bed, unable to move, anchored there by sweat. How did people ever sleep in heat like this? She kept seeing the Captain of the *SS Korrigan*, his skull pressing through his brittle yellow skin, his leering mouth. *Wait till July.* But it was still only the beginning of June. Her nightgown stuck to her body, and her hair hung in tight, damp curls upon her forehead. Then, as she turned over, seeking some miraculous panel of coolness in the bed, she heard the cries.

At first she thought the cries were taking place inside her head, the product of her fevered sleeplessness, but when she raised herself on one elbow and listened she could tell that they were coming from the open window. Surely it could not be Montoya again? She fought her way clear of the sheets and leaned on the window. The shutters stood open, a vain attempt to stimulate the flow of air. She peered out.

The nights in this place reminded her of no other nights; they had a demonic beauty all their own, in which both industry and nature played a part. There would be moons of strange proportions, sometimes gilt, sometimes scarlet, tilted at drunken angles in the sky. Like cups with no handles, or faces cut off just above the eyebrows. Even the clouds could send a shiver through her. They were thin and silver, rare apparitions. They lay parallel to one another, in horizontal rows, like surgical instruments on a country doctor's wall. The wind, though soft, almost imperceptible, blew on shore and then off shore with the regularity of a watch for which each beat was six hours. It ebbed and flowed, just as the ocean did; it was like a tide happening in the air. Monsieur de Romblay had told her that they had to run the smelter so it worked in concert with this phenomenon. The smoke that was given off by the plant – the effluence, as he liked to call it – contained a lethal dust that could shower down on the town's inhabitants, creating illness and disease. 'And quite frankly, my dear,' he had spoken behind his hand, though his eyes twinkled with a kind of mischief, 'we've got enough problems with the

Indians already, without poisoning them into the bargain.' And so the smelter ran at certain hours of the night, dictated by the winds, and the smoke was ferried safely out over the gulf. During these hours you could hear the constant grating and clanking of machinery, as if something were being broken rather than made. It no longer disturbed her; it had come to seem familiar, almost reassuring. But some nights they timed it wrong, and the wind changed before they had a chance to shut the smelter off, and a glittering dust, the finest particles of copper that you could imagine, would float down through the atmosphere, settling on rooftops and trees, the ships that lay at anchor in the harbour, drunk miners on streetcorners, sleeping dogs, and the world would take on a supernatural, gilded look, as if some god had been at work with paints.

Tonight the sky was dark, the ocean almost invisible below. She could still hear the cries, but she could see nothing. She slipped a robe over her nightgown and picked up a fan to ward off the mosquitoes, then she pushed her bare feet into a pair of *huaraches* and tiptoed out of the room and down the stairs. She opened the screen door; the clatter of night insects grew louder and more shrill. But she could see nothing from the veranda either.

She ventured down the steps and out along the street. She knew that it was dangerous for a woman to be out alone at night – only a fortnight ago Marie Saint-Lô had been assaulted on her way back from the hospital – but her curiosity outweighed her fear. To her left she could feel the gap of darkness where the harbour lay, ships with rigging as complicated as the bones of fish, the massed black hulks of the freighters that carried the copper to America. She passed the Director's house. No lights showed in any of the windows. Then, instead of following the road round the hospital and down the hill, she walked straight ahead, into the small park that overlooked the town. The cries were louder now. She crept towards the parapet and, gripping the warm stone in both hands, peered over.

A curious procession wound its way up the hill towards her. One man had been hoisted on another's back, his head lolling, his neck offered to the sky. He had flung his arms out sideways, like someone crucified, and his feet trailed on the ground. A Mexican sombrero hid his face. About half a dozen men, Indians mostly, capered behind him, pointing fingers, drinking, chattering. In their hands they carried an assortment of bottles and machetes. Every now and then the man who seemed to be impersonating Christ uttered a cry or a groan from beneath the hat. Each utterance was greeted with a chorus of jeers and whistles.

She sat for a while below the parapet. It was like an illustration from the Bible. The rocks, the moonlight – Christ. All the colours were cold, metallic. She did not move. Gradually the cries grew fainter; the men must have retraced their steps.

Somehow the sight of the procession had depressed her. The depression had an edge of grime to it; it was as if she had dirt inside her head, dirt that could not be washed away. A flash of lightning showed her the range of mountains behind the town. They looked too close; they looked built. She stood up and brushed the dust from her skirts, then turned and walked back towards the house. She felt that she was being followed. There are children behind me, she thought. Children are walking in my shadow, but they're not mine. My children are buried at crossroads in the dark. I stirred their ashes with a stick. My children fill my shoes. Time, they were chanting. Time, time. She braced herself and turned. A stray dog brushed against the folds of her robe, thrust its damp nose against her wrist. Three men had died of rabies in the last two weeks. She walked on, hands clasped in front of her. She could hear the wretched animal behind her, paws ticking on the cobblestones.

When she entered the bedroom, Théo was sitting on the edge of the bed. Looking at him in his nightshirt, with his bare calves and his tousled hair, she felt an absence of tenderness. Only impatience at his heaviness, frustration at his immobility. As if he were some dead weight that she was trying with all her might to shift, but could not.

'I woke up. You were gone.' He spoke in the short, dazed sentences of someone who was only just awake.

She shut the door and moved towards the bed.

'Where were you?' he asked her.

'I went outside to get some air.' She smiled vacantly. 'There wasn't any.'

'That noise,' and he was frowning now, one hand in the hair at the back of his head, 'what was that noise?'

'Some men. I think they were drunk.' She took off her robe and hung it over the end of the bed. 'Go to sleep, Théo. Go back to sleep.'

'Have you seen Señor Wilson?'

Mama Vum Buá's jaw swung sideways in a graceful arc. At the end of the arc, she spat into the dirt.

Suzanne tried a different approach. '*El Americano?*' She mimed a hat in the air above her head. Then, feeling foolish, a moustache.

'No.'

The Señora was standing outside her restaurant, with her elbows cradled in her hand and her blue eyes blazing between their swollen lids. Her gaze shifted from Suzanne's hair to her cheek to her nose. Then down to her mouth. Settling at last on her left hand. One forearm disengaged and the Señora pointed.

'How much?'

'It's a wedding-ring. It's not for sale.'

The Señora shrugged. 'No American.'

For a moment Suzanne thought Mama Vum Buá was holding Wilson Pharaoh to ransom, and the price of his release was her gold ring. But that would have been ludicrous. Probably it was just that the Señora was more interested in her jewellery than in her questions.

Suzanne had woken that morning thinking of the last time she saw Wilson. He had fled, as if running from a ghost. He had not visited her since. She wanted to explain the circumstances surrounding Montoya's letter, how it was only a piece of vanity on her part, an entertainment. Together they could joke about it. Together they could dismantle the bomb. Sitting in cane chairs on an afternoon later in the month, one of them would turn to the other and say, 'This hour that I am spending with you is a jewel.' She could already hear the laughter that would follow.

After her lack of success with Mama Vum Buá, she decided to try the hotel where Wilson stayed. She remembered that it was called the Hotel La Playa and that it overlooked the square where the church was being built. The only building that fitted his description was a shabby, two-storey structure on Avenida Manganeso. Three steps led up to a narrow veranda that had buckled and splintered in the heat. A row of chairs stood with their backs to the wall. All of them were missing either seats or legs, or both.

She stepped through the doorway and found herself in a courtyard that was open to the sky. The walls had been painted a sickly shade of green. Two Indians hunched over a round table in the corner, moving pebbles across the surface. There were piles of crumpled money at their elbows. They did not look up.

She walked over to a hole in the wall and peered through. A Mexican was sitting facing her. He had a thin, mournful face, with dark lips and the high, arched eyebrows of a pantomime fiend. A cracked glass half full of some clear liquid stood on the table beside him.

'I'm looking for Mr Pharaoh,' she said.

The man did not say anything. She could hear vultures on the roof above.

'Mr Pharaoh,' she said slowly, in case he had not understood. 'I'm looking for Mr Wilson Pharaoh.'

The man scratched one of his forearms.

'Do you know where he is?'

The man swallowed half the contents of his glass and smiled sadly. He did not seem unfriendly. It was just that he would not speak to her. Perhaps he was simple, she thought. Or dumb.

She wanted to leave a message for Wilson but she had neither pen nor paper. And there would be nothing like that here, even if she could have asked for it, even if she had received an answer. She turned away, biting her lip.

Another Mexican had appeared in the lobby. He wore a pair of blue-tinted glasses and a suit of brown clothes that resembled a uniform. He had a face with too much flesh on it. He was stooping over a piece of cake, one hand cupped to catch the crumbs.

'Can I help you, Madame?' He spoke French.

'I'm looking for Monsieur Pharaoh,' she told him.

'The American?'

She nodded.

'He's not here.'

'Do you know where I can find him?'

'I'm afraid not, Madame.' His mouth hung open. The gaps between his teeth were filled with the cake that he had just devoured.

'If you see him,' she said, 'would you be so kind as to give him a message?'

'But of course.' He dusted his hands and, removing his blue spectacles, moved closer. 'I would be delighted.'

She did not like this familiarity of his, but she had no other choice. 'Tell him that Suzanne wants to speak to him. It's urgent. Tell him,' and she paused, trying to think of words that would be remembered, words that would bring him back, 'tell him that I miss him.'

A smile spread over the man's thick lips like butter. He talked past her shoulder to the other man, who was now peering through the hole in the wall. A few fast words of Spanish, followed by coarse laughter.

'I beg your pardon?' she said.

The man switched back to French. 'I was just saying. Mr Pharaoh is a very lucky man.'

She chose not to dignify his impertinence with a reaction. Instead, she turned and walked calmly out of the hotel. As she crossed the street she could hear him laughing and calling after her in French, 'I miss him, I miss him.'

3

Wilson had no idea where he was going. One of his eyes had misted over. The other was closed and swollen; he must have struck some wall or door or table with his face. Every time the mule stumbled beneath him, his head pealed like a great cracked bell.

He had woken that morning sprawled on a bank of sandstone and pumice at the back of the Bar El Fandango. Daylight had come down like an axe and split his good eye apart with one clean stroke, as if it were a piece of wood to feed a fire. He did not want to think about why he had drunk with such seeming greed for his own annihilation or why, on waking, he had saddled up and ridden out of town in the direction that would present him with the greatest hardship, namely south-west, towards the desolate pastures of the Vizcaíno. He did not want to think about reasons.

He must have dozed off as he rode, or else he took a wrong turn. As he came through a narrow pass, it was not desert that he saw but sea – one shot of pale liquor in a rough brown glass. He had found his way to San Bruno, that cluster of cactus-shacks and fishing-huts which clung to the sun-blasted shore some ten miles south of Santa Sofía.

That San Bruno should offer sanctuary was no small irony. In times past, men had been drawn to this stretch of coast by the promise of a night of love. The women of San Bruno were twice the size of other women, except in one miraculous respect, and they wore skirts of black pearls which, when unfastened, fell to the ground with a sensual, hypnotic click. There was no man alive who could resist the sound – though it was likely to be one of the last they heard. For it was here that men were captured for their seed and butchered afterwards. Their corpses were heaped into barges known as bone ships, along with any male offspring, then cast afloat on currents that would carry them southwards, to the ocean, to oblivion. This had always been a dangerous country for men. Just stories, of course, legends that had grown in the otherwise unfruitful soil; the only skeletons on the village shores these days were the skeletons of fish – but still. A man could not ride into a place like San Bruno without the vague feeling that he might be inviting his own extinction and that immortality was by no means guaranteed.

It was strange then that the first person he should see as he cleared a mesquite grove and rode up a track towards the village was a priest. The priest was sitting at a table made from bits of driftwood. The wall behind him, a kind of salmon colour, revealed the true state of his vestments. They were stained and faded, torn in places too, as if he had fought his way through cactus thorns on foot. At his right hand lay a pack of playing-cards, weighed down by stones in case the unthinkable happened and the wind blew. This priest no longer trusted anything at all; or maybe he had lost so much that he was taking no chances with the little he had left. A priest in San Bruno, Wilson thought, as he rode up to the cantina. It was a rare sight. The nearest mission was Mulege, some thirty miles to the south.

He looped the reins over his mule's head and tied them to a post that held the roof up. He stood in the shade, one shoulder against the wall. He watched the priest picking at a plate of fish.

'Morning,' he said.

The priest grunted, but did not lift his head.

'Are you a priest?'

'What's it to you?'

'You look like a priest.'

The priest raised eyes that were the washed and naked blue of a sky after rain. 'And you look like you lost a war.'

They had both lost wars. The priest's hair was drained of colour and prickly as ice-plant. His blue eyes seemed related to the Señora's. But that man would be dead by now, long dead. Another of the same breed, though. Priests who had turned religion on its head and cast the Lord out of the garden of their bodies.

Wilson knew the stage that the man had reached. He himself was somewhere similar. That moment when you let go of one thing and reach out for the next. You're not sure where the next thing is or what it looks like; for all you know there might be nothing there at all. You wait. In the silence that follows there's no expectation of what might happen, only abandonment of what came before. Halfway out, no going back. How that place could hurt, that half-way house. Its rooms were haunted, lonely; rain through the roof and voices on the stairs. Sleep would have been a blessing, but sleep was something that happened somewhere else. You lay awake. You hurt. And you couldn't see how things would ever change.

He gestured at the only vacant chair. 'Mind if I sit down?'

'You got something to say, you can say it standing up.' But the priest had wearied; his voice did not burn with the same fire as his words.

Wilson sat down, removed his hat. He sighed.

The priest stared at him a moment longer, as if considering an act of violence, then he bent over his fish again. He worked on the skeleton with the precision of a watchmaker. He did not seem to be eating the fish but, rather, mending it.

'Maybe you could do something for me,' Wilson said.

The priest won a piece of grey meat from the net of bones and poked it into his mouth. He studied Wilson as he chewed.

'You could listen to my confession.'

The priest began to cackle. Bits of fish danced on his tongue.

Wilson leaned forwards, forearms on the table. 'Father,' he said, and he heard a threat buried in the calmness with which he was speaking now, 'I need it done.'

He was too astonished at his own resolve to notice how the priest responded. This whole scene, in fact, was taking him by surprise.

'Are you a Catholic?' the priest asked him.

'What difference does that make?'

Another cackle, but it faded fast. 'I'd like to finish my lunch first. You got any objections?'

Wilson sat back. It seemed as if some fragment of his desperation had got through. He lit the butt of an old cigar and felt the smoke rake over the back of his throat. If he had judged this wrong he would have been dead by now.

He sat in the midday heat, and smoked.

It was a while before the priest pushed his plate away. Wilson could not be sure, but he suspected that the priest had used the time to gather himself. He was the challenge that the priest had been expecting, a moment of truth. But he was early. He felt rather guilty about arriving during the man's lunch.

A boy appeared at the table, grime around his mouth and one ear torn. 'Anything else?'

'What else is there?' the priest asked.

'There's coffee.'

'Coffee.' The priest snorted in contempt. 'Bring me another bottle.'

The boy took his plate away, scraping the bones on to the ground outside the door. There was a flurry of cats.

The priest turned to Wilson. 'Do you have another smoke by any chance?'

'I've got a butt, that's all.'

'I'd appreciate it.'

Wilson reached into his waistcoat pocket and produced an inch and a half of two-week-old cigar. It was his last smoke, but he did not begrudge it to the priest. He held it out across the table. The priest stuck it in his mouth and leaned into the flame that Wilson struck for him. He took a deep draught down into his lungs.

The boy with the torn ear stood another bottle and two glasses on the table. The priest uncorked the bottle, poured two drinks. He pushed one in Wilson's direction.

'On me,' he said.

He sucked down another lungful of smoke. 'Well,' he said, 'let's hear it.'

Wilson told the story of Suzanne Valence from beginning to end. His first sight of her, their first meeting. He talked of his infatuation, then his love. Her trust in him. His hypocrisy, his lust. He took the knife of his desire and turned it on himself. He twisted it deep. Revealed the vision of her ring slipping from her finger. Her clothes slipping from her body. The vision of her naked between the sheets that smelt like hot, sweet grass. Naked on sharp fields of lava. Naked under the bright-orange branches of the elephant tree. He did not spare the details. Nor did he spare himself. He wanted everything out in the open, known.

By the time he had finished, the sun had altered its position in the sky. The priest was staring at him, a curved fold at the corner of his mouth, one eye slightly narrowed. It was the closest he had come to smiling.

'I don't understand,' he said.

Wilson stared back across the table. 'What do you mean?'

'I don't understand what happened.'

'I told you what happened.'

'Everything?'

'Yes.'

'In that case I don't understand what you're confessing.'

The boy stood another bottle on the table. The priest poured himself a drink. He drank it off and placed his empty glass next to the bottle.

'Have you slept with this woman?'

'Of course not.'

'So what is it that you're confessing? A conscience? The unique ability to resist temptation?' The priest cackled again. 'Abstinence?'

Wilson did not like the sarcastic tone. 'I'm confessing sins committed in my head.' He picked his drink up, drank it down.

'In your head?' The priest ran a hand through his hair, then reached for the bottle. 'In your head,' he repeated. Still holding the bottle, he gave Wilson a look that seemed to come at him from around a bend. It was as if the priest's eyes had to turn a corner just to see him. 'If you're a sinner, then you're the purest sinner I've ever come across,' he said. 'By Christ, if you're not the purest.'

'I want absolution.'

'You don't need absolution. You just need to forget.'

Wilson fixed the priest with a steady look.

'What the hell.' The priest put the bottle down and began to make signs in the air, but as his hand dropped from his head towards his heart he toppled sideways off his chair. He lay in the dust, among the fish-bones. He did not move.

Wilson knelt beside the priest and seized his shoulders. Shook him. The priest's head lolled on his neck. His eyes fell shut like a doll's. But a pulse was beating in his wrist. He was still alive.

The boy with the torn ear pointed at the three empty bottles lined up inside the door. 'He drank them for breakfast. It's a wonder he could speak to you at all.'

Wilson hauled the priest into a sitting position, propping him against the wall. Then he walked over to his mule. There was nothing more that he could do in this place. He untied the reins and mounted up.

The boy came and stood below him. 'He won't remember you. When he wakes up, you'll be nothing but a dream to him.' He grinned up at Wilson, one eye closed against the glare.

Wilson turned his mule round and rode out of the village. He wanted it behind him, lost in memory.

He headed inland, towards Comondú, which lay some thirty miles to the west. If he did not stop to sleep he would be there by daybreak. The drinks that the priest had forced on him blazed steadily behind his eyes. The boy's words stayed with him. The hours he had spent in their company had given him the curious feeling that he had been alive once, and had then passed on, and that all this had happened long ago.

He was not sure that he could have offered proof of his existence, if he had been asked for it. He had been well and truly undermined by the encounter, and the width and harshness of the landscape that now surrounded him did nothing to restore the balance.

4

Towards evening, when the sun had dropped behind the ridge and the Mesa de Francia lay in cool, mauve shadow, Suzanne picked up her fan and her parasol, and left the house. There had been no word from Wilson Pharaoh, and she began to doubt whether her message had ever been delivered; she did not trust that gloating Mexican, with his thick lips folded back upon his face and his pockets stuffed with cakes. She could not now be sure whether Wilson was in the town at all. But, thinking of his promise to ride with her to San Ignacio, she found it hard to believe that he would have gone without her.

She had followed the dirt-track that the miners used, high into the stony pastures behind the Hôtel de Paris. Away to her right she could see a railway line climbing in lazy curves towards the mine entrance. The landscape was barren, industrial, unfinished. Work had been suspended on the church that day, owing to an Indian festival, but Théo had still contrived to spend the entire morning at the site. Since four o'clock he had been confined to his study. He was conducting some research into stress factors; he wanted to impress Monsieur Eiffel with his zeal on their return. When she asked if he would like to take a walk with her, he looked at her with incredulity. It seemed he no longer understood even the simplest and least threatening of her desires. Which made her wonder whether, in fact, he ever had. In Paris, with its wealth of distractions, she had never noticed. But the harshness of the light in this new place had revealed differences between them, and had thrown those differences into sharp relief.

Before leaving for Mexico she had bought a sketchbook from the artist's shop behind the Rue Fontaine and, during the voyage, she sat on deck and recorded her impressions in water-colour. She captured the conical green hills of the Azores at sunset, Tierra del Fuego's celebrated glaciers, ports like Panama and Buenos Aires, Santiago with its almond trees in bloom. But there was one page, in her opinion, at least, that stood out from the rest; she had painted it during their passage through the South Atlantic.

She had been thrilled when Théo and the Captain took the decision to sail round Cape Horn. She knew of its reputation, and it had not disappointed her. She remembered the first storm descending, the moment it began – a black cloud moving up from the south and swallowing the sky. Suddenly they could not hear each other speak.

She did not know how long it had lasted; time soon lost all meaning in the constant darkness. One morning, her mind almost visionary with lack of sleep, she ventured up on to the bridge. It was then, in that dim light, that she saw a sight that she would never forget. They were about fifteen nautical miles north-east of the Cape, and it was beginning to exert its influence. The ship would disappear in front of her and it would seem as if they must be sinking, but the bows would heave and lift, and they would scale a wall of water that was higher than a house, and then, when they reached the summit, there would be a hush, a kind of stillness, and she would catch a glimpse, under the boiling sky, of waves in their thousands, each one a mountain capped with snow, then down they plunged, the body of the ship protesting, down into the depths once more.

It was during one such moment that she heard a cry. She could not be sure, but she thought it had come from outside, somewhere below. She waited for the ship to rise, and heard the cry again. And then, peering through the glass, she could see what it was. The figure of a man lashed to the railings, not twelve feet from the bows. The ocean curled over him and slammed across the foredeck, but he would always appear again, head tipped skywards, white foam rushing past his ankles. Each time they pitched down the steep slope of a wave, he threw his head back and she heard him laugh. Yes, she was sure that he was laughing.

'The damn fool,' the Captain was muttering behind her. 'I'll have his hide for this.'

The Captain did not warrant her attention; she was too preoccupied with the man on deck below. It was a passion similar to hers, a passion she had always been taught to conceal, to deny. Men buried what was precious in themselves and thought that women should do the same. Sometimes, when Théo made love to her, she had to take the sheets between her teeth so that she would not cry out. What Théo felt was muffled, sheathed, contained. She could only sense it, as if through many layers of rock. You would need dynamite to get to it. While hers rose up in seconds. Crackled on the surface of her skin and lifted every hair.

And afterwards sank down, beat slowly through her womb, the wings of a swan at dusk.

The next morning, when the storm had settled, she sat in her cabin, swathed in blankets against the cold, and painted the man with the green waves curling heavily above him.

Three weeks later, in a hotel in Santiago, Théo picked up her sketchbook and leafed through the pages. The contents were probably much as he had expected – flowers, figures, scenery; he commented politely on several of her efforts. Then he saw the picture of the man lashed to the railings and paused, as she had known he would. He asked her how she had come to choose the subject.

'It was inspired by the storm.'

'Is he being punished?'

'No,' she said, 'he's enjoying himself.'

And Théo had laughed, thinking that she was teasing him.

Their minds were engaged on two different levels. There was only, at times, the habit of a link between the two. In company, of course. In public. The part of him that had understood her had shrunk, and was on the point, she felt, of vanishing altogether.

Some stones rattled down on to the track behind her. She turned to see Montoya standing ten yards away.

'Captain,' she said, 'you startled me.'

His eyes had a flatness about them, a dead quality, like the ocean on a humid day, like oysters. His face hung mournfully about the collar of his scarlet tunic. 'Did you read my letter?'

She said that she had.

'Well?' he said.

'Well, what?'

'Will you come away with me?'

She did not answer.

'My uncle has a ranch in Venezuela.'

She suppressed a smile and turned away from him.

'Don't laugh at me. I mean it.' He stood beside her now. He had taken her arm.

'I'm sorry, Captain. You don't understand.'

'Come away with me,' he begged her, 'please.'

'You seem to have overlooked one rather important fact,' she said.

'What's that?'

'I'm married.'

He saw no obstacle. 'Leave him.'

'For you?' She had to laugh.

'Leave him.' He was staring down at her. 'We could go now. My carriage is waiting behind the rocks.'

She drew back, and he was left with one hand outstretched, like someone offering assistance. She walked away from him. The layer of cinders sprinkled across the slope of the mountain had deepened in colour. It could have been a field of crushed plums.

When she had moved some distance up the hill she turned to look at him again. She saw that he had drawn a gun. It was not aimed at her. He held it slackly, the muzzle pointing out across the railway line.

'What's that for?' she said.

He did not reply.

She could not believe the feeling of calmness that had flooded through her at the sight of the gun, nor could she make the slightest sense of it.

'Are you going to shoot me?' she said.

His mouth opened, as if he were about to speak, but then it closed again. He turned on his heel. She stood still, watched him go. It was not long before he had vanished round a bend in the track.

There was a shot. The echo crackled across the loose stones of the mountainside. She picked up her skirts and ran back down the hill.

His horse sprawled in a pool of blood, its hindquarters flickering. It had been harnessed to the carriage as usual. When the horse fell, the carriage had toppled; it lay on its side, one wheel ticking as it revolved. Montoya stood over the animal, the gun still in his hand. The blood expanded in the dust. It moved less like something liquid than like something solid that had melted. It moved, she thought, like lava. She could already hear the flies gathering.

He spoke without looking at her.

'Did you think it was me?'

She turned her face away from him, as if from an insult, and began to walk back down the hill, towards the town.

He shouted after her. 'Would you have cared?'

When she opened the screen door she was surprised to see Théo standing in the corridor. He was dressed in his formal evening clothes. His white tie hung, as yet unfastened, round his neck. His lips were pressed together in such a way that they had almost disappeared.

'Are you going out?' she asked him.

'We're due at the de Romblays' house in five minutes.' It had taken all his strength to keep his voice level.

'The de Romblays' house?'

'For dinner.'

Of course. It was Friday night. A tradition had been established on the Mesa del Norte: the French would gather at the Director's house and pore over the events of the preceding week. Recently Suzanne had begun to think that she was in danger of becoming an item on the agenda.

'I forgot,' she said.

His eyes moved past her face, moved downwards. 'Look at you.'

She had ripped her skirts on a cactus as she ran down the hill. The toes of her glazed kid boots were scuffed and dusty.

'Where have you been?'

'I was looking for Monsieur Pharaoh.' It was the only piece of recent truth that she could think of using.

'He's gone.'

This jolted her. The promptness, the certainty, of his response. She stared at him so hard that he felt compelled to speak again.

'He's left town.'

She asked him how he knew.

'I went to see him.' Turning away from her, he faced the mirror on the wall. He began to fasten his tie.

'You went to see him?' she said. 'Why?'

He would not answer. His chin lifted, the knot tightened around his neck. The quick, sure movements of his fingers seemed calculated to provoke her.

'He's no friend of yours,' she said. 'In fact you hardly know him. Why would you go and see him?'

Still he would not speak. And, as she stared at him, she thought she understood. She suspected a conspiracy to quell her, to tether her, to bring her to heel, with Madame de Romblay as the architect and Théo as the engineer. It could only be done by enforcing her isolation, by removing her one true friend. They had brought some pressure to bear on the American. They had used his goodness, his nobility, against her. She looked into her husband's face and saw no anger there. No, all that righteous anger had been chased away. Now there was only the refusal to acknowledge guilt.

She took the mirror off the wall and let it fall from her hands. It split into three almost equal pieces, as if it were something to be shared. Then she ran past him, along the corridor and up the stairs. She flung herself on to the bed.

'Suzanne?' She heard his voice in the hallway below. 'Suzanne?' The voice had moved closer. 'What about dinner?'

'I'm not coming.'

Since the incident with the napkin, she had divided the community. The men, with the exception of François Pineau, treated her much the same; they put it down to her comparative youth, high spirits, one too many glasses of champagne. But the women, less softened by illusion, less gullible, had not forgiven her. She could already see Madame de Romblay rising from her brocade divan and moving forwards to greet her, to gloat over her, to condemn. She could not face it. The sight of that woman's plunging breasts would bring the bile flooding up into her mouth.

'But – '

'Tell them I'm sick. Make something up.'

Her tears scalded her cheeks. She knew that he would stand in the doorway with a puzzled, faintly indignant, air. She knew he would not comfort her.

When her crying had died down and she could listen to the house again, there was no sound. He had gone.

She woke up in her clothes and called his name. There was no reply. Moonlight showed her fragments of the room: the doorhandle, a mirror, one edge of the water jug. The house had the silence of a landscape buried under snow.

She raised herself on one elbow. The moon lay on its side, the part in darkness visible, charcoal against the black night sky. She could not tell how late it was. A clock chimed in the parlour. Twice, for the half-hour. Half-hours always sounded lonely somehow. They were the furthest it was possible to be from something that was definite. Not linked to any hour of the day or night. Uncertain, incomplete. Marooned in time.

She lay back on her pillows, one arm behind her head, her left foot fitting against the muscle of her right calf. Her eyes travelled up the pale curving folds of the mosquito-net and on up the string to the brass hook, visible only as a glint, embedded in the ceiling. She imagined Théo comfortable. Sitting on the de Romblays' veranda with a glass of Sauterne and a lit cigar. She watched smoke flurry off the tip. He would also be looking at the moon. She could almost hear his voice – the measured pronouncements, solid sounds. He would be home soon, in his own good time. She was glad that she knew where he was, and could imagine him. She turned to face the wall and fell asleep again.

When she woke, he was sitting on the bed. The room seemed darker now. He had extinguished all the lamps in the house, and the moon had fallen in the sky.

'Théo?'

'Yes.'

He was still angry. She could tell from that one word, the way he had snapped it off like a piece of rotten wood.

'I'm sorry about earlier. I was upset.'

He said nothing. He just sat against what little light there was, his head and shoulders framed by the window, smelling, as she had thought he would, of sweet wine and cigar smoke.

She shifted in the bed. 'Don't hate me.'

Her words hung in the heavy air like a church bell at a funeral. The way that tolling lingered. You could never quite identify the point at which it stopped being heard and started being imagined. It occurred to her that falling out of love would be like that. It also occurred to her that she had lived much of her life in fear of that uncertainty, that moment of transition, that imperceptible withdrawal. He had not noticed her at first. He had not even seen her. Sometimes she had such doubts. She feared that she might become invisible again, that he might leave. Was that why she had insisted on coming with him? Because she felt she could not risk his absence? Absence made the heart grow colder. Absence made you disappear.

'Théo,' she said, 'please forgive me.'

'Why is it with you that there is always something to forgive?'

He was holding on to his anger; he would not let it go. There was no need for error, no excuse for it. Behaviour should be accurate to within one-tenth of a millimetre. Perfection was attainable. He still had not turned round, or even moved.

She sighed. 'I don't know.'

She had gone about this the wrong way. He hated any form of pleading or apology; they only compounded the offence. At last she saw that penitence would get her nowhere.

He rose suddenly, moved towards the door.

'Where are you going?' she asked him.

'I'm not tired.'

She waited until he had left the room and then lay down. One cord of orange light unravelled against the wall. The conveyor belt must have started up. Yes, she could hear it: the distant grinding and clanking as bins of coarse ore were borne towards the crushers. What was valuable would soon be taken out. The rest would be drained off and dumped.

Her eyes drew back into the room. A china jug for water, a cake of soap, a chair. In the darkness they looked worthy of her trust, almost noble in their simplicity.

She felt a clenching inside her. A tightening, a shrinking. Like the place where a rope is tied, the place they call a knot. She had said too much to him; she had gone too far. He must have something to answer for, surely. He could have felt the need to apologise, to explain himself, to ask forgiveness. Why did the burden always seem to fall on her?

She thought she might be blind. All she could see was dazzle, one solid sheet of it. Like being too close to the doctor's waistcoat. She lifted her head. It was the sunlight beating through the window, skidding along the floor, right into her just-opened eyes. Her own house then. Upstairs, presumably. And Imelda kneeling beside her, feet tucked beneath her dress. A look on her face that you saw in churches; her concern, which must have spread over several hours, had assumed the aspect of a trance. She could smell the girl's spicy skin.

'Are you sick, Madame?'

'No, I was just resting.' She wanted to smile, but her face resisted. The foolishness of being found, like an animal, on the floor. She sat upright, leaned against the wall. 'Is Monsieur Valence still here?'

'He's downstairs, Madame. He's having breakfast.'

A smooth crimson groove encircled half her wrist where a bracelet had bitten into her. She must have been sleeping on her hand.

'Do you need anything, Madame?'

'Would you make me some of your tea?'

She was not convinced of the healing properties of the drink, but she knew that Imelda took great pleasure in preparing it, and the taste had become a source of amusement to them both. It was another way of setting Imelda's mind at rest, a touchstone for a mood. She listened to the girl's light footsteps dwindle.

The argument came back to her. The anger – his, then hers. *Why is there always something to forgive?* She had left the bed without another word. Sat at her dressing-table and searched the mirror for her face. All the lamps had been extinguished; moonlight would have to do. Some powder first, to give her skin a shocked and ghostly look. A dab of rouge to strengthen it. She knew he was standing somewhere behind her, looking on in utter disbelief. Well, good. She took her time over the jewellery, changing her mind more than once. At last she settled on a necklace of emeralds and pearls, three amber bracelets and a cameo brooch. Touching perfume to the inside of her wrists, her throat, the lobes of her ears, she rose from the stool and left the room. Her performance only lasted until the moment when she closed the bedroom door behind her. Then she sank down on the floor. She was exhausted, bored. She had wanted him to follow her, but she had suspected all along that he would not. Not a sound carried through the door to where she sat. She did not even hear him undress, climb into bed. At last, surrendering, she lay down in the corridor, her head cushioned on the loose sleeve of her robe.

She heard Imelda mounting the stairs with her herb tea. She climbed to her feet. Her head felt like a dead weight on her shoulders, dull as a pumpkin. In the bedroom she poured water into her china bowl and began to wash the rouge and powder from her face. Imelda entered the room behind her. The chink of a cup and saucer on the dressing-table, a sigh as that day's clothes were laid across the bed.

When she walked into the parlour, Théo was smothering a yawn. She wondered if the clink and jangle of her bracelets had kept him awake; she must have tossed and turned on that hard wood floor all night. But he greeted her as if nothing had happened. All but asked her how she had slept. This ability of his to forget any unpleasantness, though something of a relief on this occasion, she often took to be a form of cowardice. It occurred to her that he must have stepped over her to reach the stairs that morning. She was beneath contempt, quite literally. She felt her anger flare, as sudden as a struck match. She was surprised that it had lasted through the night, surprised that she had slept at all with such a simmering below her skin. But then it died away again, blown out by weariness. She sat down at the table. She poured some coffee, spooned a few thin slices of fruit on to a plate.

'There's a letter,' Théo said, 'from Monsieur Eiffel.'

'What does he say?'

'Shall I read it to you?'

In this simple question, she heard his desire for a truce, his longing to restore the balance.

'If you like,' she said.

She knew that Monsieur Eiffel would serve as his apologist. Their marriage might be disintegrating, but otherwise, in all other fields of endeavour, Théo was excelling himself. So, actually, everything was all right. The letter could not have arrived at a more appropriate time.

Théo began to read, his voice lowered, his eyes avoiding hers. It was as she had anticipated. Eiffel praised him for his efforts in the most testing of conditions; he had every confidence in Théo's ability to complete the assembly to the satisfaction of everyone concerned. He mentioned several projects that were presently engaging his attention: a proposal for a Paris Métro, based on the London model; an observatory intended for the summit of Mont Blanc; an underwater bridge to cross the Channel. There followed a brief discourse on buoyancy and equilibrium. Her eyes moved to the window. Vultures paddled in the air above the ridge. She did not notice when it was that Théo stopped reading, only that he had. He was looking where she was looking.

'Something must have died,' he said.

'Yes,' she murmured. 'Something did.'

She could see his mother, during one of her frequent visits to their house on the Rue de Rivoli. Madame Valence had an invulnerable air about her, the effect, perhaps, of the severe dresses that she favoured, steel-grey and veiled in crêpe. She resembled an engine of war that could be wheeled on to any battlefield and would always find the weakest point. Her eyes closing in on Théo, her only son, as, studying his hands, he said, 'We are trying, mother.' 'Trying?' Madame Valence's gaze shifted to her daughter-in-law. 'Is something wrong?' 'Nothing's wrong, Madame,' Suzanne replied. She saw Madame Valence tighten her lips, signalling her scepticism, and arch her pencilled eyebrows slightly as she returned to her embroidery.

The questions had begun six months after the wedding, when Suzanne showed no signs of having conceived. 'And when shall we see a little one?' Madame Valence would ask, her light-hearted words masking an interest that was gruelling, that could, on occasion, seem like greed. As the years passed, the mask was dropped, all semblance of light-heartedness abandoned. A kind of quiet panic took its place. Suzanne did her utmost to ignore it – but sometimes she dreamed that Madame Valence had devoured her children.

Her eyes still fixed on the ridge, she pictured the horse's corpse with vultures hooked into its flanks, their wings spread wide for balance. Their beaks lurched downwards, ripped ungainly holes in the glossy coat and then jerked sideways, trailing bowels and intestines on the ground. The stench of blood had reached her nostrils. She brought her fan up to her face and moved the air away.

Théo was reading the letter again, in silence now. As he neared the end, he looked up.

'He mentions you, Suzanne.'

'What does he say?'

He took out his watch. 'It's getting late,' he said. 'I must go. Here.' Handing her the letter, he excused himself and, rising from the table, left the house.

His haste seemed natural until her eyes fell on a sentence close to the bottom of the page: *I have no doubt but that your decision to take Madame Valence with you has by now been vindicated, and that she has proved herself a most worthy and beneficial addition to the community.* She came close to laughing out loud. Such savage irony. No wonder Théo had not read the letter to the end. No wonder he had left the house with such alacrity.

And yet, a moment later, she found herself curiously touched by the words. There was someone who believed in her, someone who thought she was of value. She read on: *I remember well that, during the construction of the Douro Bridge in 1876, I travelled to Portugal myself, together with my wife, and stayed in a villa on the outskirts of Oporto. It is a time that I still think of to this day with great fondness.* His wife had died, of course, some few years later, and he had never married again. He had come to rely more and more on the company of his faithful eldest daughter, Claire.

Two summers ago Suzanne and Théo had been invited to spend a week at Monsieur Eiffel's house in the South of France, the Villa Salles at Beaulieu-sur-Mer. She remembered walking in the gardens with him one afternoon, through cloisters, between clipped hedges, past stone lions, the scent of lemon and hibiscus sharpening the air, sunlight on the lawn, fountains of bougainvillaea. He had always treated her with the utmost courtesy, and his sober and impassive features, which you saw in photographs and which so many people feared, would soften whenever he set eyes on her. In private he was self-effacing, genuinely unimpressed with his achievements; he did not act the famous man at all. That afternoon, in the gardens of the villa, he had entertained her with stories from his youth – dancing the quadrille with English girls, swimming across the Seine at night. His most humiliating year, he said, was 1860, when four girls, three of them blonde, rejected his proposals of marriage, all in the space of seven months. They laughed together over his misfortunes, dwarfed as they were by what had happened to him since.

'They did not know what they were turning down,' she said.

He fixed her with his blue eyes, the fingers of one hand moving thoughtfully among the silver threads of his goatee. 'Do you think that would have made a difference? If they had known?'

She smiled. 'It's hard to say. If you cannot see something, then perhaps it is not for you.'

This must have sounded a little sententious, yet he indulged her. She could tell that she amused him, that he was stimulated by her company, and she sometimes wondered if he did not see in her some incarnation of his previous desires.

A knocking reached down to where she was, among her memories.

'Imelda?' she called out.

There was no reply. Imelda would be elsewhere in the house, making the beds upstairs or in the kitchen hut, preparing lunch. She rose from her chair and opened the door herself. Montoya was standing on the veranda. It seemed that every time she answered the door she answered it to him. He must have waited until Théo left for work. He must have been watching the house.

It was intolerable, of course – and yet she did not feel that it was intolerable. There was no conviction in this thought of hers. It seemed passed on, second-hand; it might have belonged to someone else. Suddenly she felt as if nothing could disturb or worry her. She thought she owed this new strength to the letter she had just read and the memories that it had provoked.

But she had been slow to break the silence that lay between them. He spoke first.

'I wanted to apologise for my behaviour last night.'

Appearing in person like this was an impertinence, she decided, in that she could not simply ignore it, as she might have ignored a letter or a note. It forced her to be civil, diverted her from any blunt response. Appearing in person was a form of manipulation, nothing less. It was clever of him, she had to admit; she almost admired him for it. Though she doubted that he knew what he was doing.

'I behaved disgracefully. Will you forgive me?'

She let her eyes drift beyond him, out to the west, where the vultures would still be feasting. Of the two events, his shooting of the horse and his arrival at her front door, it would have been hard to say which was the more unlikely.

'I would like to recompense you.'

His forehead shone. Her continuing silence had brought perspiration to the surface. But why should she make things easy for him? She owed him nothing.

'To recompense you for any distress you might have suffered by inviting you to accompany,' he was beginning to stumble over the words, 'accompany me on a cruise in my submarine.'

'Submarine?' she said. 'I don't think so.'

'We'll be leaving at eleven o'clock, from the south quay.'

She looked into his face. His eyes were as soft as a dog's. He was begging for lenience.

'You killed your horse,' she said.

'The south quay,' he said. 'At eleven.' And, removing his plumed hat and bowing low, he turned away from her and walked back to his waiting carriage.

5

Wilson did not want to set eyes on Santa Sofía again until the church was finished and those responsible for it had boarded a steamer back to Paris. He would spend the time examining his map, trying to read some significance into its markings, giving it one last chance to prove itself. If he had found nothing after a month he would return to the town. He would burn the map and make a parcel of the ashes, then he would set out for America. His first destination would be his father's grave in Silver City. The parcel would be opened there, the ashes scattered. He would also change the inscription on the stone. Strike out 'STILL' and put 'DONE' in its place. 'DONE LOOKING'.

A few miles out of San Bruno he came across a band of Indians. They were heading north. They had heard that white men were handing out free houses and asked if Wilson knew anything about it. He tried to warn them that the houses were not free, that they were only given in return for labour, but they could not understand his medley of signs and dialect. He was able to buy food, though, trading his hunting-knife for a few strips of sun-dried beef and a sack of hard biscuit known as *pinole*. This would keep him going on the journey west. He could supplement the diet with prickly pears, which would soon be coming into season, and any fresh meat that he could kill – snake or bat or lizard.

At Comondú, he rested for a day. He climbed down to the bottom of the canyon where a black stream ran over smooth stones and tropical plants grew, green and secretive. He washed his clothes and laid them out to dry on slabs of lava. He found a scorpion that was the colour of grass when it decays. It did not move all morning; it seemed pinned to the rock like a brooch. He bathed in a deep pool, his eyes drifting up the sheer sides of the gorge to the sky above. He willed himself to think only of what he could see: the plants, the rocks; that strip of sky. He resisted memory. It was like a kind of hunger, the hollowness that he began to feel. He filled the *bota* on his saddlebow with water. On he rode, the trance holding.

Then things began to go awry.

First his mule split a hoof. The next day, as he rode through a viznaga grove, one of the curved thorns ripped his sack of *pinole* from ear to ear; he lost more than half the contents before he noticed. There was nothing for it. Hauling on the reins, he headed north-east, back towards the coast.

His mule grew steadily more lame. In the end he had to lead the beast. It was the middle of June. The sun dropped on the land like a weight; the air crumpled in front of him. Luckily the moon was full. He could walk all through the night in a bright, metallic daylight, but as soon as a thin wedge of colour opened on the horizon he began to look for shade. He would wake in the early afternoon with flies camping in his nostrils, on his lips. He could find nothing to eat, and his supply of water was running low. He had heard of men lost in the deserts of New Mexico who cut their mules' ears off and sucked the blood. He hoped it would not come to that.

One evening, climbing through a canyon, he saw a streak of glittering substance in the low cliff to his left. His stomach ached and his tongue was so dry that it creaked in his mouth, but he could not pass it up. You just never knew. He tethered his mule and scrambled up the slope to take a closer look. It was onyx. Some jasper too. Not worth a whole lot, but it might pay a few debts. He worked with a hammer and chisel, the ringing eerie as the light shut down. After an hour he had filled a small panier with crystals.

It was dusk by the time he finished, and the old Indian who stepped out from behind his mule had him jumping backwards in alarm. He had thought himself so alone; he had forgotten there could be anyone else. The old Indian grinned and waggled a hand. He wore a cloak and hat of untanned deerskin, and carried a bow and arrow slung over his shoulder. His sweat smelled of damp ginger. He could speak no English, no Spanish either, only a language that was full of teeth and spit. He kept joining the tips of his fingers together and cramming them into his mouth. Wilson thought he must be hungry. In despair he showed the Indian the rip in his *pinole* sack and spread his hands. The Indian beckoned. He led Wilson to a shelter at the head of the canyon, just four poles driven into the dirt and a covering of wild flag. A fire crackled out in front; a mongrel sprawled close by. There was water – covered with ants and flies, but drinkable. There was food too. A clay plate of toasted cardon seeds, some aloe heads baked in ashes and half a dozen white grubs, which were as thick and long as Wilson's thumb, and tasted something like bacon. The Indian talked incessantly; sometimes he seized Wilson by the sleeve, sometimes he raised his face to the sky, mouth wide open, as if astounded by the sound of his own voice. Wilson understood nothing that was said, but he nodded when the Indian left gaps, laughed when he laughed. It was a small return on the food he had been given.

That night they slept on the ground beside the fire. Wilson was woken once, when the mongrel answered the barking of a jackal further up the ridge. Then again, when he heard the old Indian talking in his sleep. He opened his eyes. The Indian was lying on his back, one hand gesturing in the air above his chest. The hand black against the starlit sky. Less like a hand than an absence of something. The shifting of an empty space. A starlessness. He had so much to say; one evening had not been enough.

In the morning he took Wilson round the property. There was a small enclosure at the back, fenced off with cardon ribs, where he grew corn and beans and red peppers. He showed Wilson artefacts that he had made – tools, woven mats, jewellery fashioned out of crystals, bone, the teeth of animals. He wanted Wilson to buy a necklace, but Wilson had no money. Towards evening, afer sleeping through the afternoon, Wilson asked for directions to the coast. The Indian scraped lines in the dust beside the fire. When Wilson walked off down the canyon, the Indian watched him go, nodding and grinning and jamming the fingers of one hand into his mouth.

Two days later the sea appeared, some ten miles to the east. He recognised the country now, a ridge, a canyon, another ridge, the folds in the land that lay to the south of Santa Sofía. He tried to calculate how long it had been since he had left the town. He thought it must be about ten days.

He approached through Montoya's domain, passing the ranch, the soldiers' garrison, the cemetery, and stood at last above the narrow valley that was El Pueblo. A few clouds fanned out against the sky, white wing-feathers, bones refined by countless tides. The town lay below, flat and tawdry, crushed by heat.

His father had stood as he was standing now, on a hill to the east of San Francisco, and looked down at the tents pitched in the meadows, streets of painted wooden houses, the spilled silver of the harbour. The city had changed and grown in the years that he had been away. San

Francisco, 1879. A wry smile bent across his father's lips. He had come face to face with an old adversary.

Though it would hurt him, Wilson let the memory run. When they arrived outside the small house on Piano Street, his mother would not let them in. Neither of them. She stood on the threshold, her hair still smooth against her skull, but grey, her eyes dull, as if she had spent her days in pain. But her grip on the door betrayed no weakness of any kind.

'What do you want?' She was talking to her husband for the first time in seven years.

'Constance,' he said. 'I'm home.' The habit of a spring in his heels, but no power there, no conviction. Just one twang, and then silence.

She shook her head. Her smile was bitter as the taste of acorn bread. She had just realised the meaning of her name, the irony of it. The joke had been on her throughout her life. Now it was on him.

'You've got a home someplace, maybe,' she said, 'but this ain't it.'

'Constance – '

She rounded on Wilson. 'The same goes for you.'

'But I did like you said. I brought him back.'

'It don't take five years to bring somebody back.'

'I had to find him first.'

'You found him,' she said, 'then you stayed with him.' It was unreasonable, what she was saying, but there was truth in it.

'Constance – ' His father had shuffled forwards.

'No,' she said. 'It's too late.' The door closed in their faces and they heard the shooting of bolts.

'Well, I'll be damned.' Arthur Pharaoh turned this way and that on the stoop, not unlike a cat settling. But there would be no rest for him, not now. 'Well, I'll be damned,' he said again.

Then they walked back down the street and booked into a travellers' hotel.

It was the first time that Arthur Pharaoh had ever left the house on Piano Street because he had no other choice. It had taken him years to summon up the courage to go home and face his wife. All that apprehension, all those years – for what? His surprise converted into anger. 'I'll be *damned*.' He was angry as he walked away that morning. At being thwarted. At being denied the chance to own his life, with all its wrongdoing, all its shame. At the same time there was part of him that could not help but feel relieved. He had been spared the reckoning; he could continue as before. By nightfall he had come full circle, seeing the rejection as a kind of triumph. In their hotel room, as Wilson lay down to sleep, his father gave him a pointed look, as if he had known all along that going back would serve no useful purpose. The next morning, they left for Virginia City. His father did not know it then, but he would never see his home again. Wilson did not want to dwell on that. He turned his eyes back to the seat of his own pain, the town that lay sweltering below.

His breathing quickened as he saw the spire lifting above the rooftops, sharp and pale-red, and his relief was also the slow cracking of his heart. Was the church finished? Had she gone? He no longer knew the difference between what he was hoping for and what he dreaded. Then he noticed scaffolding at the far end of the building. The roof still needed work. He whistled to his mule and flicked his hat across her rump. Her ears tilted gamely forwards. Together, they started on the downward path.

It was shortly after noon. Only the shuffle of their boots and hoofs, the jingle of the reins, to break into the silence. He passed a woman dozing on her porch, a silver edge to her jaw, her face shining like a picture under glass. On the corner of Avenida Aljez the seeds on the trees had shrivelled into black half-moons.

He noticed smoke rising in a trickle from the bakery. It was just about the only thing moving. It was also strange. Jesús never baked during the afternoon. He must be on to something.

Wilson paused in the doorway. Jesús was stooping over his oven, a few sticks of straw in his fist. He whipped the door open, threw the straw inside. It flared red, and then withered, turning to cinders in an instant.

'Jesús?'

'Well, well.' Jesús stood up. 'You're back.'

'Could you spare me some water?'

Jesús pointed to an earthen pot behind the door. Wilson removed the lid and scooped the water up in both hands. No words could describe the taste of cool fresh water after two weeks in the desert. He drank three handfuls and stood back, gasping.

'Good trip?' Jesús asked.

'I wouldn't call it good exactly.'

'No gold then.'

'None.'

Jesús swept the straw cinders from the floor of his oven and shut the door. 'I've been experimenting with temperature.'

Wilson sat down on a sack of flour and prepared himself for another lecture. He would have listened to a lecture on anything right then. It was just such a blessing to take the weight off his blistered feet, to lean against a wall, to stretch his legs out in front of him.

'See, what you're looking for is a heat that's flexible,' Jesús began, 'a kind of spring in the oven. You've got to raise the temperature, hold it steady for a few minutes, and then relax it. It's all in the timing.'

Wilson nodded.

'If your heat's achieved too fast,' Jesús explained, 'and the oven gets too hot, then you burn your bread – '

'I've seen that,' Wilson said. 'I've even eaten it.'

' – but if your heat's sluggish and the oven isn't hot enough, you don't kill the yeast.' Jesús was pacing the stone floor of the bakery, his shoulders hunched, his pale hands moving in the air. They seemed to summon all Wilson's fatigue. He could feel his eyelids dropping.

'Your dough rises and rises. Then, suddenly – *plof!*' and one hand sprang open, 'it collapses. What you pull out of the oven is an embarrassment. Flat as a pancake, hardly bread at all. Three days in a row I baked flat bread. I hadn't realised.'

The last thing Wilson heard as his head fell forwards on his chest was the beginning of a digression into the subject of moisture, something about a brick wrapped in a damp cloth, something about a bowl of water. When he woke, Jesús was working at his kneading-trough, the muscles bulging in his heavy calves as he trod up and down. The day had darkened in the doorway.

'That was very interesting, Jesús,' Wilson said. ''Specially that bit about the brick.'

Jesús looked up, his feet still marching in the dough.

'You don't understand the first thing about bread. You've spent too much time in the desert,' he said, 'addling your brains.'

6

Suzanne could not bear to look at any part of the sky. It stretched above the town, taut and brilliant, the sun a core of brightness at the centre. Everything in the house was hot to the touch: the chairs, the walls, the plates – even the clothes that Imelda had laid out for her that morning. There seemed to be no escaping it. She could only think of sleeping under the fan as a way to pass the hours.

Then, towards eleven, Montoya's carriage drew up outside. It was driven by the same man as usual, uniformed and taciturn, his body trussed with ammunition-belts. She had left the house almost before she knew it – the heat took the decision for her – and was immediately rewarded with a breeze as the carriage moved off down the street. A hot breeze, true – but any breeze was better than none. She began to try and imagine what a cruise in a submarine would be like. Under the water, she thought. Away from the sun. She was already smiling, in anticipation. It would be cool under the water. It might even be cold, like winter. It was the first time she could remember wanting to be cold, the first time she had ever thought of a shiver as a luxury.

The waterfront was crowded with children, all hoping for a glimpse of the submarine. They were being kept at a distance by a number of Montoya's soldiers. When they saw Suzanne, though, they clamoured round her, hands opening and closing like sea anemones. She gave them lemon bonbons and some worthless French coins. Fights broke out. Her driver had to scatter them, his whip curling and snapping in the air above their heads.

She was ushered through the military cordon and out along the south quay to where the submarine lay moored. It was the strangest machine. Built from curving iron plates, dark-green, the shape of a cigar. 'PACIFIC PEARL COMPANY' had been painted along one side, but the white letters had peeled, flaked away, and the word 'PACIFIC' was half gone. Montoya stood inside what resembled a funnel, only the top half of his body visible. She called down to him. He glanced round. All his features seemed to leap.

'I didn't think that you would come,' he said.

She watched him climb out of the submarine and mount the stone steps to the quay. He wore white, a simple, high-buttoning jacket and a pair of ducks; his head was bare. He looked young and efficient. You would never have thought he was the kind of man who would shoot a horse for no reason.

He stood in front of her, his eyes shining, yet forlorn. Any hopes he may have had were always haunted by a fear of impending disappointment.

'Everything's ready,' he said.

He led her down the steps and on to the curving outer shell. The heels of her boots rang on the metal.

'And it works?' she said.

'So they tell me.'

She climbed backwards down a vertical ladder and found herself in a narrow metal chamber. Montoya followed, his shoes clicking on the rungs, the soles, she noticed, hardly worn. He fastened the hatchway after him by spinning a wheel that looked like part of a bicycle. Light filtered down, conducted by two tiers of glass eyes. The chamber had been painted grey, but the walls bristled with levers and faucets and winches, and they were all bright-red, the colour of his uniform. She smiled to herself.

A Mexican ducked through a steel doorway and asked Montoya a question. Montoya gave him a curt nod, then turned to her.

'That's one of the crew,' he said. 'We have six men on board. Four to drive the propellor-shaft, one to control the pumps and valves, and one to navigate.'

He guided her forwards, into the nose of the craft, a cramped space with two folding leather seats bolted to the floor and a single round window, about a foot in diameter, that looked straight ahead. This was the observation room, he told her. While he went aft to issue orders to the crew, she took her place on one of the folding seats. In the window she could see the water of the harbour, almost on a level with her eyes. A tremor ran through her as she realised that they would soon be travelling beneath the surface.

The vessel shifted; the quay backed silently away. The water rose and fell, a steady rustling against the outer shell. They passed into the shadow of a freighter. The compartment darkened. She could see the side of the ship rising steeply above her, its hull studded with molluscs and barnacles. She was struck suddenly by the smallness of the vessel to which she had entrusted her life. Just for a moment she found it hard to breathe.

As the two arms of the harbour opened wide in front of her, offering the sea, a muted roar, like air being forced through a narrow gap, started somewhere beneath her feet. She was relieved to see Montoya appear in the chamber and sit down beside her.

'Is everything all right?' She hoped she had not conveyed too much of her alarm.

He smiled. 'They're opening the valves to let the water in,' he said. 'That is what will take us down.'

Take us down? It sounded threatening, almost final.

And it was too late to change her mind. The valves were already open and admitting water, and the ocean was rising in the window, and this time it did not drop again. They were beneath the surface now. The rustle of the waves against the vessel ceased. A hush descended – the silence in a wood at dawn. All she could hear was the creaking of the metal plates, a kind of birdsong, and the rush of water into the ballast-tanks below.

A shoal of blue-and-yellow fish curved past the window in a slow, smooth arc. Her apprehension lifted; wonder took its place. Other fish, much larger, came and hung in front of her with gaping mouths, their bodies cut from beaten tin. They gazed through the glass at her, quite motionless, as if fascinated, but if she moved her head or hand they vanished instantly.

Montoya showed her a row of gauges on the wall behind her. Lit by phosphorus, they glowed like ghosts' eyes in the gloom. One recorded the air pressure, another measured depth. The needle flickered on the '30' mark; thirty feet of water stood above their heads. And they were still diving. She returned to her seat and the hypnotic window. Rafts of sunlight leaned down through water that stretched out on all sides, clear as air. A ceiling overhead, a floor beneath; shells scattered on the sand like toys. She could imagine walls too, in the distance, still too far away to see. They might have been moving through some vast hall, the inside of a cathedral, perhaps – a place where voices echoed, a place where mysteries could be revealed.

'How long can we stay down here?' she asked.

'There's enough air for three hours,' he said. 'We could travel to the mainland, if we wanted to. That would not be difficult at all.'

She gave him a warning glance. He began to talk instead of how he had acquired the submarine. How he had seen it, lying on a beach near Cabo San Lucas, abandoned. How he had bargained with the scrapdealers, a Mexican and a Portuguese. How they thought that he was mad.

But she was only half listening. He had just reminded her that he could not be trusted. It occurred to her that nobody knew where she was. Not Théo, not even Imelda. Nobody.

They were turning in a half-circle now, manoeuvering to breach a reef. As they slid through a gap in the coral, its walls as intricate as lace, she saw something flap past overhead, a huge moving shadow, a cloak with a cruel mouth. She drew back from the glass, but her eyes were still fastened on the monstrous wallowing shape.

'What was that?' She had risen to her feet, one hand against her cheek.

'You're very privileged,' Montoya told her.

She asked him why.

'It was a manta ray. You don't often see them.'

He joined her at the window. They both stared through the glass at a world that now seemed empty, chilling. As if all life had fled.

He told her of the local fishermen's beliefs. Rays stood guard over the oyster beds. They were feared by anyone who had ever dived for pearls. They could measure more than fifteen feet across, and were known for their guile and their ferocity. They would appear from nowhere and hover in the water above a diver, cutting his supply of sunlight out. Plunged in sudden darkness, the diver lost his bearings. Made blindly for the surface. But the ray would be lying in wait. It would wrap the diver in its powerful folds and crush the life out of his body. Some said it could devour a man with its horned beak. Others said that it killed for the joy of it and that, when the struggle was over, it simply left the corpse to other creatures of the deep. One thing was certain: a man who came across a manta ray was unlikely to be seen again.

She had been shuddering at the thought of being smothered in those cold blankets of flesh, and that phrase of his, *killed for the joy of it*, muttered like an incantation on the scene, and she had not noticed how he had moved nearer to her. Suddenly he was standing much too close. And had taken her hand and drawn it up towards his mouth. And was kissing the inside of her wrist, the place where excitement could be measured, the place where her life beat. Pulling away from him, she caught her dress on a handle and the sleeve tore. He took one step towards her, and then stopped. His eyes had darkened. She stood facing him, her back against the cold curve of the wall. Such fury possessed her that she was quite incapable of speech.

He reached up, touched a bright-red lever. 'I could let the water in,' he said, 'and drown us both.'

It did not matter to him that he would be drowning his crew as well. Horses, men – all forms of life could be disposed of. Only he existed, and his love for her. There was no other world.

'If you lay another hand on me,' she said slowly, 'I will see that you are whipped.' She paused for a moment. 'Like a dog,' she added. She did not know where she had found the words.

He had been smiling, but then she saw some nerve give way. His eyes lightened, and he moved to the far side of the chamber, his chin turned in towards his shoulder.

'All I ask is that you come away with me – '

Her voice cut into his. 'Turn the ship round. Take me back.'

'If you could only see – '

'Take me back,' she said. 'This instant.'

He left the observation room, ducking through the narrow steel doorway. She was aware of having to sustain her fury and sustain it visibly, otherwise she might never leave this place.

Hours seemed to pass, with nothing happening. She turned round once, saw two men toiling over a wheel.

She put her face close to the window. At last a glimpse of sunlight, pure and undiluted. A rush of foam, fountaining against the glass. The torn edge of a wave. But she could not allow herself too much relief. Not until she stood on solid ground. She held her fury tight, a valuable possession, something nobody could take from her.

Footsteps rang on the metal floor behind her, and she knew that it was Montoya who had entered.

'Your husband,' she heard him say.

She did not look up. 'What about my husband?'

'He's old.' Montoya stared out through the window, smiling as the town came into view. 'Soon he'll be dead.'

She did not understand what he intended. Though she could see his horse rear back in its traces, a bullet driven deep into its brain. She could see the horse crumple on the ground. She could see its hind legs twitching and the creeping pool of blood.

'And then,' he said, 'I'll be waiting.'

She tried to keep her voice steady. 'As soon as we get back, I am going to write to the Mexican Government,' she said, 'and have you removed.'

His smile remained. 'I love you. You do not know how much.'

Through the foaming glass she saw the two arms of the harbour reach out to embrace the craft. It would not be long, she thought, before they were moored against the south quay. It would not be long at all.

7

'Wilson?'

He had heard her voice so many times. Shifting on his bed of stones at dawn. At midday, as silence settled like the wings of vultures on the land. At dusk too, in the crackle of a fire.

The ache that rose through him split him clean in two. He remembered the epileptic miner and his vision of a painted man. Later that night Pablo had mentioned some pictures on a cave wall a few miles north of town. Tall men. Each one painted in the way the epileptic had described. Half their bodies red, half black. And Pablo had told him why. Half of you belonged to this world, he said, half to the next. But maybe it was simpler than that. Maybe it was love that had done it. Maybe love had cut them down the middle.

'Wilson? Is that you?'

He turned in his saddle. She stood below him in a lemon dress whose hem caressed the dust. Her face tilted upwards in expectation, her green eyes shining from beneath the shadow of her parasol.

But he could not look at her too closely. Instead he sent a swift glance looping across the iron rooftops of the town. And spoke away from her.

'Did I miss much?'

She smiled up at him. 'Only me, I hope.'

He allowed her this.

'Where have you been?' she asked.

He lifted an arm and pointed towards the graveyard. 'South of here,' he said, 'then west.'

'Were you successful?'

'No.' He stared down at his hands. The cracked leather of the reins chafed against the inside of his fingers. 'Well,' he said, 'I did find something.'

He reached into the saddlebag behind him. Took out a small parcel wrapped in cloth. And handed it to her.

'For me?'

He nodded. 'Open it.'

She began to unwrap the parcel – carefully, as if even the rags were valuable. And now that she had turned her attention somewhere else he could look at her. He was surprised by what he saw. A brittleness. Something that could give at any moment. Like the clay that the Indians had to dig through for the copper. You could crumble her between finger and thumb.

'It's beautiful.'

She held up the piece of turquoise that he had given her. He had thought of her as soon as he found it. Some quality it had, she had it too. Turquoise was just a name for that place between blue and green. Close as you could get with something as clumsy as a word. He saw her the same way. Unnameable, inaccessible, unique.

Her eyes lifted the colour of the stone into her face.

'Why have you been avoiding me?' she said.

He denied it.

'You have,' she said. 'You've been avoiding me.'

'I've been away, that's all.'

She was shaking her head. 'You've never lied to me before. Don't lie to me now.' Something in her was crumbling, breaking up; she wrung her hands. She was the only person he had ever seen who actually wrung their hands.

He pointed at the turquoise, as if it were evidence of his good faith, but no words came to him. His hand faltered, moved up, adjusted the brim of his hat.

'It was that letter,' she said, 'wasn't it.'

He felt foolish, perched above her, looking down. A dumb man on a lame mule. He wished that he had never returned.

'It shocked you.'

Then he was lying on his back. He thought he must have fallen from the saddle, but, looking up, he saw no mule, no sky. Just a ceiling. He was lying on his hotel bed. Fifty yards from where the dream had taken place.

He lay still, assembling things. It seemed to him that, if he went to the window and looked out, she would be standing in the street below, wearing the dress that he had dreamed her in. It seemed that she would have to be.

He climbed to his feet too fast. He had to steady himself, one hand flat against the wall, and give the darkness time to lift. Then he moved towards the window, peered down.

The street was full of men. They were heading west, towards the main square, some with pickaxes in their hands, others holding spades. Not for work, though, but for violence. No longer tools, but weapons. They were moving in one determined body, arms and faces smeared with clay. He could hear a low droning sound, like a nest of wasps trapped under a bell jar.

He stepped back into the room and sat down on a chair. A fly landed, damp feet on the corner of his mouth. He shook his head. He feared to know the meaning of those men who filled the street, with their features sharpened at the edges, notches cut by a million resentments. He did not want to understand the purpose of the crowd. His dream still seemed real, and what was real, dreamt. He no longer trusted what he saw.

Her voice rose out of the droning of the men. *You've been avoiding me. You have.* And though he had his reasons, all listed, catalogued, all marshalled in his head, none of them stood up in daylight, not one of them stood up. Not reasons, but excuses – and weak at that. The dream had served his own true thoughts up to him like a plate of bitter roots.

Another lesson from his father, this time on the subject of women: 'Don't never take up with another man's wife.'

It was Wilson's first time in the mountains. He was twenty-three, twenty-four. They had no money that year, not even enough to go panning for gold. Instead they headed north, took jobs logging in the redwood forests, all through the fall, all winter too. Hard work, and no strong drink allowed. Only tea with no milk, two cups enough to brown your teeth. And no women either. Hence the talk.

'One summer I was working in the docks, unloading pineapples from Hawaii, five dollars a ton.' His father was sitting on a split log, three other men around him. A river rushed below, swollen with melted snow from higher in the mountains. Spring in Oregon. 'This woman came up to me. I'd seen her before, worked with her husband further up the coast. Nice-looking woman. She comes up to me and says, "How about you and me go down behind the warehouse when you get off?"' His father sighed, flung a woodchip into the river. 'That's the trouble right there. She wanted to spit in her husband's eye, and that was all I'd be if I went with her.'

'So did you?' This came from a grinning, gap-toothed man with forearms as thick as some of the wood he felled.

'Sure I did,' his father said. The others roared and nodded; the chuckling was a long time dying down. 'But I shouldn't have,' his father reflected. 'That's how come I learned.'

He took an old cigar stump out of his shirt with slow fingers, bit the blackened end off, spat it out, and stuck the rest in his mouth. He did not light it, though. He just sat there, moving his teeth around it, and watched the river run.

'She was a green-eyed woman,' he said at last. 'You reach for the door to leave and suddenly there's a knife in your ribs. There's only one way to leave a green-eyed woman, and that's in a coffin.' The truth of this only struck him after the words had left his lips and he nodded, in recognition. Then he dragged a match across the sole of his boot and lit the stump.

And here Wilson was, a generation later, trying not to follow his father's example. Way past wanting to, though. Way past. He roused himself, moved to the window again. The street had emptied but for one drunk Indian. The Indian was so drunk that he walked in the slow curves of a snake. He had the big splayed feet that the Cocopah tribe were famous for. A pig was rooting in the weeds beside a house.

What would his father have said?

Wilson sat his father before him in the room and gave him a cigar to smoke. A whole one. Then he put the question.

'Say the woman who wants to go with you, it's not because she wants to spit in her husband's eye, it's just because she's lonely.'

His father studied him from the bed, his eyes sharp across the air between them. They were used to looking for gold, those eyes; trained to pick out the smallest fragments. Something that was practically invisible could still be worth money. His father lit his cigar. Wilson could almost smell the smoke.

'It don't make no difference in the end,' his father said. 'Sometimes the most good you can do for someone is, don't even spare them a thought.'

'But if she's lonely – '

'Don't make no difference.'

Wilson turned away from him.

Through the open window he heard a rush of noise rise from the main square, a thousand voices raised as one. It came out of such a stillness, so suddenly, so loudly, that it was like a change of weather in the sky, that blast of wind which always brings a storm.

8

Ignoring the offer of a carriage, Suzanne walked away from Montoya. Just walked away from him. Up the stone steps, along the quay and out across the waterfront. She passed a group of soldiers lounging outside the customs house. The air was filled with orange dust; the sun hung behind it, still as a fish and cut from the same clean tin. The streets were silent. It was the hour when people slept. She turned the corner into Avenida Cobre. Only then did she begin to shake. She had held herself so tense and now it was over. Her teeth chattered, both hands trembled; she might have been running a fever. She stood in the shadows, pretending to adjust a glove.

She could only remember shaking like this once before and that was when Theo had first made love to her. Such unlocking of her body after years of holding back. Such a flood of desire. All round her blood and out through the part of her that he had entered. Because he had taken her in hands that she had dreamed about. Hands that were like miracles, the way they touched her in the darkness. It was as if he already knew each curve and hollow. As if he had always known. His hands telling her what his lips could not. Not just fulfilment, but a kind of proof. Confirming her instincts of that summer evening when she stood in the doorway and watched him talking to her father. It was Théo she wanted, only Théo; nobody else would do. And it was Théo she had to think of now. Théo who must be warned, protected.

She found him in the church, his frock-coat folded on a stack of stained-glass windows, his shirt-sleeves rolled. He was deep in consultation with Monsieur Castagnet, and did not notice her.

'Théo?'

He turned with a look of exasperation on his face.

'I need to speak to you,' she said.

'Does it have to be now?'

'Yes.' She apologised to Monsieur Castagnet, who tactfully withdrew.

Théo walked her back towards the entrance. He told her that he had almost finished. Perhaps she should return to the house and rest a little. He would see her soon.

She shook her head. 'It cannot wait.'

His eyes lifted to the roof. She knew what he was thinking. What new outburst of hysteria is this? What specious drama, what absurdity? He might even have been appealing to the Lord God for deliverance – except for the fact that he did not believe in Him, of course.

'Théo,' she said, 'I'm afraid.'

He sighed. 'What are you afraid of?'

'I think there may be an attempt on your life.'

Her words brought his jaw down sharply; he swung round. This was more than he had bargained for. 'For heaven's sake, Suzanne.'

'I'm perfectly serious.'

He stood in front of her, his shoulders framed by the high, square doorway of the church. 'All right, tell me. Who is going to make an attempt on my life?'

'Montoya.'

Still standing there, he began to laugh.

'Whatever else he might be,' Théo said, 'Montoya is a military officer with a code of honour. He also represents the Mexican Government. He is hardly likely to go around killing people.'

She was on the point of telling him about the horse when a shouting distracted her. She could see a crowd of Indians marching up Avenida Manganeso. There was a small man in a beret at the front. He was chanting the same words, over and over again, and the crowd was answering, this second voice threatening and monumental, like the shifting of a mountain.

'There may be trouble.' Théo called to a small mule-drawn carriage that was waiting in the shade. 'Take the carriage and go home,' he said. 'Wait for me there.'

This time she obeyed him.

One thought struck her as she climbed into the carriage, and it afforded her some relief: he had been too preoccupied and then too shocked to notice that her sleeve was torn.

Almost four hours passed before Théo returned. She was lighting the lamp in the drawing-room when she heard him mount the steps to the veranda. The wick had blackened with use and would not catch.

Frowning, she held the splint against the wick until the flame burned down to her fingers. Then, finally, it spat and fizzled, the same sound as something browning in a pan of butter, the same sound, only softer. She turned the flame down low so she could watch the day fade in the window. Kneeling on the floor, she could see the sky, a mauve vault streaked with red, and the mountains black beneath. She dropped the burnt-out splint into the ashtray and rose to her feet. Théo was standing in the doorway, his frock-coat draped over his arm. He did not attempt to mask his weariness. It mirrored hers.

'You're safe,' he said.

She nodded. 'They were carrying a man.'

'A man?'

'He was dead.' She saw the man again, lying on the hands of the crowd. His body twisted as if, like some washerwoman's cloth, it had been wrung out.

'I hope it didn't upset you.'

She shook her head. 'The people were very quiet. They bumped against the side of the carriage. It was like being in a boat in water.'

Théo moved forwards into the room and took his place in the chair by the window. He was silent for a while, then he leaned one elbow on the arm of the chair and ran his hand through his thick black hair. Then simply left it there.

She walked towards him, placed her hand on his. She felt a soft jolt of surprise go through him, then an acquiescence. In that still moment she wished with all her heart that his love could equal hers. It would have been so simple then. Everything would have been simple. She would reach out sometimes and yet she could not span the distance between them, a distance of only a few feet – and him a builder of bridges. She smiled down at him, her hand on his, his head still lowered. Her love for him seemed edged in a strange nostalgia, almost a regret, as if she had already moved beyond it, to a place where it was memory.

They must have looked like statues in the room. She withdrew her hand, stepped back. Adjusted the lamp's reluctant flame.

'Was it a funeral?' she asked him.

'Of a kind.'

In a low voice he related the events that he had only heard about that afternoon. There had been a disaster at the Providencia Mine, six miles north-west of the town. During the night-shift the main shaft had collapsed and three Indians had been killed. Others had been injured.

Spokesmen for the Indians were claiming that the company was at fault. The timbering in the tunnels had always been inadequate, they said. The working conditions were intolerable. The company had no interest in the welfare of its labour force. And so on.

'Is that true?' she asked.

Théo shrugged. 'It depends who you talk to. Morlaix says the Indians were careless. He puts it down to inexperience.'

'Morlaix,' she said.

'I know. But it's a dangerous business. Do you remember what de Romblay said the other evening? We're not a charity, he said.'

She did not remember, though she could well imagine words of that sort emerging from the Director's lips.

'If I were an Indian I would be upset,' she said. 'To put it mildly.'

Théo nodded. 'In any case, they've laid down their tools. Three of the four mines have suspended operations.'

Leaning forwards, one hand cupped in the other, he stared at the lamp. The flame leapt in the glass shaft and settled back. The window had darkened behind his head.

'My men are frightened,' he said. 'Everything's come to a halt. And we had almost finished –'

She moved to the window and looked out. She could hear voices rising up from the streets of El Pueblo, but it seemed to her that they were distant and could be contained. She felt as if she had slowed down, like a clock that needed winding. Nothing could disturb her – no news, no recollection. She imagined the voices sealed inside glass jars.

'And now there's Montoya,' Théo said.

She turned from the window. 'What about him?'

Théo lifted his eyes to hers. 'He's offered to shoot the ringleaders. Personally. In fact,' and he smiled grimly, 'he's practically insisting on it.'

'I don't understand,' she said, though she was afraid that she did.

'It's political. He wants to demonstrate the good faith of the Mexican Government.' Théo shook his head. 'He wants to provide some tangible evidence of the spirit of co-operation that exists between his government and ours.'

'But shooting them.'

'I know.'

'What do you think will happen?'

Théo shrugged. 'Montoya's meeting with de Romblay this evening. De Romblay will attempt to discourage him.'

There was silence while she thought back over the events of the afternoon.

'He may not be so easy to discourage,' she said.

While Imelda was preparing their bedroom for the night, arranging the mosquito-nets and trimming lamps, Suzanne noticed the dress that she had worn on the submarine that afternoon. It had been folded and now lay draped over the back of a chair. She walked over to the dress and picked it up.

'Imelda?'

'Yes, Madame?'

'I'd like you to have this dress.'

The girl's dark eyes shifted sideways, took cover in the corner of the room.

'It got torn today,' Suzanne said. 'Look.' And she showed Imelda the place where the sleeve had caught on the scarlet lever. 'It's no use to me now.'

'I could mend it for you,' Imelda said, in her uncertain French. 'It's not so difficult.'

Suzanne had to smile at this show of devotion: the girl's wide eyes, her wide unblemished forehead. There was no way of explaining this to her.

'You mend it if you like,' she said, 'and when you've mended it you can keep it.'

At last Imelda took her at her word. She lifted the dress in her arms and poured a long slow look of wonder down on to the mass of shimmering silk. Her face might have been a jug of cream.

She was so overwhelmed by the gift that she was halfway to the door with it before she remembered to thank her mistress.

'I will be so beautiful in this dress, Madame. People will notice me.'

The door closed behind her.

Smiling faintly, Suzanne sat down at her dressing-table. As she let her eyes wander among the perfumes and lotions that she had brought with her from Paris she noticed something lying forgotten on her hand-mirror: a piece of palm leaf bound with string.

Last week she had visited the market that was held at the foot of the hill each Wednesday. Just a row of stalls with roofs of untanned leather, yucca pulp. One woman had welcomed her below a canopy. It would have been impossible to guess the woman's age; her face had the texture of brown paper that had been screwed up tight then opened out again, spread flat. She wore a jacket of pelican feathers which Suzanne had openly admired.

After inspecting everything from a pickled bat's head in a jar to a piece of crystal that would keep demons away, Suzanne chose a remedy for soothing troubled nerves. Though neither woman spoke the other's language, they managed to communicate with hand signals and bits of broken Spanish. The nerve remedy was made from a plant called maguey, which the woman had gathered on the slopes of the Volcan las Tres Vírgenes. One secret part of the plant had been dried in the sun and then crushed into a fine powder. She should drink it just before she went to sleep, two pinches in a cup of water, and the night would slip by like a snake over a stone. As Suzanne turned to leave, the woman reached out and took hold of her sleeve. In the same shattered Spanish and with the aid of a few unmistakable gestures, she explained that she also sold love potions. Some were for women, some for men. Passion was guaranteed, she said. Suzanne was smiling when she left the tent. She had just had a thought. This must be where Madame de Romblay went.

She lifted the palm-leaf packet out from among her many jars and bottles, and carefully untied the string. The powder lay inside, all flattened out, and smooth as icing-sugar. She touched it with one finger, tasted it. Stale – like chalk, or plaster. She sniffed at it. It did not smell of anything at all.

That morning in the witch's tent, a week ago, seemed as remote as history. If she could only talk to someone. Wilson Pharaoh, with his slow face and his crooked teeth and his hands too big on the end of his wrists. He was good and kind. She had never imagined that ordinary Americans might be like that. She had only read of gunfights and liquor. But this American, he lifted his hat to her and wiped his hand on his trousers before he shook her hand. Also, sometimes, he said, 'Gee'. He would have listened to her; he would at least have tried to understand. But he had gone. A strange numb dread invaded her, and her limbs felt heavy, bolted on to her body. She looked at the powder lying in its leaf. Two pinches in a cup of water.

On her way downstairs she passed Théo's study. He was bent over his desk. She could hear the scratching of a pen on paper. He would be writing another letter to his mentor, Monsieur Eiffel. In the parlour she saw Imelda, searching the sewing basket for a cotton thread to match the silk of her new dress. Imelda did not notice her either. It was so quiet in the house. She rested one hand on the fine wire-mesh of the screen door and looked out into the dark. She listened to the creaking of a gecko on the veranda. She could imagine it, pale-yellow, almost transparent, with eyes like black rubber, moving in silent spasms towards a fly.

Upstairs in her room once more, with the door closed, she reached for the powder and stirred two spoonfuls into her glass of water. She drank it down. Then she lay back and waited for the promised sleep to come.

9

17 Calle Francesa,
Santa Sofía,
Lower California,
Mexico

22nd June, 189 –

My dear Monsieur Eiffel,
   It was with great delight that I received your letter of the 2nd of April
and I thank you for your prompt reply, especially considering the weight
of your responsibilities at the present time. The projects that you mention
certainly seem of sufficient importance to be worthy of your attention;
a Paris Métro is, in my opinion, long overdue and will bring a new
freedom of movement to a city that has become congested, both with
pedestrians and vehicles. Moreover, the technical problems involved
should prove most challenging – a challenge to which the Compagnie des
Établissements Eiffel will doubtless rise with its traditional competence
and ingenuity.
   One problem that has been occupying me in idle moments is the
problem of insulation. Some members of the community have expressed
a degree of concern regarding the high temperatures which they fear may
occur inside the church during the summer months. Monsieur Castagnet
and I have put our heads together and we have, I believe, come up with
a most satisfactory solution. We have decided to use the local pumice
stone which is abundant here owing to the volcanic nature of the land,
and should prove extremely effective when ground into a fine powder
and inserted between the panels (Monsieur de Romblay has already
placed at my disposal certain machinery at the smelting plant for this
specific purpose). The lightness and porosity of the stone make it an
ideal material for insulating both the walls and the roof, and I feel
confident that it will dispel, once and for all, the anxieties of everyone
concerned.
   You may remember that I referred, in a previous letter, to the new spirit

of eagerness that prevails among my workers. This mood was temporarily soured last week when I returned from lunch to find a Mexican soldier administering a beating to one of the Indians. It was a beating of such untrammelled savagery that I felt compelled to intervene, at some risk to my personal safety, since the soldier in question had lost all semblance of control and succeeded in striking me a blow on the forehead before he could be overpowered. When he had regained his senses, I asked him what the Indian had done to merit such punishment. He became stubborn, almost mulelike, referring over and over again to the laziness of the Indians, their primitive ways, their stupidity; in short, he could give me no satisfactory answer. I determined that he had been acting solely out of prejudice and dismissed him immediately, an action which caused quite a stir on the site, there being no love lost between the Indians of the peninsula and the mainland Mexicans. I realise that this dismissal may upset the Mexican contingent and weaken the security of the site, but I would rather lose another box of bolts than see a man beaten for no good reason. In any case, one might say that we profited from this unpleasant incident: the Indians were most grateful to me for coming to their defence and redoubled their efforts, working with an industry and vigour that was quite unparalleled.

Even as I write, however, a pall of uncertainty hangs over the town. Last night one of the mine's principal tunnels collapsed, costing the lives of several Indians. Many others are still in a critical condition. The situation is volatile, to say the least, since charges of negligence have been levelled at the company. Many of my own men are related to the mining families, either by tribe or by blood, with the result that all work on the site has had to be temporarily suspended. I trust this tragedy will not greatly affect their morale or interfere with the completion of the church, which is now only a few days away. I find myself wondering how much of the unrest and irrationality that I have witnessed can be attributed to the climate, which has become almost intolerable of late. The great heat that we are currently experiencing is usually associated with the months of August and September and I feel that I can speak for both myself and Madame Valence when I say that we envy you the mildness of Paris in June. I can only hope for some respite in the days to come.

On glancing through your letter once again, I notice that it took far less time to reach Mexico than we did, from which I surmise that the trans-Panamanian Railway has resumed operations. Welcome news indeed, if true; I do not think that I could face Cape Horn a second time – though my wife will no doubt be disappointed! My first hope is that the present situation eases and that our work is brought to a successful conclusion. This is a long letter, Monsieur, yet it will not be sufficiently long if it leaves you in any doubt as to the continuing zeal of my endeavours and the profound respect with which I have the honour to be your humble and obedient servant,

Théophile Valence.

10

Wilson spent the early part of the evening in the Hotel La Playa. He occupied himself with small, painstaking tasks. He mended a shirt. He cleaned his round-nosed shovel, sanding the place where the blade had worn to silver. He sharpened his pick and oiled his rifle. He wanted to rid himself of the dream about Suzanne: her explicit beauty, her poignant, unexpected brittleness. It was his mind more than anything that he was working on.

Outside his window the streets were quiet. Every part of the mining operation had shut down. The natural sound of the land descended. That wide, desert silence. Air standing tall and glassy on the soil. Air shocked by heat. The silence had rarely been heard in the town before, and there were some who had to bury their heads beneath their pillows. Others picked fights because fights made noise. From his balcony Wilson watched a man running along the Calle Majore with his hands clamped over his ears. One of the man's moccasins fell off, but he did not stop. It lay in the street, the wrong way up – an emblem of his fear. Most people were frightened of silence. Maybe it was because they could hear the fragile loop of blood in their veins. Maybe they thought it was death coming in his soft shoes. Creeping closer, closer still. Sitting in his room up on the first floor, Wilson had the feeling that the Indians were turning the silence to their own advantage. They were used to it, after all; it was their element. It was their masters – the Mexicans, the French – who had brought sound to the peninsula.

He stood up and stretched. Hung his shirt over the back of a chair, leaned his shovel and his pick against the wall, wrapped his rifle in a rag. But still he could hear her voice accusing him. *You've been avoiding me.*

'I've been away,' he said, 'that's all.'

He was talking to an empty room.

It was no good; he could put it off no longer. He left the hotel and started up the hill to the Mesa de Francia.

On the Calle Francesa the silence had a different quality, denser, more deliberate. It was not silence that had fallen so much as silence that had been striven for. It was like held breath. There was nobody parading up and down beneath the trees, nobody drinking on the veranda of the Hôtel de Paris. The French sat inside their houses, quarantined by apprehension and uncertainty.

And suddenly he did not know why he had come. He stopped in front of the steps that led up to her house. Turned away, turned back. Then turned away again, his mouth dry and all his courage, or whatever it had taken, gone. He saw his father, standing at the window of a boarding-house in Denver. He heard his own voice reach across that dusty room; he heard the words that he had promised his mother he would say.

'Maybe we should think about heading home.'

Shirt-sleeves rolled, one forearm resting on the sash, his father was staring down into a sunlit street.

'We could rest up for a while. I could get a job. Playing piano, like I used to.'

His father was still staring, down into that sunlit street.

'The Empire would take me on – '

At last his father turned back into the room. His eyes seemed to have darkened and expanded. 'You forgot, didn't you?'

'Forgot what?'

'You forgot.'

He could not look away from his father's face. He could not speak. His right hand closed around the stone he carried in his pocket. Smooth stone, from the River Gila. Smooth, smooth stone.

His father sat down on the bed. 'Let me remind you. He pulled the shirt off his back, the buttons scattering, and there were the scars, gnarled, almost black, a stack of sticks piled for a fire.

The shirt caught round his elbows, his father began to weep. 'I can't go back,' he was saying, 'how can I go back?'

It was another three years before he was ready, and by then it was too late.

One bat jinked past, as if the air were full of obstacles. Wilson tipped his face till it was level with the sky. The stars glowed and faded, glowed and faded. They made him feel ill.

He had to think.

He hid in the narrow strip of land that separated Suzanne's house from the house next door. Stood with his shoulderblades against the wall, sweat crawling on his skin. There were two windows on this side of the house. One dark, one lit. The light thrown like a playing-card on the ground. A shadow passed between the window and the lamp. He inched closer, risked a look inside. Monsieur Valence stood over his desk, sealing an envelope with a bead of scarlet wax.

Wilson edged along the south wall, careful to avoid the needles of the century plant. He ducked beneath the flight of stairs that led down to the kitchen hut. Two dark windows, then another playing-card of light. The north side of the house. He did not recognise the room. A girl with black hair sat with her back to him. He could not see her face, only the nape of her neck and one hand curving away from her body, returning, curving away again. She might have been a marionette, her body motionless, one hand controlled by a secret string. Lifting himself higher, he saw that she was mending a dress of Suzanne's. He moved on, reached the front of the house once more. He noticed a lamp burning in a window on the first floor. He saw a shadow swoop across the ceiling. That was where she must be. And it was all he could know of her tonight, that lamp, that shadow. But it was a comfort to be close to her, and then imagine. It was enough. He would sleep now.

On his way back down the street a voice called his name. He looked round. The doctor sprang from his veranda as if he had been fired from a bow. He did not glitter this evening. He did not shimmer or shine. He was dressed in a surgeon's coat, plain white, with no adornments.

Wilson felt the need to explain himself. 'I was just out walking,' he said.

'On a night like this, Monsieur Pharaoh, it would be wiser to stay at home. May I join you, though?' The doctor chuckled, rubbed his hands.

'Please do. You're going to the hospital, I take it?'

'I have been there all afternoon. But there is more to do. Much more.' The doctor danced along the empty street on the points of his toes like a young girl learning ballet. 'You have heard, presumably?'

Wilson nodded.

'A terrible business. A tragedy, in fact. Three fractured legs. A crushed pelvis. More cracked ribs than I can count.' He let out a sigh that seemed at odds with his excitable gestures and his light balletic walk.

'How many dead?' Wilson asked.

The doctor threw him a wary glance. 'No figures have been released.'
Wilson did not pursue the subject. They passed the de Romblays'
house. A carriage stood outside, attended by a man with rows of bullets
gleaming on his chest.

'Montoya's,' the doctor said.

He told Wilson that the Director had already spent almost three hours
trying to persuade Montoya that it was unnecessary to kill anyone. That,
far from restoring order, it would ignite a situation that was highly
flammable, provoking hostilities on the streets of Santa Sofía, if not
anarchy. A state of affairs which Montoya, with his handful of soldiers,
would be powerless to remedy. But the young Mexican seemed wedded
to the idea.

'Do you know what he said?' The doctor leapt in front of Wilson,
showing all his teeth in an astonished smile. '"I will shoot them down,
like dogs."'

'Has he lost his mind?'

The doctor did not take the question lightly. 'It's possible.' He
sighed again and resumed his place at Wilson's shoulder. The two men
walked on.

When they reached the hospital, the doctor bounded up the stairs
and then spun round, addressing Wilson from the veranda. 'And your
foot, Monsieur. How does it feel?'

Wilson smiled. One broken foot after all this talk of legs and ribs and
anarchy. It hardly seemed worth mentioning.

'It's fine,' he said. 'Just fine.'

A momentary gloom descended on the doctor. 'Well,' he said, 'that's
something.'

Seventeen dead. That was what the Indians were saying. They had
gathered in the Hotel La Playa, shouting and spitting, clutching at the
air, their faces brassy against the pale-green walls. The lobby bubbled like
a cauldron with their voices. They did not pay Wilson much attention as
he climbed the stairs to bed.

When he reached the top, he noticed a strip of light beneath his door.
It was wavering – bright and steady one moment, almost invisible the
next. Somebody had lit a candle in his room.

The door was ajar. He could hear voices coming from inside. A woman's, then a man's. He moved closer, testing each floorboard for creaks
before he took a step. Then shoved the door open and stood in the gap.

It was the men he noticed first. He thought he had seen the tall one before. On the waterfront, maybe, or in the bar. A jaw like a horseshoe, hard and curved. Bloodshot eyes. The other one, a foot shorter and dressed in miner's rags, did not register.

'Welcome home, American.'

In the corner of the room, half shielded by the door, stood La Huesuda, bony as ever. She had a snapped-off chair-leg in one hand. Her mouth tipped sharply upwards at the edges and her thin nose glistened. Far from showing any signs of guilt, she seemed to have found some benefit in his appearance, seemed to be relishing the fact that he had caught them in the act.

'You've just been on a trip,' she said, 'haven't you?'

Wilson did not deny it.

'Find anything?'

'Not really.'

She stepped forwards. 'No gold?'

'No.'

The taller of the two men came and stood next to her. His only weapons were his height and the bunched fists that swung like lead weights on the end of his arms. He was looking at Wilson, but he spoke to La Huesuda.

'You believe him?'

Her mouth turned upside-down.

'Who are these men?' Wilson asked her.

'My brothers.'

Wilson looked at each of them in turn. 'Are they descended from Amazons as well?'

He saw the tall man's fist loop towards him. The room burned yellow for a moment. Then he found that he was sitting on the floor, the tall man standing over him.

'Actually, they're half-brothers,' La Huesuda said.

The short man began to rummage in the knapsack that hung on the wall. His hand emerged with a wedge of onyx.

His face twisted in a triumphant sneer. 'Thought you said you didn't find anything.'

Wilson climbed to his feet. The inside of his head shimmered and hissed. 'I was looking for gold,' he said, 'not onyx.'

'Onyx?' the tall man said. 'I never heard of that.' He was studying the knuckles of his right hand.

'Still, it must be worth something,' the short man said.

'Is there anything else?' La Huesuda stepped over to the wall. She had wrapped her small head in a scarlet shawl. Her nose protruded from her face like a knife stuck in a door.

Snatching the knapsack off the wall, she turned it over on the bed. A collection of lesser minerals, the fruit of his two weeks in the desert, spilled across the mattress. There was jasper and chalcedony, some crystals of cumengeite, and the onyx. They looked prettier and more valuable than they might otherwise have done. He had been working long hours on the stones, drawing the colours and markings out through polishing. It had been one of his methods for trying to remove Suzanne from his memory. It had not worked. He had ended up meditating on their beauty and then, by association, on hers.

'This is robbery,' he said.

La Huesuda turned to him, the black shapes of her two half-brothers lurching in the room behind her. 'Yeah, well,' she said, 'I had some personal misfortune recently.'

'What happened?'

'Someone destroyed my balcony.' She smiled to herself, teeth touching the wet curve of her bottom lip. 'It was a foreigner, I think. An American, if I remember right.'

Wilson said nothing.

'I'm asking for contributions,' she went on, cackling now. 'Just so happens I thought I'd start with you.'

'But I told you. They're not worth anything.'

'So what are you worried about?' She snapped her fingers in the air beneath his nose. He could smell raw onions, bacon fat, the genitals of sailors.

He sighed. 'I collected them. It was a lot of work.'

'As I said. A contribution.'

But he did not want to lose the crystals. Lifting the idea from his dream, he had decided to make a present of the best ones to Suzanne when they were finished. They would be souvenirs for her to take back to France with her. His only way of remaining in her memory. Touchstones. In his frustration, he had stepped forwards.

The taller of the two men stood in front of him again, his bottom teeth overlapping like a hand of cards, his bunched fists dangling against his thighs. There was a foot of stale breath between them.

The corner of the room exploded as the short man broke a bottle.

Wilson appealed to La Huesuda. 'I told you that I'd mend your balcony,' he said. 'Don't you trust me?'

'Trust you?' La Huesuda said.

The room was filled with mocking laughter.

Wilson looked from one face to another. All the mouths the same shape, all the laughter identical. Here was the family resemblance that he had been unable to see earlier on.

11

Suzanne could see the house, high on the cemetery ridge. She saw the long white wall ribboning across the land, and soldiers lying among the rocks, asleep or dead. Beyond the house, below it, lay the sea, an aching shade of violet. It was dusk.

A crowd moved up the hill towards her. There must have been at least five hundred people. The dirt-track could not hold so many. They spilled out across the slope, scrambling over rough terrain. An urgency, as if they were late for something.

She thought of hiding, but there was nowhere. Only stones the size of heads or fists, and the house in the distance, standing out against the sky, the graves like bruises on the ground. Only the dead, it seemed, could hide.

But they did not see her.

She stood on a bank above the track while they moved past. Women took the lead, their heads wrapped in black scarves, all softness gone. Silent the women were, with tight mouths, and the silence was more frightening than sound. Some had pickaxes in their hands. Others had spades. Sticks. Chains. Kitchen things.

The men followed, in workshirts streaked with clay and stiff wool trousers. She could smell them as they passed. Their clothes were company-issue, worn for weeks on end. Sweat, oil, urine, garlic, sperm. At dances you could smell it too. When you sat on a hard wooden chair against the wall and the couples went whirling past your face. It was always the men that you could smell. She stepped backwards, covering her mouth and nose. Still they did not see her. Their eyes all pointed different ways. Their fists beat at the air, as if the air were a door and they were trying to get in.

Then she was standing in the house.

She knew this part. No lamps lit in the hallway, only moonlight falling through a high window. A shine on anything that was smooth: the tiled floor, the curve of a banister –

The stairs.

They brought him down feet first. Hoisted on their hands, he seemed to undulate, a cloth stretched over poles, a snake on stony ground. She could not look into his face.

He was wearing the scarlet jacket with the silver epaulettes – his own pride, other people's mockery. His feet were naked, though. His boots were now the property of two different men. They wore one each. Later they would fight to make it a pair. Down the stairs they carried him. Along the hall. Out into the night.

It would happen in the cemetery.

She watched the crowd swarm along the ridge. Something else was being carried. The long oak table from the dining-room. She asked what it was for. One Indian shrugged. Another chuckled, but would not say.

Clothes were lifting into the air, short flights against a sky that ached. Tunic, breeches, undershirt. They were stripping him bare. She saw a silver epaulette spin through the darkness, vanish into someone's outstretched hand. Sometimes, through the crowd, she caught glimpses of the body he had wanted to show her. Pale as a peeled fruit. She had to look away. But, whichever way she turned, it was still there, in front of her.

There were knives now. Sticks too. Kitchen things.

All along the ridge the miners had lit bonfires so she could see the colour of his agony.

Up the table came, propped against a cairn of stones. And he was pinned to the dark wood, with nails through his wrists and ankles. The crowd had learned their Christianity too well. His belly had been opened lengthways, ribs to groin, and his guts tumbled downwards, over his genitals, in one bright coiled pulp. Served up on his own table like a feast.

And they had painted him. One half of his body red, smeared with his own blood. The other black, daubed with ashes from the fire. Flies were beginning to settle on his wounds. Her eyes jumped all round the sky. Would vultures soon be circling? She was not even sure that he was dead.

And in the house below, two women dancing, dancing –

She woke on her back, breathing fast. Perhaps she had run from the cemetery to where she lay. Perhaps she had run all the way. Her nightgown was drenched; she might have swum an ocean in her sleep.

Her gift had returned and it was stronger than ever. She could hardly bear the weight of it. They would kill Montoya. She knew that now. And knew it with absolute certainty. In one sense, it had happened already. She did not know what power she had to alter things. She only knew that she had been handed a responsibility. She must go instantly, and warn him. The past had no place in her decision. She did not care for him, but still she could not let him die.

She reached for her clothes.

'Where are you going?'

Théo had woken up.

But she did not stop dressing.

'I have to warn him.'

'Who?'

'Montoya.' She spoke with some impatience. This was no time for words.

She had never told Théo about her dreams. They had vanished the moment that he made love to her and it would have been difficult to talk to him of something that was no longer there. It would have been like accusing him of theft. And besides, he was such a rational man. He was too rational, for instance, to believe in God. Such mysteries were for women; men had science. What point would there have been in telling him of premonitions? He would only have presented her with a series of facts and arguments to explain what she had experienced. It was too exhausting even to contemplate.

She was opening her wardrobe to choose a dress when Théo took her by the arm.

'Just think,' he said. 'Think for a moment.'

'There's nothing to think about,' she said.

He was trying not to raise his voice. His seemingly bottomless patience had the look of weariness. 'The town is not safe. There are people wandering the streets, looking for revenge.'

'Exactly,' she said. 'That's exactly why I have to go.'

As she lifted a dress from the wardrobe he reached round and snatched it from her hands.

'You're not going anywhere, Suzanne.'

He stood in front of her with his head lowered, like a bull that might charge. She could not believe his stubbornness, his stupidity. He could not see for reasons. Facts had blinded him.

She threw herself at him, fighting to reclaim the dress. He held it away from her, used his other hand to keep her at bay. He was too strong for her. She rushed towards the bedroom door instead. She would cross town in her lace petticoats if need be. But he seized her by the wrist as she ran past him and her arm almost leapt from its socket. She cried out in pain.

'Be quiet,' he said. 'Do you want everyone to hear?'

She twisted in his grasp. 'Let me go.'

He pinned her to the bed, bruising her slender muscles along the inside of her arms. He placed a hand over her mouth.

'You're hysterical.'

She tried to shake her head, deny it, but his hand was pressed so hard against her mouth that she could not use the lower half of her face at all.

'You're making a fool of yourself. And of me.' The skin below his eyes had sagged. He was ageing. It no longer had the power to move her.

'You're not going to see Montoya, or anyone else. You're staying here, in this house.' He shook her to make sure that she was listening. 'You're not leaving. You're staying here. Do you understand?'

But he's in my dreams, she wanted to shout. He's dying in my dreams. She tried to force the words out through her eyes, but he only pressed down harder with his hand.

12

Mama Vum Buá cooked Wilson some breakfast as usual, but she would not speak to him. Her blue eyes seemed clouded and remote. He thought she must be in mourning for her people. They had died in a land that was foreign to them, a land with no rivers and no mercy: it had leaned on their spines until they snapped; it had climbed into their mouths and nostrils; it had killed them itself. He did not try to reach down into her grief. It was not his place. Besides, he had his own to deal with. Trivial beside hers, but there nonetheless. His crystals had been taken. They were gone, every one of them. He had nothing to give Suzanne. He ate his tortillas in the shade of the quince tree, content to be left alone.

It did not last long. The girls soon came clustering around his table. The Señora had warned them not to leave the property that day, and they were bored.

'Tell us something,' First, the tallest, said.

Wilson pushed his plate away. He sipped at his coffee, then wiped his moustache. 'You know, it's funny,' he said, 'but I do happen to have a story for you this morning.'

'Tell us,' First said.

'Yes,' the others clamoured, 'tell us.'

He leaned back in his chair, hands folded on his waistcoat. 'Once upon a time,' he began, 'there was a very beautiful woman. She had green eyes that were as green as the leaves on trees and lips that only the most beautiful words came out of and hair that was long,' and he hesitated for a moment, 'and black. The beautiful woman lived in a big house, high up on a hill, and she was married to a man who was very important. The man built buildings for the king. All sorts of buildings. Palaces, mansions. Churches too.'

Wilson looked up. The girls clung to the edge of the table, their eyes wide and solemn.

'The beautiful woman and the important man did not want for

anything,' he went on. 'They ate the best food in the land and drank the best wine. They had servants to wait on them, hand and foot. They slept in sheets that smelled like the grass in summer. They had gold too – plenty of it. But the beautiful woman wasn't happy – '

'Why wasn't she happy?' First asked.

'Because her husband didn't love her,' Wilson said. 'He was too busy. He never bought her presents or told her she was beautiful. In fact, he was so busy, he hardly even noticed her at all. All he could think of were his palaces, his mansions and his churches.'

Wilson drained the last of his coffee and emptied the bitter grounds on to the dirt.

'Well,' he went on, 'the beautiful woman didn't know what to do. Her eyes that were as green as leaves began to turn brown, like leaves when they're about to fall. The words that came out of her lips were no longer beautiful. Mostly no words came out of her lips at all, just silence. She was so unhappy and so bored that she almost wished that she was dead.' Wilson leaned forwards, over the table. 'Then, one day,' he said, 'she met a man – '

'Was he a prince?' First asked. She was standing beside him now, one hand on his shoulder.

Wilson smiled. 'No. He was a poor man. He lived in the valley, at the bottom of the hill. He was a poor man, but he was good. And, as time passed, the beautiful woman and the poor man became friends. They told each other stories. They talked and joked and laughed. And slowly the beautiful woman found a little of the happiness that she had lost. And slowly the poor man fell in love with her. He fell in love with her eyes that were green again, green as the leaves on trees in summer, and he fell in love with her hair that was long and yellow – '

'Black,' First said. 'It was black.'

'Yes, black,' Wilson said. 'Her long black hair. And he fell in love with her lips that only the most beautiful words came out of. But she didn't fall in love with him – '

He faltered. Sometimes, riding on the prairies, you saw a storm coming towards you. There was that feeling of the world closing down in front of you, a kind of blindness. Strange, because you could see the blindness coming. That was the feeling he had now.

'She didn't fall in love with the poor man because she was still in love with her husband,' he went on slowly. 'She loved her husband, even though he was never there – ' He paused again, thinking hard.

'Maybe that made her love him more,' he said, half to himself. 'Because she missed him so. Because he wasn't there – '

The story was closing down in front of him. There was nothing he could do. He struggled on.

'Now it was the poor man who became unhappy, the poor man who sometimes wished that he was dead – ' Wilson looked round at the girls. Their faces offered up to him, bowls to collect the story in, and held perfectly still so as not to miss a drop. His mouth opened, closed again. He shifted in his chair.

'Then what happened?' First said.

He stared into the sky above their heads. 'That's the end.'

'What?' Second shouted.

'That can't be the end,' First said calmly. 'Someone's got to live happily ever after.'

'How does it end?' Second was shouting.

Wilson sighed. 'I don't know.'

Under the table Eighth began to cry.

'I'm sorry,' Wilson said.

He knew how they felt. He found it hard to accept the fact that there was no more story. Like them, he wanted to believe that it would have an end, and that the end would be a happy one. He turned his tin mug on the table, trying to imagine it. He could not.

The story had got him nowhere. All he had realised was that his life was not a fairy-tale. Maybe no one's was.

Eighth was still whimpering beneath the table.

At last the girls drifted away, scuffing at the dirt with their bare feet and muttering among themselves.

Towards eleven Wilson left Mama Vum Buá's place and set out along the waterfront. A boat from San Pedro was unloading a cargo of mine timber. He watched a log swing through the air and down into a nearby railway truck. Minutes passed and yet he did not move. Another log swung down. Some of the girls' disappointment had stayed with him; he could not shake it. The day seemed spoiled now.

As he turned to cross Avenida del Mar he found his passage blocked by a procession. Five bodies lay in the back of a flatbed cart, with their arms folded on their chests. Their eyes had been left uncovered. Their eyes, wide open, stared up into the sky. The dead men's families walked behind the cart. The women had cut all their hair off and painted their skulls and faces white. They were naked but for skirts of flax. Behind them came the other members of the tribe, people of every age. Wearing bits of rag and deerskin, they crept along the street in a kind of standing crouch and the sound that rose from their throats was anguished and repetitive, something like weeping, only without the tears. 'Hu – Hu – Hu – Hu.' They were beating their heads with stones. The blood was flowing down their cheeks, over their breasts and shoulders, down on to the ground. Each man and woman wore a mask and cloak of blood. In all his life Wilson did not think that he had witnessed anything more terrible than this quiet and determined mutilation. A hush had fallen on the town. Only the wheels of the death cart and the shuffle of bare feet and the weeping with no tears. It was a long time before he could bring himself to cross the street.

He walked slowly in the direction of the bakery. Up Avenida Cobre, past the Plaza Constitución. Though it was morning, he could see no smoke rising from Jesús's roof. He peered in through the doorway. Jesús and Pablo were sitting side by side, like two people who had lived out their allotted years and were now waiting, infinitely tired and resigned, for that one final event. Jesús slouched on a flour sack, the heel of one hand pushed into his cheek so the flesh rumpled. His free hand dangled, as if it had been snapped at the wrist and was now useless. Pablo was staring at the ceiling with dull unblinking eyes. His hands rested in his lap, one thumb tapping sporadically against the other.

Wilson took a seat opposite the two men. The bakery felt cooler than usual and he could see why. The oven door stood open on its hinges. No fires burned inside, no heat pushed out into the room; just ashes. It looked as if no baking had been done for centuries. The air did not even smell of bread.

'I came here to be cheered up,' he said eventually.

Pablo snorted. 'You came to the wrong place.'

'I don't think there's a right place,' Wilson said, 'not today.'

There was a silence.

Jesús sat up, folded his arms and sighed. All traces of flour seemed to have been removed from him. No white rims to his fingernails, no white cracks on his knuckles. His hands were hands, not ghosts. But this was death for Jesús, not life.

'Not baking today?' Wilson asked him.

Jesús sighed again. 'You know that wheat flour I use?'

Wilson nodded.

'Usually it's shipped over from the mainland every week. But what with all this trouble, shipments have been cancelled. No shipment, no flour. No flour, no bread.'

'What are you going to do?'

'There's nothing I can do,' Jesús said, 'not until it all blows over. And I was this close,' he added, lifting a hand and narrowing the gap between his finger and thumb to a fraction of an inch. He leaned on his knees and stared down at the floor. 'It's no time to be running a bakery, that's for sure.'

'Or a bar,' said Pablo.

There was another silence, still more gloomy than the last.

'I saw the funeral procession,' Wilson said.

Pablo lowered his eyes from the ceiling. 'Beating themselves with stones?'

Wilson nodded.

'They always do that,' Pablo said.

Ever since the accident, he went on, the town had been running a kind of fever. And, as with any fever, there had been periods of delirium. An Indian girl who lived just up the street had been vomiting clay. Her parents claimed to have found grains of copper in her vomit. There was also, he announced, with a grim smile, the possibility of a volcanic eruption. Sparks had been seen rising from the main crater of Volcan las Tres Vírgenes. That had not happened for more than thirty years. Meanwhile, in the shanty town at the back of El Pueblo, a woman had given birth to a child that had no eyes. 'At a time like this,' the mother had been heard to say, 'maybe it is better not to see.' And, as if the five deaths were not enough, there was Montoya's provocative announcement. Which, though it had been issued privately, seemed to have found its way into every shop and bar in town.

'I'm almost ashamed to be a Mexican,' Jesús declared.

'The man's insane.' Pablo crossed his legs and rested one elbow on his knee. 'That's the trouble with the Government, though. Díaz has sold out. If you're foreign, they'll do anything for you. If you're just plain Mexican, forget it – unless you come from some rich family, that is. No wonder people've started calling him Perfidio. Shoot them down like dogs!' He shook his head. 'You're right, Jesús. It's not a good time to be a Mexican.'

'Mind you, I wouldn't like to be French either,' Jesús said, 'not at the moment.'

Pablo spoke to Wilson. 'That reminds me. Somone left a message for you the other day.'

'A message? Who?'

'That Frenchwoman. The blonde.'

Wilson's heart turned a somersault.

'You know,' Pablo said. 'The wife of the man who's building the church.'

'What did she say?'

A slow smile changed the shape of Pablo's face. 'She said she wanted to see you. It was urgent. She said she missed you.'

'Is that all?'

'Isn't that enough?'

'When was this?'

'I don't know,' Pablo said. 'Last Friday. No, it must have been the Friday before.'

'But that's almost two weeks ago. Why didn't you tell me?'

'You weren't here.'

'I've been back since Wednesday – '

Pablo shrugged. 'It was so long ago. I just forgot. And besides,' he said, 'a lot's been happening.'

Wilson stood up. His promise to look after her. That dream about her talking to him in the street. His visit to the house, and then not entering. *She said she missed you.* He paced the bakery floor, his heart still jumping. Two weeks ago. Two weeks. He sat down. Stood up again.

Pablo had been following his movements with some interest. Now he turned to Jesús. 'Do you remember the night Wilson left town? The night he got drunk?'

Jesús nodded.

'You remember we were wondering about a woman?'

'What about it?'

'Well,' and Pablo leaned against the wall and smiled the same slow smile, 'I think we just had a breakthrough.'

Stalls and tents had been set up outside the houses. Sprigs of amaranth hung upside-down from the eaves; glass lanterns housing hand-rolled tallow candles swung from poles. There were fortune-tellers and knife-grinders. There were women selling strips of fried meat, maize tortillas, bowls of beans. There were games of chance. The air had a roasted smell. El Pueblo, on a Saturday.

Wilson paused to watch an Indian healer. A sick woman sat on a stool, her hands braced on her knees, her eyes blank and glassy. First the healer blew into her face through a short tube. Then he danced in front of her, muttering a chant. Finally he reached up with a sharp stick and cut into her forehead. Wilson turned away before it was clear whether or not the cure had worked. He had seen enough blood spilled for one day.

A few yards further on, a woman clutched at his sleeve. One hand curled beneath his chin, words spluttering and gushing through her few remaining teeth like water forced through rocks. He understood that she was selling potions that would instil courage and resolution. When she realised these qualities did not interest him particularly, she told him that she could save his teeth. His hair too; his virility. She could stop him growing old. She could help him fall in love.

He shook himself free. 'I don't need that.'

In truth, he did not know what he needed. He was aware only that he was moving from one distraction to another. Nothing was being resolved. Maybe he should have asked her for a potion that would put his mind to sleep.

As the light began to fade, he allowed himself to be caught up in the mass of Indians who were making their way towards the main square. Monsieur de Romblay was due to speak at six o'clock. Nobody knew what to expect. The mood of the crowd was a blend of anger, grief and curiosity. Wilson could not believe the sheer weight of numbers in the streets. Then he remembered that Pablo had spoken of people coming into town from further up the coast, from settlements inland – from all around, in fact. Disasters were magnets: people were always drawn in their direction.

By the time the crowd delivered Wilson to the edge of the Plaza Constitución, it was almost dark. A clear night, no moon yet. Stars the size of snowflakes. Boys perched in the branches of the plane trees, whistling to one another, trading information and insults, their voices hoarse as crows. The square had filled with men. Some were drunk already, and staggering. They wore machetes slung at an angle through their belts or dangling flush against their thighs. They were drinking from clear bottles whose contents Wilson was all too familiar with. The previous night there had been an outbreak of rioting in El Pueblo. In order to save his bar from destruction, Pablo had been forced to hand out more than fifty pints of liquor free of charge. The only surprise was that the Indians still had any left. Scanning the faces,

Wilson noticed an almost total absence of women. He thought this an ominous sign.

A murmuring, and heads began to turn. Feet stamped on the baked ground. Monsieur de Romblay was entering the square in his director's carriage, his face, in profile, gliding smoothly above the dark heads of the crowd. He had a driver, and another man sat next to him, an Indian, but otherwise he was alone. No military escort, nothing provocative.

He climbed out of his carriage, vanishing below the surface of the crowd, seeming to drown for a moment, and then emerged again, and mounted the steep staircase to the bandstand. He held up his hands in an appeal for silence. The Indian stood beside him, darting glances at his face. The noise died down. An uneasy quiet took its place.

Monsieur de Romblay produced a sheet of paper from his pocket and unfolded it. He cleared his throat.

'*Señoras y Señores –* '

A chuckling. There were no ladies present.

At least the Director was speaking in a language that most could understand, though. He might make a fool of himself, but, equally, he might win some respect.

Now the Indian had taken over. He was an interpreter. Each time Monsieur de Romblay completed a sentence in Spanish, the Indian repeated it in dialect. This was sound diplomacy. Though restless, the crowd was listening.

Monsieur de Romblay was appealing to the Indians' good sense. He regretted from the bottom of his heart the recent tragedy and suggested that the suffering should be shared by all the people of the town, irrespective of race or colour. The French doctor and his nursing staff, each one an expert in their field, were working round the clock to make the wounded comfortable.

'What about the dead?' an Indian shouted. 'Are you making them comfortable too?'

There was a ripple of bitter laughter.

But Monsieur de Romblay did not acknowledge the interruption. It was possible he had not heard. He declared that the families concerned would all be compensated for their tragic losses. He promised an immediate review of the safety regulations and a pay rise in the near future. Here he paused and looked up, almost as if he were expecting some applause.

'The near future?' snarled the Indian. 'When's that?'

Monsieur de Romblay continued, unperturbed. He urged the Indians to show forbearance, to keep calm. Hot tempers had never achieved anything constructive.

'And while I am on the subject of hot tempers,' he said, 'I would like to apologise for the behaviour of Captain Montoya – '

He got no further.

A rocket fizzed across the square and, tangling with a plane tree, seemed to wrestle with the leaves. Sparks dripped on to the heads of Indians beneath. The crowd parted and swirled in two directions. Someone lit a firecracker. Monsieur de Romblay ducked, his hands thrown up around his head. There were screams. A machete flashed through the air like a piece of lightning. Wilson turned one shoulder sideways and tried to ease back through the crowd. But people were surging forwards now. He saw the bandstand railing buckle. The Indians were chanting slogans in which the only words that could be distinguished were 'Montoya' and 'French'. Monsier de Romblay withdrew to the Mesa del Norte in a flurry of promises and pleas, most of which went unheard.

Wilson found himself on the south side of the square. He walked down Avenida Aljez and then turned left into an unlit side-street that led to Avenida Cobre. It was not clear whether the Indians had misunderstood Monsieur de Romblay's apology, or whether they had simply run out of patience. Probably he had not been wise to mention Montoya's name. It was a pity. It had not been a bad speech up until that point. But now Wilson could foresee another night of looting.

Something struck him on the back. He turned round. A rock lay at his feet. He looked up into the hostile faces of half a dozen Indians. He could not be sure that they were miners, and that worried him. They looked more like Indians from further north. It was a dark street. There was too much space around him. He could hear the knife-grinder's cry: 'Sharpen your blades, sharpen your blades.'

One man stepped forwards, a spade resting on his shoulder.

'You shouldn't ought to be in this part of town,' he said softly. 'You should be up on the Mesa del Norte.'

'Yeah,' came a second voice. 'What are you doing down here?'

'I live down here,' Wilson said.

The man with the spade shook his head slowly. 'French don't live down here.'

'I'm not French.' Wilson was balancing himself. Trying to pick the right moment to run for it. Their words were like a fuse that had just been lit. The explosion would come. No amount of talking could change that.

'Not French?' said the man with the spade. 'What are you then?'

'American.'

'Like fuck.'

'There's no Americans here,' came a second voice.

'They're all in America,' came a third, 'where they belong.'

The man with the spade tilted his chin towards his shoulder. 'Shut up.' The chin swung back. 'You're French, you are. I can tell.' Again the chin tilted. 'What is he?'

'French,' came the shout.

But Wilson was already running.

He had to lose them, and that would not be easy. On Calle 5 he burst through a gathering of miners. They split apart like fruit. They watched him go. He turned down Avenida Manganeso. He knew that he could not expect any help. Nobody helps a running man. A running man is always guilty. His foot hurt. He came round a corner, saw the church. In there, maybe. He ducked through the side door. But they had thought of it. Before he could hide, they were in front of him. Behind him, too. He tipped his head back on his neck, trying to regain his breath. The spit had thickened in his throat. His clothes stuck to his skin. He could taste blood.

He was surrounded by armed men. Some had picked up iron bars and bits of scrap metal from outside. One had a cross. The man with the spade still had the spade.

He could see the night sky through the open windows.

'This is a church.' He felt he had to point it out. But it brought him back from the stars' cool sanctuary. His heart was trying to elbow its way through the clutter of his ribs.

'So what,' somebody said.

'It's a holy place. Nothing bad can happen here.' Thinking he might vomit he had to squat down, hang his head. He heard somebody spit.

'We don't believe in that.'

They would not listen to a word he said. He was French. He was done for. A dog groaned and sidled out.

'Besides,' said the man with the spade, 'it's not even finished yet.'

Laughter rebounded off the walls. The man with the spade was right. It wasn't finished. Wasn't holy yet. It could prevent nothing. The spade lifted high into the unconsecrated air.

'Wait.'

The voice had come from somewhere further out. The voice of the night sky. The stars had intervened.

An Indian broke the circle of men. Wilson could not see his face.

'This man isn't French.'

'What is he, then?' the man with the spade said.

'American.'

A murmuring began. The new voice had authority. Doubt had been planted.

'He's the one who went with that whore and then her house fell down. Remember?'

The man with the spade was thinking.

'I remember,' somebody behind him said. 'He was walking around with a broken foot. It had a rose on it.'

'That's the one. He's got nothing to do with this. He's not part of it.'

The murmuring grew. Some men shuffled in the dust, shamed by the weapons in their hands. Some had already thrown them down.

Wilson felt the ground beneath his hands, how smooth it was, how even. It had been levelled off, ready to receive the tiles. Then the altar would arrive. Then a lectern, rows of pews. There would be order, worship – peace. He could feel the sweat cooling on his forehead, on his clothes.

He sat on the floor of the unfinished church and gave thanks to that old inability of his to hold his drink. He paid tribute to Pablo, who had supplied the liquor, and to the pair of Seri Indians who had drunk him into oblivion. He sang quiet praises to the Bony One, the rottenness of the wood throughout her house, the weakness, in particular, of her balcony. He applauded the vices of gambling, intemperance and fornication. He owed his life to them.

When he looked up, he saw the Indians moving away across an almost empty square. He heard somebody crack a joke about the church not lasting long if that American stayed inside. He heard the laughter that came after. He began to smile. He had just identified the Indian who had spoken up for him. It was the epileptic from the bar. The man whose tongue he had freed.

He sat on the ground and smiled, and the dog that had slunk out earlier returned and, settling down beside him, rested its nose between its paws, sighed once and went to sleep.

13

At long last there was the illusion of a breeze.

Suzanne was riding up into the silence of the mountains. The town lay behind her, sprawling in a bowl of dust. A ship's horn called from the harbour, but she shut her ears to the sound. She would only listen to herself from now on; she was done with any other kind of listening. The horse's hoofs clinked on the stones; a cactus sent a thin green scent into the air. She was receiving everything around her with such clarity. That house had clouded her. Thoughts had snapped off like the tails of lizards in those airless, silk-lined rooms. Thoughts had dehydrated on the hot wooden floors.

It hurt to hold the reins. She looked down at her hands. She had bruised the knuckle at the base of her thumb, and her palms were flecked with splinters, all angled the same way, like rain on window-glass. One of her fingernails had torn; it was still attached, but only by a hinge. Théo had locked her in the bedroom. It was hard to believe that it had happened; it seemed so crude. But the pain in her hands kept reminding her that it was true. He had stood on the other side of a locked door and pleaded with her through the wood.

'It's for your own good.'

But it was not her own good that she was thinking of. That was the whole point.

'Open the door, Théo.'

'I had to do something. You were hysterical. You wouldn't listen to me.'

'Just open the door.'

'Not until you've calmed down. I told you, it's dangerous outside. You could get killed.'

He did not even have the courage to talk to her face to face. He had to keep a door between them. He was weak.

As she stood in the room that morning, no longer speaking, she had remembered the day that she had spent on the water with Wilson Pharaoh and the fisherman. With the village of San Bruno on the port bow, Wilson had told her about a tribe of female warriors who were said to have inhabited the peninsula long ago. They had lived according to one simple, brutal philosophy: the power of life belonged to women alone. Men had not been given the power, and were envious. They coveted it, assaulted it, corrupted it. They were a force for destruction, and should be treated as such. The women would capture men, but for one purpose only: to breed from them. Afterwards the men would be put to death. In legend the women were believed to be giants, a tribe of Amazons, though there was no evidence to support this. In fact, Wilson had said, laughing, there was no proof that they had ever existed at all. They might simply have been a nightmare in the minds of men.

'Suzanne?'

Her silence must have disconcerted Théo, but she would not speak to him. A door between them, closed by him, the key in the keyhole turned by him. He was a jailer and a coward. Something else that Wilson had said came back to her. It was about the Indians who now inhabited the peninsula, whose existence could not be disputed. Apparently they had no understanding of the concept of marriage. They did not have a word for 'to marry' – or even a word for 'jealousy', for that matter. They had the word 'husband', he told her, but it referred to any man who was known to have abused a woman. She heard Théo sigh, then turn and walk away. She heard the stairs creak. She saw the key, one shining object at the bottom of his pocket, as if she had a jackdaw's eye. A jailer and a coward. He would never touch her again. The decision was like a bright weight dropping through her brain.

She must have fought the door for an hour. She wrestled with the handle; she shoved and pummelled at the panels. The wood resisted her. She cut her thumb on an uneven hinge and it was so hot in the bedroom that her blood dropped all over the floor. It would not stop. She crossed to the dressing-table and bound the wound in a clean handkerchief, then she pulled the carpet over the blood that led like a trail through the room. And, bending down, straightening a corner, heard footsteps in the corridor. Not Théo's, though. Softer than Théo's. More tentative.

'Imelda? Is that you?'

'Yes, Madame.'

'Could you open the door?'

'I can't, Madame. I have no key.'

'There's only one key?'

'Yes.'

She turned away from the door. It had lost its function; it might just as well have been a wall. The window was her only hope. She removed the screen. Outside, it was another identical morning. A view of rocks – some brown, some ochre. A view of sea, all tight and pale. She could smell engine-oil, fish-blood, anchor-chains. Her marriage was over. The love that had bound them had dissolved. Their house no longer had a soul.

Hands on the windowsill, she peered down. Below her was a slanting roof of tin. If she could drop down and somehow keep from slipping, she would be halfway to the ground. She sat side-saddle on the sill, and then let go.

Her heels skidded; she lost her balance. She landed on her hip, began to roll. But the pitch of the roof was shallow. She dug her fingers between two sheets of corrugated tin and held on. In the silence that followed she could hear the roof adjusting to her presence.

She sat still, trying to rehearse her next move. There were three wooden stanchions supporting the veranda on this side of the house, she remembered, each stanchion shaped like a Y. She would have to crawl or slide backwards and then feel for the place where the stanchion joined the roof. If she could just win a foothold in the crook of a Y, then she would be able to ease herself over the edge and climb down the stanchion to the wooden rail where the carpets were hung out to air.

In a few moments it was accomplished. She had not been seen, nor had she done herself any further damage. She stood on the pale-green boards of the veranda, jasmine twisting up the wall behind her. Her mind emptied suddenly and she glanced down. The front of her dress was smeared with rust; the white satin had an odd, scorched look, as if it had been held too close to a fire. She realised she could not risk the street; if anybody saw her like this, she would be locked up again – and probably in the hospital this time. And the path that led along the backs of the houses would be no safer: Florestine Bardou spent part of every morning on her back porch, creating yet another waistcoat for her husband. There was only one direction open to her, and that was down the slope, towards the company offices and workshops.

She left the veranda by the kitchen stairs and, lifting her skirts an inch, began to pick her way down the barren hillside. The sun leaned on her bare head. At one point she heard voices, and had to hide behind a rock. Four Indians passed within a few feet of her. One of them wore a beret. She had seen him the day before, leading the march up Avenida Cobre. They seemed to be pointing at the doctor's house. They did not notice her.

At the bottom of the slope she slipped through a wire fence and into the alleyway between two buildings. The sudden shade was like a benediction. She stood against a wall and looked around. Pools of oil shimmered. Broken cement-blocks lay in heaps. She had to try not to think about her hands. How much they hurt her. How she was carrying bits of the house in her skin. The wall trembled at her back. She found a window and, peering into the building, watched fire arc downwards through the gloom. The molten copper flowed from a ladle near the roof into a huge cylindrical drum. She saw Pierre Morlaix standing below. His silver hair marked him out. It was then that she realised the extent of her own visibility, dressed in white silk, soiled though it was. She hurried down the alleyway. Behind her, she heard the drum begin to turn.

She crossed a factory yard and hid in the gap between a warehouse and a stack of railway sleepers. All in all the circumstances favoured her. With the Indians on strike, there would be fewer people about. Less chance of being seen. She edged past a padlocked door and, rounding the corner, found herself in a passage that led between two high walls of blackened brick. And there, at the far end of the passage, bleached by the sunlight, was the piece of luck she needed. Bleached to the colour of a ghost, but real enough. A horse.

She moved towards the horse – slowly, so as not to startle it. Its head swung in her direction, curious. She recognised it now. All black, with two white fetlocks and a white blaze on its forehead. It belonged to Monsieur de Romblay. She even knew its name.

'Normandy,' she whispered.

She pushed one hand against the sleek muscles in its neck.

'There, Normandy, there,' she whispered as she untied the loosely knotted reins. Still whispering the horse's name, she fitted one foot into the stirrups and eased up into the saddle.

She rode through the gates and out on to the cinder track that ran between the office buildings and the sea. Nobody called after her. Nobody had noticed. She had not liked taking the Director's horse, but it could not be helped. And he would thank her later.

Her first idea had been to ride to Captain Montoya's house and warn him. But that would have been a mistake, she realised, a terrible mistake. It would be far better to ride in the opposite direction. To put as much distance as possible between herself and the event. For she now believed that it could not happen if she were not watching. Without her, the table could not be raised against that cairn of stones. Without her, the naked women could not dance.

This new belief had come from nowhere, with the force of a revelation. Her dream's appendix. Ride away from the town; ride up into the hills. It was the only way to save his life.

14

Back in his hotel room Wilson sat with his boots on the table and his guitar cradled in his hands. He had decided to put the finishing touches to that song of his. It would complement her message to him, which he had got so late. It would be the tune of their reunion.

He was still tinkering with the first two lines when somebody rapped on the door. He jumped so hard, his thumb caught in the strings. An edgy, chaotic chord. He put the guitar down and reached for his shovel. If it was Indians again, they'd be in for a surprise this time. The same went for those half-brothers of the Bony One. The blade's edge had a blunt grin where he had cleaned the dirt away; the steel gleamed. It was rapidly becoming a traditional weapon in town. But it would do the job, no question. He had seen men killed with far less elegance.

'Who is it?' he called out.

He stood to one side of the door with the shovel raised.

'It is I. Monsieur Valence.'

'One moment.'

He leaned the shovel against the wall and, looping his suspenders over his shoulders, tucked his shirt into the waistband of his pants. What could the Frenchman want? It must be urgent, for him to venture down into El Pueblo on such a night. He opened the door. Valence peered through the gap.

'I'm sorry to intrude on you.'

Wilson held the door open. 'Come on in.'

Showing Valence to a chair by the window, he was momentarily embarrassed by the poverty of his surroundings.

'You're taking a big risk coming here,' he said. 'I was almost lynched tonight.'

Valence sat with a straight back, both hands balanced on the carved head of his cane. He had the stillness, the solidity, of a piece of furniture. A dresser, maybe, or a chest of drawers. A place where things were tidy, ordered, stored. And yet Wilson had the feeling, looking at the man, that if he slid a drawer open, any drawer, then chaos would be revealed. Moths. A nest of mice.

'You have a nice view of the church,' Valence said.

Then he fell quiet again.

'Is there something I can do for you?' Wilson asked eventually.

Valence began to tell him about a priest who had visited the site during the first days of construction. The priest had delivered a sermon to a gathering of Indian workers. Afterwards one of the Indians had approached the priest. The Indian was curious about the new building. He wanted to know what it was. 'It's a church,' the priest said. Then, so as to make himself quite clear, he added, 'A house of God.' 'A house of God?' The Indian looked puzzled. 'What does God want with a house?' The priest gazed at the Indian with an expression of kindly tolerance. 'It's a place where we can go and meet Him,' he explained. 'You too will be able to meet Him there.' The Indian's look of puzzlement remained. 'But I thought you said that God was everywhere.' There was a silence, then the priest suddenly remembered that he had an important engagement on the Mesa del Norte. If he did not leave immediately he would be late.

'It's not the first time the Indians have got the better of a priest,' Wilson said with a smile.

But Valence did not seem to have heard. He was still staring out of the window.

'Suzanne has disappeared,' he said.

'What?' Wilson was not sure that he had understood.

'My wife, Suzanne. She has disappeared.'

'When?'

'This morning.'

'Where did she go?'

'I have no idea.'

Both men were still, one sitting on the chair, the other standing over by the wall. There was the power and secrecy of this information between them now, binding them the way blood does. It was as if they had suddenly become fingers of the same hand.

Valence began to mutter in his own language. Wilson stepped forwards and put one hand on the Frenchman's shoulder.

Valence looked up. 'I'm sorry. You cannot understand.'

'Could she be somewhere in the town?'

'I don't know. She stole a horse.'

Wilson had to smile. His father may not have trusted green-eyed women, but he would surely have warmed to a green-eyed woman who could steal a horse.

'It is not a laughing matter, Monsieur.'

The Frenchman's eyes had mustered some hostility. Wilson chose to ignore it.

'If she stole a horse,' he said, 'she could be anywhere.'

She could be dead, he thought. Nobody rode out into that landscape without knowing its secrets and its dangers – even somebody who seemed blessed, like her. The heat of the sun, the dearth of water. There was no mercy in the land. It would kill you as soon as look at you.

'I thought perhaps,' and Valence was lifting his face again, in hope this time, in supplication, 'that you could find her.'

Wilson turned away.

Valence rose out of his chair. 'You understand the country. You know it.' His voice dropped, like someone taking cover. 'You are her friend.'

When Wilson did not reply, Valence spoke again. 'Am I wrong?'

'You're not wrong.'

'Then for the sake of friendship.' Valence spread his hands. 'You have to.'

Wilson shook his head. There was no avoiding her. It did not matter which way he turned. She was round every corner, at the end of every street. If she did not appear in person she appeared in what was being said. When he closed his eyes to keep her out, she stepped into his dreams.

'I'm not sure,' he said slowly, 'that you're in any position to make demands.'

'I don't follow you,' Valence said.

It was too late for Wilson to hold back now. 'If you had truly loved your wife,' he said, 'she would not have gone.'

The Frenchman's face tightened.

'What do you know about it?' he said.

'I know enough.'

The two men stared at each other without speaking. The silence thickened in the room.

Then Valence turned away, one hand thrust into his hair. 'She loved me first. I could never – ' He had walked into the corner of the room. He was facing the wall.

Wilson could not think of anything to say.

'If I loved her, she always loved me more. I wanted balance, equality. She would not allow it.'

Valence swung round. 'I knew she should not have come to Mexico with me. I knew that it would be difficult. But she insisted. She can be so strong.' He smiled. It was a hopeless, foolish smile, deformed by circumstance. It was not something that he could really permit himself. 'She said it was the place of a wife, that she should be with her husband.'

'And isn't it?'

Valence shrugged. 'It depends who you listen to.'

'Maybe you're the wrong man for her,' Wilson said.

'And who is the right man? You?' Valence was almost glacial. His confessions had given him strength.

'No.' Wilson looked round at his rented room, his few belongings. And had to chuckle. 'No,' he said, 'not me.'

And suddenly he found the way forwards. This was nothing to do with love. A man had come to him and asked for help. It did not matter which man, what help. He had no right to turn the man away.

'I'll need a mule. Mine's split her hoof.'

'You will do it?'

'Yes.'

'I will find a mule for you. Immediately.'

There was no reward for Wilson in the Frenchman's sudden animation, in his gratitude. If anything, it exhausted him.

'And provisions,' he added. 'I'll need food and water.'

Valence had one hand on the door, but then he saw that Wilson had not finished. 'Is there something more?'

Wilson occupied the centre of the room. 'I'm her friend. You know that. What you don't know is, I love her.' He saw that Valence was about to speak and raised a hand to silence him. 'It's all right. She doesn't know. I haven't told her and I don't intend to. She will never know.'

Valence had not flinched from Wilson's painful gaze, nor from the knowledge of his secret, but now he lowered his eyes. His voice, when he finally spoke, was soft as the dust that rolled along the bottom of the walls.

'You are also the wrong man?'

Wilson nodded slowly. 'Yes.'

'Come to the main office in two hours,' Valence said. 'I will be there, with everything you need.' He left the room, closing the door behind him.

Wilson sat down on the bed.

'But it's you she loves,' he said, 'and I'm not so sure that you deserve it.'

When he looked away from the door, she was standing in the corner of the room, next to the wooden frame that held the washing bowl. She had changed into another dress. There was nothing strange about that; it was another day, after all. He had not seen the dress before. It was geranium-red, with trimmings of black lace and black buttons at the cuffs.

'You didn't hear any of that,' he said.

She did not move except to reach up with one hand and push a curling strand of hair away from her forehead. Her eyes were paler than usual, chalky, almost grey, and her skin had such clarity, it was like shaped light.

'I'm not feeling too good,' he told her. 'I'm going to need your help.'

Still she did not move. Her hands were almost touching the sides of her dress. He could see the air between her fingers.

'You'll have to show me the way,' he said.

Then he lay down on his bed and slept.

15

It was long ago, somewhere in Paris. There were chestnut trees, their branches weighed down with pale blooms. She noticed the fragrance pausing at their table, then its absence as the wind blew. She watched her two hands taking one of his. His hand that could lift her trembling to the surface of her skin, then sink her deeper than she had ever been. And she could hear her voice.

'I love you, Théo. I really do.'

'Yes, yes.' His hand withdrew.

The strength of what she felt embarrassed him.

A gust of wind; the fragrance of the blossom gone.

There had only been a few who had not been impelled by her into some needless hostility or withdrawal, and she had thought him one of them – but he was not. There was Monsieur Épaules, if that was truly his name. She was always returning to him, perhaps because she had never been able to. That sense of life falling short, an incompleteness that would last for ever. She could see him climbing the stairs with his burden of water. Tilting in the silver pails, solid and opaque, like ancient coins or medals. And his secret vial on a cord inside his shirt. That bitter taste. That promise of a future.

But this was not a good time to be thinking of him.

'No,' she murmured, 'it is not a good time for that.'

She looked around. Orange boulders littered the ground. The air stood tall and still. She had no hat, no parasol. She had no water.

She pulled on the reins; the hoofs stopped. Flies settled on her face, the backs of her hands. She tore a square piece out of her skirt. Placing it over her head, she tied the two ends beneath her chin. A simple headscarf. It would afford her some relief. She had to keep going, though. Inland, always inland. Sooner or later she would reach the mission at San Ignacio. Sooner or later she would drink from the cool green waters of Kadakaamana. Two days' ride, she remembered. But how long had she been riding for already? She could not recall how many times the darkness had come down, or even if it had at all. She laid her hand against the horse's neck.

'I'm sorry, Normandy,' she whispered.

She shook the reins and they moved on. Through fields of boulders and cactus. Past trees with pale-green trunks and spindly branches of grey and amber. Towards the volcano. Its flanks of charcoal and violet, moulded like the muscles on the haunches of a lion. This was where the makings of her nerve remedy were gathered. Under whose influence her dream had been delivered in its entirety. Not what she would have called a peaceful night. No source of peace to her at all. Though still some distance off, the mountain rose so high, it made her feel giddy. She had to look away.

There came a time when she could only think of things that made her weep. Monsieur Épaules, alone in the darkness of the stairwell, his silver buckets empty. Théo with his back turned late at night. Wilson Pharaoh playing the piano in the rain, his fingers slipping on the keys. And her own two children, who had never even drawn a breath. Her first child, burned in a ragman's brazier at a crossroads in Les Halles. Her second, two inches long and lying on her palm. That seedling eye, those streaks of redness. No he, no she. Just something that had failed.

Her tears scalded her face.

And the brown pelican which flew so close to the water that its shadow almost touched its belly.

Her tears.

That barrenness inside had led her to believe that nothing could be changed, inside or out. His love was weak and hers would never be enough. Nothing between them could be sustained. Everything between them died.

Yet there was still the memory of setting sail from Le Havre. That crisp December morning, ice and sunlight gilding the handrail as she climbed aboard. It was her first time on a steamboat, unless you counted that trip down the river the summer before, when they had moored at the Pont du Jour and dined on fried gudgeon and the sour green wine of Surèsnes. The open sea delighted her. She had looked back on her life – the dances, the opera, the races – and wondered how it had been possible to breathe at all. She remembered taking Théo's arm. They stood on deck and watched the spray rise off the waves.

'So,' he said. 'You're happy now.'

She had laughed. The word did not do justice to her feelings. 'You were so selfish,' she said, 'to try and keep me from all this.'

It was not a reprimand, of course, but an expression of her elation and he had taken it as such, smiling down at her, moving his hand to cover hers, then lifting his eyes to the horizon and filling his lungs with clean, cold air.

Moving his hand to cover hers.

The sun stared into her eyes. The horizon duplicated itself in the heat like a stack of plates. From a distance the orange boulders looked as if they might all be the same size, but up close every single one was different.

'How can you bear it?' she had asked him recently, in the calmest voice that she could muster.

Théo glanced up from a list of the church's components. 'Bear what, my dear?'

'The fact that all the parts are the same. All perfectly identical. Every section the same length, every hole drilled to within a millimetre. Every time.'

He was smiling. Though she was attacking him she could see that he was flattered by her familiarity with his work.

'You're talking about perfection,' he said. 'If it's attained, it should be celebrated, admired. It's not something that you have to bear.' And he looked at her in that quizzical way he had, as if he suspected that she might be teasing him.

She raised her eyes from the coarse hairs of the horse's mane. The sky was one exhausting wash of light. She had tried thinking a woman's thoughts, which were always, it seemed to her, excuses or apologies: he has his work; he is making discoveries; he needs my understanding. But a cry had always risen up in her: Discover *me*. Perhaps she should have made small parcels of her love, been miserly with it. Perhaps she should only have offered it when it was wanted. Begged for. Earned. But how could she, with her feelings for him so generous inside her? You might as well tell trees not to blossom in the spring, a river not to flood its banks. You're talking about perfection, he had said. Was her love so imperfect, then?

There was a ridge ahead of her. She could not tell how far away it was, but it seemed to her that beyond it she would find the mission. She would pause on the crest of the ridge, her face bathed in the last soft light, and she would look down and there it would be. One hundred thousand palm trees. The cool green waters. Kadakaamana. There, as promised. What relief there would be in that still moment. What peace.

The horse stumbled, dropped its head. She could feel its bones stagger in its skin. She shook the reins with the little strength that she had left. She touched its flanks with the heels of her boots. She could hardly speak because her lips had turned to stone.

'Normandy,' she whispered. 'We're almost there.'

16

The party that had gathered outside the main office of the mining company to wish Wilson Pharaoh well was necessarily small, owing to the lateness of the hour and the pressure of events. Of the four people present, only Monsieur Castagnet appeared calm. Monsieur Valence paced up and down, the cinders crackling beneath his polished shoes. Madame Bardou stood close by, her face so drained of colour that her lips looked as dark as an invalid's. It was not just Suzanne's disappearance that had upset her. Late that afternoon the Bardous' house had been broken into, and more than a dozen of the doctor's waistcoats had gone missing. Clinging to Madame Bardou's arm, and flushed with the drama of the situation, was Madame de Romblay. As Wilson mounted the mule that Valence had commandeered, she spoke to him, her eyes dilated, almost gloating.

'I hear you were attacked.'

Wilson smiled grimly. 'They thought I was French.'

'My God,' she said, 'what will become of us?'

Madame Bardou's hand had risen to her throat. 'You're not hurt, I hope?'

'No, ma'am, not a scratch. But thank you for asking.'

Wilson leaned down to adjust a stirrup strap. It had been impossible to keep track of what was happening; reports varied wildly. He had been woken from his nap by the sound of hammering – not the church this time but Mexicans, nailing bits of wood over their windows. Towards midnight, as he crossed town to meet with Monsieur Valence, he ran into Pablo. Pablo was in his element, meddling with fact and fabricating rumour.

'The fat man,' he said, his eyebrows lifting high on to his forehead. 'The Director. Have you heard?'

'What about him?' Wilson said.

According to Pablo, Monsieur de Romblay had been taken ill as he left the Plaza Constitución that evening, and had been rushed to hospital. Then, as the doctor reached for his scalpel, Monsieur de Romblay exploded. Right there, on the operating table. A nurse was killed by flying organs. The doctor only survived because he was wearing a magic waistcoat, the one made out of sunlight and diamonds. There had been some trouble on the waterfront as well. The customs house had been looted, and someone had uncovered Ramón's secret stockpile. Not just ordinary goods like sugar and flour. Luxuries too, which must originally have been intended for the French. Silk pyjamas, for example. Goose-liver pâté. Armagnac. And then, less than an hour ago, two of the five dead miners had come back to life. They had been seen on Avenida Aljez, leaning casually against a tree, their hands and faces lit by soft green flames. What else? Oh yes –

'Don't tell me,' Wilson said. 'The Amazons are coming.'

Pablo held his hand out in the air. Wilson had to shake it.

'But seriously, Pablo.'

'Well,' Pablo said, 'there has been some rioting on Calle 14.'

This Wilson could believe. The Mexicans would not be boarding up their windows for nothing. If the French had any sense, they would do the same, despite the heat.

It was from Castagnet that Wilson learned of recent developments on the Mesa del Norte. In the wake of his abortive speech, Monsieur de Romblay (shaken, but in perfect health) had been trying to resolve all disputes in private conference. At one point during the proceedings Montoya had pulled his pistol from its holster and fired a bullet into the Director's dining-room ceiling. The bullet had passed through an electric wire and fused every light in the house. The three Indian spokesmen who were waiting in the hallway – they would not sit down at the same table as the Mexican – were plunged into darkness. One Indian claimed to have heard thunder. Another talked of an eclipse. Offerings of amaranth and crushed obsidian would have to be made at once, they said. To Coatlicué, to Humming-Bird-on-the-Left – and to Jesus Christ as well: in circumstances as mysterious as these, it was best to leave nobody out. De Romblay and Montoya had repaired to Castagnet's house and were believed to be close to reaching some kind of understanding. In the hospital across the road the doctor was performing surgery on an injured miner; amputation of the leg seemed likely. Of resurrected Indians and revelations at the customs house, Castagnet knew nothing. There was a sense in which Suzanne's disappearance could be seen as conforming to a pattern. It could have been truth or rumour. It was yet another symptom of the town's delirium.

Monsieur Valence coughed into his fist. 'You're quite sure that you will go alone?' he asked.

Wilson nodded. 'It's what I'm used to.'

Monsieur Castagnet stepped forwards, one hand on the reins. He stroked the mule's nose. 'Do you have everything you need?'

'Compared to what she has – ' Wilson did not finish the sentence.

'True,' Castagnet murmured.

'What I still cannot understand,' Madame de Romblay said, 'is why she stole my husband's horse in the first place. That horse is valuable. He paid more than a thousand francs for it.' She was looking at Monsieur Valence, as if she expected an explanation.

But Valence, deep in a turmoil of his own, had not noticed. 'I don't know how I'll sleep tonight,' he said.

Wilson smiled bleakly. Sleep did not seem a possibility for anyone.

Madame Bardou offered him her face once more. Her hair was curling in the humid air.

'Which direction will you take, Monsieur?'

He had given no thought to this at all and yet he found that he already knew the answer.

'I'll be heading inland,' he said. 'West.'

Five hours of darkness remained when he set off along the cinder track that led out past the lumber yard and the smelting plant. When he had passed the two brown trains he glanced behind him. The French were still standing outside the gates, four figures dwarfed by buildings and machinery. They looked like a fragile race, a race in danger of extinction. He found himself feeling a kind of pity for them as he rode on.

It was a moonless night, not at all the kind of night that he would have chosen for a journey through the awkward country of Cabo Vírgenes. In some places the coastal plain that divided the mountains from the sea was no wider than the track itself. To the left you passed canyon after canyon, reaching down from the mesa, high and waterless, behind. The land was only fertile in one respect: minerals had been found in such abundance that names could not be made up fast enough. It was here that the company had established many of its mines. To the right lay a gravel beach and waves that always sounded tired: *flop*-flop *flop*-flop *flop*-flop. An hour went by before he saw the turning that he had been looking for; it wound its way up into a district known as Soledad, and then climbed higher still, towards the pass that cut through the Peninsula Range. He breathed a sigh of relief. It was a narrow path and he might easily have missed it in the dark.

No sooner had he started up into the mountains than his worries began. The mule felt uncertain under him. She had been borrowed from the company. She would be used to pack work, the same routes every day; it was possible that she had never left the town before. He cursed himself for not having asked. The trail he was taking was the most direct. There were tight bends, steep slopes, sheer drops. It called for surefootedness and a steadfast disposition. But they were only just above sea-level, and already the mule was laying its ears back and looking to escape. That could be fatal in a country where the only sideways turn was likely to be over a precipice and down five hundred feet.

He went on for as long as he dared, stopping to make camp when the track widened to form an oval. It was dark as a hand of black cards, and there would be rock-falls ahead. He would rest here until the sun came up. Stepping out of the saddle, he hunted through his knapsack for a length of rope and tied the mule's forelegs together so she could not bolt. Then he poured some water into the crown of his hat and set it on the ground in front of her. She dipped her head and drank. Stars jostled in the sky between her ears.

He built a small fire, filled the kettle. While he waited for the water to boil he ate a few mouthfuls of jerked beef and followed it with some fresh dates which the doctor's wife had pressed into his hand. Later, he unpacked his bedroll and lay down, a cup of sugared tea heating a circle on his chest. Part of him knew that there was no time to waste and wanted to panic. Part of him cursed the mule. But he had to lock that part away. It would do Suzanne little good if he was killed before he got to her – and besides, it could not be more than a couple of hours until dawn.

The mule shifted sideways, almost tripped. He calmed her with his hand. Then he threw some brushwood on the fire, enough to keep the jackals away while he was sleeping.

Wilson peered into the distance, eyes screwed against the glare. The Volcan las Tres Vírgenes rose out of a monotonous plain. There was no sign of life, human or animal. The Vizcaíno Desert. A wilderness of thorns and stones. A place to try your faith.

'She is married, you know.'

Only yesterday afternoon he had been sitting in the Hotel La Playa with Pablo and Jesús. Pablo was making entries in the ledger. His hair, slick with pomade, shone white where the light ran over it. Jesús was testing the reflexes in his left knee with a failed baguette. The bread was stale, hard as wood; the knee was not responding. From time to time a vulture dropping landed with a soft slap on the lobby floor. The two Mexicans were teasing him about Suzanne.

'I know she's married,' Wilson said. 'In fact, I was the one who told you.'

'You Americans,' Jesús said.

'I've done nothing to be ashamed of,' Wilson said.

Pablo glanced up. 'I don't know. You Americans. No scruples.'

'You can't talk,' Wilson said, 'calling this place the Hotel La Playa.'

'What's wrong with Hotel La Playa? It's a nice name.'

'Yeah, it's a nice name,' Wilson said, 'but where's the beach?'

Pablo returned to his ledger. A couple of figures demanded his immediate and close attention.

'You're in the middle of the town,' Wilson said, 'and you call it Hotel La Playa. You're not even on the waterfront.'

'It's salesmanship,' Pablo said. 'You wouldn't understand.'

'Hotel La Playa?' Wilson said. 'There isn't a beach within five miles of here.'

Another vulture dropping slapped on to the floor.

'I must do something about a roof,' Pablo said.

Jesús shifted on his chair, anxious suddenly. 'What if the French find out?' he said. 'About you and the Señora?'

Wilson sighed. 'I told you. There's nothing in it.'

'They'll crucify him,' Pablo said, with relish. 'Absolutely crucify him.'

The mule dipped her head and began to snap at the shoots on a mesquite tree. Wilson let her eat. He had been travelling since dawn without a break. Two hours' sleep, and only his memory for entertainment. He had decided not to think about how to find Suzanne. He would just ride to San Ignacio, zigzag-fashion, so as to cover the widest possible area. He chose not to dwell on the fact that she did not know the way. There was a point at which he had to throw his lot in with everything that could not be counted on. It was nothing new for him. This journey put him in mind of other journeys. Leaving San

Francisco on foot to look for his father had seemed no less foolhardy, no less desperate. His mother standing on the corner of Piano Street, wrapped in a shawl against the April wind. 'Find the good-for-nothing. Bring him back.' With a country three thousand miles wide to choose from! But Constance Pharaoh knew her husband. He told lies that were remembered. He left a trail in people's heads. Out on the open road Wilson soon found women who wanted his father dead. Men who had laughed so hard, their faces were still marked with it months after.

Now he thought about it, he seemed to have spent his entire life on missions where the chances of success were so remote that he could not actually imagine it at all. And yet he had developed qualities along the way that had stood him in good stead: intuition, tenacity, patience too. *In patience wisdom can be found.* A Navajo scout had told him that, one winter in Zuñi. That man had taught him plenty. How to move from one part of yourself to another. How to listen to the part you chose and hush the rest. A bent nose and a turquoise amulet. A bottle of Taos lightning. A voice no louder than the desert wind. That was the most that he could summon of the man, and yet the lesson had never faded. Maybe because he had a picture of it. Maybe because he saw patience as a kind of ore and wisdom as the gold that it could yield. It was a good thing for him to know and to remember, seeing as how he was descended from a line of tense and brittle men.

It was late afternoon and he had ridden through the heat, twelve hours of it, when he thought he could see a white dress lying on the ground ahead of him.

He did not believe it.

It was what he wanted to see, and it was just like the land to conspire with his mind and fake it for him. It must be water, then. A puddle on the ground.

But out here?

His eyes swept tall cactus, orange rocks, the sheet glare of the sky. Returned. It was still there. A glimmer. A reflection.

It could not be her – surely. For one thing, it was too soon. For another, there was no sign of the horse.

As he drew closer, though, he saw the vultures. Then he knew for certain. They looked like smudges of black ink on the cactus spires. They looked like mistakes; they should not have been there. He dug his

heels deep into the mule's flanks and urged her forwards. The ground
was almost level here. She did not complain.

In one motion he jumped down and looped the reins around the
branch of an elephant tree. He swiftly gathered rocks and hurled them
at the vultures. They took off as if they were made of sticks and cloth.
They ambled away through the air on clumsy wings, indifferent to his
anger, untouched by it.

He dropped to his knees beside her. Opening the lid of his tobacco tin,
he held the shiny metal to her lips. The faintest smear of condensation
formed. Now he was inches away from her he could see a weak pulse
beating in her neck. He brought the water up to her mouth.

As he moistened her lips, her eyes opened. Rolled backwards, then
seemed to focus. He felt that she could see him.

'Suzanne?'

Her lips were scorched and split, dried blood in the ridges. But they
had moved a fraction. He bent down close to her.

'Who – ' Her voice cracked.

'It's me,' he said. 'Wilson.'

One of her hands curled in the dirt. Blood had blackened on her
thumb. He had never imagined that she could be so injured.

'You – '

'Slowly,' he said. 'Take it slow.'

His ear grazed her lips.

'You came – '

His eyes drifted, blurred.

Her face turned sideways; she was looking along the top of the ground.
'I had so much love in me,' she whispered, 'and no one wanted it.'

He lowered his head. His tears fell among hot cinders.

17

Suzanne could see a woman standing at the water's edge. The woman wore nothing but a skirt of black pearls. The water washed across her feet and then withdrew. The woman smiled. A slow smile, a smile with pure pleasure in it. She knew where the power of life ended and the power of death began. She had drawn the line.

Suzanne lifted an arm to wave but her hand stayed motionless in the air beside her ear. She did not call out, not yet. She just waited, knowing it would not be long.

Slowly. Take it slow.

Life, she comes from nowhere. Behind, above, below. Some place our eyes are not looking at. Death, she walks right up to us. We see her coming. Every step, every sway of the hips. Every inch of the way. Death, she wears a black pearl skirt.

Suzanne opened her eyes. Until she opened them she had not known that they were closed. It was like having a choice. Two worlds. One on this side, one on the other. Her eyelids were the border, were the door. The sky was darkest blue in front of her. Then something landed on her face and made her blink. Not pearls, though almost as miraculous.

Rain.

Beads of it dropping all over her skin, her dress, the ground. Some necklace had broken up above. And the sky still darkest blue, and not a cloud in it.

The woman turned her face and smiled in recognition. A smile that said, One of our own. Turned and walked towards her, wrists knocking against her hips, hips swaying lazily. That smile. A skirt that swayed and clicked. The power of life.

Her feet left no prints on the sand.

She was thirteen and running in the long grass. The woods outside the town. That green smell of rain on leaves, rain on the trunks of trees. That hard sound, as if the rain were solid – not water falling from the sky, but coins or buttons. God's purse, God's sewing basket. Her friend ran beside her, and everything bad had been undone. All life handed back, all the simple joys released. The rain poured off her arms and legs, and she looked down at herself, among green leaves, among black trunks of trees. She looked as if she had been polished. She looked like something valuable. To be treasured. Something that would last for ever.

Drink it up. All up. It will keep you strong.

A man kneeling beside her. She knew him. He lifted his hat to her and wiped his hand on his trousers before he greeted her. He had come to take her to the cool green waters. She smiled behind her lips. It could not be far now. They were almost there.

Everything settling, everything arranged. All movements gradually diminishing. Even the rain seemed to be touching her more gently now, like the light from distant stars.

Her husband, whom she would always love.

She wanted to say something about happiness, such happiness as she had known. Her lips moved, came as close to words as they could. Which was not even close. The air stood still in her throat. Her tongue not even there.

She blessed him in his absence. She blessed him. He had never been anything less than kind.

So. Are you happy now?

The sky was darkest blue in front of her. The black pearls sown and scattered on the land. This knowledge had been revealed to her. A knowledge that would grow in her. The knowledge of her power.

The woman walked towards her, hips shifting lazily. Somebody who wanted her.

One of our own.

18

The first rain in months. In years. And out of a clear heaven too. Wilson tipped his head back, felt it beat against his forehead, eyelids, teeth. He had heard that this could happen. A *chubasco*, they called it. Canyons became rivers. Coyotes drowned; whole settlements were swept away. And afterwards a spring would come. A spring that was momentary, improvised. The barren landscape bristled with shoots and blossoms. The desert would turn green. That was what they said. He had listened but he had never known quite what to believe. Maybe it was no more than a traveller's tale, the kind of lie his father used to tell.

But here it was, all round him. And not just drizzle either. Sheets of it between him and everything. Loud bucketfuls tumbling out of the sky. The mule had tipped her head to one side and she was snapping at the rain with her chipped teeth, the way a cat snaps at a blade of grass.

And then it stopped. As suddenly as it had started. The sky still clear above, the sky still blue. Before he had time to fill his canisters. Before he could even take his hat off and turn it upside-down. He listened to the land settling into its new shape. Creaking as the water ran over it and into it. It was already vanishing. Soon there would be no evidence that it had rained at all, and he would be another traveller with a tall tale.

He looked at Suzanne. Her face streaked with dust that had turned to mud, her blonde ringlets matted.

She was whispering something. He had to bend down, put his ear close to her mouth.

'Water – '

'You want some water?'

She shook her head. 'Green – '

'Green? Green what?' He bent still closer. His ear grazed her lips.

She tried to swallow. 'Green water – ' Her chin lifted. 'Ka – ' She could not say it. All those syllables. Then her voice found its way clear. 'You promised.'

He washed her face and neck with torn-off pieces of her own damp dress, then he threaded his hands beneath her body and carried her over to the mule. As he heaved her up into the saddle, her head fell back against his sleeve. He tried to coax a little water through her lips, but her throat was too swollen. It just spilled out again.

He climbed into the saddle in front of her. The mule staggered. He fitted his hand against the muscle of the mule's shoulder. Spoke a few words into her ear. When she had found her balance, he lashed Suzanne to his back with a length of rope that circled them three times. Then he placed her arms around his waist. He had to keep her from slipping sideways, falling to the ground.

She was still trying to say the name.

'It's all right,' he said. 'I heard you.'

'I understand,' he said.

He thought of the mission church, solid as the land itself, the masonry tinged with pink. He could remember sitting in the town square, beneath an Indian laurel tree. That huge vault of foliage. One of many men, just sitting. Relishing the shade. Father Lutz had offered him a pomegranate. 'It's from my garden.' He could still taste that fruit, its jewelled pieces sweetened by the volcanic soil in which it had grown. He had stayed in a whitewashed room. Stone floors, the walls bare, the furniture carved from some dark wood he did not know. At dusk he had walked among the palms, beside still waters. He remembered how it had felt to be there. His thoughts seemed blessed. His life became a psalm.

And there would be this advantage: he would not have to lie to her.

She sat behind him, her face turned sideways, one cheek resting between his shoulderblades. At last the sun was dropping through the sky. The heat bore down, a weight upon his head. The air so still that he constantly imagined movement. He was riding into his own tall shadow.

There were lava-fields now, shades of charcoal and maroon. Like raised roads, they curved towards him. This was where the elephant trees put down their roots. Perverse trees, to choose such desolation. Nothing else grew here. From a distance the lava looked smooth, but up close you saw that it was flakes of rock stacked tightly, pages in a book. And each flake sharp as glass; they could slice through boot leather, horses' hoofs. He let his eye climb towards the mother of the fields. Its slopes striped with lava stains. The shocked blue air above the crater's edge. The last time it erupted had been a century and a half ago. But the air did not forget.

Suzanne was murmuring into his back. He could not understand what she was saying. He supposed it must be French – though even English, in her condition, might not have been intelligible. He had a sudden picture of the inside of her head: a cage of brightly coloured birds, their wings cramped by the bars and weakening, folding around their bodies, as if they were cold. Delirium. There could be no other explanation for the insistent, soothing murmur of her voice. She could have been comforting a child.

Her head slipped sideways, knocked against his elbow. He had to reach behind him with one hand and heave her upright. During the next few hours this would become a habit. One of those habits that you don't remember later. But at the time it's the only thing you know.

The world was turning over. Sky, ground, sky.

He must have been dozing, chin on his chest. Moments above sleep, and moments just below. No clear dividing line. No sense of the difference. Then the rattle of shale and stones, and the mule disappearing from under him.

Blue, brown, blue. Brown. Blue.

He was lying next to Suzanne, tangled in rope, as if he had been delivered to her side by some clumsy angel. The sky had darkened; the day was burning low. He lay still, waiting for pain to start. But his head ached, and one knee. That was it.

He sat up.

'Suzanne? Are you all right?'

She had grazed her forehead in the fall. Blood slid from a gash above her eyebrow and sank into her hair. He took his shirt-tail, worked to staunch the flow.

They had been riding in the shadow of a wall of rock. To their left the ground dropped away, sharply in some places, to a valley hundreds of feet below. A sunlit plain, strewn with boulders. And, in the distance, mountains. A burnt colour, toasted. He looked up, tried to figure it. The track must have given way. A kind of landslide. But they had not fallen far. Ten feet, at the most. He could only think that the rain must have weakened the ground. Driven wedges into it. Cracked it as cold water cracks hot glass. They were lucky not to have fallen further. Not to have broken anything. There was no great subtlety about the way death reached for you sometimes. Take his father.

The mule was standing a few yards away. She seemed unharmed. Perplexed too, if a mule could know perplexity. It was in the angle of her jaw, somehow, the gap between her ears. He turned back to Suzanne. And it was then, still smiling at their luck, that he noticed the colour of the soil around her head. He sat quite motionless, all previous astonishment nothing compared to this.

Gold.

A lifetime of winters came tumbling through his memory, as if the rain had seeped down into his mind as well, as if the past itself were crumbling. All the hardships, all the disenchantments. You travelled by foot into unknown country. There were no roads, no guides. You had to carry everything you needed in your hands or on your back: food, clothes, tools. You slept with your head between two stones to cheat the arrows of Indians who might be on your trail. You woke before dawn, your threadbare blanket stiff with frost. You dug holes, washed earth. Pay-dirt, mostly. A diet of snakes and acorns. Unleavened bread that sank a weight in your belly but did not kill the hunger. Tea made from muddy stream-water or dew or melted snow. Loneliness, cold, disease. And so little to show for it. So very little in the way of reward. You felt like those pelican robes the Indians used to wear, Indians who lived on river estuaries, the Gila, the Colorado: feathers on the inside, blood facing out. Life that hard, feelings so raw; all the pain faced outwards. It was enough to break a man. More than enough.

And now this.

Some rain, a landslide; the work of a few moments. And not even his work. He could hardly say that he had found the gold. It had been presented to him.

He squatted down, reached out. It was in large pieces, and in a perfectly smooth, pure state. He could only think that the force of the rain had prised it loose, and that same force had washed the ore away and left the metal free. Some of the grains weighed several ounces; they were closer to nuggets than to grains. It put him in mind of Mariposa gold. One of his father's friends had dug it up. Wilson had held that gold in his hand so long he might have been learning it by heart. His father had been proud of his reverence that day, boasted to his friend that prospecting ran in the family.

That reverence came back to him as his gaze moved up to Suzanne's face. Her lilac mouth, all cracked and bleeding. Her skin as dry as paper. Her green eyes slumbering behind burned lids. But her head crowned in gold, which was the way he had always imagined her, somehow. He remembered times when he believed that he might bewitch her with his stories, that he might talk his way into her heart. He did not come close. Even Valence, in the Hotel La Playa, had seemed humbled for a moment, as if he had been faced not with a question but an emperor. And yet that was what she still longed for, still lacked. Some love to match her own. The kind of devotion that did not waver – like worship with all the distance taken out. Something she could understand, accept, return.

'Suzanne?' He had a secret for her.

Her eyelids opened.

'Look.' He showed her the gold. 'It was here all the time.'

Though her mouth must have hurt her, she found a way to smile. 'Mr Pharaoh,' she whispered. 'Very lucky man.'

It would be just the way he had said it would be. The last sunlight angling almost horizontally across the valley. Half the palms in shadow. Half still green, and edged with gold.

'There, Suzanne,' he said. 'Look there. Below.'

Her eyes rose above his shoulder. Far-sighted, bloodshot, chalky-green. And one word reached his ears.

'Down.'

The mule needed no encouragement. Maybe she could already smell the water, imagine the lavish quenching of her thirst. Down they plunged.

It was night when they came to the place. A lake – and yet it had the dimensions of a river. Narrowing in the distance, as if it flowed on from here to the sea. Dark palms leaning inwards, the lake's banks narrowing. And the grass that he had spoken of, sedge grass: tipped in silver, massed like spears or lances – an army at the water's edge.

Kadakaamana.

He turned in the saddle to see her face. Her eyes, still open, stared as if entranced. He saw that they would wither now and die. Her eyes would blow away like leaves. A movement across the iris startled him. But it was only a reflection, the fingers of a palm branch fidgeting. Her lips, though parted, would not speak again.

He heard hoofbeats coming from behind him. He urged his mule forwards, into the shadow of the palms and out along the grass that sloped down to the water. Once concealed, he let the mule dip her head and drink. He watched the stranger passing, a hunched figure on a pale horse. He waited until the paleness was lost among the trees. The mule's neck arched; she was still drinking. Ripples moved out across an otherwise smooth surface. As if the lake were being peeled.

Under the palms, in that evening stillness, he could feel her against his back. No heart beating, just a warmth that would not last. A weight that would diminish. He slid out of the saddle. Grass beneath his feet after an age of dust and stones. Sweet, yielding grass.

When he reached up for her, she toppled sideways, down into his arms. He carried her to the water's edge. Returning to the mule, he collected his rifle, his pickaxe and his spade, and uncoiled the rope from the saddlebow, the same rope that had bound them together, the same knots that her life, like some contortionist, had slipped. He carried the rope and the tools to where she lay. It was only then, as he kneeled beside her, that he noticed how swollen her ankles were. He unfastened her shoes and eased them slowly off. She would not be needing shoes, in any case. The floors of heaven would be soft. He laid the rifle and the tools lengthways on her body, then he reached beneath her with the rope and pulled it through. She had never weighed much; they would be more than enough to take her down. He folded her arms across her chest. She seemed to be holding his rifle, his pickaxe and his spade for him. They were her charge, in her safe-keeping. Now and for ever. He lifted her again and, stooping among the sedge grass, laid her on the water as if it were a bed and took his hands from under her. She seemed to wait there for a moment. She could have been lying on solid ground. Then, smooth as clouds across the sun, the water moved to cover her. And chattered as she sank. Washed the dirt from her. The dirt of the wrong loves. The dirt of his lack of faith in her. Washed it all away. Wrapped her up in what she had dreamed of. Better than any sheets or arms. Now she would be cared for, honoured, pure.

He lifted his eyes from the place where she had been. The night was still new. Dogs barking, a child's laughter. Stars prickled in a sky that had sent, miraculously, rain.

Use the hours of darkness.

His mind torn loose. Cut from his body, floating, separate. It did not seem to be his own. All he could see were women with their shaved heads painted white. Sorrow beyond weeping, grief beyond tears. The relentless violence of stones. The mask and cloak of blood.

Use the darkness while it lasted. In the light there would be suffering. Out into the land he rode, the dust and plants still cooling from the day. Out along the tracks that he had put down earlier. Into the desert with the mission bell ringing in the air behind him, a sound as rich and round as fruit.

She's dead. I buried her.

Was it right or wrong, what he had done? It had felt right. It would look wrong. It was her wish, and yet it amounted to a treachery. He had been sent by the French to find her, bring her back. In his faithfulness he had betrayed them. In telling her the truth he would be telling them a lie. But he knew where his loyalties lay. Not with those doomed people standing on the road. Not with them. He was beginning to understand his father. His honesty had its roots in his father's many deceptions; his consideration in his father's utter fecklessness. And yet –

I buried her.

One fact that pulled in two directions. The spirit that divides against itself. Some might argue that he had committed a crime. But crime ran in the family. Especially the kind of crime that had two sides to it, that cut two ways. Look at my father, he would say. Well, I'm my father's son.

He felt her against his back, and turned sharply to see nothing. Other times he felt her slipping and reached behind him. His hand met empty air. But he could not shake her presence. It was as real as the mule was – her cheek against his shoulderblades, her head by his elbow. He saw black water rippling. He saw her eyes float free like leaves. The face they left behind was smooth and mad. There came a time when he no longer dared turn round.

A jackal barked in the distance. One soprano cough, then another. The volcano loomed, a bulk against the sky. He had to keep it on his left. Every once in a while his hand passed almost absent-mindedly across the pouch where he had put the gold. The night grew softer, another presence, warm and close, as if he were lying in bed and a face had lowered over him. Eyes patched with shadows. A needle like a splinter of the moon between his father's fingers. He cried out. The desert took the cry and swallowed it. Towards the end his father had begun to believe in his own punishment. All his misfortunes had been earned. Any apparent fulfilment of a dream was only another persecution in disguise. Hope became a poison to him; he lanced the place inside himself where it had lived, and drained it out of him like pus.

Wilson lifted his eyes. The day was breaking, wedges of rose and pale-yellow in the eastern skies. He was not fooled by it. There had been another morning once. A morning of sardonic beauty. Dawn on the Natchez Trace, some thirty miles south of Vicksburg. His father up and whistling. One hand in the mane of a stolen chestnut mare, the other on his hip. A fire crackling. A twist of steam above the kettle. They were only a few days into September, but the air had a fall snap to it. The smell of frost's first explorations in scorched summer grass.

And then the trees moved. Gave birth to men with rifles. One man wore a star that made him God. Two others took his father and flung him face-down in the grass.

The Marshal stood over him, legs wide apart, as if he might open the flap of his pants and piss.

'Pharaoh, you done fooled with the law.'

For some reason his father was grinning. The butt of a gun soon wiped that off.

'Ain't the first time,' the Marshal said, 'but it sure as hell is going to be the last.'

He was right about that.

They tried and sentenced his father so quickly that the sun did not even change position. Right there, among the soft colours of dawn and the birdsong and the fall's first frost. And him still kneeling in the grass, as if someone had told him he was in a church.

When the punishment had been decided on – a matter of one question, followed by a nod from the Marshal; it was the usual one – his father was hoisted to his feet. The two men ripped his collar clean off and split his shirt open on his back. Then they pushed him up against a live oak, face into the bark. Tied rope to one wrist, passed it around the trunk and tied it to the other wrist. Then they stood back.

'Don't he just love that tree,' one said.

'Ain't seen a woman in a while,' said another. 'What's a man to do?'

There was a third man who was not laughing. His pale eyes raked the grass. 'What about the boy?'

The Marshal shook his head. 'Boy don't need no whipping. Be a lesson to him, watch his pa.'

Be a lesson all right.

The darkness had drained away. Up came the sun again. Seemed it was everywhere that he was heading. Rose gone now, all yellow gone.

Just glare. Thorns tearing at his legs. The land was trying to weigh him down with tools of its own. Tied its heat and drought to him. Tied it inside as well as out. They had no water left. He chewed viznaga pulp instead. Through glass air he saw an arrow tree. Its fruit was blindness. He would not sleep just yet. Would not sink down. Just one more mile. And when he thought that mile was done, one more. Sun on face and hoofs on stones. Mile after mile she clung to his back, murmuring her own dead language.

His head lifted suddenly. He must have fallen asleep again. They were not even moving. Just standing in the heat.

He dug his heels into the mule's flanks. She took a step. He dug his heels in once more. He no longer knew the why of it. Not the French, not the gold. Not the ghost he carried on his back. But on they went, across the barren plain, their shadow slowly overtaking them.

The sun was high when they cut his father down. But he had not been looking at his father. He could not. Instead he had been looking at the man who was sitting by the fire. Staring at the man. A tightness reaching from his stomach to his throat. A tightness that was like an ache. The man had a length of metal, not much longer than a toasting fork, and he was holding it over the flames. He watched it carefully, head tilted on one side, eyes narrowed against the smoke, turning it and turning it in the hot part of the fire, as if he were cooking some tender morsel and it had to be done just right. The two other men brought his father across the grass. His father breathing hard, as if he had been running. But his legs dragged, and the toes of his boots pointed at the ground. They took his shooting hand, told him to make a fist and raise his thumb. The Marshal stood some distance off, among the trees. He was staring out across a stretch of open country, a cigar wedged horizontal in his mouth. Smoke curled, almost slavish, past his face. He did not acknowledge it. The two men held his father by the upper arms as the rod was lifted, glowing, from the fire. A quick hot sound: one raindrop landing in a pan of fat. His father struggling, and then still.

The Marshal stared out across the open country.

Be a lesson.

His shadow lengthened on the ground. He was heading for a gap in the mountains, a gap he thought he recognised. Looked like the space between fingers and a thumb. But the plain laid out in front of him seemed endless. Mind the only thing moving. Turning and turning in a fire. Man on a doorstep, fat in a pan. He was seeing white hills, the Cajon Pass in February. Ice hanging from the bridle bits. Teeth chattered in your mouth as if your head were bone and nothing else. You could not get the shiver out of you. And riding north, towards Alaska. Worse. The winter plains, smooth as ironed linen. Soot-grease smeared beneath your eyes against the glare of snow. You had to paint your canvas overcoat to keep the east wind out. Seemed like a kind of heaven to him now. Mind turning in a fire. A quick hot sound. The smell of sealed meat. A ghost clung to his back, delirious. Her shoes swung from the saddlebow. He could not look. The hoofs of their four horses dwindling, his father lying in the grass. His back a mesh of red against the green. And they had written on his thumb. Letters that would bind their lives together. 'Happy Times,' his father would always say. 'That's what it stands for. Happy Times.' He could not look. Her laces threaded neatly through the eyeholes. Her heels shaped like sheaves of wheat. He had helped his father to his feet, laid cool dock leaves on the wounds. His father's eyes more painful than his back. Grapes without their skins. A layer gone, the nerves exposed. All the hope drained out of him. All the pain of that moment facing out.

He could not look.

He thought he must have missed a turning in the dark and ridden into hell. A church was burning. He could see the leap of flames inside. The walls glowed red.

He did not stop.

Windows burst as he passed by. Stained-glass lay in fragments on the street; the mule's hoofs crunched over it – saints' haloes, a disciple's agony, the Lord Himself.

The night was being held against a branding-iron; he could feel it trying to twist away, avoid the crimson tip. Men stumbled past him with blood and ashes on their faces, the corners of their eyes and mouths pulled wide. Two humorous sounds: a pop and then a twang. Something bright flew past his ear. And then a jangling, a splintering. He looked over his shoulder, saw the spire lean down.

A man ran up to him. He was brandishing something that Wilson mistook for a rifle. Only it was golden. The man was shouting.

'Look,' he was shouting. 'I've done it. Look.'

He smiled down at the man and nodded, then he pushed the heel of his boot into the mule's ribs. There was only one destination, and this was not it. He could not stop now. If he stopped, he might never make it.

The ground tilted upwards. All the shouting faded.

Then a face swooped out of the air. No body, just a face. White under its black hat. Skin looped beneath the eyes. He could not remember the face's name.

'It's a miracle. We had given up all hope.'

Hands were fumbling at his clothes. He fought to lift his head. To tell the truth.

'She's dead,' he said. 'I buried her.'

Another face. Another language. The words that she had murmured. French?

'I found her. We rode to the water. Then I buried her.'

His vision cleared.

He saw the faces that surrounded him, still as moons in the black air, and awful in their stillness. Only the red light flickering across their foreheads, cheekbones, jaws. His own fingers playing some fast piece. But there was no music that he could hear, no tune.

'She was sitting right behind me.' He reached backwards with his hand. Set her straight in the saddle. 'She was sitting right there.'

Only the faces, hanging in the darkness.

'You don't believe me? Look. I've got her shoes.'

Still the faces.

He began to laugh. 'Did it rain here?'

JULY

1

2nd July, 189 –

My dear Monsieur Eiffel,

I scarcely know how to begin. During the past few days we have been exposed to scenes of barbarism and destruction the like of which I hope never to see again. The church is damaged beyond repair. I find it almost impossible to accept that all our good work has been undone.

Then, as if that were not catastrophe enough, Madame Valence disappeared. She was out riding when her horse, startled by gunfire, bolted into the inhospitable desert behind the town. She was missing for a full three days, and would certainly be dead by now, but for the valiant efforts of an American, who knew the country and was prepared to risk his life on her account.

There is little more to say. I am taking her away from this place. We are leaving tomorrow, on a steamer bound for Panama. If news should reach you before I do, I beg you to give it no credence. The events that have befallen us are terrible enough already, without the distortions and extravagance acquired by numerous tellings.

I trust that you will forgive the incoherence of this letter, taking into consideration the utterly dispiriting circumstances under which it was written. Only know that I remain your most humble and obedient servant, and that I have done my utmost on your behalf.

I am yours, respectfully, etc.,
Théophile Valence.

2

Through a light curtain of dreams Wilson heard a ship's siren. The first note short, the second longer. Then, some time later, two more notes, of equal length, but fainter. Opening his eyes he saw windows high up in a pale-yellow wall and a fan revolving slowly, like a piece of hypnotism. The air feathered down on to his face.

'Ah. Monsieur Pharaoh.'

The doctor was standing at the foot of his bed. He was wearing a waistcoat that resembled a garden in summer: pale-gold roses planted in a field of green.

'It is I. Dr Bardou.'

Wilson smiled faintly. 'Who else would wear such a waistcoat?'

'Why, Monsieur Pharaoh,' the doctor said, laughing, 'you are certainly making an excellent recovery. Nobody would ever guess how close you came to death.'

But Wilson's eyes were still absorbed by the pale roses. 'I thought they'd all been stolen.'

'All except this one.' The doctor fingered the brocade. It glinted in the hushed light of the ward.

'Do you know who did it?'

'I do now.'

It transpired that Wilson had timed his departure well. For the following three days it had been – and here the doctor paused, one of his hands climbing past his ear as he tried to conjure the right word from the air; then he snatched, his hand closing in a triumphant fist, as if the word were a fly and he had caught it – it had been *pandemonium*. Three days of looting and burning in El Pueblo, three days of murder and mutilation. Most of the Indians' rage had been directed against Mexican targets – the military garrison, the customs house – but still the French had feared for their lives. No women had been allowed to venture forth alone. Monsieur de Romblay had issued firearms to all the men.

'Sounds like I was safer out there,' and Wilson gestured towards the window, 'in the desert.'

The doctor smiled.

Only with the arrival of a detachment of *rurales* from Guaymas, he said, did the unrest finally come to an end. The men had sailed through a storm (El Cordonazo could always be relied upon to strike when it was least convenient). Their faces had the awful, yielding pallor of bread that had been soaked in milk; their uniforms, usually so dashing, so appealing to the ladies, were elaborately embroidered with vomit. Still, less than an hour after disembarking, they were marching through the streets of El Pueblo in a show of force, some mounted, and armed with sabres, some on foot with muskets. That same night, the 29th of June, the Indian rebels swarmed east along Avenida Manganeso. They were forcing air between their teeth, making a sound that was like a flight of locusts or a viper's hiss. In their fists they wielded bows and arrows, broken bottles, the legs of chairs. Their bodies glittered strangely as they advanced towards the waterfront, glittered and glowed. The Mexicans had been expecting a motley band of savages. They began to mutter among themselves. One of them was heard to wail, 'They're wearing armour.'

'Your waistcoats,' Wilson said.

The doctor nodded grimly. 'They thought that wearing my waistcoats would keep them safe from harm. They thought that was where my powers came from.'

'And it almost worked – '

'Almost.'

There had been a moment when a number of the *rurales* turned away as if to flee. Then one young soldier kneeled quickly, fired. One of the glittering Indians crumpled. Reassured, the Mexicans let fly with a volley of musket-shot and fourteen Indians dropped to the ground at once. The rebellion was crushed in a matter of hours. The Indians who survived the battle were treated with a brutality for which the *rurales* were notorious. Some were thrown into railway trucks and transported to a canyon five miles north of town where they were shot. Others were only marginally more fortunate: they were shipped to the mainland, destined for labour gangs in the Yucatan jungle.

It seemed to Wilson that he must have ridden into the aftermath. He could quite clearly remember the screaming and the blood, sabres slicing through the smoke, church windows strewn on the ground like jewels.

And the ghost of his love still murmuring against his back.

'Suzanne – ' Suddenly he did not know what to say.

'Yes?'

'I found her, then – ' He paused. He would have to lie. 'Then – then I don't know.'

'You brought her back. She was tied to you, with a piece of rope.'

'I brought her back?' Wilson gaped at the doctor. It did not seem possible. His memory curled, folding inwards on itself – one long wave breaking, back into the past.

'It was a miracle,' the doctor said. 'Not just that you found her, but that she was still alive.'

'But – ' Wilson could see his shovel and his rifle upright in her arms. He could hear the water chatter as she sank. 'I thought she died – I thought I buried her – '

'You were delirious, Monsieur. Heatstroke, dehydration – '

'And now?'

'Now what?'

'Where is she now?'

The doctor opened his hands; he might have been releasing captive butterflies. 'She's gone.'

Wilson stared at the doctor's empty hands. He could not speak.

'She left this morning,' the doctor said, 'with her husband. I advised against it. In my opinion, she was not well enough to travel. She needed rest, as you do. But he would not listen.' Stepping forwards, the doctor adjusted the metal apparatus that stood beside the bed. 'The sooner she returns to France, the better. That is what he said.'

Wilson suddenly noticed the bottle of clear fluid above his bed and how it fed down a tube into his arm. 'What are you doing to me?'

'Salt solution. To replace what you lost. You will be a new man.'

Wilson doubted that. His mind would still be old. His mind and what was in it.

He lay still, watched the fan revolve. Then he closed his eyes. The air beat softly at his eyelids.

Not dead, but gone.

The knowledge floated down. Was there a difference – for him? He was not sure. He felt the knowledge settle in his head. He had never imagined that grief could weigh so little, or desolation be so gentle. It was like being covered in the finest gold leaf.

'You're something of a hero, you know,' he heard the doctor say. 'It's not every man who would have risked his life like that.'

'If you don't mind,' Wilson said, 'I'd like to sleep now.'

When he woke the next day, there was a huge area of blue at the edge of his vision. He altered the position of his head on the pillow. Monsieur de Romblay was sitting on a chair beside his bed. It was the frock-coat that was blue, with a loop of gold, the Director's watch-chain, slung like some elaborate vein between his heart and his liver. A white lace neckcloth billowed at his throat. He was muttering to himself under his breath. From time to time he would fall silent, lifting his eyes to the ceiling. Then he would smile and his chin would tumble downwards; he would continue with his muttering.

At last he noticed that Wilson's eyes were open. His smile puckered, the corners of his mouth tucking into his cheeks. His feet shifted on the floor.

'I was just working on a speech. We're expecting the Mexican Foreign Minister here tomorrow.' He grasped Wilson's hand. 'It's good to see you looking so well, Monsieur Pharaoh.'

'Good of you to come, sir.'

'How are you feeling?'

'Much improved.'

The Director nodded. 'I assume that you've heard about our,' and he paused, 'our difficulties?'

'They'd already started when I left.'

'Of course.' The Director adjusted his lace neckcloth. 'I have never known such carnage,' he said, 'not since my days as an engineer with the Army.'

Everyone who appeared at Wilson's bedside seemed eager to furnish him with their own version of the events and each version differed. With Monsieur de Romblay, there was no sartorial angle, of course. Instead he talked at great length of his diplomatic initiatives and how, given their failure, he felt that he should shoulder some of the responsibility for what had followed. He had been left with no option but to declare a state of emergency, he said. Nonetheless, many heinous crimes were committed, many barbarities. None more disturbing, perhaps, than the lynching of Captain Montoya.

'They killed him?'

'Oh yes.' The Director grimaced. 'But the word "kill" does not adequately describe what they did to that unfortunate young man.'

Wilson did not need to be told. He was familiar with the way in which Indians exacted vengeance; he knew that it would have been brutal and humiliating beyond his imagination.

Happily, the Director continued, when he saw that he would be hard pressed to sway Montoya, he had cabled the authorities at Guaymas, requesting urgent reinforcements. The response had been most impressive. Once order was restored, he had announced a substantial increase in the miners' basic wage, then he had introduced a raft of new safety regulations. The miners were due to go back to work any day now. He had kept the soldiers on, billeted in Montoya's house, in case of further trouble. But he felt confident that the episode was over. There had been numerous letters of apology from the Mexican Government, even one inviting him to Mexico City to discuss the crisis, signed by Don Porfirio himself.

'As I said, the Foreign Minister is due tomorrow,' Monsieur de Romblay concluded. 'He's profoundly embarrassed. Hence the speech.'

'I can think of nobody better qualified to reassure him, sir. Everyone remarks on the high quality of your public speaking.'

The Director's hand fluttered among the folds of his lace neckcloth. Then, in an attempt to conceal his pleasure, he rose to his feet and turned away.

After a moment's silence, Wilson spoke again.

'I have a question.'

Monsieur de Romblay's face loomed over the bed once more, all benevolent attention.

'The church,' Wilson said. 'Was it destroyed entirely?'

'Not entirely. But it's badly burned.'

The Director explained that scaffolding materials had been piled against an inside wall, chairs too, fence-posts – anything combustible. Then somebody had set the lot on fire.

He sighed. 'It will be built again, of course. Perhaps next year, perhaps the year after. When things are less sensitive.' He turned to Wilson and his face brightened. 'But I did not come here to burden you with all this unpleasantness. I'm here to express the gratitude, not only of Monsieur and Madame Valence, but of the whole community.' He leaned forwards. 'I would like to know,' he said, 'how we can repay you for what you did.'

'There's no need. Madame Valence was a friend.'

'All the same, Monsieur. It was a heroic act. We feel that it should be recognised.'

Wilson stared up at the ceiling fan. It revolved at a speed that allowed him to distinguish the individual blades. The air dropped on to his face in soothing layers.

'What can we offer you,' and the Director's voice had softened, 'as a token of our indebtedness?'

Wilson brought his eyes down from the ceiling. 'I'd like some wood.'

'Wood?' The distance between Monsieur de Romblay's features seemed to expand.

'Oak, if you have it,' Wilson said, 'though I guess pine would do.'

3

The green light of evening.

Across the lawn the palms showed black and spare against the sky. There were no waves in the Bahía de Limón tonight – just a slight swell, a restlessness, as if the water were a single, gleaming sheet and some creature stirred beneath.

It would rain before long.

Angling her chair so that the light fell across her writing paper, Suzanne dipped her pen into the inkwell and began.

> Hotel Washington,
> Colón,
> Panama
>
> 19th July, 189 –

> My dearest Wilson,
> I do not know whether this letter will ever reach you. I have to believe that it will. Still, writing gives me a disturbing feeling, as if I were speaking to an empty room –

She paused, looked up. Imagined him.

His flat-crowned hat, its curling brim. His shocked blue eyes beneath. Eyes that looked as if they had witnessed atrocities, or miracles. At times they had seemed to distance him, to place him at one remove from reality. Then she could see why some might think of him as a simpleton, a dreamer – a laughing-stock . . .

Yet he had saved her life.

The thought opened a space inside her head. A landscape that was featureless, where nothing could find purchase.

She tried to imagine thanking him and saw his boots begin to shuffle in the dust. She watched one hand wander from his pocket, touch his hat.

She lifted her eyes to the window. Beyond the palm trees, on the horizon, black clouds heaped above a narrow blade of land. That would be the coastline, stretching north. Bahía de las Minas. Cristóbal. The sky had darkened. Green light seeped through one last gap.

We arrived in Panama after nine days. I did not see much of the city, though we did take a drive along the Avenue Balboa and spend a few moments on the seafront, looking out towards Taboga and the islands beyond. There were many white pelicans floating on the water. To the south the mountains were covered in a light cloud. It was very beautiful. And it seemed quite natural to be sitting there, just looking, saying nothing, perhaps because it was the kind of thing we used to do –

A knocking at the door interrupted her. She looked round.

'Yes?'

When there was no response, she laid down her pen and rose to her feet. She opened the door. Two hurricane lamps, already lit, stood at her feet.

She peered down the corridor. It was tall and narrow; the walls, panelled in cheap wood, had been treated with a dark varnish. She caught a glimpse of a boy in a white shirt, close to the top of the stairs.

'Thank you,' she called out. '*Gracias.*'

Back in her room, she placed one of the lamps beside her on the writing desk and then sat down again.

Wilson, it was so strange for me to find myself in a country where there are trees and flowers, where there is life. In fact, it has been a strange journey altogether, undertaken in a kind of trance. I am suffering from headaches; it is possible that I am still feeling the effects of our ordeal in the desert, though it could be a change of climate, I suppose, since Théo has been ill as well –

A kind of trance.

She had woken in a small white room, not knowing where she was. Her bones lay buried deep below her skin; they felt as if they had been down there for centuries. Her mouth hurt when she tried to speak.

There was a constant humming in her ears which she found comforting somehow. She did not need to have the sound identified.

It was days before she learned that it was engines. That she was on a ship.

As her strength returned she left the cabin, but the voyage south made almost no impression on her. She slept much of the time, in a striped canvas chair. When she was not asleep, she watched blocks of shadow edge across the bleached boards of the deck. The second officer would bring her iced water in a jug.

In Panama City Théo heard that a steamer was sailing from the port of Colón on the east coast the following afternoon. Hoping to escape the heat, they took the night train. A journey of fifty kilometres lasted almost seven hours. She remembered the day breaking, darkness lifting from the jungle. Light that was pale and tropical, like oysters or muslin. Massed trees, sticky with mist. A river sliding past huge knotted roots, its surface solid, seamless; it could have been a length of polished wood. She saw a bush adorned with white flowers of such a size that she could only stare. One blast from the train's whistle and the flowers rose into the sky.

Herons.

As the mist began to burn off, Théo woke from a nap and looked at her, his eyes dark in his exhausted face.

'I've been dreaming.'

But he did not elaborate.

Instead he turned to face the window where broad trenches were now visible, gouged through the terrain. The soil was the colour of tea.

'The canal,' he murmured.

Suzanne gazed out.

This was all that now remained of de Lesseps' attempt to build a waterway through Panama. It had taken him eight years to admit his mistake; by then the scandal had muddied even Monsieur Eiffel's name. Yet the cleared areas were already growing back; banana leaves and lilies draped pieces of abandoned machinery. The shame of the French was being covered over, as if the land itself were embarrassed on their behalf.

Théo contemplated the scene with a kind of morbid relish.

'They say that twenty thousand men died out here.'

The landscape offered him no solace, no evidence of mercy or redemption. He could see only disaster, and it was everywhere he looked. It was as if his failure had taken its rightful place in a whole hierarchy of failures.

And one failure, it seemed, could breed another. In the shipping office in Colón, they were told that there was no boat. Not for another week. When Théo tried to argue, the man just shrugged his shoulders, a slow, watery gesture that seemed to render them powerless, that was like being drowned. They had no choice but to book into the Hotel Washington, and wait.

On their first evening, Suzanne took a seat on the veranda. As the sun began to set over the Caribbean, Théo joined her. A march by Sousa blared and crackled from the graphophone in the dining-room. She wondered whether she ought not to be talking to Théo. Instead she listened to a French anthropologist tell a story about some trees that he had discovered in the province of Chiriquí. 'They were extraordinary,' he said. 'Quite square.' She presumed he meant the trunks. When he had finished his story about the trees, he launched into another. This time it was frogs. Golden frogs. He was a thin man, tubercular, with earnest lines between his eyebrows and the distinctly irritating habit of constantly swirling his drink around inside his glass. She found that his stories did not surprise her. In fact, she was not sure that she was capable of feeling anything as abrupt as surprise. Certainly it would take more than a few square trees.

When she retired to bed that night she glanced across at Théo. They had scarcely exchanged a word all day. She wondered if the anthropologist had noticed. Weren't anthropologists in the business of noticing such things?

The lamp at her elbow began to smoke; she had to adjust the flame. Then she dipped her pen into the inkwell and continued.

From Panama we took the railroad (built by Americans, apparently!) to Colón on the Atlantic coast, which is where we are now. There is little to do here but rest; the good doctor would approve, no doubt. We leave tomorrow, on a steamship bound for New York – an eight-day voyage, if everything goes well –

The door opened and Théo entered. He hung up his hat, leaned his cane against a chair, then glanced across the room at her.

'A letter?'

She nodded.

'Who are you writing to?'

'Monsieur Pharaoh.'

Standing in front of the mirror, Théo adjusted the lapels on his frock-coat. 'Make sure you post it in the morning,' he said. 'There won't be another chance for a while.'

She watched him settle in the armchair with a newspaper. The walls behind him were papered in green-and-gilt, mould blossoming above the picture-rail. Dictionaries filled the shelves. Works by Cervantes too. The size of the books wearied her; she had to look away.

'How was your walk?' she asked.

'It was hardly a walk,' Théo said, peering over his paper. 'I sat on the quay most of the time. There were two Chinamen playing a game of dice. One of them was blind and the other one kept cheating.' Théo forced a laugh.

He was attempting to amuse her, she thought, but he could not summon the enthusiasm necessary to make what he was describing come alive. Or perhaps the incident had depressed him.

He turned back to his paper with a frown. After scanning the front page, he folded it in two and laid it aside.

'It's seven o'clock,' he said. 'Perhaps we should go down.'

They ate in the hotel dining-room – a vast, deserted room with white walls and a tilting wooden floor. Huge gilt mirrors increased the sense of desolation. The orchid on their table sent a thin but sickly fragrance into the air. Outside, the usual evening rain began to crash against the trees.

'You were lucky,' she said.

'Lucky?'

'With your walk.'

He reached into his pocket and took out his watch. 'It always seems to rain at the same time.'

Somewhere in the hotel a shutter banged.

Then two young men ran up the steps. They stood in the hotel lobby, laughing and shaking the water off their clothes.

Suzanne watched Théo tuck his watch back into his pocket. He seemed so delicate, though it was she who was supposed to be the convalescent.

Since leaving the shores of Mexico, Théo had been sleeping poorly. Night after night he woke up bathed in sweat, his bedclothes drenched; also he had developed eczema on the back of his hands. She did what she could, sitting beside him in the darkness, laying cool cloths against his brow, but she did not have the strength to nurse him properly. During the daylight hours a calmness stretched between them, a silence that felt bottomless, a kind of exhaustion. It was not uncomfortable; rather, it was as if they had been admitted to a place where words did not apply. She was not sure what had happened to her love for him. It had been withdrawn, concealed from her. Only charity remained. She moved about with hollow spaces inside her. Her limbs weighed almost nothing. It was like the feeling she used to have after communion when she was a child, a feeling of sublime emptiness that had somehow been received, been granted, that was greater, infinitely greater, than what had been there before.

The shutter banged again. She looked up. Théo was staring at the piece of beefsteak on his plate.

'This meat,' and he grimaced.

'It's terrible, isn't it?'

He nodded.

'I can't even get my knife through it,' she said.

'Why did we order steak,' he said, 'when there is all this fish – ' He gestured towards the windows and the dark arena of the ocean that lay beyond.

As his hand returned, it knocked against the table's edge. A glass tottered, almost spilled. He did not notice.

'I'm sorry,' he said. 'About everything.'

He was staring at his plate again.

She saw that he had not meant to speak. Those last few words of his had startled him.

'Théo,' she said, 'you have nothing to be ashamed of.'

Still he would not look at her.

She leaned forwards. 'Nobody could have done more.'

The rain was louder now, a constant roar against the roof. Their waiter was closing shutters on the north side of the room.

'But Monsieur Eiffel,' Théo said. 'It was my responsibility – '

She reached across the table for his hand. 'You wrote him letters, didn't you?'

He nodded.

'Regularly?'

'Yes.'

'Then they will be your witness,' she said. 'Those letters. They will vouch for you.'

She sat back and looked at him. Just looked at him.

'And me,' she said at last. 'I, too, will be your witness.'

His eyes lifted to her face. They seemed filled suddenly with a curious benevolence – as if he were old and she were very young, as if the fifteen years between them had grown to fifty. And yet, paradoxically, some gap appeared to have narrowed, some barrier had been removed. She had a sudden image of the tree that she had seen from the train, those birds which she had taken to be flowers, and the moment when their petals turned into wings, and they rose up out of the foliage, and flew.

After dinner, they retired to the veranda, where the anthropologist awaited them. The two men lit cigars. Suzanne excused herself, using words that Théo had given to her earlier. 'I have a letter to write. It must be finished by the morning.'

She left the two men blowing smoke against a curtain of rain.

Climbing the stairs to her room, she heard laughter. Three women were grouped around an open doorway on the landing. They were Cuña Indians. Each woman had a black stripe running from her hairline to the tip of her nose – a sign of beauty. One wore a dress of orange silk. As Suzanne passed by, the woman in the orange dress reached for her hand.

'Ah,' she said, 'you are married.'

Suzanne smiled; she could not think what else to do.

Still holding Suzanne's hand, the woman turned and spoke to her companions. They were listening, murmuring what sounded like agreement, but they were staring at Suzanne, their wide eyes rimmed in purple paint.

Then the woman in the dress turned back again. 'We say, if we are married, we are very happy.'

She let go of Suzanne's hand – but reluctantly, as if it were something of her own that she was parting with.

Suzanne moved on towards her room. Fitting the key into the lock, she looked back down the corridor. The women were still watching her, their eyes filled with drowsy fascination, a kind of awe.

'Good-night,' she said.

Their faces did not alter.

It was not until she was sitting at her writing desk that she remembered the open doorway and how she must, at some point, have glanced inside because she could now picture the man who had been lying on the bed.

He was dressed only in his underclothes. He was stretched out beneath a fan. His black hair moved on his forehead.

She took up her pen and dipped it into the ink, but it was several minutes before she began to write.

Do you remember how we used to sit on the veranda of the Hôtel de Paris and try to imagine rain? I think we always failed. How we longed for it, though! Well, it is raining tonight in Panama; it is raining so hard, in fact, that it is splashing through the closed shutters, soaking the floor under the windows. Outside, the streets are rivers –

She paused with her pen in mid-air.

Suddenly she believed that the letter would reach him. She could see the doctor darting into Wilson's hotel, his waistcoat glittering, his moustache-tips needle-sharp. 'Monsieur Pharaoh,' he would be breathing a little hard, 'a letter for you. From Panama.' Then Wilson turning the envelope in his slow hands. Would he know who it was from? Would he guess? She thought he would read it upstairs, in the room that she had never visited, or at Mama Vum Buá's place, perhaps, with a cup of grey coffee in front of him and the Señora's dark-eyed girls plucking at his sleeve. Later, perhaps, he would sew it into his jacket lining like that map. Carry it with him, to America.

It hurts me that I could not see you before I left, Wilson. I am not sure that I would have known what to say to you if I had. I know now, though. I want to tell you that you have given me a second life, a new place to begin, a new tranquillity. I cannot thank you enough for that.

I have a favour to ask. Would you write to me occasionally, just a few words, so that I may have some news of you? I enclose my Paris address in the hope that you will not deny me this. I am so grateful for your companionship, Wilson; in truth, I do not know how I would have managed without you.

Goodbye, my dear friend. I shall never forget all you have done for me. I must stop now, for it is after eleven o'clock and this must be posted in the morning.

I am yours, with the greatest affection and gratitude,
Suzanne Valence.

She took the blotter and rolled it across the page. Then, folding the letter once, she tucked it into an envelope. She would address it care of the doctor. She could no longer remember the name of that hotel in El Pueblo; in any case, she did not trust the place.

The letter in her hand, she sat quite still and listened to the rain.

Outside, the streets were rivers.

'You have finished?' Théo was smiling down at her. She had not even heard him enter.

She nodded.

He stood behind her chair.

'Out there, in the desert,' she began, 'when I was out there,' and then she faltered.

One of Théo's hands moved slowly upwards, touched her neck. Or not so much touched, perhaps, as came to rest.

'I almost died,' she said.

'I know.'

She stared down at the letter she had written. The words blurred on the envelope.

'I know,' he repeated, still more softly.

She felt his lips descend, his breath against her hair.

'Suzanne.'

4

The morning Wilson left the hospital, he walked to Mama Vum Buá's place for breakfast. Sweat had soaked his flannel shirt before he was halfway down the hill. The dense heat of July. He had forgotten how immovable it was, how still; how it could hold a smell. Today it was beached weed, the rotting shells of crabs. Eight hours, even in the shade, could turn a piece of fresh meat green; eight hours, and the meat would be alive with maggots.

When he turned into the yard he found La Huesuda sitting at his table, three empty plates in front of her. For once he had no reason to flinch from the encounter. She was wearing a gingham dress of faded blue, earrings made from drilled coins and a red paper rose in her hair. She gave him a neutral look; he could have been a tree, or a dog, or a ship with no sailors in it. He put one hand on the back of a chair.

'May I?'

She shrugged.

He pulled the chair out, eased down into it, stretching his legs under the table.

'You're looking well,' he said.

'Riots do have their advantages.' She aimed her fork at the Mesa del Sur. 'All these new soldiers in town.'

'It's strange,' he said, 'but I was just on my way to see you.'

He saw the light of business flare up in her eyes.

'Not for that,' he added quickly.

The time had come for him to keep his promise to her. He intended to build her a new balcony, he told her, and a flight of stairs to go with it.

'The French are giving me the wood. As much as I want.'

She stared at him sidelong, across the bridge of her nose. Her teeth glistened on her lower lip.

He would start the following day, he said, if that was all right. He

was still weak, he warned her; it might take a while to complete
the job.

She had not stopped staring at him. At last she spoke.

'I don't like jokes like that. I don't think they're funny.'

'I'm not joking.'

Her earrings jingled as she pushed backwards from the table.
'Pompano's right.'

'About what?'

'You've been in the desert too long. Your brains have cooked.'
She moved away across the yard, shaking her head and muttering
to herself.

'I'll see you tomorrow,' he called after her.

But she did not believe it; she just kept on walking.

He heard the creak of a door-hinge and shifted on his chair. Mama
Vum Buá stood behind him, her fists dug into the fat on her hips.

'What do *you* want?' she said.

'Some eggs'd be good.'

She fired a ball of red spit into the dirt. 'You're late.'

'I'm lucky to be here at all.'

'Not that lucky.'

He did not follow.

'There's no eggs,' she told him.

'How come?'

The Señora jerked her chin towards the quay. 'That skinny bitch just
ate the lot.'

Pablo was sitting in the lobby of the Hotel La Playa when Wilson
walked in. One elbow on the table, his cheek propped on his hand,
he was tapping the rim of a glass with a long grey key. Some mornings,
silence was difficult for Pablo – more of an affliction than a choice.
Wilson consulted his watch. Eleven minutes to go.

He took a seat at the table. After a while he noticed something moving
at the top of the stairs. A black hunched back, a shuffling of feathers. He
stood up, walked over. Through the banisters he saw a vulture hobble
across the landing.

'Did someone die in here?' he asked.

Pablo did not answer.

Wilson pushed his face against his sleeve as the stench of droppings
reached his nostrils. That smell, he had forgotten it; sometimes it was

so bad, you had to tie a rag over your face. He had been spoiled in the hospital. Retreating to the table, he sat down again. There were still five minutes till midday.

His thoughts turned back to Mama Vum Buá. As she cleared his breakfast plates away that morning, he had spoken to her again.

'I heard the church burned down.'

A smile slid out of the right side of her mouth. 'I heard that too.'

'You don't seem too upset about it,' he said.

The smile shrank. 'What are you getting at?'

In that moment, he suddenly remembered what the Director had told him. It had not been a spontaneous act of violence. It had taken real determination. He thought of Mama Vum Buá's grudge against priests. They had corrupted her family. They had polluted her with their blue eyes. If anyone had reasons for burning the church, she did. Especially since it was being built by Monsieur Valence, a man who had insulted her cooking.

He looked up at her. 'Apparently somebody piled wood inside the building, then set fire to it – '

The Señora's head swung sideways and she spat.

'I don't know anything about that,' she said.

The clock on the roof of the company store began to strike. Wilson had never expected to learn the truth from her, but that sly smile spilling from her mouth intrigued him. She smiled so rarely. Had Monsieur Valence been justified in his suspicions? For the first time, it occurred to Wilson that she might actually have poisoned the Frenchman. Deliberately.

As the twelfth note died away, Pablo stood up and walked to the cupboard where he kept his liquor. His eyes lifted to the landing; the vulture was still up there someplace, shuffling its feathers in the gloom.

'It's ever since the riots,' he said. 'Can't seem to keep them off the streets.' He brought a bottle over to the table. 'Talking of streets, have you heard the latest? They're thinking of naming a street after Montoya. The place where it happened. They say it'll be a kind of memorial.'

Wilson had to slow him down. 'Where what happened?'

Pablo took Wilson through the events in detail, as Wilson had known he would. Montoya was returning from Frenchtown after another round of discussions with de Romblay when he was ambushed by a crowd of Indians. Such was the Indians' fury that they tore the carriage to pieces with their bare hands. They stripped Montoya of his uniform and nailed him to one of the wheels. For more than an hour they dragged him through the streets. They believed his suffering would act as a kind of poultice, drawing out the suffering of their people; his anguish would replace their own. Afterwards they took him to the park. There, on the dark corner where the Calle Majore met Avenida Aljez, not two blocks from the hotel, the Indians got out their knives. Montoya was still conscious when they cut him open and threw his intestines on the ground. It was their version of a crystal ball. Nothing like the guts of a Mexican aristocrat to give you an idea of the future.

Wilson grimaced. 'How did it look?'

'Peaceful. Or so they said.' Pablo uncorked the bottle and poured two shots of liquor. He pushed one across the table.

Wilson drank it down.

Pablo offered him another, but Wilson shook his head.

'It took him two hours to die.' Pablo poured himself a second drink and swallowed it. 'People who live on that corner, they can still hear the groaning.'

Wilson leaned back in his chair. He did not want to think about Montoya. He followed a crack as it meandered up the pale-green wall. The square of sky at the top burned white.

Later that afternoon, the two men made their way to the bakery. Along Calle 3 and then right, up Avenida Cobre. People were sitting on their porches, faces slackened by the heat. The mood in the streets was leaden. It reminded Wilson of oceans after storms. All that exhausted water. Spaces had opened in the town's young memory. For some they would be grotesquely detailed, graphic – food for nightmares; for others, blank. He was not sure he would have called it peaceful. More like numb.

His eyes lifted to the graveyard on the hill. Montoya. Some soldiers from the garrison. And then the Indians, too many to be counted. In 1879 he had spent a few weeks in Virginia City. People always used to tell him that the first twenty-six bodies buried there were murdered men. Life was furious in a new town; nobody had time to die of natural causes.

In the bakery Jesús was sitting with Luis Fernández. Wilson and Luis shook hands. Pablo arched an eyebrow at his younger brother, then leaned against the wall and picked his teeth. Over glasses of black coffee and angel cakes baked fresh that afternoon, Wilson learned of Luis's appointment to the post of customs officer.

'So they killed him too,' he murmured.

'Ramón was asking for it,' Jesús said, 'hiking import duties like he did.'

'And all those bribes he took.' Pablo shook his head.

Luis kept silent.

Wilson noticed how slim Luis was, and how there were no pockets to his pants.

'Just the same,' Jesús was saying, 'I wish they'd found some other way. That was a full day's baking – and I never got a penny for it.'

Medically speaking, José Ramón had suffocated. The Indians had held him down, and forced cake into his mouth and nose; they had done such a thorough job that, during the autopsy, Dr Bardou found icing in the customs officer's lungs. Not only that but they gouged out his eyes and filled the sockets with marzipan. Then they chopped his hands off at the wrist so he would not be able to accept any bribes in the afterlife. As Jesús said to Pablo. 'Imagine what they would have done with a baguette.' But he had only made the one at that point, of course, his first –

Wilson interrupted. 'I think I saw you, the day I rode back into town. You were waving something.'

'That was the day he did it,' Pablo said.

Jesús nodded. He had heard the guns that afternoon, but he had assumed it was fireworks – some festival which he had, in his excitement, forgotten all about. He did not realise the truth until he dashed out into the street waving his baguette and promptly lost the end of it to a Mexican lieutenant's sabre.

He led Wilson over to the row of shelves behind his counter and drew the cloth off the glass case where he always used to keep his doughnuts. And there it was, resting on green velvet, tapering and golden at one end, brutally truncated at the other: the first baguette.

Nose close to the glass, Wilson examined it. He tilted his head one way, then the other. Then he nodded and stepped back.

'The doctor must be pleased,' he said.

'Free medical treatment for life.' Jesús beamed. 'Not just me, either. The whole family.'

Putting on another pot of coffee, he asked Wilson what his plans were now that he was well again. Wilson told him about the balcony that he was going to build for La Huesuda.

Pablo smirked. 'He'll get it for nothing from now on.'

'That's a relief,' Jesús said. 'We won't have to pay for him any more.'

The three Mexicans roared with laughter.

'I'm not interested in that,' said Wilson, grinning.

'No,' Pablo said, 'of course you're not.'

For the remainder of the month Wilson worked on La Huesuda's house, starting at daybreak every morning. Monsieur de Romblay was most amused when he discovered the purpose to which his materials were being put.

'And she's a friend of yours,' he said, 'this prostitute?'

Wilson demurred. 'More of an acquaintance.'

'An acquaintance?' Monsieur de Romblay smiled. 'In France, of course, it's an art, to be accomplished in love.'

'In America,' Wilson said, 'we don't generally talk about it.'

He had to keep love in mind, though, as he laboured: love's requirements, love's demands. He cut stairs that would be wide enough for any drunken sailor's boot. He reinforced the handrail; it would not give, even if someone leaned against it, vomiting. And the balcony could take the weight of half a dozen men with ease (for those nights when La Huesuda entertained the garrison).

She still could not believe it. Most days she walked into the middle of the street and stood there staring up, her hands spread on her hips, jaw dangling. Then, as she got used to the idea, even thrilled by it, she began to reward him with glimpses of her skinny body; robes fell open by mistake – or sometimes she would just forget to dress. These were the favours that Pablo had predicted. When Wilson politely turned her down, she laughed. 'What's the matter, American? Afraid you might break something else?'

From where he was working, two storeys up, he could watch her go about her business. Out along the waterfront, with her wishbone legs and her eyes like avocado skins gone bad. One hand thrown up in front of her, the fingers splayed, her body tilted at the waist, she would taunt the crews of ships that lay moored along the quay, then swirl away, her bones rolling and jumping inside her dress. La Huesuda.

'So tell me, Wilson. What kind of women do you like?' Suzanne's voice. Softened by white wine from underneath the house.

'You, Suzanne.' He must have blushed.

He looked inland, towards the ruined church. Its fire-blackened walls, its windows emptied of their glass.

'You.'

A slow smile had spread across her face. 'You're a gentleman,' she said. 'Really. You are.'

He shook his head. She thought that he had seen her question as a chance to pay her a compliment, and she had been genuinely flattered by what he had said. She had not realised. It was not a compliment; it was a declaration. It was the torture he had inadvertently devised for himself, that he could never allow her to understand him.

At the time, in the impotence of knowing that he loved her, it had frustrated him. Now, though, he could only see her simple absence of resentment, a touching gratitude. Life had been too watery, too grudging – too meagre altogether. He stared at the blackened walls, the spire leaning to one side. If he had been her husband, he would have built a church, not for some remote god, but for her, in her honour, to her glory, and would have considered it no blasphemy at all.

He put in long hours on La Huesuda's house. His hands blistered and then hardened. He could feel his body strengthening. The details gave him pleasure: a dovetail joint, an edge planed level. The steps climbed steadily heavenward.

Some mornings Jesús would stop by with a baguette. When Wilson snapped the bread in half, steam drifted upwards from the soft interior. Other times the Vum Buá girls would visit. They had not forgotten his story, but he was still lost for an ending. One day they came to him with a proposal: suppose the beautiful woman decided to marry the poor man, not for money or for jewels, but simply because he made her happy. Wilson thought this an admirable solution. The girls promptly invented a new game: the wedding. Wilson had to be the poor man, of course, and he was told to kneel on the ground throughout the ceremony. The girls took it in turns to be the beautiful woman, standing at his shoulder. First always played the priest, since only she knew the words. For confetti the bridesmaids used sawdust, which there was plenty of. In the middle of one wedding, just at the moment when the rings were being exchanged, long shadows fell across the bride and groom. Still on his knees, Wilson looked round. La Huesuda's brothers stared down at him, their foreheads dented in the sunlight. The girls scattered; Wilson reached slowly backwards for a hammer. But the two faces opened, and rows of stained teeth showed. 'No hard feelings, mister.'

July slipped by, and his thoughts began to move northwards. There was a kind of nostalgia lodged in the wood itself. The scent that it released into his nostrils as he worked put him in mind of Upper California. He could see forests of fir trees climbing the slopes behind a town, the tip of each tree sharp, the sweep of the forest even in the glittering fall light. He could hear the deep tolling of the surf at night as the ocean rolled shorewards, and the absolute silence between each breaking wave. He could feel the tug of the land in his blood.

Wilson sat on the doctor's veranda sipping tea from a china cup. When he had told Bardou, the day before, that he would soon be leaving (Monsieur de Romblay had secured him passage on a steamer bound for San Diego), the doctor had insisted on a full medical examination. Wilson had spent most of that afternoon reclining on a bed in the surgery while the doctor peered into his throat, tapped his kneecaps, scrutinised his pupils, measured his pulse, took his temperature and listened to his chest. After almost an hour, Bardou stood back. His hair, his waistcoat and his teeth conspired in an effortless display of brilliance.

'You are healthy,' he declared. 'You have my permission to leave town.'

Wilson helped himself to another slice of lemon sponge, then turned to Madame Bardou. She was pouring him a second cup of the almond infusion which, according to the doctor, was not only refreshing, but extremely beneficial to the liver.

'This cake is delicious,' he said.

Madame Bardou's wide forehead lowered. Her smile had scarcely reached her lips before it was gone.

The doctor echoed Wilson's compliment, then steered the conversation from cake to bread. Since Señor Pompano had mastered the baguette, the doctor's life had become, he said, a model of contentment. In fact, things were looking up generally. Only yesterday, five of his waistcoats had been recovered. In poor condition, admittedly, but what could you expect when Indians had worn them into battle? Wilson asked him what he proposed to do with the waistcoats.

The doctor did not hesitate. 'I will frame them.'

When Wilson suggested this might be a little gruesome, the doctor disagreed. He argued that it was his duty to preserve the waistcoats.

'After all,' he said, tilting his face towards Wilson, the tips of his fingers joined beneath his chin, 'they have become a part of history, have they not?'

Wilson pictured the brocade. Punctured, ribboned, stained with blood. The brutal evidence of musket-shot and sabre-blades. Men had believed in that glittering cloth. It had betrayed them. Maybe the doctor was right. It was a kind of lesson. History.

He shifted on his chair. 'That reminds me,' he said. And, reaching into his pocket, he took out a piece of malachite.

Looking at the crystal, he had to smile. He could remember how the gold had looked when he first found it. Large pieces, in a perfectly smooth, pure state. Stream-rounded, almost. He had forgotten about it until the day he was discharged from hospital and he was handed his possessions. When he undid the straps on his knapsack and reached inside, his hand emerged with a piece of malachite. He reached inside again. Some copper ore. He shook the contents of his knapsack out on the hospital veranda and sat back on his heels. At first he thought he had been robbed – but what thief would have bothered to replace gold with rocks, let alone with malachite and copper? Besides, the nurse assured him that his possessions had been kept under lock and key. No, his eyes had played a trick on him that afternoon. The sun, slanting low across the desert, had lit both the crystals and the ore with a deceitful yellow glow. Some would make fine beads if they were carved and drilled. Others would turn the flames of a fire green. But they were not what his father had been looking for.

He held the malachite out towards the doctor.

The gap between the doctor's eyebrows narrowed. 'For me?'

Wilson nodded. 'I found it in the desert. In my delirium I thought it was gold.'

The doctor laughed. 'All the same, it's rather attractive.' He turned the crystal on his palm.

'Do you remember my promise to you?' Wilson said. 'About the nugget?'

'Yes, I do. But I never thought – '

'Nor did I. Not really.' Wilson stared at the mountains that had kept their secret from him. 'I guess that's about as close as I got.'

Towards sunset Bardou saw him down the steps. After thanking the doctor once again, Wilson walked back along the Calle Francesa, his eyes following patterns in the cobbles. Each stone cut by hand. Then shipped all the way to Mexico.

When he glanced up, it was dusk. That wash of supernatural light before the darkness dropped, a violet glow that altered as you watched. There was a woman in a pale-yellow dress walking along the road ahead of him. He recognised the dress; it had lilies of the valley stitched on to it, which stood for happiness returning. They were the only two people on the road. Any moment now the night would crash down through the sky. He recognised the dress and broke into a run.

'Stop,' he cried. 'Wait.'

The woman stopped where she was, but did not look round. Not until he caught up with her did she turn. It was a face he did not know. A round, young face. A slightly startled smile.

'Yes?'

'I thought – ' He was stammering; his hands cupped empty air. 'I thought you were someone else.'

The girl did not seem alarmed, only sorry to have disappointed him. She bit her bottom lip, lifting her shoulders in a little shrug.

'Who are you?' he asked.

'My name's Imelda.' She held the skirt out sideways in the air and let it fall again. 'Do you like my dress?'

'Yes,' he said. 'I do.'

'Do you think I look beautiful?' A sudden shyness lowering her eyes.

'Very beautiful.'

Her face lit. She turned away.

'Good-night,' he called after her.

Her voice floated back over her shoulder. 'Good-night.'

He stood there, watched her walk away from him, the pale dress fading, settling, sinking down into the darkness.